E

"A skillfully written first novel with the narrative voice, knack for dialogue, and plot movement of a veteran author."

"The thrumming question of faith—how can there be a good God in a world so full of pain beats at the core of the book. A page turner that is not easy to put down. By the end of *The Reason*, you will understand that question in an entirely new way.

KAY CAMPBELL, *The Huntsville Times*

"Sirls sets the narrative hook deep with intriguing characters and a multi-layered plot that asks you to 'only believe' when everything else tells you not to. Prepare to laugh! Prepare to cry! Prepare to be inspired and renewed!"

GAIL WELBORN, *Midwest Book Reviews*

"Readers everywhere will identify with these characters' experiences. An incredible story of second chances and seeing the bright light of Christ shine through in the darkest hour. William is using his own second chance at life to remind us of God's love. This is a must-read for anyone who needs a reminder of what God asks of us: only believe."

PETE WILSON, pastor and author of *Plan B* and *Empty Promises*

"*The Reason* is one of those rare books whose characters reach off the pages and take you by the heartstrings. It demonstrates an unwavering faith in God that was an inspiration to me."

KIMBERLY BROWN

"*The Reason* will serve to fortify your faith and reassure you of God's constant love and incredible power. If you are not yet a believer, this book will open your eyes to the possibilities of God that can manifest in any and every part of our lives."

CHRIS SONKSEN, lead pastor of South Hills Church, founder of Celera Church Strategy Group, author of *In Search of Higher Ground and Handshake*

"*The Reason* will serve as a reminder that God wants us to do our part, to only believe, and to leave the outcome (good or not) to Him because He, ultimately, always knows what's best!"

JACQUELINE LYNCH, associate pastor, Loma Linda University Church

"*Of Mice and Men* meets *Brian's Song*. *The Reason* is a powerful story that delivers message after message."

THOMAS LANE

"While I love to read, I'm generally not into Christian fiction. *The Reason* is an exception. It is a gritty story about everyday people who are believable and easy to relate with. It had me both laughing and crying at times as a good book should. I would recommend it to both believers and non-believers alike, but non-believers—be cautioned. You may have to really rethink and question why you don't believe in the God of the Bible."

MARK DREW, California Baptist University

"Pay attention to each and every page or you will miss something. William Sirls is about to take you on an emotional rollercoaster ride that ends in an answer that far too many are still blind to."

KELLY ANDERSON

"*The Reason* is an outstanding effort to communicate the love of Christ."

THOMAS AYERS

"A book you will not forget. A clever tearjerker that invites you to think as you turn page after page."

D. JAMES

"The people in the small town of Carlson come to life fully. They made me laugh and cry. A book as rich and engrossing as *The Reason* can make you forget your own problems."

PATTI HOGUE

"Draws you in with its richly written characters and maintains an intense, almost eerie vibe throughout the story. *The Reason* is a uniquely compelling tale."

RUSSELL BRADLEY FENTON

"*The Reason* will grab you at the beginning, wrap its arms around you, and keep you guessing until the end. Have your Kleenex handy and then only believe."

M. MYERS

"Anyone reading this book will identify with at least one character with an invitation to change."

JAMES STEERE

"May this book turn out to be a blessing to an unheard number of more people as it was to me."

MICHAEL STEDMAN

"*The Reason* is an intriguing tale of diverse personalities and problems that will lead you to twists and turns that are entirely unexpected."

LORENE MILLER

"The book started off very well, even had my heart pounding in the opening scene in the church . . . but as soon as I realized it was about Alex having leukemia, I almost put the book down. I have a very difficult time reading/watching books/movies where children are hurt. On top of that, one month ago I lost a best friend to leukemia. It seems that God's timing was perfect for me reading this book! I certainly sense His Hand in it. Looking back, I am blown away by the slim chance that 'I' ended up reading 'your' book. That you ended up being connected with me, when it could have been countless others. There are no such things as 'chances' with our God! I would highly recommend your book to anyone, and will definitely do that. Thank you for letting me have the privilege of reading it."

LIZ ZELLER, director of biblical counseling and
director of growth classes, Harvest Church, Billings, MT

"A tangible reminder that God is with us, loving us, and guiding us towards him if we only believe."

KAREN MORTON

"Nothing I say could capture what this book meant to me."

BETH HENSLEY

"Believable characters whose life lessons will truly inspire you. I can't wait to read it again."

EMILY SCHMIDT

"Brilliant. Simply brilliant. I don't know what else to say. I've never cried like this reading a book before and you will too."

MELANIE JOHNSON

"These characters became people I cared about. I lived the story with them and enjoyed the difference God made in their lives."

TED J. KOZIATEK

THE
REASON

A Novel

WILLIAM SIRLS

BroadStreet
P U B L I S H I N G

BroadStreet Publishing Group, LLC
Racine, Wisconsin, USA
BroadStreetPublishing.com

THE REASON
Written by William Sirls

Scripture quotations are taken from the NEW KING JAMES VERSION. Copyright © 1982 by Thomas Nelson, Inc. Used by permission. All rights reserved; the King James Version of the Bible; and the HOLY BIBLE: NEW INTERNATIONAL VERSION*. Copyright © 1973, 1978, 1984 by International Bible Society. Used by permission of Zondervan Publishing House. All rights reserved.

Publisher's note: This novel is a work of fiction. Names, characters, places, and incidents are either products of the author's imagination or used fictitiously. All characters are fictional, and any similarity to people, living or dead, is purely coincidental.

ISBN-13: 978-1-4245-5136-1 (softcover)
ISBN-13: 978-1-4245-5137-8 (e-book)

Cover design by Steve Fryer at stevefryer.com
Interior by Renee Evans at reneeevansdesign.com

Printed in the United States of America
16 17 18 19 20 5 4 3 2 1

DEDICATED TO ALL OF US
WHO NEED FORGIVENESS.

ONE

It was the second time in fifteen minutes that the power had gone out at the church, and it was noticeably darker this time.

Brooke paused—to wait for the lights to come back on—and stared at the three strange shadows that hovered against the fellowship hall's vaulted ceiling. Something about them seemed alive.

She glanced over at her five-year-old son, Alexander, and removed her earbuds, noticing the wind had stopped howling. "You okay, buddy?"

"I'm not even scared," Alex said bravely. He gave her a reassuring smile and waved the small rag he liked to use when he helped her dust.

Brooke turned off her smartphone and pressed the vacuum's power button a few times. Nothing happened. She shook her head and looked back up at the ceiling. The shadows had somehow become one.

The weatherman on the morning news had said they may be getting some storms, but when she, Alex, and Charlie had come up from the house to clean, only plump, white clouds and a bright sun filled the southeast Michigan sky. But it had been windy. *Really windy.*

And now the wind was gone.

"It's too dark," Alex whispered. "Charlie is gonna be scared."

"He'll be okay, baby," she said. "The lights will come back on soon."

"But the sky just did some big thunder," Alex said. "You couldn't hear it with your music on."

"Charlie!" she yelled, taking Alex's hand and moving quickly across the room toward the tall double doors that separated them from the sanctuary.

Though Charlie was thirty-eight years old and big as a tree, thunder terrified him. Even with his familiarity with the church, all his safe places had surely been erased by the darkness and terror flooding his small mind.

She opened the doors and walked into the sanctuary. It was dark, but not nearly as dark as the fellowship hall. It was perfectly quiet.

"Charlie?" Brooke said, glancing up toward the front of the church. She heard nothing, but could feel Alex pulling on her pant leg.

"Look, Mom," he said.

She turned, and her eyes followed his index finger, pointing at the two-paned glass doors that served as the main entrance. Brooke squinted and cocked her head to the side. She had never seen the sky that color before.

She took his hand again, walked to the doors, then leaned against one to push it open.

It was deadly still outside. The air was thick and had a strange smell to it. The clouds were now a dark gray and the sky behind them an eerie crayon green, casting down a steady shadow of the same color over everything she could see.

"We better take cover," Brooke whispered, holding the door. She gazed out at the fifteen-foot wooden cross, centered on the church's front lawn. Beyond the woods, she could hear spirited rolls of thunder approaching off the shore of Lake Erie. There was no way in the world Charlie would have come out here, let alone try to make it over to the house.

"I want to go back inside," Alex said, letting go of his mother's hand and wrapping his arms around her leg.

Brooke took a deep breath and tilted her head up again to stare at the sky, wondering how much time they had. She looked down the hill at the house, which now seemed far away. More thunder sounded in the distance. Louder this time.

"Charlie!" Alex shouted. There was panic in his small voice.

Brooke looked back over her shoulder into the church. She leaned her head against the door and waited for Charlie to jump up from between two pews, as he'd done hundreds of times before during hide-and-seek.

"He won't come out, Mom," Alex said. "You know how he is when he's scared."

"He has to be around here somewhere." Brooke took one more look outside. She picked her son up and stepped back into the church, letting the door close behind them. "We have to find him fast, Alex."

She walked along the length of the back pew and stopped when they hit the center aisle. Brooke could see the push sweeper lying on the floor up near the pulpit. Charlie had obviously abandoned it when he heard the first crack of thunder.

Brooke put Alex back on his feet and tried to listen for Charlie.

She looked back at the main entrance. It had clearly gotten darker, and beyond the door's plated glass, lightning flickered gently, as if God were flashing the porch light for someone who had just missed his driveway.

"Charlie!" Brooke yelled again.

"Charlie!" Alex echoed.

They turned and slowly made their way up the main aisle, taking turns calling Charlie's name and looking for him in the darkness between the pews.

"Maybe he did make it down to the house," Brooke said, glancing back at the front doors. The sky had gone from green to black.

They both flinched at the thick volley of thunder that coincided with a flash of lightning, like an X-ray of the church's front lawn.

"I don't like this," Alex said, sounding on the verge of tears.

"It's okay," she said, still staring at the front doors. She held her hand out behind her for Alex to take. He didn't.

"I'm over here," Alex whispered.

Brooke turned around and could barely see him. He was nothing more than a small shadow kneeling in the pew. "What are you doing?"

13

"Praying we find Charlie."

Brooke kneeled next to him and struggled to slow her breathing. *Please, Lord, keep us safe.* She put her arm around Alex and pulled him closer. She could feel his heart pounding against her palm.

Alex squeezed her arm and closed his eyes as she pulled him closer still. She kissed the top of his head as a violent peal of thunder boomed directly over the church.

"No!" Alex cried.

"Let's go," Brooke said, taking his hand. As they rose, she thought she heard something over the rain. It was dark, but she could vaguely make out some of the shadows around them. The pews. The dim outline of windows. A stack of rarely used folding chairs against the wall. They stepped into the aisle, and Brooke proceeded to look mechanically to her left, and then to her right, her head's slowly shifting movements like a low-end security camera.

She saw little, but she definitely heard something. *Charlie.* He was crying. But the sound of him was drowned out by thunder so loud it reverberated in her chest and the wind that had returned with a vengeance.

"Make it stop!" Alex begged, grabbing hold of her leg again.

She turned to comfort him and a flash outside caught her eye. Another finger of lightning darted across the grounds, and Brooke flinched as the entire front lawn disappeared in a brilliant flash of reddish-orange light. It was gone before she could shield her eyes, and the deafening blast that followed shook the building, sending them both instinctively to the floor. She draped her arms around Alex. He was trembling, but she didn't blame him. Whatever had just happened outside was unlike anything she had ever seen or heard. They needed better cover—to get out of this big space.

"Charlie!" she yelled, standing, then picking up Alex. "Where are you?"

There was no response.

"What if he's hurt?" Alex cried.

"What in the world?"

"Do you see him, Mom?"

Brooke squinted at the glass of the front doors.

Something was on fire outside. Flames seemed to float about ten feet in the air, then rapidly weakened under the assault of the constant rain.

"What's that?" Alex asked. As he spoke, the last of the fire went out.

"I think it was the cross."

"Oh no," Alex said, like a concerned old man. He leaned his head on her shoulder. "Please, let's hurry. Let's find him."

She raised her finger to her lips. As they waited and listened, all Brooke could hear was the tapping of the rain on the windows.

"A car's coming," Alex said. Headlights made their way up into the parking lot of the small church.

"It has to be Shirley and Pastor Jim," she whispered. A clicking sound came from the other side of the building, restoring the power.

Only two of seven lights were on in the sanctuary, offering them no real improvement in their ability to see Charlie, but they both breathed a little easier.

"I like that better," Alex said.

"Me too, little man."

They heard a humming sound coming from somewhere in the building and looked at each other.

"What's that noise?" Alex asked.

"I think it's the vacuum cleaner over in the fellowship hall. I must've left it on when we lost power."

Alex smiled and she kissed the top of his head again. There was more thunder, but it seemed to be fading. The storm was easing away, and now Brooke was sure she could hear Charlie.

"I hope the dumb lights stay on this time," Alex said. "I wish they—"

"Shh," Brooke said, moving slowly toward the front of the church. One dome light cast a soothing glow over the altar, the old Wurlitzer piano and the hand-carved pulpit.

She tilted her head and lifted her hand. She definitely heard someone sniffle.

"We need to find Charlie," Alex said, as if she'd forgotten.

"We just did." Brooke ran her hand through Alex's bright red hair. Charlie was up in the nave, lying down between the last two pews, where the choir sat. All she could see of him was the white, size twenty-one tennis shoes on the carpet, sticking out past the end of the bench.

Brooke carried Alex up to the choir stalls and stepped into the row in front of Charlie's hiding spot. She lowered Alex to stand on the seat cushion above Charlie, and they both leaned over and looked down.

Charlie Lindy was perfectly still, flat on his back, with his eyes closed and his hands over his ears.

"There you are, big guy," Brooke said. "It's okay, Charlie."

Alex started giggling. "You big fraidy cat, Charlie!"

"It's okay, Charlie," Brooke soothed. "The storm is about over."

Charlie opened his eyes and looked up at them. Thunder rumbled in the distance, and he immediately shut them again.

"It's all right," Brooke said. "It's going away."

Charlie reluctantly opened his eyes again, and they darted from side to side. He slowly sat up and lowered his hands from his ears. He smiled at Brooke and pointed at the light switch behind her.

"You got it, big guy," she said.

"You're a big fraidy cat!" Alex laughed, jumping up and down while holding out his arms for Charlie to take him.

"I think we were *all* afraid," Brooke said as she turned to switch on more lights.

"No!" Alex yelled, his voice echoing off the church's white brick walls.

Brooke spun around and found herself staring straight into Charlie's barrel-like chest. His right arm extended firmly out to his side like a thick branch. At the end of that limb, two feet above her head, Alex dangled helplessly facedown as Charlie's mammoth hand held him by the backside of his tiny Levis. She smiled and put her hands on her hips.

"Okay!" Alex shouted, followed by a playful giggle. "Okay, Charlie! You're not a fraidy cat!"

Charlie grinned and effortlessly flipped Alex upright to sit on his enormous shoulders. Alex balanced himself by hanging on to one handful of the giant man's cropped blond hair and another handful of his left ear. Charlie's oversized fingers wrapped carefully around the boy's thigh to hold on to him. His other hand slowly lifted, opened, and then revealed a single TicTac, which Alex snatched up.

Brooke was giving Charlie a thumbs-up when Shirley Lindy came through the door. Shirley wore a plastic blue poncho and pulled out a tissue to wipe away the small beads of water on her wire-rimmed glasses.

"Hello there, Alexander," Shirley said, looking up at him.

"Hi, Mrs. Lindy," he said. "We couldn't find Charlie and he scared me!"

"Me too," Brooke said. "Where is Pastor Jim?"

"I left him out front," the older woman replied.

"What's he doing out there in the rain?" Brooke asked.

"We have a little problem." Shirley reeled in her right index finger, silently inviting them to come and see.

Brooke was the first outside as Shirley held the door for a ducking Charlie, who still had Alex saddled on his shoulders.

A fog had rolled onto the property, and the storm had been reduced to a misty drizzle. Brooke's breath clouded before her mouth and nose. But her eyes were on Pastor Jim.

"Oh no." She sighed. "I saw this happen."

Brooke slid her arms around Shirley's shoulders as Alex lowered his chin to the top of Charlie's head.

Pastor Jim knelt in a shallow puddle with his head down and hands resting on the top half of the large wooden cross that lay on the ground.

Lightning had struck.

TWO

Thirty-six-year-old Kaitlyn Harby sat on a corner barstool at The Pilot Inn. She was halfway into her first Bacardi and Coke and wished she could smoke a cigarette. She took a deep breath and ran her finger slowly down the side of her glass. She hadn't had a smoke in over five years and knew the craving wouldn't last long. It felt kind of good to be in control of something, at least.

Despite being one of the area's most popular watering holes, the storm had made it a slow night at The Pilot. The sticky smells of stale beer that usually haunted the hundred-year-old bar and diner were minimized by both a light crowd and a splintered mop handle that propped the back door partially open, allowing rain-fresh air to waft through. Only one of the televisions was on, making it a little darker than usual, and The Guess Who's "No Time" was playing a little too loudly from the corner jukebox. Kaitlyn wasn't sure why she only liked listening to old songs. She guessed that they made her think of her father and the short amount of time she'd had with him.

She shook it off. This wasn't going to be another one of those nights where the promises she had made to herself once again ended up in small pieces scattered all over the floor of the bar. The song ended to the sarcastic applause of an overweight man in his midfifties. A trucker? A construction worker? His fat, sausage-like fingers held a bottle of Bud Light as he slammed four quarters down on the edge of the pool table, securing his rights to play the current game's winner. He glanced back at Kaitlyn with eyes as gray and worn as his face, giving her the once-over. It didn't bother Kaitlyn. Men had always looked at her. Though the cigarettes and booze hadn't been kind to her appearance, she took a fair amount of consolation in her ability to still turn heads.

She rested her chin on the palm of her hand and then looked up. In the long mirror that ran the length of the wall behind the bar, she could see one of her only *real* friends, Lila, The Pilot's owner, walking through the saloon doors that separated the two halves of the bar and diner.

It was good to see Lila, all six feet and two-hundred-fifty pounds of her. They had known each other for over fifteen years now and Lila had spent the bulk of that time not just bartending, cooking, and bouncing, but also doing a pretty solid job of limiting whatever Kaitlyn drank at The Pilot. This helped Kaitlyn keep the secret part of her life bottled up. *Enable* was the word Lila liked to use, even though it bugged Kaitlyn.

"I had a feeling I'd find you here," Lila said, taking off her coat as she stepped behind the bar.

"Not sure how to take that," Kaitlyn said.

"You can take off if you want, Vince!" Lila shouted to the far end of the bar, letting the bartender know she was here. She grabbed the fountain gun and filled a glass with water before turning back to Kaitlyn. "That was some kind of crazy storm, huh?"

"It was somethin," Kaitlyn said, tapping at the side of her glass with a fingernail. "Let's have another rum and Coke. And before you ask, it's only my second."

Lila dropped her elbows on the bar and then pointed toward the pool tables. Kaitlyn turned her head and caught the eye of a man over by the jukebox, staring hard at her. It wasn't the kind of look she was used to, the soft perusal of a would-be lover. It was like his eyes drilled into her. Saw her. Knew her.

"I think you've got a fan," Lila said, stepping back and grabbing a bottle of Bacardi from behind the register.

Kaitlyn nodded toward the man. He was a little too thin for her liking, had wavy brown hair, and appeared to be in his early thirties. Jeans. Navy pea coat. And boots that told her he was but another construction worker out to blow off some steam. He had a pool stick in one hand and what looked like an apple in the other. And he continued to stare. Though Kaitlyn wouldn't consider him to be an eye-catcher, he had, for whatever reason, caught her eye.

"Why is he looking at us?" Kaitlyn asked, turning back around. "And why would he bring an apple in here?"

"He ain't looking at my old bag of bones," Lila said.

"I'm gonna get him to come over here." Kaitlyn flashed him the little smile that never failed.

"Just don't leave with him." Lila gave Kaitlyn a warning look.

"What's that supposed to mean?" Kaitlyn asked, poking at Lila's shoulder. "I'm gonna behave."

"Looks like we're gonna find out. Here he comes."

Kaitlyn watched the man lean the pool stick against the wall and put the apple in the front left pocket of his coat. He didn't break her gaze the whole time, and even though she was burned out on construction types, she couldn't take her eyes off him. He sat a few seats down, nodded at Lila, and then resumed his examination of Kaitlyn, making her even more curious.

Something seemed different about this guy. His eyes were a soft green, yet cast subtle hints of authority. Even though he hadn't shaved in what looked like a couple of days, his grittiness came across as clean and pure. She had never seen anyone quite like him.

"He certainly has your attention," Lila whispered. "Don't be so obvious."

"He is beautiful," Kaitlyn said.

Lila laughed. "Beautiful? I've never heard you say that about a guy before. He doesn't seem like your type. Too skinny. Too . . . average."

"Look at him. He's unreal."

"What are you talking about?"

Kaitlyn leaned forward, and then shifted toward him.

"Hi there," she said softly, in open invitation.

She waited, but he didn't say anything.

"Strong, silent type," Lila whispered.

Kaitlyn took a sip of her drink. She didn't like being ignored.

The least he could do was reply. "Why are you staring at me?" she asked, this time a little louder.

The man didn't move.

"Why don't you just take a picture?" Kaitlyn said, waving her hand back and forth in front of her.

"Are you talking to me?" the man asked calmly.

"Oh my goodness!" Kaitlyn said. "You can talk!"

"You want me to take a picture of you?" he asked, a hint of a smile bending the corner of his mouth.

"No," Kaitlyn said, her voice changing from the curious to the more playful one that she had more confidence in. "I just wondered why you were staring at me."

"I'm not staring at you," he replied.

"Oh yes you are," Kaitlyn said. She winked at him and hoped Lila didn't catch it.

He gave a little shrug. "No, I'm not."

"Then what are you looking at?" Was he mental? Or was this part of his game?

The man lifted his hand off the bar and pointed his pinky finger right at what Kaitlyn thought was her head. "The TV."

Behind Kaitlyn, against the far wall on a flat screen television, a magician was attempting to crawl through a solid piece of glass that served as the front window of a department store. Kaitlyn tried covering her face with her hand as she wished she could steal the magician's thunder by disappearing into thin air.

"I am such an idiot," she mumbled, dropping her hand and ducking her head.

"Sorry," Lila said to the man, putting her hand on Kaitlyn's arm. "Please excuse her. She's a little tipsy."

"No, I'm not," Kaitlyn said. "I told you I'm only on my second drink. Two more is my limit."

"Relax," Lila whispered. "I just saved you."

"That's okay," the man said, as if he understood. "It happens."

"Jukebox time," Kaitlyn said, standing and looking down at the floor. It was the first excuse she could think of to get off her stool and out of the man's sight. She knocked on the bar top. "Get me and our new friend a shot of Jäger." She was hoping that maybe the drink could serve as an apology to the man.

"Okay," Lila said.

Kaitlyn stood a few feet behind the pool table and fed a pair of dollar bills to the jukebox. She laughed out loud. *The only time I really want a guy to look at me, and he isn't.* She ran her hand through her hair and peeked back toward the bar. Lila was pouring the shots, and the guy with the apple was still staring—at the television—when she felt a hand settle on her back.

"Need help picking out some real music, sugar britches?"

Kaitlyn turned around, and the fat trucker coughed out a syrupy laugh right in her face.

"Excuse me?" she said.

"Who taught you how to pick out music?"

So he didn't like her taste in songs. She ignored him and scanned the jukebox for some more oldies. Maybe she could pick out another classic—something that would stick real well in Truckerman's fat head. She made her final selection and as she headed back to the bar, Kaitlyn gave the fat trucker a look that suggested pool wasn't the only game he'd lose tonight.

"I'm gonna step to the other end of the bar and get out of your way here," Lila said.

"You gonna leave me alone with this guy?" Kaitlyn asked, tilting her head toward the man at the bar.

"He seems all right," Lila whispered. "And by the way, he didn't want the shot."

"I'll change his mind."

"Just behave." Lila leaned her forehead toward Kaitlyn's and lifted a delicate brow in silent warning.

"I will," Kaitlyn said, rolling her eyes. "I'll yell if I'm feeling naughty."

"You do that."

Kaitlyn sat back down and quickly polished off one of the shots. Apple man was still glued to the TV when she turned to him.

"I think I owe you an apology," she said. "I thought you were looking at me and I guess I kind of wanted to talk to you."

He didn't respond again. He just kept staring.

Kaitlyn knocked on the bar and raised her voice over Foreigner's "Dirty White Boy." "Will you quit staring at that stupid television? I'm trying to apologize to you."

He carefully crossed his arms. Kaitlyn found it difficult to take her eyes off of him while silently wondering what it was about him that she was drawn to.

"I'm not staring at the television anymore," he said. "Now I'm staring at you."

"What?"

"You heard me," he said. "And I have a feeling you know why."

Kaitlyn felt a tiny chill dance across the side of her neck and stop just under her chin. She ran her palm along where she'd felt it and tried to look back at the man. But she couldn't.

"It's not like you to be bashful, is it?" he asked.

She didn't like the way he asked the question. If it was flirting, it wasn't fun. He hadn't moved, but somehow he seemed so much closer. Too close.

"You have never been the shy type," he said.

The way he said it was calm and with no emotion, but some of that authority she sensed in those green eyes had underlined all seven words. She tried to look at him again and couldn't, but now she knew why. She looked down and closed her eyes. He knew her, knew about her past. She heard the legs of a barstool pushing back. There was a pause, then evenly paced steps.

He sidled up next to her.

"Tell me why I was staring at you," he whispered.

The man had found a way to take a lifetime of indiscretions and balance them neatly on the point of a needle. Each time she tried to look at him, it poked at her, exposing everything about her, while injecting paralyzing doses of shame.

"It's okay," he said.

No, it isn't. It's another bad day, and I'm kidding myself about ever quitting drinking. A four-drink limit was a nice start, but it will never be enough to drown it all out. I'm going to get drunk tonight.

And by tomorrow, I will have forgotten about how my conscience let me believe that this guy . . .

Kaitlyn opened her eyes. "Look. I don't know who you are or what you want, but let's go back to silent staring. Okay? Better yet, let's just go our own ways."

She edged off the stool and reached out to pick up the other shot. But as she did, she felt his warm hand gently take her wrist. That little chill raced across her neck again and moved into gooseflesh that crossed her shoulders and spread down her back.

"That's enough, isn't it?" he asked, guiding her hand and the drink back to the top of the bar. "You're okay."

As he gradually let go of her wrist, for the first time in her life, she felt like she really was okay. But that made no sense. She shivered. A tear slipped down her cheek, and Kaitlyn closed her eyes. She couldn't deny it; she was at complete peace. The bar had gone quiet, and she could feel him standing next to her. The tear dripped off the side of her chin, then more quickly followed. She couldn't stop them. She didn't want to. Everything was okay. No, *perfect*. Even though she was weeping.

"I would like to show you something," he said.

Kaitlyn opened her eyes and the man leaned against the bar and reached into his coat pocket. He pulled the apple out and placed it in front of her.

"What do you see in this?" he asked.

Kaitlyn couldn't speak.

"It's okay," he said. "Tell me what you see."

She was mesmerized by the fruit's immaculate shine. She had never seen one with such a perfect shape, and its bright red color looked as if it had been painted on. It even had a tiny leaf attached to its green stem. It almost seemed fake—as if it belonged in a dining room display at a furniture store. She hesitantly picked it up and held it, confirming that it was, in fact, flawlessly real.

"Tell me," he repeated kindly. "Tell me what you think of it."

She turned it slightly in her hand, and part of the man's reflection appeared in it. Her arm fell to the bar, and the tiny hairs on the back of her neck stood on end as she looked at him. She wanted to say more, but only managed three words: "It is beautiful."

He tapped on the side of the apple and looked right at her. "What do you think would happen to this beautiful apple if it had a worm inside of it?"

She paused for a moment, wiping away her remaining tears, leaving smudges of eyeliner on her shirtsleeve. "I don't know. It would eat it up?"

"Yes, it would," he said, placing his hand directly on top of hers. "Forgive."

"Forgive?" she whispered.

"Kaitlyn, I want you to learn to forgive."

He turned and slowly walked away from her, making his way out the back door.

Kaitlyn picked the apple up off the bar and hurried after him, staring out the window to the rear parking lot. She watched him climb into the cab of an old Ford F-150 and pull away. But one question rang in her mind, above the rest.

When did I tell him my name?

THREE

L et's just turn around and go back," Brooke said as she and Shirley
stood in the center of the heavily wooded Church Road, a half-
mile passage of sand, pea gravel, and white stone that didn't make
it on most maps. Beyond the arrivals and departures of Brooke and
the Lindys, the only other traffic the road saw was from the few who
came to church on Sunday or the occasional jogger looking for a
shortcut into the park that ran along Lake Erie.

Shirley turned back to Brooke. "I'm sorry, honey. My darn arthritis is working overtime this morning."

"No worries," she said. "I'm not in the mood to walk this morning anyways. I'm freaking out about Alex."

"He's going to be just fine," Shirley said. "You're just being a
good mother."

"He got another bloody nose last night after everyone went to
bed."

"Poor baby. Isn't that the third or fourth in the last two weeks?"

"More like seventh or eighth."

"Maybe they'll have answers for us this morning at the hospital."

"We'll see," Brooke said. "But why would they want us to come
back for blood tests?"

Shirley glanced at her watch. "What time are we supposed to
be there?"

"Seven forty-five."

"I'm sure the tests are just part of a normal routine."

"Routine for what?" Brooke closed her eyes and pinched the

bridge of her nose. She didn't like the way it sounded. "You think it's something bad?"

"Not at all," Shirley said, putting her arm on Brooke's shoulder and pulling her in for a quick hug.

Brooke forced a smile.

They made a right into the narrow driveway that led through the trees and to the twenty-acre patch of land, all St. Thomas property. At some point, church members had probably hoped they'd one day need to expand, build a larger sanctuary, a huge parking lot. Sadly, there was little need for that. But Brooke was still glad it was here and that she lived there with her adopted family. With the rolling hills, the deep forest, the little church and cozy house, it always made her feel at peace. Like she'd discovered someplace secret, sacred, hers. Whenever she heard someone say "God's Country," she thought of St. Thomas Church and the land surrounding it.

And then the cross came into view. Or what was left of it. She had to look away.

"I know Alex is going to be fine," she said. "But the cross won't be. Look at that thing."

"Don't worry about the cross," Shirley said. "It can be replaced."

"With what? Our good looks? We don't have the money to fix it."

Shirley didn't respond and neither of them said a word until they reached the end of the driveway near the house.

Shirley pulled an envelope from her pocket. "I forgot to put this in the mailbox, and if I don't do it now, I'm liable to forget again."

"Let me take it back down there," Brooke said.

"I may take you up on that," Shirley said with a smile. "See you in the house in a few minutes."

Brooke glanced at the envelope, an electric bill, and ran down and put it in the mailbox. When she made it back up the driveway, she went up on the porch and stopped, looking through the front window. Pastor Jim was sitting in the old La-Z-Boy with his braille Bible in his hand. She suspected he was rehearsing his sermon for Sunday.

Brooke smiled and glanced back up the hill toward the church, thinking of him in there, preaching one of his sermons. Her smile faded and she looked back through the window at Pastor Jim. For the first time ever, she was glad he was blind; she didn't want him to see the wreckage on the hill.

She took a step back on the porch and remembered the way the cross had been. It stood so tall, and there was something about its polished wood and placement on the lawn that left her feeling safe, protected. Pastor Jim always told her that it was her choice to go to service, and every Sunday morning, it was impossible for her to not stop and stare at the cross before she walked in.

But now it'd been blown in half, with the bottom part still sticking out of the ground. Most of the top of the cross lay facedown in the wet sod. A separate piece was a few feet away.

She blew a puff of warm air into her hands and grabbed the door handle. It was never locked, so she turned the knob and stepped inside.

"Hey, hey," she said, closing the door behind her.

"Hello, kiddo," Pastor Jim said, pivoting the chair in her direction. He was wearing an old T-shirt that fell over a pair of flannel pajama bottoms. He closed the Bible and brushed his salt-and-pepper hair back with his hand. "That was a short walk on this bright and early morning."

"We've got to get ready to take Alex to the hospital."

"I offered to drive, but the idea didn't go over too well with Alex."

"Ha-ha," Brooke said, shaking her head. The pastor hadn't been allowed to drive for years. "By the way, since when is seven in the morning bright and early for you?"

"Seven is pretty early."

"She knows as well as anyone in this house that you're the first to rise," Shirley said, entering the living room from the kitchen. Brooke noticed the limp had gotten worse. *Arthritis must be really bothering her today.* Shirley leaned over and kissed Pastor Jim on his forehead. "This man wakes me up every single morning. I can't remember the last time he slept past five."

Pastor Jim stood and hiked his thumb in the direction of Shirley's voice. "I figured she would be used to it after all this time. You think she's getting ready to trade me in, Brooke?"

"I would, if I were her," Brooke said.

"Don't tempt me," Shirley said with a teasing lilt to her voice.

"Never gonna happen," Pastor Jim said, holding out his arms for a hug, which Shirley was quick to give. Brooke wished she had someone in her life to hug her like that. The look in Pastor Jim's eyes was usually hard to read, with the gray film that covered them, but right now they said loud and clear, *I cherish my wife.*

"Where're Alex and Charlie?" Brooke asked.

"I think they are downstairs," Pastor Jim said.

Brooke stomped a couple times on the floor and then walked over to the closet to retrieve her son's coat. "Let's go, Alex!"

A series of little footsteps scurried up the stairs. The door opened, and Alex skipped over and hugged his mother's leg. "Hi, Mom!"

"Hey, buddy," she said.

Alex proudly lifted his chin as he let go of her leg. "When blood came out of my nose yesterday, it didn't even hurt."

"I know," she said, pinching his cheek. "How did you get so brave?"

His hazel eyes squinted, and the freckles that had been sprinkled around his little nose seemed to hunch together. "I don't know, but you said I can get some chocolate milk from the store today."

"That's right," Brooke said, holding open his Detroit Tigers jacket. Alex backed into it and put his arms through the sleeves, which were about three inches too short.

"Looks like somebody needs a new coat," Shirley said. "Maybe Santa will bring you one."

"No," Alex said. "He's getting me a bike that doesn't have baby wheels on it."

Charlie dipped under the top of the door as he came up from the basement. He smiled and waved at Brooke.

"Hey, Charlie," she said.

The big man walked over and handed Brooke Alex's matching Tigers baseball cap.

"Thanks, Charlie," Brooke said. She stopped buttoning halfway up the coat and put Alex's cap on the way he liked it, backward. "We need anything else from the store?"

"Just the Pop-Tarts and two gallons of milk," Pastor Jim said.

"Okay," Brooke said. "We'll be back in a few hours."

"I think maybe Charlie wants something," Shirley added, nodding at her son.

Charlie was holding his TicTac container up in front of his face. He stared at it for a few seconds like he had never seen it before. There were two left.

"I think you are right," Brooke said.

Charlie opened the lid and poured out the two candies into his other hand. He reached down and gave one to Alex, and then leaned his head back and dropped the last one in his mouth. He held the empty container back up in front of his face, then slowly turned to Brooke.

"TicTacs, Charlie?" Brooke asked, smiling.

Charlie took a step toward her and stopped. The top of his head was just under the edge of the ceiling fan. He stuffed two fingers into his front pocket and then took another step toward her. He held out his hand and gave her a nickel and three pennies. His eyes began to blink quickly as a broad grin slowly stretched across his face in what could only mean *Yes, please.*

"Let's bolt," Brooke said.

Brooke held the screen door and waited for Shirley as Alex walked outside. She glanced up at the church and then turned back to the three Lindys, who were standing next to one another in the center of the living room. Shirley was smiling at her with eyes that were much easier to read than Pastor Jim's. Despite having a blind husband and a seven-foot, three-hundred-fifty-five-pound son that hadn't spoken a single word in his life, her eyes were sending a message that was loud and clear.

I'm the luckiest woman in the world.

• • •

"We're gonna be so late," Brooke said, leaning her head against the window.

"They will understand," Shirley said. "Quit worrying."

"Easier said than done. But I'll do my best."

"Thatta girl," Shirley said.

"You okay back there, buddy?" Brooke asked.

"He's out," Shirley said.

"But we just left." Brooke turned and looked in the backseat. Alex was sleeping with his head turned to the side, making his red eyelashes look extra long. He was snoring lightly, and he held the rubber SpongeBob he scored with his Happy Meal the week before.

"How late were you guys up?"

"Too late," Brooke answered, closing her eyes and shooting up a quick prayer for good news at the hospital.

It was normally only about a ten minute ride from the Lindy house to downtown Carlson, but they were stuck behind a train on Old Gibraltar Road, a county-neglected minefield of potholes, gravel, and oily sand. Despite its horrendous condition, the wooded two-mile stretch was the shortest and most commonly used route to North Jefferson Avenue and the city's two banks, one gas station, and string of mom-and-pop businesses that were separated by unoccupied buildings.

At the tail end of North "Jeff" was the hospital and Carlson's number one producer of unemployed people, a partially functional assembly plant, now operating under the tax-friendly pseudonym of "Auto Trust." Brooke did a couple year stint there before moving on to become a nail tech at the Downriver Mall in Lincoln Park. Even though the three hundred a week she earned was less than half what she had made at the plant, she liked doing nails, and the time it gave her with Alex—as well as less need for childcare.

"Pastor Jim hasn't said a single thing about the cross," Brooke said. "Not one word."

"How many times have you ever heard him complain about anything?"

"Like, never," Brooke said. "What's the plan with it, then? What are we gonna do?"

31

"Not sure," Shirley said, taking her turn to look back at Alex. "James said that everything happens for a reason and that regardless of what it is, God is with us and will make something good come from it. But you are right. James isn't exactly the type to ask why it happened or why us."

"Of all the places for lightning to hit," Brooke mumbled, glancing up at the flashing red lights that were attached to a pair of worn-out posts that looked like they were about to fall over. *This crossing is in serious need of a gate. It's a miracle nobody's ever gotten creamed by a train.* Not that this particular train was going to get anybody. It was dead stopped. She let out a long breath of frustration. She looked at what had to be Detroit gang signs scratched repeatedly on the side of one of the boxcar doors, then read one of the painted tags. "Guess what, Shirley?"

"What?"

Brooke pointed at the train and read words spray-painted in purple and underlined in black. "HUBBA IS ALL DAT."

"Oh yeah?" Shirley laughed. She pointed to their right and read huge gold letters. "BOBBY IS A . . . uhh . . ." She glanced at the sleeping child behind her. "Something really bad."

"I knew that," Brooke said casually, "but more importantly, THE NURSE IS EASY."

"KAITLYN IS HOT," Shirley said as they waited for the train to pass. And then she sighed. "I don't appreciate women being called that. I wish young men would be more respectful nowadays."

"Good luck with that," Brooke said, lifting her hand back toward a different train car. "Maybe you need to GET HIGH IN JULY."

"Never touched a marijuana cigarette," Shirley said as the dinged-up freight train began to pick up speed. "Check that one out, Brooke. One of our graffiti guys must have taken an art lesson."

Against a colorful backdrop, painted in perfect block letters, were the words: ONLY BELIEVE.

"Wow," Brooke said. "I wonder how long it took to do that."

"Don't know. Had to be awhile."

Brooke turned around and smiled. Alex was rubbing his eyes and finishing a yawn. "Hey, buddy, that was a short nap."

He fumbled for his SpongeBob and then looked right at her. "What does it mean that Kaitlyn is hot?"

"Nothing, buddy." Brooke smiled, put the car in drive, and as they made their way over the tracks and headed up Old Gibraltar, she turned the stereo up and sang "Magic Man" along with the radio.

FOUR

Macey Lewis strolled into the waiting room of the free clinic on the first floor of East Shore Community Hospital. It was always busy down here, but today it was packed, even at this early hour. She guessed that the forty seats were a couple dozen shy of what was needed.

Since she wasn't in a rush, for once, she took a place in line in front of the receptionists' window and waited to drop off her file. She didn't mind hanging out here; standing in a room full of colds and sprained wrists practically felt like a vacation, compared to her normal life.

She looked down and smiled at a little redheaded boy standing in front of her. He hid behind what was probably his mother's leg and then peeked back out at her.

"Hi," she said.

He kept smiling. She guessed he was about five or six, and she'd seen his brand of shyness a thousand times before.

She turned around and perused the room. Grandparents, parents, teenagers, and children talked and thumbed through year-old issues of *Time*, *National Geographic*, and *Highlights*. Over in the corner, a school of minnow-sized fish were gliding back and forth in an aquarium, casting a hypnotic spell upon a handful of onlookers.

There was a tap at her hip. A little girl, maybe a year older than the redhead, was looking up at her. She had thick, curly brown hair and matching brown eyes that did more than hint she wasn't quite feeling like herself. Her cheeks were red and raw, and Cheetos residue accented her chapped lips and runny nose.

"How did you get so pretty?" Macey asked.

"I dunno," the little girl said with a tiny voice and shrug. "I like your shoes." The girl knelt down and tapped on the light blue logo of Macey's brand-new Nikes.

"Why thank you, sweetheart. I just got them yesterday. I like yours too."

A large woman, wearing a Detroit Pistons sweatshirt, abandoned what appeared to be her two other children and hurried over to apologize for the little girl. "I am so sorry."

"No worries," Macey said. "She sure is a cutie."

"Thank you," the woman said. "She can be a handful, though."

The redhead came out from behind the other woman's leg. He was another cutie. Actually, all the kids in the clinic were cuties, but she hoped to never see any of them again. The boy stepped up next to her and pointed his index finger at the girl and her mother as they walked away. "She has boogers in her nose."

"Alexander!" the woman said, turning around and picking him up. *Yep, that's his mother.*

"She *really* has boogers in her nose, Mom."

Macey quickly exchanged smiles with the mother, who shook her head in what seemed like a mild form of parental embarrassment. "They tell it like it is, don't they?" Macey said.

"Particularly this one," the woman answered, tugging on the bill of her son's ball cap. She looked like she was going to say something and then stopped.

"Our cross got hitted by thunder," the little boy said.

"What, sweetie?" Macey asked.

"He's talking about the storm last night," the mother said. "Do you mind if I ask you something?"

"Go for it," Macey said.

"How long does it take to become a nurse?"

"Oh, I'm not a nurse," Macey answered, holding up a manila folder. "I'm only down here dropping this off. But I think it's a little over four years."

"Thanks," the woman said. "I thought you looked a little bit young to be a nurse. My bad."

35

Macey was used to hearing that. She smiled back, knowing full well that with her ponytail and no makeup, she didn't look a day over eighteen. If she had a dollar for every time someone said they thought she looked too young, her student loan balance would probably be half what it was. Wearing the same, comfortable, bright orange scrubs the third-floor nurses would be wearing that day, she figured she probably *did* look a little bit young to be a nurse.

"It was on fire," the boy said. "I didn't see it, but it was."

"What was on fire? The cross?"

"Yeah," the mother said. "It's in front of our church. It got struck by lightning."

"It got whacked in *half*," the boy said.

"A cross got hit by lightning?" Macey asked.

"And it smells funny," the boy added. "Mrs. Lindy says we can't 'ford to fix it."

"That's not her problem," the mother said. "Shh."

"It's okay," Macey said. "You know it's really none of my business, but the church's insurance will probably cover that. You should check."

"Yeah," the mother said. "We don't have many people at our church. We kind of don't have that much insurance anymore."

A cross they can't afford to fix? What were you thinking, God? I don't understand you. But one thing she *did* understand was not being able to afford things. *Been there, done that.*

"I want to help you fix it," Macey said. The words hadn't made it off her lips before she regretted it.

"Really?" the mother asked, her eyes wide.

No, not really. I don't have to be the one that fixes everything. I don't have the time and wouldn't even begin to know how to help you.

"You can fix it?" the redhead asked, his eyes lighting as if she were going to orchestrate a miracle for him.

"I'm not sure," she said, smiling and not sure why it was impossible to say no. "Why don't we find out?"

. . .

Dr. Zach Norman leaned over the edge of the third-floor nurses' station and dropped a stack of folders on the desk. "Will someone please tell me when that noise is finally going to end?"

Kaitlyn knew his question was directed at her, sitting behind the nurses' desk, updating patient records by inputting notes from the rounds into the computer. "If I had to guess, Zach, I'd say the noise will stop when the job is finished." She paused for a few seconds, confident that it wasn't her sarcasm that bothered him. It was the fact that her eyes had never left the pile of charts. She could feel his irritation across the counter.

The noise that Zach referred to was created by the construction workers—working on the hospital's new $28 million administration wing. It was in its twenty-second of twenty-four scheduled months, and Kaitlyn knew it had been the bane of the doctor's ability to concentrate—the relentless tapping and pounding of hammers, the humming and buzzing of dull saws and worn-out drills, and the painful screech of metal ladders unwillingly dragged from the steel beds of trucks. He needed to get over it. It wasn't that bad, even when you drank seven days a week.

"Seriously," he said, snapping his fingers and still waiting for her to look at him. She didn't. "How can you work with all that racket?"

"I ignore it. Try concentrating on your patients, Doc, and quit being so fussy. We've got a ward full of kids today. Let's think about them instead of you for a change, huh?"

Out of the corner of her eye, she saw him cross his arms. "You know, Kait," the doctor said under his breath, as another nurse left the station, "I'm really not in the mood today. And by the way, in the halls, I think it's best if you refer to me as Dr. Norman."

"I apologize for questioning your authority, *Doctor*," Kaitlyn said. Her eyes left the chart, and she stared straight at him, exercising a greater authority only the two of them could understand. "If you want to play that way in the *halls*, you can refer to me as Nurse Practitioner Harby."

He sighed, lifted his hands in surrender, and dropped his elbows on the counter. "Sorry. I've got a rippin' headache. Let's start over. Would you care to join me for lunch, Nurse Harby? My treat."

You've got a headache?

"I think I'll pass, Doctor," she said calmly, picking up the top chart again.

"C'mon, Kait." He sighed. "For Pete's sake, now we can't even go to lunch?"

"Looks that way."

"Isn't today pizza day?"

"Yep."

"You are turning down pizza?"

She studied him. She should steer clear of him, but she was starving and she did love the cafeteria's pizza. And she *had* been a little hard on him, if he had a headache. "Okay. Give me fifteen minutes to check on two patients and I'll join you."

● ● ●

Kaitlyn wasn't sure which decision was worse—hers to join Zach for lunch or the cafeteria's to serve baked beans with pizza.

She rolled her eyes as he fidgeted with his napkin. Of course, pizza in itself was beneath "the great doctor." She watched as he took another bite out of his salad before washing it down with a tidy sip of the four-dollar bottle of imported water that he had brought with him.

Everything was beneath Zach. Beneath him and his Mercedes convertible, his Rolex, his eight-thousand-square-foot house, and his seven-figure brokerage account.

It was going to be impossible for her to get through this lunch without explaining for the umpteenth time what had happened to "them" and why she didn't want to be with him anymore.

Though her answer would never change, the way he asked the question always did.

"Do you know how many women out there would be interested in what I have to offer?" he asked.

"Sounds like you already know the answer," she said, peeling little chunks of green pepper off her second slice of pizza. "I'm sure there are way too many to count."

"For crying out loud," the doctor said. "I should just give up."

"That would be a good idea."

"Kaitlyn," he whispered loudly. "Just tell me."

"Tell you what?"

His fingers drummed along the side of his water bottle. "Tell me what I have to do to make you happy. Tell me and I'll do it."

"That was actually pretty good," she said matter-of-factly. "Have you been reading *Cosmo* or something?"

"Don't be ridiculous. C'mon, I'm trying here."

"I just find it interesting that you never even came close to asking me these things while we dated. You always—"

"Hi, kids!"

Kaitlyn was spared by Macey Lewis, who invited herself to join them for lunch.

"Am I interrupting anything?" Macey asked.

"Of course not," Kaitlyn said, offering a half-hearted smile and a subtle look of thanks.

"Not at all," Zach added. Kaitlyn saw his disappointment. No doubt he would harass her about the intervention later.

"That's some fancy water there, Zach," Macey said, pointing at the plastic bottle. "I'm sure you can tell a huge difference between that and the cheap stuff us common folks drink."

"Actually, I can," he said. "You keep up the good work, and you'll be able to afford this stuff someday."

"I'm doing my best," Macey said. "I'm begging you to be patient with me, boss man."

Kaitlyn grinned. Macey was the only person at the hospital who would ever get away with talking to Zach like that. Even though he was the one in charge, he gave Macey all the space she needed on the pediatric floor for one simple reason—she was a brilliant doctor.

"How about that weather last night?" Macey asked, squinting and tilting her head toward Zach.

The weather? Kaitlyn thought. Macey either asked a legitimate question or was trying to hint to Zach that it was better to talk about anything other than his relationship with Kait.

"I haven't seen anything like it in years," Zach said, taking the hint with a lift of his chin.

Macey leaned back in her chair. "I sat on my deck and watched the storm for twenty minutes before I realized I had left the top off my Jeep." She laughed. "My car seat is soaked. I'll have wet-butt for two weeks."

"Wet-butt?" Zach repeated. "Real classy, Dr. Lewis."

"The news said that over half of Carlson lost power last night," Kaitlyn said.

"Lost power and produced one dead cross," Macey added.

"One dead cross?" Kaitlyn asked. "What do you mean?"

"Ran into some people this morning down at the free clinic. Lightning hit the cross at their church and literally cut it in two."

"What church?" Kaitlyn asked.

"St. Thomas, I think," Macey answered.

St. Thomas, Kaitlyn thought. She knew of the church, but was much more familiar with the old road it was on.

"God firebombs his own house?" Zach asked. He snickered and turned to Kaitlyn.

She didn't like that look. He was also doing his close-mouthed smile that she hated. Even though she only ever went to church for weddings, funerals, or Christmas Eve, her pleas for Zach to join her had gone unanswered. She wanted to be a better person, to go more and believe that there was something better, something that could help her be who she was *during the day* . . . all the time. But for Zach, science had somehow put God out of a job, so talking about faith was about as important to him as holding hands or sharing his true feelings.

She was glad their relationship was over.

"God just didn't firebomb it," Macey said. "He did it to people who can't afford to fix it either. Go figure."

"Their insurance should help them out on that," Zach said. "Unless Santa Claus is their agent."

"I told the woman the same thing," Macey said. "But it sounds like they don't have any insurance."

"What are they going to do?" Kaitlyn asked. "People are going to pull up to the church and see half a cross?"

"Not for long," Macey said. "We are going to help them."

Zach rolled his eyes. "How are you going to do that?"

"I haven't figured that out yet. I just know I need to help."

"Listen to me, guys," Zach said. "Work with me here."

Kaitlyn clenched her pant leg and held her breath. Zach's "work with me here" was his way of saying, *I'm right and about to prove it. If you disagree, you'll end up feeling pretty stupid.*

"Stop me when I say something you disagree with," Zach said. He pointed at Macey. "Let's say there was an omniscient and loving God."

"There is," Kaitlyn interjected.

"That *loving* God let that cross get hit by lightning, and he knew they couldn't afford to fix it. So why are you fixing it if God wanted it to happen?" He turned and looked right at Kaitlyn. "Unless, of course, he's just a terrible shot." He laughed over his own joke.

"Maybe God wants us to step in. To help," Macey said. "It's a chance to show kindness."

Zach let out a scoff. "Don't you have far bigger things to do, Macey? Like save a kid's life?"

Kaitlyn shook her head at him and placed her napkin neatly over the untouched baked beans on her plate. "You have such incredible compassion, Zach. I've really missed it."

"What's that supposed to mean?" he asked, glancing between her and Macey. "You guys are missing my point. Just look at things we wade through here at East Shore every single day. All I'm saying is if there is a God, he's a bully, I don't like him, and I don't want anything to do with him."

"If God's only a bully," Macey said, "why are you a doctor, cleaning up his messes? Why even do what you do?"

He sighed heavily, clearly growing uncomfortable with the conversation. "There is no God," he said, with a shake of his head. "And I help sick kids get better for only one reason."

"Why is that?" Macey asked.

"Because I can."

Macey picked up his bottle of water and gave him a look that seemed to suggest she wasn't all that impressed with it. "Let me hit you with another worn-out question, and then I want to be done with religion for the day." She crossed her arms. "If there is no God, what happens to us when we die?"

"Yeah, Zach," Kaitlyn said, curious to hear his response.

"C'mon, guys," he said. "You're clearly not in the right mood for thoughtful dialogue."

"I want to hear your answer," Kaitlyn said, ignoring his attempt to exit the conversation just when it was getting good. "What will happen to *you* when *you* die, Zach?"

"It's simple," he said, giving her that irritating smile once again. "Remember what it was like before you were born?"

She squinted and looked at Macey, who shrugged. "Of course not."

He lowered his hands and tapped on the table. "Death is just like that."

Kaitlyn noticed that Macey recoiled a little from his answer. She also noticed how quiet the cafeteria had just become.

Macey tapped back at the table. "We are still going to help them fix that cross."

"Exactly who makes up *we*?" Zach asked.

"Me and whoever I round up," Macey said, pointing her finger past him and Kaitlyn. "Maybe I can get some of them to help."

Outside the cafeteria window, a handful of construction workers were in the temporary parking lot, sitting in the bed and on the tailgate of a rusty old Ford F-150, laughing and eating their lunch.

"Oh please," Zach said. "Good luck with that."

"I'll help," Kaitlyn said.

"You guys are crazy." Zach rolled his eyes and crossed his arms. His smile fell. "You are serious, aren't you?"

"Yes," Macey said.

"Why?" he asked. "Just tell me why. Don't we have enough to do around here?"

Kaitlyn took his arm and did her best to duplicate his irritating little smile. "Because we can. And if we have the power to help, and a need is presented, doesn't that require any doctor to step up . . . including you, Dr. Norman?"

"Me?" he said as he ran his hand along the side of his face and shook his head like he couldn't believe what he was about to say. "I guess you can count me in too."

FIVE

Later that afternoon, Macey sat alone in the quiet of a small laboratory. As she leaned in toward the room's only functional microscope, she was thinking about Zach's statements about death and God. He was wrong, and even though he was a jerk a lot of the time, a big part of her still felt sorry for him. *Such a hopeless, helpless stance, to try and go it alone . . .*

She raised her head and then gently rubbed her eyes before peering back through the lenses at the tiny specimen on the slide below.

The free clinic had ordered the tests, and a computerized whole blood cell counter had already generated the results that were sitting on her desk. Regardless, she still had to be sure.

Though she had yet to prove the machine inaccurate, it was of the utmost importance to her that she saw things for herself.

She held her breath and turned the slide slightly.

Maybe, just maybe, this is the time it will be wrong . . .

It didn't take her long to recognize what she didn't want to see.

Modern science wins again. Wishful thinking loses.

Macey quickly flicked off the microscope lamp and made her way out of the lab toward her small office a few doors down the hall. She squinted against the harsh hallway lights and struggled to keep the pulse in her head from pounding in direct concert with each step she took.

Another migraine. She looked at her watch. It was only two fifteen, and what was already a long day ahead was about to get longer.

As she opened her office door, she immediately reached for

the dimmer on the wall. With a turn of her wrist, the unbearable brightness became a soft, soothing, and therapeutic component of a routine she had developed over twenty years of trial and error at managing the pain. It normally began with dimming the lights, then massaging her temples, taking some medication, and then finally putting a cold washcloth on her forehead.

With a little luck, she wouldn't vomit, and a potentially paralyzing headache would be manageable within three to four hours.

She looked up at the ceiling and tried to keep her head still as she slowly lowered herself into her chair at the desk in the corner of her office.

Macey closed her eyes and placed her hands over her face to slowly massage her temples with the pads of her thumbs. It wasn't helping much. Worse, her stomach was beginning to roll.

When she opened her eyes, she found herself looking directly at a blank calendar on the wall in front of her. The pulse in the back of her head was thickening into a series of hollow *thuds*.

Next to the calendar, on top of a black metal filing cabinet, were a few framed pictures of her and her friends having fun in what she considered to be the good old days: Parasailing a little too close to the coastline with Kimmy Miggs, Kathy, and Samantha in Key West. Skiing with Lauren and Lindsey in Park City; Lindsey was leading them into "the death chute," a two-story drop onto a fifty-degree slope. Bungee jumping alongside a waterfall with Keith, James, Matt, and Doddie in the Smoky Mountains.

Her eyes rested on the last one, a picture of her sitting in an "herbal" club in Amsterdam with the whole gang. She was surprised at how well she still remembered that vacation. They must have burned through a pound of weed that week.

Those were the days when she had a life.

That was ten years and $140,000 in student loans ago.

One-hundred and forty . . . grand.

Her headache was getting worse. She looked up at the ceiling, wondering if it was all worth it. She gripped the side of her chair and then reached inside her purse to grab her bottle of migraine medicine. It felt too light, so she shook it.

Empty.

"You have to be kidding me," she whispered, glancing at the clock on the desk. The pharmacy was on the first floor, and the headache would make the walk practically impossible. Slowly, she laid her arms out on the desk and put her head down on them.

There were four quick knocks at the door. She heard each one as a hammer to the head, but hoped it was Kaitlyn.

"Come in!" she called, immediately regretting raising her voice. It felt like the back of her head was going to explode.

The door opened and then quickly shut.

"You are a savior," the doctor said. "Can you run down to the pharmacy for me—"

"Dr. Lewis?"

It was a man's voice.

She hastily lifted her head to see a strange man standing in her office. A construction worker, by appearances.

"Can I help you?" she asked, trying not to appear overly startled. And hoping she wouldn't vomit in front of him.

"Actually," he said, "I was wanting to help you." He gave her a small smile.

"Listen," she said sternly. She stood and crossed her arms. "I'm having kind of a rough day. Why are you here, and what do you want?"

The man stepped closer. "I was hoping to help," he said, pulling a folded piece of paper from his pocket.

"Help me with what?" she asked, frowning.

"With this," he said, holding up a sign.

NEED HELP WITH DAMAGED CROSS AT CHURCH
PLEASE SEE DR. MACEY LEWIS, 3RD FLOOR
PEDIATRICS, BETWEEN 7:00 A.M. AND 3:00 P.M.

A wave of relief ran through her, and she smiled. "Wow, that was fast! I just gave that sign to one of your superintendents after lunch. But shouldn't we leave the sign up? I was thinking we'd need a few guys—"

"I think I can handle it," he said, using a tone that suggested he was going to be the *only* volunteer. "I'm pretty good at this sort of thing."

"Sorry if I seemed rude," she said, finding herself oddly drawn to his green eyes. "I'm not feeling too well this afternoon."

"You weren't rude," he said.

She held out her hand. "I'm Macey Lewis."

"I'm Kenneth."

"I haven't even contacted the minister yet to let him know we'd like to help. I guess I wanted to see if I could gather a group first. You know, before I got his hopes up. So far I have two doctors and a nurse, which sounds like the beginning of a joke . . ."

He gave her a tender smile and lifted his hands. "And now someone with a little construction experience."

"I'm relieved," she said, nodding. "I'm going to contact the minister today and see when we can go over and take a look."

"Sounds good," he said.

Macey shrugged. "I'm not really sure how much I can pay you or what help my friends and I will be. We aren't exactly the hammer-and-saw types, but I guess it's all for a good cause."

"It's for the best cause," he said. "And you don't have to pay me. I want to help."

Macey wondered for a second if this guy was a little too good to be true. She forced a grin and waited before slowly guiding him back toward the door. "I have to get back to work here, Kenneth. Is there a cell phone I can call once I have more specifics?"

"Actually, I don't use a cell phone," he said. "Would it be okay if I just stop by around three tomorrow?"

"That would be fine," she said. "I really appreciate this, Kenneth. Thanks so much for coming by right away."

"I guess I'll see you tomorrow, then," he said, realizing he was being asked to leave.

"Three o'clock," she said.

"I'll be here," he replied. "I hope you feel better."

She smiled politely and then went back and sat at her desk. She flipped open her appointment book to get the woman's name and number who had told her about the cross. Macey's breath caught when she saw the name.

She blinked quickly and then squinted at the test results she'd just brought with her. A slight chill ran through her chest as the same name seemed to jump off both pages.

Brooke Thomas.

It appeared that she would be speaking with Brooke not once but at least twice over the next few days—once by phone and once again in person.

First, she'd call Brooke to make a plan to see about the damaged cross.

She picked up the test results from the whole blood cell count and looked at the name under "Parent/Guardian." She carefully laid it back on the desk.

She'd also be speaking with Brooke in person, along with Dr. Alisoni from the free clinic, to inform Brooke that her son, Alexander, has leukemia.

What a coincidence, she thought. She looked at the filing cabinet and once again at the pictures of her former life.

And then she glanced slowly back over at the test results and thought about a certain little redhead.

It was all worth it. The long hours. The debt. The headaches. *Kids like Alexander make it worth it.*

She stood again, snatched the empty pill container off the desk, and walked quickly out of the office to head down toward the pharmacy.

It wasn't until she got off the elevator at the first floor that she realized it.

She lifted her fingers to her temples, and then her palms slowly flattened against her cheeks. She turned around and stared at the elevator door.

Her headache was gone.

SIX

Even though it was a week into October, it was a warm six-ty-eight degrees. Brooke and Shirley were sitting on top of a metal picnic table at Lakeside Metropark, looking across Lake Erie into Canada.

Charlie was down the bank in front of them, standing next to the water, his head teetering curiously to the left and right as he watched a handful of sea gulls pace nervously along the shoreline. A light breeze came off the lake and filtered across the park, momentarily cooling the Indian summer day.

Alex was his usual arm's length from Charlie, preparing to unload two fistfuls of tiny pebbles into the water. His Detroit Tigers baseball cap was on backward, and his red bangs hung straight across his forehead. Brooke watched him as he teased the dying waves inching toward him on the shore with the toe of his sneaker, getting as close as he could. He tapped Charlie on the side of the leg and pointed at a passing freighter before turning back to her.

"Look, Mom!" he yelled.

"I see it, Alex!"

"Where is it going?" he asked, saluting the ship as he shaded his eyes with his other hand.

"I don't know, baby. Maybe Cleveland."

"Cleveland?" He looked at her like it was the first time he had ever heard that word.

"Yeah. It's a city in Ohio."

Alex sent the tiny stones flying into the lake, then quickly ran up the shallow bank. "Can we go on the swings?" he asked.

"You better hurry up," she answered, smiling and pointing over his head to Charlie, whose broad steps already had him halfway to the playground.

"Wait, Charlie!" Alex yelled, pushing off Brooke's leg before running toward the swings.

"Be careful, buddy!"

"I will!"

Alex eased into a slow-motion tiptoe about three steps before reaching Charlie. He turned around and smiled at Brooke and Shirley, holding up an index finger to his mouth in the *"shh"* position.

"Last one there is an egg!" Alex shouted. He bolted past the big man and raced toward the swings without realizing that he left the word *rotten* out of his announcement.

"Go, Alexander, go!" Brooke yelled, pumping her fist at the air.

Alex was no more than thirty feet past Charlie, running as hard as he could, when he fell flat on his face while attempting to run through a colorful pile of wet leaves. He appeared to bounce. He didn't make a sound.

Brooke's heart skipped a beat, and she and Shirley both stood. Charlie never broke his stride as he reached down and scooped up Alex, along with what appeared to be half of the leaf pile, and hoisted him to the familiar perch of his broad shoulders. They had almost arrived at the swings when Charlie suddenly stopped and turned around. Alex was smiling from ear to ear as they walked all the way back to where he had fallen. Brooke laughed. Her son looked like a human leaf picker as Charlie hung him upside down by one leg to grab the baseball cap that had come off on his fall. Charlie brushed damp leaves off the boy, then set him on his shoulders again.

Brooke shook her head and laughed before taking her seat again beside her friend.

"No need to worry about him with Charlie around," Shirley said. "That boy is like Alex's own guardian angel."

"You're right."

Two older kids were already on the swings, and Alex had probably given Charlie strict orders to make sure he swung the highest of all. As Charlie pushed, at the far end of each arc, the chains of his swing grew slack and his chair lurched. But her son was gloating and scoffing at the other boys' futile attempts to swing as high as he was.

"Not so high, Alexander!" Brooke yelled.

"It's okay, Brooke!" he shouted back, as if he believed that calling his mother by her first name would further impress his competition.

"*Brooke?*" Shirley asked. "Did your little man just call you by your first name?"

"He thinks he's a comedian." Alex had never called his mother by her first name before, and she was trying hard to not laugh when she yelled back to him. "What did you call me, Mr. Thomas?"

Alex's head popped up, yet he still seemed to debate his response. Brooke assumed it was his effort to save face with the other boys.

"Not so high, Charlie!" Brooke hollered.

As Alex swung back to where he would normally be pushed, a gigantic hand appeared across his waist and froze the swing in midflight. When Charlie finally let go, Alex shook his head in obvious disappointment as he was left to his own swinging abilities, the older boys now easily passing him up.

"Thanks, big guy!" Brooke yelled to Charlie, who waved a massive arm in return.

"Let's go for a little walk," Shirley said. "Let's see if I can keep this arthritis at bay for a bit."

"We'll be right down there!" Brooke shouted at Alex and Charlie, pointing to the shoreline. "You'll be able to see us! Yell if you need something!"

"Okay, Mom!" Despite looking exhausted, Alex swung frantically to keep up with the other boys, his voice sounding energized, happy.

Even with the warm weather, the lake smelled cold, and the Michigan autumn had hardened the sand, making their footsteps crunch as they made their way a short distance down the shore. They walked for over a minute along the shoreline before Shirley stopped. She crossed her arms and cocked her head. "You ever wonder how that happens?"

"How what happens?"

"That," Shirley said, pointing down in the sand in front of them.

Brooke laughed, and they stopped walking. Directly in front of them was one tennis shoe. It was waterlogged, coated in sand, and its size and faded light blue Nike logo made it obvious that it had once belonged to a woman. Something about it looked familiar.

"How does just one shoe end up somewhere?"

"Maybe she thought that one went out of style," Brooke joked.

Shirley laughed. "Speaking of tennis shoes, James and I need to get Charlie some new ones. That poor boy of ours must have a million miles on that old pair of his."

"I don't think he's too concerned about the latest fashion trends," Brooke said. "But if I see a pair of twenty-ones that have randomly showed up at some store, I'll call you up and we can go halves."

"You are too kind, Brooke, but you don't have to do that," Shirley said, putting her arm around Brooke's shoulders as they walked farther down the shoreline. They slowed for a moment and watched a flock of Canadian geese fly directly over their heads from the park out into the lake.

"Where do you think they are going?" Brooke asked.

"Not far," Shirley said. "Seems like this park is loaded with them year round."

Brooke lifted her left foot and jammed the heel of her shoe in the sand. She took a deep breath and then studied the whitecaps that came and went like hundreds of blinking eyes.

"Sometimes I wonder where *I* am going," Brooke said, exhaling loudly. She raised her hands to her ears and then dropped them to her sides. "And I also wonder whether or not I'm doing things right. I mean, I try to live the life we are supposed to live and feel like I'm always waiting for something good to happen . . . something special or some type of reward. But all I end up seeing are the other things—the *bad* things that have already happened and the ones that are happening right now. I know Alex is going to be fine and I believe something good will come from the cross getting hit by lightning. But when does it end? Do you ever wonder if we really got it right?"

"What do you mean, honey? Who is we?"

"Believers, I mean," Brooke said. "My parents are dead, Pastor Jim is blind, Charlie is—"

"Yes," Shirley said. "We have it right. And *you* have a beautiful healthy son, a place to live, and two old farts and their son that love you very much."

"I'm sorry," Brooke said, stepping back from the water. She removed a white-hooded sweatshirt she had wrapped around her waist and slowly pulled it over her head. "I love you guys too. I know I should be more thankful, but I just wish God would give us a break."

"God doesn't have to prove anything to anyone," Shirley said. "He's God. We aren't."

"You're right," Brooke said with a sigh. "You always are."

"I don't know about that," Shirley said, "but we better turn and head back."

As the two women walked quietly back down the shore, the sun moved behind the clouds, reminding Brooke that it was, indeed, still October. Charlie and Alex were throwing rocks into the lake. Though they were over fifty yards away, Brooke could still hear Alex laughing and making explosion noises as the rocks hit the water.

"I'm going to work on being more thankful," Brooke said.

"That's always a good idea," Shirley said. "I think I'll join you."

Brooke heard Alex laughing. She looked up from the sand, and Charlie was holding him by one arm and one leg, twirling him around from a height most kids would never experience. She smiled. *Everything is going to be all right.*

Shirley suddenly stopped and pointed down at the sand again, only a few feet away from the Nike they had discovered earlier. "When did *that* get there?"

"I don't know. It wasn't here earlier."

"It's a little creepy, isn't it?" Shirley said.

"A little? I'd call it *very* creepy."

A baby-doll had washed up on the shore, and for some reason,

Brooke couldn't take her eyes off of it. Most of its red hair had fallen out, and the lake water had stained dark circles around both of the doll's eyes. One eye had been pasted shut, and the other was half open, staring right at her.

"Hey," Shirley said. She took Brooke's arm. "Are you all right?"

"Yeah," Brooke answered as they started walking again. "I think so."

They'd taken less than a dozen steps when Brooke stopped. She turned back around and looked at the doll. She couldn't stop herself from thinking about the little girl who'd lost it. And she wondered how long the little girl cried, knowing she would probably never see her baby again.

SEVEN

Short-Term Delay
Long-Term Relief

Thank You For Bearing With Us As We Grow.

M acey slowed down and glanced up at the sign. For a fleeting moment, she found herself agreeing with Zach and his never-ending complaints.

The construction was a pain in the neck.

She looked past the sign into the fenced-in area that once served as the employees' parking lot and wondered if her old spot was still there. Maybe it was behind the cement truck, the tons of piled brick, the mounds of shredded plastic and paper, or one of the two mobile homes that now served as central command posts for the various superintendents. Any way she diced it, she had appreciated that parking space when she had it, and wished she had it back every day that she had to park two football fields away.

She looked at her watch. The appointment with the construction worker was at three in her office, which was seventeen minutes ago. She shook her head and looked at herself in the rearview mirror.

"Macey Marie Lewis," she said, "you need some time off." Even the thought of a brisk walk made her tired.

She kept giving herself a no-nonsense, you-need-a-vacation look while finding a place to park in the back corner of the temporary lot. She opened the car door and called Kaitlyn. Her cell phone was tucked between her cheek and her shoulder as she carefully repositioned a clear plastic bag over the driver's seat of her black Jeep Laredo.

"Hang on a second, Kaitlyn. I'm adjusting the plastic bag on my seat."

"Uh-oh." The nurse laughed. "The dreaded wet-butt?"

"Not today, thanks to my elegant slipcover. Did you tell him I was running late?"

"Yeah," Kaitlyn said. Something in her voice sounded distant, less confident.

"Something on your mind?" Macey asked.

"I'm fine. Why?"

"You sound flustered. Anyhow, can you tell him I'm in the parking lot and will be up there in five minutes?"

"I can't," Kaitlyn said. "He said he had to go and would try and stop by again."

"Okay," Macey said, walking past a group of huddled smokers and making her way through the revolving front doors of the hospital toward the elevators. "See you in a minute."

Macey closed her phone and exchanged grins with a glowing, red-eyed spider that hung loosely above her from a neatly shaped, white yarn web. The walls leading to the elevators were covered with confetti pumpkins, paper black cats, and a matching pair of plastic, one-toothed witches. The Halloween decor was oddly accented by the scent of roses funneling from the first-floor gift shop.

At the end of the hall, volunteer decorators from the Carlson Rotary had hung an ever-growing flock of tissue ghosts that swarmed above the elevator doors.

She looked up and noticed the lit number 5 above each elevator door. She turned to a bald, overweight Rotary volunteer at his station. "Are the elevators stuck?"

"I think so," the man said, pulling out a pair of silver-rimmed glasses and putting them on. He squinted, his blue eyes looking up. "They've been like that for fifteen minutes."

"Maintenance must have them all stopped there," Macey said. "It's a little strange they would do that right after visiting hours begin."

The man looked back at the elevators and then wrapped a rubber band around a twirled piece of tissue, forming a ghost's head. He dropped it on the counter and shrugged. "Who knows what they're thinking."

"No biggie," she said. "I'll take the stairs like everybody else. I need the exercise." She flipped her cell phone open to check the time and then headed toward the door that led to the stairwell. Behind her, all four elevators simultaneously chimed.

"Here you go!" the bald man yelled, pointing at the elevators.

Macey turned around and walked back. "Gotta love that timing."

Four doors opened at the same time. Each of the cars was empty.

"Take your pick," the man said, holding out an open palm to the four doors.

Macey stared at the elevator in front of her and hesitated before finally entering and pressing 3. She couldn't remember being the only person on an elevator at East Shore.

It felt strange.

It *was* strange.

She playfully waved at the smiling man, feeling like a kindergartener saying good-bye to her father from the bus on the first day of school. The doors closed, and the elevator went up.

She exited at the third floor and found herself turning around to watch the elevator doors close. *I don't know what it is, but something strange just happened.*

As Macey approached the nurses' station, Kaitlyn quickly put a phone call on hold and stood before pointing back over the doctor's head down the hallway. Her hand was shaking, as if she was nervous. "He just walked back into the waiting room."

"What's going on with you?"

"*Nothing.* Go to your office and let me bring him down there."

"Okay," Macey said, forming the okay sign before turning back toward her office. "Thanks, Kait."

She still had her coat on and was sitting at her desk when Zach came to the door.

"Knock, knock," he said.

"Come in." She waved him toward her without turning around. "Check this out, Zach."

He leaned over her shoulder, and she held up one of the copies of the map Kaitlyn had printed off, with directions to St. Thomas Church.

"Kaitlyn already told me about the little boy being a part of this cross business and also being a new patient," Zach said. "It's, uh, awkward."

"Awkward isn't the word," she said, shaking her head. "We are going to be working on the cross at their place on Sunday, and I'm going to be acting all happy-go-lucky while the mother won't have the faintest idea how sick her son is. Or that I'm going to be his doctor."

"Until the next morning," he said.

"When I was talking to her on the phone to arrange for our visit, she told me the clinic called and wanted them back Monday morning. You should have heard the worry in her voice."

"Of course."

Macey imagined them all working on the cross. *Hello, Miss Thomas, we are having so much fun working together today. By the way, your little boy has leukemia, but I won't be making it official until the morning, so just try to stay calm and pass me the hammer and saw.*

"I'm not going to say anything until Monday," she said.

"That's smart," Zach said. "And when they ask you why you didn't say anything the day before—*which they will*—tell them it's hospital procedure. Which it is." He pointed at her. "Remember that, Macey. *Hospital procedure.*"

There were a couple knocks on the open door, and the carpenter from the day before was standing next to Kaitlyn. He was wearing a tattered white sweatshirt, faded jeans with a hole in the left knee, tan leather work boots, and an old pea coat.

"Hello, Dr. Lewis," he said. He crossed the room and shook her hand, then introduced himself to Zach. "I'm Kenneth."

"Dr. Norman," Zach said, stiffening. Macey knew he didn't want another man around Kaitlyn and figured Zach introducing himself as "Doctor" was better than locking horns or making his mark somewhere in her office.

"I am so sorry I was late," Macey said.

"No problem at all," the carpenter said. "It gave me a chance to visit an old friend of mine that's up on the fifth floor."

"Great," she said, briefly wondering about his friend. "We are going to meet at the church when the service ends at eleven on Sunday. Will that work for you?"

"It's perfect," he said, pulling a folded sheet of paper out of his pocket. It was another copy of the map. "And my new friend here just gave me this. I'll be there."

She could practically hear the hair on the back of Zach's neck stand. She guessed Zach probably wasn't a big fan of the way Kaitlyn was looking at Kenneth either.

"Everyone appreciates what you are doing," Macey said. "The people from the church were thrilled to hear that you volunteered to help."

"And it was great of you to organize this," he said, pulling back the flap on his coat pocket to put the map back in. Macey caught a glimpse of what looked like an apple.

"None of us can save the whole world by ourselves," Zach said, "but we can at least try to do our own little part."

Kaitlyn rolled her eyes, obviously biting her tongue. Kenneth began to button his coat. "I think I know what you mean, Dr. Norman."

Macey wasn't sure what it was about those light green eyes. Actually, it was something *behind* those eyes that drew her to him. Something innocent, yet powerful.

"Have I met you before, Kenneth?" she asked. "I mean . . . other than at my office yesterday, do I know you?"

"Not as well as I'd like you to know me."

She felt herself blushing and let out a little laugh. She wasn't sure how to take that.

Kenneth stepped forward and shook Zach's hand again and

then hers. "I have to run, you guys. We will have that cross looking like new."

"I don't know," Macey said. "I guess it's really bad."

He walked back to the door and turned around. "Like new."

She liked the way he said it, and something about him was convincing. "Hey, if you believe it, Kenneth, I believe it."

"Sometimes that's all you have to do," he added.

"What's that?" Macey asked.

Kenneth didn't answer.

Macey waited. They all waited, just long enough for a strange silence to fill the room. The carpenter finally smiled at her, then shifted his eyes to Zach. He was still staring at Zach when he finally answered.

"Only believe."

There was another uncomfortable pause, and Macey turned to Zach just in time to catch a glimpse of something she had never seen before. It certainly wasn't his light brown hair, which was neatly combed back. It wasn't his crisp, white dress shirt. It was practically perfect—same as his red tie, black slacks, and six-hundred-dollar matching belt and shoes. But she had seen it, and knew exactly what it was.

Even though they were in her office, this was his territory; nobody ever dared to push Zach Norman around at East Shore Community Hospital. Still, she knew he had just been rattled. And the carpenter had somehow done it with just two words.

She glanced over at Kaitlyn to see if she was picking up on the same thing. No dice. Her nurse friend was still looking at Kenneth like he was a movie star or something.

"See you guys on Sunday," Kenneth said. He did a quick wave, took another long look at Zach, and then left.

Kaitlyn peeked out of the office, down the hallway, and ran her hand across the back of her neck.

"You okay, Kait?" Macey asked.

"Yeah." Kaitlyn nodded.

"Never would have guessed by the way you were gawking at him," Zach said.

"Right?" Kaitlyn whispered, and then it was like she came out of a trance. "Wait. What? You were gawking at him, too, Zach. In fact, I've never seen you so speechless, *Mr. Do Our Little Part to Save the World. Spare me.*"

Zach finally uncrossed his arms and whirled his index finger in a little circle like he didn't want to listen to her. "He's too young for you."

"Whatever, Zach."

Zach clapped his hands together and held them in front of his chest. "Listen, let's move beyond it. My alma mater is playing Wisconsin Saturday and I have killer seats. You guys want to go?"

"I didn't know the University of Control Freak had a football team," Kaitlyn said. "But I couldn't go anyway. I think I'm covering Jo's shift."

"C'mon guys," he said, gesturing toward Macey. "I was going to set you up with a buddy of mine from Detroit Medical. He's a prince."

"Sorry. I'm working too," Macey said. "I have to catch up on some stuff." She felt like she was *always* catching up on stuff.

"Catch up next week," he said. "Find somebody else to cover Jo's shift, Kait. The game will be fun."

"I can't, Zach," Macey said, honestly regretting it. *First chance at a date in two years and it's a double with a guy my BFF can't stand and his buddy. So much for that.*

"If I find someone for Jo, can you set me up with the prince, Zach?" Kaitlyn asked.

He gave her a frustrated sigh. "Are you telling me I should take someone else then?"

"Hmm," Kaitlyn said. "With Macey out, wouldn't that make the prince available?"

"Come on, Kaitlyn," Zach replied, patting her on the shoulder. "You know I'm better than some prince."

"Do I?"

"Of course," he said, grinning in a way that let Macey know the bulk of his feathers were back in order. "Who would take a prince over a king?"

EIGHT

The digital clock on the stove made its dinner-bell sound, letting Jim know it was 5:30 p.m., the official suppertime at the Lindy house.

He finished drying his hands and leaned back against the kitchen sink. "The news said it's supposed to be a beautiful day tomorrow," he said.

"That's what I heard too," Shirley said. "Midfifties and sunny."

"A perfect day, in my book." He felt Shirley wrap her arms around his waist and lean her head against his chest. Not many things in the world felt better than this.

"My best friend once told me something," Shirley said. Her cheek came off his chest, and he knew she was looking up at him. She nestled in again. "He told me every day is a perfect day if you just take the time to look."

"That's my girl," he said, smiling proudly. He leaned down and kissed the top of her head before resting his chin on it.

She lightly pinched his elbow. "Your wheels are turning, James Lindy. What is it?"

"How many people do you think our doctor friend is bringing with her tomorrow?"

"I don't know. Why are you asking?"

"Three others," Brooke said, walking into the kitchen. She had spent the last two hours cleaning the basement, and Jim knew her maternal stress and worry were in full bloom. There hadn't been a fifteen-minute span where he didn't hear her come up the stairs to check on Alex as he slept on the couch. "I think another doctor is coming, along with a nurse, and a carpenter."

"So around nine of us all together, then?" Jim asked.

"Something like that."

"Just curious," he said. "If you had to guess, how much do you think it would be for all of us to have lunch at The Pilot Inn?"

"I think we can afford that," Shirley said. "That'd be so nice."

"I'll chip in," Brooke said absently.

Jim knocked on the counter. He could tell she was distracted. "Stop worrying about Alex, Brooke. I promise you, he is going to be all right."

"Maybe." Brooke sighed. It sounded like she turned away. "You guys ate lunch at eleven?"

"A little earlier," Shirley said. "Alex ate a little bit of his fried bologna sandwich and then went to lie down."

Brooke paused. "So he's been asleep for six hours? He hasn't slept like this during the day since he was a baby."

"Maybe he's going through a growth spurt," Shirley said.

Brooke took a deep breath and quickly exhaled through her mouth. "Something is wrong with him."

Jim felt Shirley let go of him. He guessed that she was hugging or putting an arm around Brooke before she said, "You're going to worry yourself sick. There's nothing to do until we know more."

"If it will make you feel better," Jim added, "maybe we can ask one of the doctors to have a quick look at him tomorrow."

"I just don't like it," Brooke said. "If everything's okay, why would they want to see him on Monday?"

"There could be a hundred reasons, many of them no big deal," Jim said.

"Right," Brooke said. "You're sure he'll be okay, Pastor Jim?"

"I wouldn't say it if I didn't believe it," he said.

"I'm sorry for being such a downer today," Brooke said.

It was Jim's turn to put his arm around her. "You are not being a downer. We are here for one another."

"Yes, we are," Shirley said. "And don't forget, we also have had a little bit of experience with a child who had some rough turns through hospitals. Do you know I couldn't hold Charlie until he was a month old?"

"No," Brooke said, her tone horrified. "That's terrible."

They didn't talk much about those early years. About the umbilical cord wrapping around Charlie's neck—depriving his brain of oxygen for a "detrimental" length of time. *Hypoxia.* Those were the two words Jim remembered most. *Hypoxia* and *detrimental.* And endless days, walking hospital hallways, feeling helpless . . .

Jim laced his fingers together and tilted his head toward Brooke. "Charlie wasn't supposed to live past five. When he turned ten, we pretty much quit listening to the doctors, but not a day goes by when we don't thank God for our sweet son. Just remember God's in charge, Brooke. Alex is going to be fine."

"I can't imagine Charlie as a ten-year-old," Brooke said.

"That was twenty-eight years ago," Shirley said. "Heavens, where has the time gone?"

Jim shook his head and smiled. "Charlie was little then, at ten. A six-foot-tall pipsqueak."

Brooke laughed and Jim was glad for the sound of it. He hadn't heard her laugh in days.

"I don't know where I'd be without you," Brooke said. "Thanks, guys."

"We don't know where we would be without you and Alexander," Shirley said.

"I'm gonna wake Alex up," Brooke said. "By the way, Dr. Lewis said she hasn't been to church in years and is way overdue. She said she and her nurse friend may be coming to service in the morning."

"Praise God," Jim said. "That's certainly good news. I'm excited to meet them."

• • •

Brooke returned to the living room and sat next to Alex, who was asleep on his stomach and facing the back of the couch. She slid her hand up under his shirt. He felt unusually warm and sticky. As she rubbed his back, tiny, pin-sized red dots appeared and disappeared on his skin in the shape of her hand. She looked over at Charlie, who was completely ignoring the television. He kept looking at Alex and then at her. Back to Alex, then back to her. It made her uncomfortable.

"C'mon, Alex," she said. "Wake up, sweetheart. Shirley's going to make some mac and cheese for you." She rolled him over, and he squinted up at her. His red bangs were darkened in sweat, like a new paintbrush that had just been dipped in water.

"Where were you, Mom?" he asked faintly.

"I was at work this morning, buddy. When I got home, you were sleeping, Mr. Sleepyhead."

"Mr. Sleepyhead?" He giggled. "Where's Charlie?"

Charlie leaned over Brooke's shoulder, his eyes wide and worried, peeking at Alex. He smiled and nodded his approval, seeming to draw comfort from the fact that his friend was at last waking up.

Alex held up his hand, and Charlie high fived him. He lowered his arm and rolled back over again. As if he would go back to sleep the second she let him.

"C'mon, buddy," Brooke urged.

"Peanut butter samwich too?" he asked, his eyes still closed.

Brooke managed a small laugh. "Peanut butter sandwich too. It's done, buddy, c'mon."

When they walked into the kitchen, Alex reached up and grabbed a cookie off a plate on the counter.

"Uh-uh, young man," Shirley said. "Not before dinner."

As Alex apologized and put the cookie back, Brooke nudged Shirley and said, "At least he's getting his appetite back."

"He's just fine," Shirley whispered. "Mark my words: growth spurt."

"I think you're right," Brooke said, watching Shirley empty the balance of the noodles into a bowl for Charlie. She then ran a knife through the center of five peanut butter sandwiches—four and a half for Charlie, and one half for Alex.

Brooke took Alex's bowl and lightly tapped a few sprinkles of pepper on top and retrieved Alex's preferred eating utensil. He wouldn't dare eat his favorite meal with a fork, and he really didn't like pepper, but two-handing the Batman spoon and stirring the cheese and noodles until the little black specks disappeared had to be just as much fun as eating the food itself.

The five of them sat at the table and held hands. Pastor Jim cleared his throat. "Let's pray."

Brooke peeked at Alex, sitting beside her. His eyelids fluttered as he forced himself to keep his eyes closed. She gave his hand a little squeeze, and he squeezed it back. Sitting next to Alex was Charlie. Brooke looked down at the giant fist that held and covered her son's entire hand and forearm. She noticed how Charlie's thumb was almost as long as the space between Alex's wrist and elbow, and then closed her eyes.

Pastor Jim thanked God for the food, their family, their health, and their visitors from the hospital who would be coming tomorrow.

The prayer ended, and Brooke opened her eyes.

"Pastor Jim," Alex said. "You have a boo-boo on your head."

Brooke noticed the scratched, marble-sized bump that was partially hidden near Pastor Jim's hairline, and wondered how she'd missed it in the kitchen.

Shirley reached up and lightly touched her husband's forehead. "What happened?"

"Old track injury," he said, tapping his finger lightly on the bump. "Javelin catching."

Brooke laughed, causing Alex to giggle. Shirley didn't.

Pastor Jim leaned his head back. "It's funny. I don't know how many times I've tried it, but I just can't seem to walk into the garage with the garage door closed."

"Oh, honey," Shirley said sympathetically.

"It's all right," Pastor Jim said, grinning. "I'll most likely live. I thought I had left the garage door open. It must have swung shut."

"Uh-oh," Alex said.

"Oh, honey," Shirley said again.

"What is it, buddy?" Brooke asked, turning to Alex. His eyes were wide with a mixture of fear and excitement.

Blood was spilling from his nose.

NINE

Zach was in that room again.

He was trapped.

She couldn't breathe.

He was running frantically back and forth on the cool white carpet.

He looked and looked, but couldn't find her. Only he could save her. He was her only chance.

Time was running short. Time always ran short in that room.

At last, he could see her again in the window—that clear, thick, icy window.

Her face, that beautiful face.

Her hair flowed freely around the top of her head and the sides of her chalk-white cheeks. Her face pressed against the window and slid slowly against it. Her eyes, her frightened blue eyes, blinked repeatedly in a desperate panic.

Her hand was gliding back and forth across the window. She knocked. She wanted to come into the room.

He placed his own hand over the outline of hers and watched her lips speak words he couldn't hear—words that no one could hear.

She pounded on the window. He pounded, clawed, and kicked at the window, too, but it wouldn't open. It wouldn't break. He needed just a little more time.

She drifted back from the window, her form disappearing into the darkness beyond.

He screamed her name and popped up in his office chair. Sweat rolled off his forehead and the sides of his neck as his heart knocked at the inside of his chest.

The dream. It was back.

• • •

It was late afternoon and Macey had just removed her lab coat and hung it on the wooden coatrack she had inherited with her office. Kaitlyn had already kicked off her tennis shoes and was sitting on the couch, her legs folded beneath her.

"I'm starving," the nurse said.

"Me too," Macey said.

"I barely saw you today." Kaitlyn was giving herself a foot massage. "You were a busy girl for a Saturday. You really were catching up."

"Too busy to eat lunch."

Kaitlyn put her right shoe back on and began to massage her left foot. "Soup and salad down at the corner café with two huge Diet Cokes. What do you think?"

"Sounds perfect," Macey said. "Let's get out of here."

Zach was standing in the doorway with his arms crossed. The edge of his mouth tilted toward his right cheek as though he was biting down on the inside of his lip. "Would you ladies like to join me for dinner?"

Kaitlyn put her other shoe back on. "Nice of you to knock, Zach."

"The door was open."

"What are you doing here?" Macey asked. "Your plans for the game fall through?"

"Yeah," Zach said, his tone vague. His eyes shifted to the window. "What do you say? Dinner? My treat?"

Macey looked over at Zach and wondered what he would do if she said yes and Kaitlyn said no, but he didn't look like he was in a joking mood. In fact, something seemed off with him. Today's dress shirt had a few creases in it, and there was a small tuft of hair curling around the top of his right ear. She wasn't quite sure what was wrong, but the mighty Dr. Norman actually appeared to be having a rough day.

"You all right, Zach?" Macey asked.

He straightened and frowned a little. "Yeah. Why?"

"You look a little gray."

"You do look a bit pale," Kaitlyn added.

"I'm fine."

Kaitlyn leaned forward and crossed her arms. "Thank you for asking us for dinner, but we already made plans."

Macey flicked the desk lamp off and turned around. "But you are welcome to join us, Zach."

Kaitlyn smiled at him. "The corner café—your favorite."

Macey grinned at Kaitlyn, knowing that the odds of Dr. Norman wanting to eat at the little rundown café were the same as him wanting to eat pizza in the cafeteria. Besides, all three of them knew that he only wanted to have dinner with Kaitlyn.

"I think I'll pass," he said. "What time did you say we are meeting at the church tomorrow?"

"We decided to go to the service at ten." Macey suspected Zach's motivation for going had probably expanded into keeping Kaitlyn away from the carpenter. "But we are going to start on the cross around eleven."

"Good," Zach said.

Macey grabbed her coat off of the rack and folded it over her arm. "What'd you do with your tickets to the game?"

"I gave them to Dr. Timmins," he said.

"I didn't think Jerry liked football," Macey said.

Zach shrugged. "I'm not sure if he likes football or not. The tickets weren't for him."

Kaitlyn stood and picked her own coat up off the other side of the couch. "I saw Dr. Timmins give the tickets to Mr. Springsted."

"That's right," Zach said.

"Oh," Macey said. "You mean that little old man security always chases out of the chapel after-hours?"

"That's him," Kaitlyn answered. "The one who used to buy his wife flowers every Friday and put them by her bedside."

"*Used* to buy?" Macey said sympathetically. "Oh no, that's terrible. I heard that she was in a coma for, what—six, eight weeks? Poor thing."

"Twenty-two weeks," Zach said.

Kaitlyn crossed her arms. "Mrs. Springsted was in a coma for twenty-two weeks and got flowers *every* Friday."

"Yeah?" Zach said, squinting at her.

"That's about twenty more times than I got flowers from my old boyfriend over three years."

"Well, it looks like Mr. Springsted doesn't have to buy them anymore."

"Zach!" Macey said. That statement was a little insensitive even for him. "That's awful!"

"What?" Zach asked.

"Are you serious?" Macey puffed. "The poor woman is dead, for Pete's sake."

Kaitlyn asked, "You really *were* busy today, weren't you? You didn't hear?"

"Hear what?"

"She didn't die," Zach said.

Kaitlyn took Macey by the arm. "Mrs. Springsted walked out of here yesterday."

"She *walked* out of here?"

Zach leaned against the doorway. "Her husband came to visit her yesterday, and she was sitting up in the bed when he walked in the room."

Macey grabbed her purse off her desk, went to the door, and waited for a punch line. "You guys are pulling my leg. After twenty-two weeks in a coma? That's impossible."

"Call it what you want," Kaitlyn said. "She walked out of here yesterday."

"Twenty-two weeks?" Macey asked again. "But her mind, her strength, the atrophy—it's impossible!"

"It happened," Kaitlyn said. "Carrie Armstrong told me that Mrs. Springsted was as sharp as a tack and walked as if she had just awakened from a nap."

"Amazing," Macey said, looking back and forth at them. They were telling the truth. She had never heard anything like it. "First thing Monday, I'm going up to Seven to hear the story from Dr. Timmins. I love stories like this."

"He doesn't work on Seven," Kaitlyn said. "He hasn't worked up there in a couple of months."

"What floor is he on now?"

Macey suddenly felt as if something had brushed against the hairs on the side of her neck. Goose bumps marched down her back and arms. She thought about that strange and lonely elevator ride and how she tried to figure out why maintenance would be working on the elevators during the busiest part of the day. She could still see the same lit number, frozen above all four doors before the elevators had come down to answer her call. She remembered getting off that elevator, feeling—no, not feeling, *knowing*—something had happened.

She knew, before they said it, which floor Mary Springsted was on when she came out of her twenty-two-week coma and went home. The floor Dr. Timmins worked.

Five.

TEN

Ever think about listening to some music from this century?"
Macey asked as she and Kaitlyn turned on to Church Road on
their way to St. Thomas. "We weren't even born when half this stuff
came out. Get with the times, girl."

"Quit hatin' on the classics," Kaitlyn said, thumbing through
her smartphone she had plugged in to the stereo in Maccy's Jeep.
"That's when music was real."

The songs made it hard for Kaitlyn to drive down the road
without thinking about high school. Back in the day, the cops never
bothered coming out here, and Church Road had been the perfect
place to smoke pot, down some Boone's Farm, make out with the
boys . . . or more. All that time, she'd never made it down to the end
of the road. It practically made her itch now, passing their favorite parking area, a bare area of grass that nudged into the woods,
knowing that when she was doing all those things, God's house was
just up past the trees. *If those church people had only known,* she
thought.

That made her think about the man that called himself Kenneth. Mr. Mysterious. And the apple. When he said forgive, was he
talking about one of those boys from her high school days? One of
the many who brought her out here, to *Church* Road, used her and
then tossed her aside? Or all of them?

It's not them, she thought. *He was talking about my dad.*

She closed her eyes. That Kenneth guy didn't know her father
from Adam, but Kaitlyn knew her father was the one she needed to
forgive. *Part of being a parent is making mistakes,* she thought. *But*

when you leave half your head splattered on a wall for your eleven-year-old daughter to find, it's kind of tough to say sorry.

"The last thing my dad said to me was that he loved me," Kaitlyn said, then shook her head, her mouth clamping shut for a moment. "You just don't do what he did to someone you love."

"What?" Macey said as they slowly maneuvered around a pothole.

"Nothing," Kaitlyn said. "Just some lyrics to a song I haven't heard in a while."

"Another oldie?" Macey asked.

"Yep," Kaitlyn muttered. An oldie that wouldn't stop replaying in her head.

She wanted it to all be done. She wanted to live just one life—the one that was her on her way to a church to help people—the perky, highly respected, clean-faced nurse practitioner that made a difference in kids' lives. Not the other one. The human garbage. The drinker with all the history. The whore that wore all the makeup as if the eyeshadow was Clark Kent's glasses, separating one life from the other. The one she had convinced herself the carpenter knew all about . . .

He could see right through me, and when he grabbed my wrist, everything seemed all right. Like I was being given another chance. I could choose to do something, and if I could just do that one thing—all my mistakes would be forgotten . . .

But what is that one thing? And why didn't Kenneth say a single word to me at the hospital about our talk at the bar?

"There it is," Macey said as they reached the end of the road and turned into the driveway. "It's beautiful back here."

The first thing Kaitlyn saw was the cross on the lawn. Something about it made her afraid, like she needed its permission before entering the church.

A sense of emptiness tapped at her gut when three deer walked gracefully around the corner of the church and stopped next to the cross. That weird sense of being stared at—*just like that night at the bar*—niggled at her and she laughed out loud, quickly dismissing it.

"What's so funny?" Macey asked.

"Nothing. Just a lot on my mind."

"You sure have been acting weird the last couple days."

"Shush, Lewis," Kaitlyn said with a phony grin as they pulled in and parked the car. "I am allowed to not be myself every once in a while."

Whoever I am.

• • •

Macey closed the passenger door of her Jeep and leaned over to check her hair in the cracked side-view mirror.

"Did you want the window rolled up?" Kaitlyn asked.

"Just leave it like it is."

The air was cool, and although a lazy fog stretched out over both the parking lot and most of the grounds of St. Thomas, the sun was starting to peek through, hinting at a beautiful day ahead. The faint sound of a piano filtered through the damp air and down the hill from inside the small church. Macey threw her purse over her shoulder and walked around the front of the car.

"It starts in four minutes," she said, putting her coat on. "We better move it—and by the way, you look nice, Kait. Very churchy."

"Thanks, but I honestly can't remember the last time I was in a church."

"It's been a while for me too," Macey said, picking at a strip of lint that clung to the arm of her coat. "I hope the building doesn't crumble when I walk in."

"You think Zach is going to show up?"

"Trust me. He will be here. Particularly since I told him that you promised me that you would lighten up on him a little."

"I know you didn't tell him that," Kaitlyn said. "Zip it."

A slight frost had glazed the lawn, and the air was filled with the scent of wet pine needles. The two women were making their way up the narrow walkway leading to the church and stopped next to the cross.

"Wow," Macey said, stopping to stare in disbelief. "How is anybody going to be able to fix that?"

The cross was history. Its bottom portion was now a six-foot-high, splintered stump, looking like it still grabbed for what was once its upper half—like an arm that had been severed at the elbow. *Phantom limb*, she thought. The cross was beyond repair.

Had she seen it before now, she would never have volunteered to find someone to fix it. *It's impossible.* She studied the tiny drops of moisture that glistened like pieces of broken glass on the section of wood laying in the wet grass, serving as a temporary playground for three robins that chirped and pranced on it. She studied the quickness of the birds' pipe-cleaner legs and figured maybe they were discussing their pending vacation south. *Vacation*, she thought. *I wish I could get away for just a few days . . .*

"It's ruined," Kaitlyn said. "To get that presentable, let alone fixed, is going to take a serious fund-raising campaign. Maybe we could at least get it dragged out of here today."

"That's probably the best way to go," Macey said, shaking her head. "I'm going to buy them a new cross."

"I don't think anyone expects you to do that, Macey."

"Hi, Dr. Lewis!" Brooke called at the front door of the church. She was wearing a cream-colored dress, a black cardigan—the edges of which looked a bit frayed—and shoes that the doctor figured were reserved exclusively for Sundays. Brooke held the door open. "C'mon in, you guys; service is about to start. We'll see to that old cross later."

As they entered the church, Macey was overcome by a sense of quaintness and warmth. She immediately felt welcome. Just being there felt right. Someone tapped her lightly on the shoulder, and she turned and witnessed the largest hand she had ever seen.

"This is Charlie Lindy," Brooke said. "He is Pastor Jim and Shirley's son."

Macey looked up—and then up some more—before realizing that the largest hand she'd ever seen belonged to the largest man she'd ever seen. He was wearing a navy blue suit with a slight tear in the breast pocket, giant-sized white tennis shoes, and a dark gray clip-on tie that was slightly crooked and only came to the bottom of his ribs. She guessed his height at close to seven feet as her hand and wrist disappeared into his gentle handshake. His blue eyes blinked innocently as he tilted his enormous head, encouraging her and Kaitlyn to take two church bulletins from his other hand.

"Hello, big guy," she said. She found it difficult to break eye contact with him, knowing something was wrong with him and that she was unqualified to help him. It made her feel a little sad.

"Hi, Charlie," Kaitlyn added, looking up at him as he greeted them with another quick nod of his head.

"Would you guys like to sit with us?" Brooke asked, pointing toward the second pew.

"Of course." Macey scanned the rest of the church. There were twelve to fifteen other people. Flowers were neatly tucked in vases beneath each stained glass window. Hymnals and Bibles were all straight and tidy in their compartments behind the pews. It was clear to her that these people were doing their best on a limited budget. No insurance, she remembered. Now it all made sense.

As Brooke led them up the aisle, Macey noticed a tiny pair of eyes peeking over the edge of the pew. The little redhead slowly rose to his knees and leaned forward against the back of the bench to face them. He had on a short-sleeve dress shirt and a small, dark gray clip-on tie—a miniature replica of Charlie's. His short, red hair was gel-spiked and slightly brushed to the side. The freckles that surrounded his nose bunched together as he smiled when he spotted his mother approaching. Macey could still see his name on the medical chart. *Alexander Robert Thomas*. Within twenty-four hours, he would be her patient.

"Alex," Brooke whispered. "This is Dr. Lewis and her friend, Kaitlyn."

"Hi!" Alex shouted, pointing at Macey. "I saw you at the hospital!"

"*Shh*, buddy," Brooke said, raising a finger to her lips.

"He is so cute," Kaitlyn said softly.

"That's my son, Alex," Brooke said.

"Hi, Alex," Kaitlyn said.

Brooke pointed to the piano. "That's Shirley, and Pastor Jim will be out in a minute."

The piano music stopped, and everyone stood. Macey looked at Alex, and they exchanged grins before he took refuge behind his mother's leg.

Charlie joined them at the end of the pew. The music resumed with "I've Got a Friend in Jesus," a song that Macey remembered from her childhood. She and Kaitlyn opened the hymnals and each pretended to mouth the words, too embarrassed to have the other hear her voice. Macey secretly admired—maybe even envied—Brooke's singing voice. It was lovely, in tune.

Kaitlyn nudged her, and they both looked at Charlie, who also held a hymnal and was swaying, not singing, along with the song. Alex continued to smile mischievously and stare both of them down before adjusting Charlie's hymnal. It was upside down.

As Pastor Jim came up the center aisle, Macey saw where Charlie had gotten his height. She guessed that the minister was about six foot four, and she also admired how thin and clean-cut he was. He walked in his white and burgundy robe, shoulders back, while singing in a confident, deep baritone.

When Pastor Jim turned around and faced the gathering, Macey felt a tug on her heart. She could see his eyes from the second pew. He was blind.

"Good morning, friends," he said with a warm smile. "Please, let's greet one another."

She watched as he walked forward and to his left to the first pew and held out his hand. An older man, likely in his seventies, and close to a foot shorter than the minister, took it.

"Good morning, Alton," Pastor Jim said. He then turned his head to the frail, bluish-haired woman next to Alton. "Good morning, Pauline."

Macey felt as if she had made eye contact with him as he stepped back into the aisle and to the second row.

"Good morning," he said, "looking" right at her.

"Good morning," she said into his sightless eyes.

"I'm Pastor Jim," he said. "Thank you so much for being here today."

"Thanks for having us," she said, wondering how in the world he knew they were standing there. "I'm Macey Lewis and with me is Kaitlyn Harby."

"Hello, Kaitlyn," he said, taking her hand as everyone else in the church appeared to be shaking a hand, saying hello, or hugging someone.

When Pastor Jim returned to the front of the church, Macey noticed him look at Shirley, who lightly tapped on what had to be the highest note on the piano. *She's letting him know that she's there.*

The minister nodded, then smiled at his wife before closing his eyes. "Let's pray."

During the prayer, Macey felt like she was breaking one of God's laws by looking around the church again. People, heads bowed, were absorbing the minister's words of hope, love, and thankfulness. Little Alex was leaning against Charlie. Brooke's hands kneaded the top of her thighs, as if anxious. Macey looked back at the piano and at Shirley.

She also had her eyes open.

Macey watched the way the woman was looking at her husband as he neared the end of the prayer. She was fixed in admiration, soaking up every word he said, as if she felt each one. Shirley clearly loved her husband. They were the real deal. How long had it been since she'd witnessed such love and devotion?

The prayer ended, and Brooke went to the pulpit and started reading Isaiah 53. Macey grabbed a Bible, but Brooke was done reading by the time either she or Kaitlyn could even locate the book of Isaiah.

Alex had recaptured Macey's attention with a bashful smile as he crossed his arms and leaned back to let his legs dangle over the edge of the bench. She figured he wasn't used to seeing strangers at church, and when she winked at him, he tried to wink back, closing both eyes.

Alex slid over in the pew and tapped Macey on the leg. "My grandpa and grandma are in heaven."

"So are mine," she whispered.

"Really?" he asked.

"Really."

Brooke cleared her throat and then read Matthew 18: "Assuredly, I say to you, whatever you bind on earth will be bound in heaven, and whatever you loose on earth will be loosed in heaven. Again I say to you that if two of you agree on earth concerning anything that they ask, it will be done for them by My Father in heaven."

Out of the corner of her eye, Macey saw Kaitlyn rubbing the side of her face and then the back of her neck.

"What's going on?" Macey asked.

"Nothing," Kaitlyn whispered. "Why?"

"Something wrong with your neck?"

"Shh." Kaitlyn nodded toward Brooke, who continued the reading.

"For where two or three are gathered together in my name, there I am in the midst of them."

Macey glanced back at Kaitlyn, who had turned around to look behind them. Her blue eyes were lit up and a smile dimpled her cheeks.

Macey turned to see what Kaitlyn was staring at.

He was unshaven, dressed in work clothes, and sat perfectly still. He was leaning forward, resting his forearms on the back of the pew in front of him. But his eyes were only on Kaitlyn.

It was the construction worker. He was sitting in the back row.

ELEVEN

"Sure, Dr. Norman," the woman said. "I could probably swing by there to take a few pictures."

Zach held his phone to his ear as he sat in the parking lot of CC's Sporting Goods. The driver's side door of his three-week-old Mercedes was open, and he was relishing the new car smell that seemed to be enhanced by the clean, fall air. He eyed the ruffled, white packing paper, which was hanging out of an empty shoe box on the passenger's seat, that read "Red Wing Shoes—Since 1905." As he wiggled his toes, he was pleasantly surprised at how good the boots felt, considering their affordable $76.70 price tag, which was almost $400 less than his previous footwear purchase.

"I think it would be great press for the hospital." He closed the car door. "I can see it now on the front page of the *Carlson Herald* this coming Wednesday—'East Shore Professionals Nurse Cross Back to Health.'"

"That sounds pretty good," she said.

"Unless you can think of something better," he added, confident she couldn't.

"I think your idea sounds real good," she said. "I'll put something together for you."

"I would owe you big time." He was fully aware that he was playing a bit of a bully, but sometimes a guy had to be that way to get things done. He didn't mind playing the big wig from East Shore, which happened to be the paper's largest advertiser. It had all kinds of perks.

"Okay," she said. "What time do you want me out there?"

Zach smiled and started the Mercedes. "Hang on a second, Shannon," he said, setting the phone down on the car seat. He just had to check it. He carefully listened and noticed that he could barely hear the car's engine. Perfect. He picked up the phone. "Church ends at eleven. How about eleven thirty?"

"Okay, Dr. Norman."

"You're the greatest, Shannon. Thanks again."

• • •

"This guy is good," Kaitlyn whispered as Pastor Jim's voice resonated throughout the small church.

"Awesome," Macey responded.

"I'm asking you to be thankful," Pastor Jim said, stepping out from behind the pulpit.

Macey glanced over at Charlie, who was giving a small piece of white candy or a mint to Alex. She watched the giant man squint at a tiny clear box that he held up in front of his face. *TicTacs*, she thought.

"Be thankful," Pastor Jim repeated.

The way the minister said it actually made Macey *want* to be thankful.

She watched him pause as he slid his right foot carefully forward on the carpet, feeling for the top of the two steps, before he walked down in front of the first pew. He stopped and waited again before lifting his hands to close his sermon.

"Friends," he said, talking barely loud enough for everyone to hear. "I'm asking you to think about something. When you go home today, ask yourselves if maybe—just maybe—you spend too much time worrying about what you *don't* have, when you should be taking the opportunity to be thankful for what you *do* have." He smiled, then walked back up the steps and turned around.

Shirley began playing the piano, and the whole congregation stood, signaling the end of the service.

"He is so right," Kaitlyn said.

"Yes, he is," Macey said, once again looking around the church.

Old Alton had put his arm around Pauline, and most of the people were still nodding their heads in agreement with the message that the minister had delivered. She looked back at Pastor Jim and wished he could see the good he had just done.

"Zach's here," Kaitlyn said, holding up her cell phone. "He only texted me seven times. Good thing I had my phone on mute."

"I'll go out there and bring him in," Macey said.

"You gonna have cookies and punch?" a high-pitched voice said. It was Alex.

"You really have cookies?" Macey asked. "*And* punch?"

"Really," Alex answered. The little guy actually looked surprised that she was impressed with the menu.

"I gotta have some then," she said, reaching down for a high five, which he gladly gave. "I'll be right back, but can you help me with something?"

"Help you with what?" he asked.

"Can you take my friend here to the cookies and make sure you guys save one for me?"

"There's a lot," he said. "Charlie can't even eat all them cookies." He scooted by her in the pew and held up his hand for Kaitlyn. "C'mon, I'll show you where they are."

"You'll do that for me?" Kaitlyn asked, using the voice she reserved only for kids. She leaned over and took his hand. "Awesome!"

As Macey watched Alex lead Kaitlyn toward what looked like a small reception room, she thought about how much she loved that voice Kaitlyn had just used. How much she appreciated her friend. Kaitlyn did so much more than deliver medications, shots, and food that the kids didn't like. The kids loved Kaitlyn, and so did just about everybody at the hospital. All the staff on the third floor knew that she understood the difference between hope and hype, and that it wasn't uncommon for her to stick around after her shift had ended, normally to relieve tired parents who desperately needed an hour or so to go home and catch up on personal matters. They also knew that during some of those same hours, Kaitlyn had held the hands or stroked the heads of dying children, assuring them that they were not alone as they let go.

Brooke tapped her on the shoulder. "Did you enjoy the service, Dr. Lewis?"

"It was excellent," Macey said, watching the carpenter dip into the reception area. "I loved the part about being thankful."

"Me too," Brooke said. "Shirley and I have been talking a lot about that lately."

"I'm so glad I came. And please call me Macey."

Brooke pointed at Kenneth. "Do you guys know him?"

"He is the guy we are hoping can help us with the cross," Macey said. "He's the carpenter volunteer from the hospital."

"Cool," Brooke said. "I can't tell you how thankful we are."

"Speaking of volunteers," Macey said. "Excuse me while I run out and get the last one. He's outside."

"Okay. See you in the fellowship hall and then we'll see what we are gonna do about the cross."

"Perfect," Macey said, heading toward the door.

She went outside, and Zach was leaning on the wooden handrail that led down to the parking lot.

"Looks like you dressed for the occasion, Zach," she said, glancing at her watch. "And you're here early to boot."

"Where is Kaitlyn?" he asked.

"She's inside."

"Is church over with?"

"Just ended," she answered. "Spiffy new boots there, Zach."

"Thanks, I just picked them up."

She looked at his designer jeans, which were neatly cuffed over the top of the boots. She also noticed how well they matched the gray Polo sweatshirt that appeared to have never been worn. At the very least, it was a gallant effort on his part to resemble a man of manual labor. Regardless of what his intentions were for being there, she appreciated his efforts to actually show. "Thanks for coming, Zach."

"The newspaper will be here in about twenty minutes or so to take a few pictures," he said. "It will look good for us."

She shook her head as he walked up a few steps, blindsided by his news. "What's wrong with helping somebody out just for the sake of helping, without telling the whole world about it?"

"Nothing," he said sharply. "But what's wrong with giving some credit where credit is due?"

"Credit?" she asked.

"Good PR for the hospital certainly wouldn't hurt us," he said, looking at the cross like a motorist who had slowed to gawk at a fatal car accident. "But, whoa. Who are we trying to kid here? That thing is done."

She glanced again at the cross. The splintered pieces looked even more tattered and hopeless now that the morning dew had dried from its remains. The three robins were gone.

"Kenneth said they will have it looking like new," she said. "Remember?"

"Yeah. Right. It isn't going to happen."

"If not, I'm going to replace it."

"Whatever," he said indifferently. He sounded like he was having a bad morning.

They walked into the church, and Alex and Charlie were the only two left in the main sanctuary. Alex was jumping up and down behind the pulpit, and it looked like Charlie was putting hymnals back in place behind the pews. They both stopped what they were doing and looked back at the door.

"There's my patient," Macey murmured.

"Cute. But holy cow," Zach whispered back, staring at Charlie. "Will you look at the size of that guy beside him?"

"He doesn't speak. That's the minister's son."

Alex sprinted down the main aisle and put on his brakes in front of the two doctors. "Hi, Doc Lewis. Your friend is in the other room eating a cookie." He looked up at Zach and squinted his eyes. "You weren't at church."

"I'm sorry, buddy," Zach said, talking to Alex while staring up at Charlie.

Macey rested her hand on Alex's shoulder. "Alex, this is Dr. Norman. We work together."

Alex poked Zach on the leg. "My grandpa and grandma are in heaven." He pointed at Macey. "She already knows."

Zach didn't say anything, and Charlie's tie unclipped and fell softly to the ground. Zach picked it up and handed it back to him. Charlie smiled and stuffed it into his pants pocket.

"C'mon," Alex said, poking again at Zach's leg and then quickly pulling his hands behind his back. "Even though you didn't go to church, I'll ask if you can have some cookies too."

Alex led them through a door in the side of the chapel into the reception room while Charlie followed. At the center of the room sat a folding table covered with a stained white tablecloth, a half-gallon can of Hawaiian Punch, and a plate of what had to be fifty chocolate chip cookies. The wall to their left was lined with metal folding chairs, while the opposite wall featured an old maroon couch accented by a scratched and faded coffee table.

They walked over toward Kaitlyn, who had just been joined by Kenneth.

"So, there's my lady," Zach said.

"Ex-lady," Kaitlyn said, frowning in confusion.

Trying to stake your claim, Doc? Macey wondered.

Zach nodded at Kenneth. "It appears we have our work cut out for us with that cross."

"I'm pretty sure we will get it straightened out," Kenneth said, opening his hand in the direction behind Zach and Kaitlyn. Pastor Jim and Shirley were approaching.

"Hello, friends," Pastor Jim said. "On behalf of the congregation of St. Thomas, welcome and thank you so much for being here today."

"I loved your sermon," Macey said.

"Why, praise God," he replied. "And thank you for your kind words."

"Thank *you*, James," Kenneth said. "Your words were from the heart. They were beautiful."

"You folks are too kind," the minister said, tilting his head curiously toward Kenneth.

"That's Kenneth," Macey said.

"Hello, Kenneth," Pastor Jim said. The minister was holding a Styrofoam cup of punch, and the short sip he took didn't take much of the curious look off his face. "It's funny for me to hear anyone call me James, with the exception of my wife. Around here, I'm mostly Pastor Jim."

Alex walked in the middle of the group, tugged at Pastor Jim's pant leg, and pointed at Zach with his other hand. "Pastor Jim, that man wasn't at church. Can he still have some punch?"

"Why, of course he can." The minister laughed.

Alex looked up at Zach and pointed over at the cookies and punch as if he had just brokered a successful deal. "You can have punch if you want now."

Shirley ran her hand across the top of Alex's head as she looked at them. "I don't know what we would do without your help today. It's beautiful how people can help one another in times of need."

"Yes," Pastor Jim agreed, lifting his hands. "Bear one another's burdens, and so fulfill the law of Christ."

"Sounds like that's from the Bible," Kaitlyn said, as if she were both asking a question and giving the answer.

"Galatians 6:2," Kenneth said.

"Yes, it is, and yes, it is," Pastor Jim said, nodding and smiling. "Somebody knows the Bible pretty well to get the chapter and verse on that one. I'm impressed."

"Let's hope he knows as much about carpentry as he does the Bible," Zach whispered.

"He'll give it a go," Macey said, taking a bite out of a cookie and glancing over toward the punch table at an older couple. "And if he can't fix it, we'll be here to help make it right."

TWELVE

"Thanks, Shannon," Zach said, handing the *Carlson Herald* reporter a bill from his pocket, folded in a small square. "I wanted to give you this."

"What's this for?" She stared at it.

"Something to show my appreciation for you coming out on such short notice." *As in, a hundred bucks' worth of appreciation.* "Make it look real good, Shannon."

"I can't take this," she said. "I'll make the article look good anyway."

"Call it a tip. Take it," Zach said, glancing over at the cross. It didn't really matter that they hadn't even started on it yet, let alone had absolutely no chance of fixing it. What did matter was that he looked good in the group picture she had taken and that it be great press for the hospital. He pointed at the bill in her hand and nodded. "I insist you have that. I'm sure you had other plans for your Sunday morning."

"Well, uh, okay. Thank you, Dr. Norman," she said, taking the bill and pressing it into her front pants pocket.

"Let me know tomorrow how it's going to read," Zach said as they walked down the steps and joined the others, who were gathering around Kenneth's pickup truck. Shannon might have run the story and picture without the "tip," but he knew that now she'd feel obligated to send him a draft to review. He smiled in satisfaction.

Kaitlyn put her hand on the top of the old Ford's tailgate. "My dad used to drive an F-150 and loved it. Do you like yours, Kenneth?"

The carpenter closed the driver's side door and turned to her. "It serves its purpose, Kaitlyn, but I don't see it making it through the winter."

Zach shot a quick glance into the back of the truck. He was a little surprised that it wasn't a complete mess. "Congratulations. This is the only pickup I've seen from the East Shore job that doesn't have a case of empty beer cans scattered in back."

"Not much of a beer drinker," Kenneth said, shrugging his shoulders.

"I'm going to need some of this stuff to do my deck in the spring," Macey said, pointing at four brand-new gallons of lacquer in the back corner of the truck bed. "That's a pretty big cross up there. Think we have enough?"

"We can always get more," Kenneth said. "Let's see what happens."

Zach watched Brooke stare at Kenneth, who was smiling not so innocently over at Kaitlyn. There was something about that smile that made him uncomfortable.

Brooke pointed toward the house and said to the women, "Let's move out, ladies."

"Where are you guys going?" Zach asked.

"We need to change," Kaitlyn answered. "It's gonna take all of us to move that cross."

Macey pointed to Pastor Jim and Charlie, who had changed clothes somewhere in the church and were walking toward them. "Looks like the men are ready to go, but you're welcome to join us at the house, Zach."

"Very funny."

"Try not to get your new boots dirty," Kaitlyn added, drawing a little laugh from Macey that he didn't appreciate. As the women left, he considered jumping in his Mercedes and heading over to the club for a quick nine holes. It was a little too cool for golf, but he needed this grief like a hole in the head.

He walked around the back of the truck and turned to watch Kaitlyn walk across the lawn with the others.

"She's a nice lady, Dr. Norman," Kenneth said.

"She's with *me*, pal," he answered, not caring how it sounded. Kenneth was nowhere near as good-looking as he was, and Zach probably paid more taxes in a month than the carpenter made in a year. But there was something vaguely threatening about him. *Why?*

"No worries, friend," Kenneth said, hands up. That little smile the carpenter had shared with Kaitlyn was back. *Maybe he's just waiting for the chance to make a move on her . . .*

Pastor Jim and Charlie were standing to the side of the truck. Zach would much rather have taken them over to CC's for some new outfits instead of dinking around with the cross. The minister had on a pair of Wranglers that had to be ten years old, his white high-top Reebok tennis shoes were even older, and his Honolulu blue Detroit Lions sweatshirt had a bleach stain on it the size of a softball. The big guy had on gray cotton sweatpants with a matching top that could probably cover the hood of the Mercedes. His tennis shoes weren't quite as old as the minister's . . . *but at least a size twenty.*

"Charlie and I would like to do our part," Pastor Jim said.

"I wish I had more like you, James," Kenneth said.

"You wish you had more like me?" Pastor Jim asked. "More blind guys?"

"More willing hearts. And you see better than most."

Pastor Jim paused, as if considering his words. "Are you a supervisor, over at the construction site?"

"Something like that," the carpenter answered. "Let's get a few things out of the truck."

"Hey, Shirl," James said, turning around and putting his hands in his pockets. "Charlie and I—" He stopped and tilted his head and waited a few seconds. "She's not here, is she?"

"She went back to the house a few minutes before the rest of the women did, James."

"Yes, to change her clothes," the minister said humbly.

Kenneth took Charlie by his sleeve. "You, my Nephilim-like friend, will be a big help."

"What do you want me to do?" Zach asked.

"Can you grab this?" Kenneth asked, reaching into the truck bed and handing him a rolled-up extension cord.

"I certainly hope so," Zach answered, taking it.

"And this." Kenneth grinned, handing him a power saw to take in his other hand. It was a lot heavier than it looked.

He handed Pastor Jim a fifteen-foot piece of coiled rope and another extension cord. Kenneth guided Charlie to the side of the truck and pointed at a shovel, a pick, and a sledgehammer. He lightly touched Charlie's left hand, and Charlie reached down with it and scooped up all three by their handles. The carpenter then tapped on the end of a five-foot metal spike, which Charlie grabbed with his other hand before stepping away from the truck.

Kenneth slammed the Ford's tailgate closed, grabbed a utility belt, and buckled it around his waist. The four cans of lacquer were all that remained until Kenneth grabbed two in each hand by their handles.

"To the cross," Kenneth said.

"To the cross," Zach echoed as the four men made their way up the hill. He kind of liked how valiant it sounded.

● ● ●

Alex slid a chair over to the kitchen window and was looking out at the men as they surrounded the cross. "Can I go outside, Mom?"

"Baby, you better stick with us for now," Brooke said, lifting him up and returning the chair to the table. "Do you guys want a cup of coffee before we head out?" she asked her guests.

Macey and Kaitlyn shared a glance. Shirley wasn't changed yet, so they had a few minutes. "A little caffeine would be perfect right now," Macey said.

Brooke smiled. "It'll make us better workers. How do you take yours?"

"Cream and sugar would be great," Kaitlyn said.

"Black," Macey answered.

As Brooke poured, Macey took in the friendliness of the décor in the small kitchen. There was a chipped cookie jar on the far counter, an ancient waffle maker that had seen plenty of use, two ceramic angels, and four stained potholders with the word *Love* embroidered around the edges. A half dozen of what had to be Alex's crayon masterpieces hung on the front of the refrigerator, held firmly in place by an impressive collection of M&M-sized magnets. Most of the drawings featured the same two stick figures—one small with bright red hair, and the other huge with an oversized head. On the other counter next to a stacked set of plastic bowls was a Plaster of Paris square with what looked like a man's handprint in it. Typed on a blank business card glued at the base of the handprint were the words CHARLES PAUL LINDY—AGE 9—LOUISE GIVENS ACADEMY.

"I love this kitchen," Macey said. "It's so homey."

"Me too," Brooke replied, lifting a white paper sack of sugar from a narrow pantry before struggling to tear off its top.

"Let me help you with that," Kaitlyn said as she walked over to the sink. She glanced out the window and laughed, covering her mouth. "Macey, come look at Zach."

Macey went to the kitchen window. "When do you think Zach Norman last had a shovel in his hand?"

Brooke leaned her head toward Kaitlyn. "Is he your boyfriend?"

"Ex-boyfriend," Kaitlyn answered. "Things didn't quite work out. Is it that obvious?"

"Maybe a little," Brooke said with a grin.

"Men," Shirley said, shaking her head as she entered the kitchen. "If that man had his head on straight, he'd make sure a cutie like you never got away."

Kaitlyn smiled and poured some sugar into the container Brooke was holding before they sat back down at the table.

"Speaking of cutie," Macey said. "What do you think of our volunteer from the hospital? There's something different about him that I can't quite put my finger on. Different in a good way."

"It's funny you say that," Brooke said. "I feel a little weird around him. And I agree. It's kind of hard to describe."

Kaitlyn nodded. "He's not the most handsome guy in the world, but there is something about him that's just . . . *beautiful.*"

Macey thought again about how something odd seemed to be going on with Kaitlyn. But now wasn't the time to bring it up.

"I think he's handsome," Macey said.

"Mom says I'm handsome," Alex added.

"You sure are," Macey said.

"Yeah, I know."

"You're also very modest," Shirley added, grimacing as she leaned forward in her seat to put on her other shoe. She slowly sat back up and smiled at Macey. "Dr. Lewis, you seem like a natural around kids."

"I work with them every day."

"Oh," Shirley said. "What kind of doctor are you?"

Kaitlyn pressed her tongue to the back of her front teeth and gave Macey a look that only could have meant, *You had to know this was coming.*

"I practice pediatric oncology and hematology."

Brooke tried to help Shirley out. "That means she works on kids' rear ends."

Kaitlyn put her hand on top of Brooke's. "Actually, that's proctology, Brooke."

Brooke covered her mouth. "Duh, what was I thinking?"

"That's okay," Macey said. "I help kids with cancer."

"And she's the best," Kaitlyn said.

"I don't know about that, but I do my best."

"That must be terrible," Brooke said. "Working with sick kids like that."

"Actually, it's just the opposite. It's incredibly rewarding."

"I couldn't imagine that," Brooke said. "I mean, the stress of it all."

"What do you do?" Macey asked. The needle on her irony meter was buried all the way to the right as she began to mentally rehearse her response to what she guessed would be one of Brook's top questions tomorrow: *Why didn't you tell me Alex was sick yesterday?* Suddenly, she was hoping they could wrap up here in the kitchen and head back down to the cross.

Brooke tapped on the side of her coffee cup. "I do nails. I work over at Clippers in the mall."

Shirley sipped at her coffee, and the steam left a thin film of fog on her glasses as she looked at Macey. "You look so young to be a doctor."

"I'm thirty-four," Macey said, "but I hear that quite a bit. Brooke thought I looked too young to be a nurse."

"That's not much older than I am," Brooke said in admiration.

"I'm just glad I'm out of school and into my job," Macey added. "I love it. There's nothing I'd rather be doing."

"That's like me. I really do like doing nails," Brooke said, "but you won't see me pulling up here in a new Mercedes."

"Yeah, well, it'll be a long while before I can afford one of those either. Med school loans are my constant companion for a while."

"Med school loans and dealing with dying kids?" Brooke said, shuddering. "No thank you. I don't know how you do it."

"Honey, let's not talk about kids with cancer," Shirley said. "If we're all ready, maybe we should head back down to join the men . . ."

"I'm sorry," Brooke said apologetically. "I probably shouldn't have said that."

"That's okay," Macey said.

Kaitlyn reached her hand out to Brooke like a queen presenting it to be kissed. "What could you do with this nurse's nails, Brooke?"

Macey winked, thanking her friend for changing the conversation and then said, "Let's finish our coffee and head back out. They probably think we ditched them."

"Mom," Alex said.

All eyes moved to him and Macey's heart dropped. *Nosebleeds. Just one of the many signs of leukemia.*

. . .

Jim wished he could be of more help.

He was standing next to Charlie, about ten feet from the cross, patiently listening to the men and the sounds of their shovels as they stabbed at the ground. All he had really done so far was listen in as Kenneth instructed Dr. Norman and Charlie.

It had been dry and windy since the big storm, and apparently the muck the cross had fallen into had hardened, leaving it stuck in ground. As he understood things, it sounded like Kenneth and Dr. Norman had managed to get a makeshift noose under the very tip of what was once the top half of the cross. As soon as they could get their shovels under at least *some* of the wood that had embedded in the soil to lift it, Kenneth would say something to him and he would have Charlie, who was hanging on to the other end of the rope, pull as hard as he could to drag it out of the way. It sounded like a good plan, and regardless if it worked or not, he was thankful for his new friends and their effort.

"This ground is hard as a rock," Dr. Norman said. "And I still don't see how we are going to get these halves of the cross to stay together, once we get it upright."

This clearly wasn't the doctor's cup of tea, but God bless him for being here. Perhaps some words of encouragement would be one way he could assist. "I'd like to offer something, if you don't mind," Jim said. "From the book of Mark."

"Go for it," Kenneth said.

Jim raised his right hand. "For the earth yields crops by itself: first the blade, then the head, after that the full grain in the head."

"Good timing," Kenneth said. "Chapter four, verse twenty-eight."

"Man, you are sharp on the Scriptures," Jim said. "How long have you been a man of God?"

"Forever," the carpenter answered. "What does that verse from Mark mean to you, James?"

Jim wondered why Kenneth kept calling him James. He sort of liked it.

"I was taught that it asks us to focus on God's harvest and to enjoy the journey toward reaching our goals as much as finally reaching the goal itself. To me, it means to enjoy every moment of your life and to be thankful, because each second that you live is a gift from God."

"I like that interpretation, James."

"Thank you, Kenneth, it's nice to know that Scripture can make—"

"Ow!" someone cried, followed by what could only have been the sound of a shovel falling to the ground. "Man, that hurt!"

"What happened?" Jim asked. "Are you all right?"

"I'm fine," Dr. Norman said, not sounding like it.

"Let me have a look at that hand," Kenneth said, followed by the sound of another shovel falling to the ground and a few footsteps.

"I'll live," Dr. Norman said.

"But you're bleeding," Kenneth said.

"It's okay," Dr. Norman insisted. "I'm the doctor here, sir."

"That you are," Kenneth said. "But you should still probably run over to the house and get that cleaned up."

"We have a first-aid box in the kitchen," Jim said. "How did you hurt yourself, Dr. Norman?"

"I tried jamming my shovel down," the doctor said. "And the only thing that moved was my palm down the wooden handle."

"I'm sorry," Jim said. "Got yourself a splinter, eh?"

"Pretty good sized," Dr. Norman said. "I am going to run over to the house real quick. Looks like the gals are still there."

"And two of them a doctor and nurse," Kenneth said, a smile in his voice. "I wager a man could find all the medical care he needs in the Lindy home today."

"I'll be right back," Dr. Norman said.

It became quiet without Dr. Norman around. Jim hoped that the man's hand wasn't hurt too badly; he needed those hands to make his living. *I trust you, Lord, to see to his healing.*

"Tell me when you want Charlie to pull," Jim said. "He's pretty strong. You know he could beat me at arm wrestling when he was eleven?"

"I'm sure he could," Kenneth said.

"Just say when," Jim said, turning his head to Charlie. "I know he wants to help too."

"Let's hang on a second here," Kenneth said. "I think we're going to try something different."

"Whatever you think is best," Jim said. The sound of the front door closing at the house echoed up the hill toward them. He heard a few footsteps and then he sensed the carpenter right next to him.

"Ready to get this done, James?"

"Yes, sir."

"This shouldn't take long, now," Kenneth said.

"Really?" Jim asked, loving the young man's confidence. From what Shirley had described, he couldn't imagine this taking less than all day. "What do you want me and Charlie to do now?"

"You and Charlie may want to step back a little."

"Why is that?" Jim asked, feeling someone take him by the elbow.

"This way," Kenneth said, guiding him and Charlie back from the cross. "You guys ready?"

"Ready for what?" Jim asked. "What should we do?"

Kenneth didn't answer. Charlie was breathing faster.

From directly in front of them, Jim heard what sounded like small pieces of wood cracking, as if a large animal were walking across fallen branches in the distance on a quiet night in the woods.

Charlie gasped and put both his arms around him at the same time the noise stopped.

Jim sensed that Charlie was trying to protect him from something. "It's okay, son. It's okay."

"You guys all right over there?" Kenneth yelled.

"What was that noise?" Jim asked.

"Hang on!" Kenneth yelled. "James, why don't you and Charlie cover your ears? This will be done a little quicker than expected."

"Do like this, Charlie," Jim said, holding a hand over each ear.

But Charlie wouldn't let go of him until he took Charlie's hands and put them over his ears for him.

The noise grew louder.

Jim could hear the stress of bending wood. It sounded like someone was trying to break a thick limb off of a tree. "What is that?" he yelled, hanging on to Charlie.

Charlie grunted and then shrieked in terror at the first snap. Jim instinctively ducked and covered his head as if something were about to fall on them.

The wood seemed to cry out as the carpenter stretched, split, broke, and . . . *What is that sound?*

Charlie picked Jim up by the armpits and swiftly carried him back at least another thirty feet.

"Charlie!" he cried, alarmed at the panic in his child. "What is it, son? What are you doing?" Charlie trembled and panted.

"What's going on?" he yelled. "Is Kenneth hurt?"

Charlie's grip burned into his arm as the final ear-piercing snap ripped through the air, followed by a quick series of muffled sounds that Jim couldn't identify. *There is a row of wooden cars, and someone is gently opening and closing their wooden doors—it is definitely wood joining wood. It almost sounds like someone is doing a huge jigsaw puzzle made of soft wooden pieces.* There was no more cracking, bending, pulling, snapping, or breaking.

Charlie was still shaking as silence enveloped them. Footsteps approached.

"Kenneth?" Jim asked. "What on earth was that?"

"*That* was your cross being repaired, James," Kenneth said.

"Repaired?" Jim sputtered. "It's *done?*"

"Good as new," Kenneth said.

Jim blinked, wishing more than ever that he could see. *Even a little bit, Lord.*

"Is Charlie okay?" he asked, still feeling the sting of Charlie's grip and the distinct smell of what he thought was urine.

"Something frightened him," Kenneth said calmly. "He had a little accident. But he's going to be fine. You both are."

"Oh." An accident? His son hadn't had an accident since he was a child. Jim reached out a hand, found Charlie's shoulder, and patted it. "It's okay, son. It's okay."

* * *

Kaitlyn was wrapping Zach's hand with the gauze that Shirley had retrieved from the hallway bathroom. "You're lucky this isn't worse, Zach."

"I didn't plan on it," he said with a flirty smile. "But maybe I would have, had I known it'd get you to hold my hand again."

"What's the prognosis on the cross, Doctor?" Shirley asked.

"I don't like to be the bearer of bad news, but I don't see us finishing today," Zach said. "With only a handful of tools and four cans of varnish—I don't know—even with all the tools in the world, I just don't see it. That lightning really did a number on it."

Shirley sipped at her coffee as a half dozen lines stretched across her forehead. "It's okay. James knew it was bad. We are still extremely thankful that you'd even try to help."

Macey leaned against the table. "Shirley, I'll make sure the cross gets replaced. Nobody deserves it more than you guys."

"Oh, honey, thank you, but that's not your responsibility. What with those med school loans you mentioned—"

"Please. It'd be an honor to help," Macey said, imagining for a second that the two ceramic angels on the counter were looking at her. She noticed the unusual silence fill the room. It wasn't that uncomfortable silence, but a *good* silence.

"I'll split the cost with you, Macey," Zach said.

"We'll go thirds," Kaitlyn said.

Brooke stood up and hugged Shirley. "You know I don't have much, but what I have is for the cross."

Zach seemingly saw his chance to floor the women, primarily Kaitlyn. "Ladies, forget it. I'm paying for the whole thing, and that's all there is to it." Macey could almost hear him wondering if it was tax-deductible as soon as the words were out of his mouth.

"Well, let's go see if we can salvage it before we start scouring the Internet for crosses," Macey said. "Everybody ready?"

"I think so," Shirley said, standing up and taking her cup to the kitchen sink. "Oh my word!"

"What is it?" Brooke asked.

"Thank you, but your kind offer apparently won't be necessary!" Shirley said, leaning closer to the window. "Come look at it, Dr. Norman. It's beautiful!"

Kaitlyn reached her first and looked out the window. She glanced back at Zach. "Nice try, Zach."

"Nice try with what?"

"Why didn't you tell us the job was done?"

"What?"

Brooke was now looking out the small window too. "Looks pretty good to me," she said.

Zach joined the others as they stared at the cross up on the hill. His mouth gaped, and he slowly parted the women and craned his head forward, his face only an inch from the glass. He swallowed audibly. "It's impossible."

"Right," Kaitlyn whispered as the rest of them quickly headed toward the front door.

"But . . . but . . . it's impossible!" Zach repeated, staggering back from the window before joining Macey at the door.

• • •

The carpenter was putting equipment back into the truck when they all walked up. Macey noticed Charlie was sitting in the back of the truck with his legs hanging over the tailgate, a newspaper draped over his lap.

Pastor Jim hugged Shirley, and she kissed his cheek. "How does it look?" he asked excitedly.

"Magnificent," Shirley said. "It looks brand-new."

"Praise God," Pastor Jim said. "It must not have been as bad as I thought."

Kenneth took him by the arm. "Let's just let that last coat of finish dry, and it should be all set."

"Last coat?" Zach asked. "You didn't have time to put *one* coat on it."

"Tricks of the trade," Kenneth said.

Macey noticed that Zach couldn't take his eyes off the cross. "It—it's perfect!" he yelled. "You could not have possibly—"

"Yes, it is, Dr. Norman," Kenneth said, joining them.

Macey looked at Zach again, then up at the cross. As Shirley said, it was magnificent—standing high and shining in the sun as the wet lacquer provided the perfect finish.

"It's unreal," Brooke said.

Kaitlyn stepped forward and dreamily said, "I had a feeling he would fix it."

"It's impossible what they did!" Zach muttered, almost complaining. He rambled halfway up the hill and stopped. He had a look on his face that Macey had never seen before. Like he was crazy.

Brooke pointed at Charlie, who was walking toward the house. "Where's he going?"

Kenneth shrugged and then smiled. "His dad mentioned that we were all going to get burgers and fries when we were done. I think he's going to change."

"Let's get a close-up of the cross," Shirley said excitedly.

"Take me with you," Pastor Jim said.

"You guys did a great job, Kenneth," Macey said, her elbows up on the side of truck, gazing up the hill in a bit of disbelief herself.

"Thanks," Kenneth said, closing the tailgate on the truck, rattling the tools and the cans of lacquer as tiny flakes of rust from the bed fluttered to the ground.

Macey looked back up at the cross. It really was impeccable. She glanced over at Zach, who was still acting like a madman. Zach could be obnoxious, but he wasn't crazy. The scent of lacquer drifted down the hill toward them, testifying to a fresh application. She looked back in the truck bed again—at the cans of finish.

She could hear Brooke, Shirley, Kaitlyn, and Pastor Jim celebrating as they walked up the hill to closely examine the risen cross, but she couldn't move.

She couldn't take her eyes off the seals on the cans—*all four of them.*

"Only believe, Macey Lewis," Kenneth said, throwing a tarp over the tools and cans of finish. "Remember?"

THIRTEEN

Kaitlyn had never seen it so busy at The Pilot.
All three TVs in the bar section were on, featuring the Detroit Lions leading the Green Bay Packers seventeen to seven in the third quarter. Kaitlyn didn't know much about football, but the Lions' unusually good start to the season had made Sundays at The Pilot a weekly party, and thousands of southeastern Michiganders were uttering three words that had never made sense in the same sentence before: *Super, Bowl,* and *Lions.*

Please . . . don't let anybody I know see me today.

"Football is bad for my ears, but good for my wallet," Lila said, leaving the bar to seat them in the diner. "It makes up for the slow days." They walked through swinging doors and into a lighter, brighter rectangle of a room, devoid of TVs. Five of the booths were occupied, folks enjoying their lunches. The diner portion of The Pilot did a decent business, but not nearly what the bar did.

"I guess so," Kaitlyn said, watching as Lila slid one table toward another so they could all sit in the center of the room, between the booths.

"Everybody watch their fingers," Lila said, pushing together the last two tables and then pulling out an order pad. "Sorry about making you the center of attention. This is the best I can do with so many of you."

"This is perfect," Kaitlyn said, looking back at the swinging doors that led to the bar and secretly wishing for a dash of rum and Coke.

"You and that lady know each other?" Zach asked. "You seem like best buds."

"She has owned the place forever," Kaitlyn said. "You know I grew up in this town."

"We never came here," Zach said.

"You would never come in a place like this," she said, thinking *I came here all the time when I was dating you, Zach. And I still do.*

"I want chicken strips," Alex blurted.

"Then it's chicken strips for you!" Lila answered. "And as I'm sure you all know, we also have the best burgers in the state."

Brooke was giving her order when she handed Charlie a handful of quarters. Kaitlyn had noticed the big guy pointing at the video games when they all walked in. Charlie stood and left the table with Alex at his heels.

Zach and Macey were sitting with Brooke, and at the adjacent table, the carpenter sat across from Pastor Jim and Shirley with an empty seat to his left. Kaitlyn saw the opportunity to avoid Zach and decided to take it.

"This is fun!" Shirley said, surprisingly loud over the dim tune of Willie Nelson's "Always on My Mind" playing on the jukebox in the bar.

"Hey, Pastor Jim," Kaitlyn said, glad to see the older couple having a good time. She pointed at Shirley. "Try to settle her down. We don't want to get kicked out of here."

Pastor Jim put his arm around Shirley and pulled her toward him. "If she gets kicked out, I may just try my luck around here with one of those other women next door."

Shirley smacked him playfully on his arm and shook her head.

Pastor Jim shifted in Kenneth's direction. "Just point me toward a keeper, Kenneth. Then watch me work."

Kenneth reached across the table and tapped Pastor Jim on his arm. "I think you already have a keeper, James."

"I guess I'll probably hang on to her," Pastor Jim said. "I'd be in the dark without her!"

"You know I don't like you making fun of your blindness," Shirley said.

"Forgive me, sweetie." He gave Shirley another squeeze.

Kenneth turned slightly toward Kaitlyn and spoke so low, only she could hear. "Can you forgive him?"

A chill danced off the side of Kaitlyn's neck. It was the same chill as the one he caused the night she met him at the bar and just like the one she felt a couple hours earlier when she *knew* he entered the church.

She gripped the metal napkin holder in front of her. It felt cool to her palms as she angled it just right to see his reflection.

"Who are you?" she whispered.

"Look at me, Kaitlyn," Kenneth said.

She slowly turned her head toward him and found herself immediately locked onto his clear green eyes. Soft and understanding. She could feel her abdomen tighten as the overwhelming feelings she'd had the night at the bar returned. *He seems to know everything about me. He knows who I have to forgive.*

"Can you take these for me, handsome?" Lila asked, holding five standard bar glasses in her hands behind Kenneth.

Kenneth reached up and took the glasses without breaking eye contact with Kaitlyn. A memory flashed in her mind—her father standing in the doorway to her bedroom, smiling at her with such tenderness. She remembered his last five words.

I love you, baby girl.

Kaitlyn shot out of her seat, looking toward Kenneth, but unable to see him any longer. All she could see was her father. She closed her eyes and slowly shook her head.

"No, I can't forgive him," she mumbled. "And I never will."

• • •

Macey wasn't sure what to make of the way Zach was behaving. He seemed listless, rising to stare at the historic pictures on the diner walls, as if they were the most intriguing things he'd seen all week. When he returned to the table, he was silent and bit at his lip. "You're sure quiet, Zach. You feeling okay?"

"I'm all right," he said.

"No, you're not," she said, leaning toward him so she could whisper. She shot a sidelong glance down the table to make sure no one else was paying attention. "Tell me, Zach. How did he fix it so fast?"

"Like the minister said, it must not have been as bad as we all thought."

She could tell that Zach didn't believe his own words. He was acting like a man who knew that ghosts didn't exist, trying to explain the ghost sitting right in front of him.

"You sure?" she asked.

"Yeah, I'm sure." He gave her a drawn and tired look—an expression normally reserved for doctors coming out of nine-hour surgeries. She knew that he couldn't rationalize what had happened.

"Zach," she said, trying to get him to focus.

He tilted his head as if he hoped she had an explanation. They stared at each other and seemed to silently agree that something unusual was going on.

Zach finally looked away. "It wasn't as bad as we thought," he said again. "There's no other explanation, Macey."

"I guess you're right." He *was* right. There really was no other explanation. But it was destroyed. It looked so bad. *And, yes, ladies and gentlemen, let's not forget about those four cans of unopened lacquer. Surely a weather-beaten, lightning-singed, fifteen-foot cross would soak in at least one of the cans.* She turned her head to find that Kenneth was staring at her. And then he gave her a slow, knowing smile.

She quickly looked away at Alex and Charlie. Alex was standing on a chair in front of an arcade-type game at the end of the diner, methodically controlling the jaws of a tiny metal crane hovering over an orange ball with rubber spikes. Charlie was looking back—*gawking*, actually—at Kenneth. Charlie looked at Kenneth as if he were a magician who'd made an elephant disappear into thin air. Or took a completely destroyed cross—shredded, split, and burned by a lightning bolt—and made it brand-new. Better than new—considering the layers of lacquer that magically covered the cross in a matter of minutes.

She turned her head back toward Kenneth, who was still watching her. *Nice work, Kenneth,* she thought. *His dad couldn't see you fix the cross, and he can't talk about it. Good one there, pal. Just who are you and what are you up to?*

• • •

Kaitlyn was returning from a visit to the restroom when Lila grabbed her by the arm.

"Guess who's here," Lila whispered.

"Don't even say it," Kaitlyn said, eyeing Alex and Charlie as they played an ancient Pac-Man machine in the corner.

"Okay, I won't then," Lila said.

"I never even thought about him being here on a Sunday," Kaitlyn said. "I should have known, with the Lions playing." She sighed and turned toward Lila. "Is he drinking?"

"He just got here, but it seems like he has been, from the looks of him."

It's what Kaitlyn feared. Tim Shempner, Kaitlyn's on-again-off-again fling from days past, was pretty good at losing his temper, and when he was drinking, he was one of the best. The innocent victims of his drunken bouts of anger were normally smaller and weaker targets, his favorite once being Kaitlyn. She never wore makeup to the hospital, but in a few instances, she'd had to apply foundation in order to cover suspicious bruises.

"Maybe you should get out of here," Lila said. "Go out through the kitchen. I'll bring you your burger."

"Did he see me walk through?"

"I don't think so," Lila said.

Kaitlyn sighed. "I'm staying. And I'm not going to let Shempner push me around anymore. Plus he's too much of a coward to try anything in front of all these people."

Lila looked back at Pastor Jim and Shirley, and then at the other table. "That's great, Kaitlyn, but the last thing I need on a busy day like this is a scene in front of everybody."

* * *

Jim was trying to figure out why all old diners seemed to smell the same when he heard Shirley clear her throat.

"I'm amazed how good the cross looks, Kenneth. You certainly are gifted with tools. We never imagined it could be repaired so quickly."

"It's sometimes difficult to believe things," Kenneth said, "particularly when you don't see them with your own eyes."

"I don't know how we can ever repay you," Jim said.

"Your joy and gratefulness are thanks enough," he answered.

Jim smiled. "Where are you from, Kenneth, if you don't mind me asking?"

"A little bit of everywhere," Kenneth said.

Hmm, a wanderer. Times were tough for everyone. Maybe Kenneth had a difficult time holding a job and went wherever construction led him. Jim found himself hoping the hospital construction would keep him around for a good long while.

"It'd be nice if you could come to our harvest party on Saturday," Shirley said. "You're welcome to bring a date if you want."

Jim let out a little laugh. "Shirley, I'm sure the man has other plans for the weekend."

"I don't, actually. I'll be there," Kenneth said over the cheers of The Pilot Inn regulars next door. It sounded like Detroit kicked a field goal.

"Wonderful!" Shirley said. "That goes for you guys too!"

"What goes for us too?"

Jim thought the voice was Macey's.

"We're having a harvest party this Saturday at the church," Shirley said. "Come if you don't already have plans. Kenneth said he'll be there."

"Sounds like fun. I haven't been to a church party in ages!"

Yep. Definitely Macey.

"Wonderful!" Shirley said again. There was nothing his wife liked better than a bunch of guests to look after.

"Maybe then we can have our friend tell us how he patched that cross up so fast," Macey said. "What do you think, Kenneth?"

"Maybe I will," Kenneth said. "I think Dr. Lewis is on to me, James."

Jim smiled. "Sometimes the Lord works in mysterious ways. Even through us!"

"He certainly does," Kenneth said.

"By the way," Jim said. "After the young lady from the newspaper took our picture, why didn't you give her your name? I'm just curious."

Jim felt a hand on his shoulder and figured it was Kenneth. "Take heed that you do not do your charitable deeds before men, to be seen by them. Otherwise you have no reward from your Father in heaven."

"Matthew 6:1," Jim said, recognizing the verse his men's group had just studied a couple of weeks ago. "A hard lesson for most of us." Hadn't he even enjoyed a flash of pride when he could identify the chapter and verse as easily as Kenneth seemed able to do? "We all like a little recognition. But good for you, for living it out."

"I had a feeling you'd get that verse," Kenneth said. "I'm thinking I can stump you with another, though."

"Possibly," Jim said. He held up his hands and then pointed his index fingers at Kenneth. "But as Alex would say, bring it on."

"Do not be afraid; only believe, and he will be made well."

"It's Luke 8:50," Jim said, not feeling prideful, but fortunate. He'd been reading the Bible since he was about seven, and when he finally lost his sight for good, he ended up with a steel-trap memory and a braille Bible set to boot. By the grace of God, he was pretty sure he'd memorized most of Scripture over the years, and even spotted something the carpenter had missed.

"If you don't mind me correcting you," Jim said, "the verse ends with '*she* will be made well.' I think you may have accidentally said '*he*.'"

"Tell her," Kenneth said. "It's very important that you remember that. Please don't forget."

"Tell who?" Jim asked, sitting back.

"Tell her to only believe, and *he* will be made well."

"Tell who?" Jim repeated.

The carpenter remained silent.

"A puzzle?" Jim asked, drumming his fingers on the table. "Something you want me to figure out on my own? I won't forget the verse. It's Luke 8:50. But who to tell?"

There was a little pause and then a warm hand took his wrist.

"Give it a day or so," Kenneth said. "I think you'll figure it out."

• • •

"What do you think you guys are gonna be for the harvest party?" Brooke asked. "You don't have much time to figure it out."

"Adults are dressing up too?" Kaitlyn said, thinking about the last big Halloween party she attended. It was close to ten years ago at The Pilot. She also remembered not remembering where she woke up on November 1. "I have no idea. After years of working with kids on the hospital ward, I have a few options. What about you?"

"I'm going as Dorothy from *The Wizard of Oz*," Brooke said. "Alex is gonna be the scarecrow, and Charlie is gonna be a big tin man."

"He is perfect for that!" Macey said, sitting up straight in her chair and taking a deep breath. Next to her, Zach was reaching into a bowl of Goldfish crackers with a pained expression.

"Look at me," Zach said. "I'm so hungry that now I'm eating this garbage."

Alex wedged himself between Macey and Zach and was staring at Zach. "Hey, mister," he said while tugging on Zach's sleeve.

"Hey there, sport," Zach said.

Alex pointed at the small bowl of Goldfish. "Why are you eating those?"

"It's a little snack before the food comes," Zach answered. "Want some?"

"No way," Alex said, pointing back at the half-filled bowl. "Mom says there is pee on those goldfishies. People don't always wash their hands after going to the bathroom and then they eat these with their dirty hands."

Kaitlyn hid a smile.

"Alexander!" Brooke said.

"But you said that there—"

"Enough, Alexander! I'm sorry, Zach."

Zach choked down the ball of half-chewed pulp in his mouth. "It's all right," he said, picking up his glass of water. He studied the cleanliness of the glass and then took a drink.

Alex looked wide-eyed at Zach. "It's pretty gross, isn't it?"

Zach nodded his head and set his glass back down.

"Sorry about the wait, everybody!" Lila said, placing a huge tray of Pilot Burgers on the crease that brought the two tables together.

"Where is mine?" Alex asked.

Lila put a plate of chicken strips in front of Alex, who clapped in delight. "And these are for you, Alex."

"No sauce for me," Alex said, lifting his hand to the stocky waitress the way a Roman emperor would address his subjects.

"You can keep my sauce too," Macey said.

"Shall we join hands real quick before we eat?" Pastor Jim asked.

The nine of them joined hands and Pastor Jim began the prayer.

"Lord, thank you for bringing us together today, and thank you for the additional blessing of new friends, and for showing us that regardless of the obstacles we face, we can come together and—"

"Well, if it isn't The Pilot bimbo!" someone called. The other customers in the diner immediately fell silent. Everyone in their party looked up to the swinging door and a drunk man, weaving his way toward them. "Here I was thinking you saw me and left, but no! You're in here hiding!"

"Who the heck is that?" Zach said.

At the sound of Tim Shempner's voice, Kaitlyn felt like she'd just stepped barefoot out into the snow.

Even most of the bar seemed to fall silent on the other side of the doors, with the exception of the televisions. Kaitlyn reluctantly looked up to see Shempner marching toward their table. He wore a plaid shirt over a gray T-shirt, which hung over dirty jeans. It looked like he hadn't shaved in three days, and his grease-stained fingers were resting across his beer gut.

How did I ever think he was cute? Horror flooded her chest at the thought of what was about to come down. *Why didn't I go when Lila suggested it? But I just said I'm not going to put up with stuff like this.*

Even though you couldn't smoke in the bar, a half-finished Newport hung out of his mouth, and when he arrived at the table, an inch of dirty gray ash broke off and fluttered down to the floor.

Kaitlyn stood, determined to hold her ground. "Not today, Tim. Go back, now. Back to the bar and leave us be."

"Only if you come with me," Shempner crooned. "Or are you gunning for one of these poor fools to buy you a rum and Coke so you'll go home with them?"

"Please, Tim," Kaitlyn said, turning to Pastor Jim and Kenneth, who were now standing.

Shempner dropped a heavy hand on Charlie's shoulder and then glared at Brooke. "Oh, lookie here, everybody. They brought the big retard with them today! The preacher's boy! God is great! God is good! He wasn't too good to you, was he *reeetaaard?*"

Charlie reached in his pocket for his TicTacs. He offered one to Shempner, who mindlessly slapped the container out of Charlie's hand, scattering little white candies across the table and floor.

Charlie stood to retrieve the small plastic container, and Shempner grabbed his arm and squeezed it. "You stay put, boy! I didn't say you could leave! Sit down!" Charlie froze.

Shempner laughed then, so hard tears streamed from his eyes.

The rest of them remained silent. Zach stood and took a step toward Shempner, but for some reason, Kenneth reached out and took Zach by the arm.

"Why are you doing this?" Zach asked Shempner.

"Shut up, fool!" Shempner yelled at Zach, all traces of humor abruptly leaving his face. He looked savage, mean. A shiver ran down Kaitlyn's back as he pointed to Kenneth. "He just saved you from a beatdown."

Kenneth calmly crossed his arms, drawing Kaitlyn's attention. *Do something*, she thought. *Why did you stop Zach? Please, one of you do something . . .*

Charlie turned cautiously toward the safety of Pastor Jim and Shirley. He smiled at the mere sight of their faces.

"Hey, retard!" Shempner screamed. "Are you deaf, too, boy? I said, sit down!"

"Please, Tim," Kaitlyn pleaded. "Let's go outside and talk things over. C'mon . . ."

But Charlie spotted the tiny plastic top of his TicTac container on the floor directly behind Shempner. Excited by his discovery, he jerked forward, but before he could reach it, Shempner slapped him across his left cheek.

Charlie stood straight up and covered his face with both hands.

"No!" Alex screamed.

"He was coming after me!" Shempner cried. "I've got witnesses!"

Brooke stood. "Stop it!"

Shempner stepped closer to Charlie and lifted his hand, causing Charlie to flinch. Shempner then let out a crazy laugh and lowered his hand. "Turn the other cheek, preacher's boy!"

Pastor Jim started to step forward, but Kenneth grabbed him by the arm as well, bringing him to a stop.

Charlie held his hands over his face. He was trembling and peeking down at Shempner through his fingers.

Brooke edged between them and slowly pulled Charlie's arms down. "Shh, shh," she soothed. "It's okay. I won't let him hurt you anymore, Charlie." He had a red handprint on the side of his face. Two tears slowly trickled down his cheeks.

"What did he ever do to you?" Kaitlyn cried.

Shempner let out a scoffing noise. "I should kick the tar out of you and him!" he screamed, stepping back toward Charlie.

"Just try, Tim!" Kaitlyn cried, turning to face him. "Just try, here, in front of all these witnesses you're so fond of noting. Hopefully it will land you in jail where you should be!"

"Why you . . . ," he sneered, pulling back a fist.

"Twenty seconds, Tim! You have twenty seconds!"

It was Lila. She barreled through the doors and came up behind Shempner, two-handing an aluminum baseball bat, waving its top back and forth as if she were waiting for a curveball. "You leave within fifteen seconds or I'll start playing T-ball with your head."

Kenneth took a step toward Shempner. "I think she means business, friend."

"Shut up. I'm not your friend."

"You are down to ten seconds, Tim," Lila said.

"You gonna take this whore's side, Lila? You know how she is."

"Who are you calling a whore?" Zach said.

"Five seconds, Tim," Lila said, the barrel of the bat trembling. "Don't ever show your face in The Pilot again."

"If me and my buddies quit drinking at this dump, you would go out of business."

"I'll take that risk," Lila said, lowering the bat. She stepped right up next to him and whispered something only Kaitlyn could overhear. And after she finished, Shempner straightened, gave her a long look, then turned around and slammed through the saloon doors.

Lila gave them all a self-satisfied smile. "Sorry about that, folks. I'll see that he doesn't return. Please, go back to your meal. It's getting cold."

Kaitlyn just stared at the saloon doors, wondering why she couldn't ever send Tim Shempner off like that. As Lila walked away, the waitress's words played over in Kaitlyn's mind:

Don't stay away forever, Tim. I'm begging you. You know who my friends are. Come back just one more time, and I promise that you'll walk funny for the rest of your life.

Kaitlyn could hear Alex crying. She turned and he was clinging to Charlie's leg. Charlie picked him up, and Alex kissed the man on his cheek and hugged him. "You okay, Charlie?" Alex asked.

Kaitlyn took Charlie's hand and looked up at him. "I am sorry he did that to you, Charlie." She reached up and wiped the tears from his cheek, feeling the weight of his pain and embarrassment, and then stroked Alex's arm. "It's okay, Alex. Charlie is all right."

But it felt anything but all right.

And it was all Kaitlyn's fault. *What did Charlie ever do to hurt anybody? And little Alex . . .* Tears clogged her throat.

She looked down the table. As if it wasn't already horrifying enough, she was about to lose it, in front of everyone. The minister, his wife, Macey, Zach and . . . Kenneth.

The carpenter stared into her eyes, but she quickly looked away. *Forgive him? Who? Tim? Not in this lifetime.*

Who was Kenneth to come here, anyway? Judging her?

What right did he have?

* * *

They ate quietly as the Packers scored on the last play of the game to beat the Lions twenty-one to twenty. By the sounds of the disappointed fans, those in the bar had all but forgotten the drama next door.

"I feel badly about what happened," Shirley said.

Jim noticed that Kaitlyn didn't respond. Was she offended by his wife's words?

"You all right, Kaitlyn?" he asked.

"She went to the restroom right after that man left," Shirley said. "Doctor Lewis followed her in and then came back, but Kaitlyn still hasn't returned."

He could hear the two doctors talking with Brooke in low tones at the end of the table next to them. "I didn't know she wasn't here," Jim said. "I guess we can be thankful it didn't get any worse."

"True," Kenneth said. "And everybody is okay, including Charlie."

"Praise God," Jim said. "We should pray for that Tim fella. I hope something happens to help him find his way."

"Hey, James," Kenneth said. "Let's let it go and try to enjoy the rest of this day. Let me see you smile. Remember that new cross."

He was right. They couldn't let evil overshadow the light of this amazing day. Jim grinned and held out his hand, warmed when Kenneth took it. "I'm glad we met, friend. I feel like I've known you forever."

"I feel the same," the carpenter said. He paused, still holding his hand. "And, James, I need you to remember to do something."

"Oh, don't worry," Jim said. "You want me to tell someone about Luke 8:50."

"I'm not talking about 8:50 anymore," the carpenter said, pulling his hand away. "When it happens, promise me that you will never tell anyone about it."

"Tell them about what?"

"About 7:16."

"From which book?" Jim asked, hearing Kaitlyn return to the table. He thought he could smell liquor and swallowed a wave of disappointment. He opened his mouth to say something, at the same moment he felt Kenneth's warm hand wrap around his wrist once again.

"Give it a little time," the carpenter said, lightly squeezing Jim's wrist before letting go. "I think you'll figure 7:16 out too."

FOURTEEN

Macey knocked and waited while studying the thick, brass nameplate on the office door that read "Percival J. Timmins." She took a quick sip of her coffee and found herself wondering if there was anyone who had been at East Shore longer than Jerry Timmins. In his thirty-five years here, Timmins had established himself as a no-nonsense doctor; a straightforward, what-you-see-is-what-you-get human being; and a devout Christian. She liked him, as most people did.

The door opened, and Timmins smiled. "C'mon in, Dr. Lewis."

"Hello, Jerry. Thanks for taking the time."

He glanced at his watch and then guided her to a chair that was angled to the side of his desk. "I'm usually not busy at this hour." He smiled again. "Zach Norman taking care of you down there on Three?"

"As well as can be expected. Zach actually called in—he isn't feeling well."

"Really?" Timmins said. "Our model of health called in sick? That's a first."

"Yes, it is."

"I'm gonna close this window," he said, walking swiftly to the other side of the room and then cranking a small handle at the window sill. "It feels like we're going to have an early winter."

"I'm still trying to figure out where summer went," Macey said, admiring the agility and speed that Timmins still possessed. She guessed him to be around five foot nine, 160 pounds, and he was still in what she thought to be excellent shape. Despite being sixty-six years old, he didn't have a gray hair on his head, and he kept that hair in a tight brush-cut, not unlike the one she assumed he had during his two tours as a medic in Vietnam, doing what he referred to as "patching up wounded teenagers."

She glanced around the office. The faint aroma of Lemon Pledge accented the spotless office that she already considered to be military-clean. Behind the desk she noticed a photo she'd not seen before of a handsome young man in a military officer's uniform. "West Point?" she asked, pointing at the photograph.

"Yes," Timmins answered. "That's Michael. It was taken about eight years ago."

"You must be proud."

"As proud as a father could be," Timmins said, pausing. "We lost him in Iraq."

Macey clenched her teeth and gave herself a swift internal kick for not remembering that Timmins had a son who'd been killed in action. "Oh, Jerry, I'm sorry."

"Don't be," he said calmly—almost too calmly, she thought. "Michael's with God."

"With God," she repeated.

"Yes," Timmins said. "You know, Macey, we don't always understand why, but certain things happen for a reason. Including what happened to Mary Springsted."

"Yes," Macey said, straightening up in her seat. "I mean—twenty-two weeks in a coma, and she just gets up and walks out?"

"Just like that," Timmins said, snapping his fingers crisply.

"But, Jerry, five months in a—"

"Just like that," he repeated. "Mr. Springsted walked into his wife's room twenty minutes after visiting hours started, and then immediately came running out, screaming like a madman, yelling for us to come. Carrie Armstrong and I rushed down there, and when we entered the room, little Mary Springsted was sitting up with her legs hanging over the edge of the bed." Timmins shrugged his shoulders and then crossed his arms. "It's that simple."

"Simple?" Macey chirped. "She was in a coma for five months. *Five* months."

"Mrs. Springsted was speaking with perfect clarity and said she wanted to get out of bed. Carrie and I asked her to lay back down so we could examine her, but she'd have none of it. She stood right up and looked at us like the suggestion of an exam was nuts. Why? Because she felt perfectly fine."

Macey tugged nervously at her ear. "That's unreal."

"Agreed. But I assure you, it was most real."

"But her mind . . . her muscles, the atrophy . . ."

"I know."

Macey sipped her coffee again. "Twenty-two weeks? It's impossible, isn't it?"

Timmins grabbed a peach-colored mug off of his desk that had the words "I love Grandpa" printed in dark blue letters on its side. "How about a warm-up?" he asked.

She handed Timmins her cup, and he walked toward a small kitchenette in the corner of the office. "And then there were the bedsores," he said.

"Bedsores? What about them?" She knew it was a chronic problem that doctors and nurses faced when treating comatose patients; the skin simply began to break down.

Timmins picked up the pot of coffee that was next to the sink and then immediately put it back down. "They were gone, Macey. Gone."

"What do you mean?"

Timmins turned around and brought his hands to the sides of his face. He suddenly seemed uncomfortable. He took a deep breath, and his cheeks puffed out as he exhaled. "I'm telling you, Dr. Lewis, that we treated her bedsores every single day. And then came that day, the day she woke up. They simply weren't there anymore. They were gone."

Macey brought her hand to her chin, reminding herself of *The Thinker*. "Jerry—how do you explain it? What you are describing seems impossible."

"But it's not impossible. This isn't some second-hand story. The fact remains that it happened, and I *saw* it happen. Mrs. Springsted stood up, and her husband said they were leaving and that nobody was going to stop them."

"Keep going," Macey said, noticing an open Bible next to a magnifying glass on the desk.

"Mrs. Springsted finally agreed to let us take a look at her." Timmins paused for a few seconds and then shook his head again. "I really don't know what to say, Macey. She was fine—mentally and physically. As Carrie said, it was like she had just awakened from a nap."

Macey blinked. She thought as highly of Carrie Armstrong as a nurse as she did of Kaitlyn. "Okay, Jerry, tell me—what is your medical explanation? What are you going to put in her file?"

"Explanation?" he said. "Well, it's not entirely unheard of for someone to come out of a five-month coma. You know that."

"I understand, but for her to *walk* out the same day? That's inexplicable, right?"

"In my thirty-five years, I've had six patients come out of comas longer than three months, and I've read about dozens of others. In each and every one of these cases, you're looking at months of physical therapy, and normally an equal—if not greater—amount of mental and emotional rehabilitation. I really don't believe that you will find a single documented case anywhere of someone just getting up and walking out the same day, let alone . . ."

"What?" she asked.

Timmins closed his eyes and his brow was furrowed, as if he were deciding if she could handle the truth.

"Jerry?"

He looked her straight in the eye. "Let alone waking up in *better* physical condition than when they entered the hospital."

"Until Mary Springsted?"

"Exactly," the doctor said. "I'm telling you right now that Mary Springsted walked out of here not only in better shape than when she arrived, but in better shape than she had been in for over a decade."

"I don't know what to say," Macey said, leaning to the side of her chair. "How do you explain *that?*"

Timmins took a deep breath. "I believe that man—Mr. Springsted—was down on his knees at the chapel literally every single day, praying. He prayed and prayed, and then prayed some more that God would heal his wife." Timmins brought his hands together. "And I believe his prayer was answered."

"You really think that's what—"

"I *know* that's what happened."

Macey grinned, but she wasn't really sure why. "That *God* did it?"

"Yes," he said. "Another one of those unexplained parts of that plan we don't understand—that we can't understand."

Macey held her coffee with both hands and bit down lightly on her bottom lip. "I don't think I'd tell Zach Norman that, Jerry."

"Why not?"

"I'm not sure he would believe you."

Timmins nodded and then looked down in a way that she found peculiar. "Sometimes things happen to people, and they choose not to believe."

"What do you mean?"

"Let's just say if Zach asks, I'm still going to tell him what I believe really happened."

Macey got up and walked over to the window, catching herself trying to spot the old Ford pickup. "But *medically* speaking, what do you tell Zach?"

"Nothing different than I've told you. That there are things that are bigger than medicine—and as much as we doctors hate to admit it, bigger than us." Timmins tilted his head, and the corner of his mouth rose. "Other than that, what happened to Mary Springsted is impossible. There is no other explanation than God."

Macey felt a wave of religious claustrophobia. It was all a bit much. "So, what is Mrs. Springsted's follow-up?"

Timmins smiled. "I'm sorry to impose my beliefs on you, Macey."

"That's not it, Jerry."

"The Springsteds said they'd think about coming back in on

Wednesday to let us check Mrs. Springsted out, just to make sure everything is okay. But they won't be here."

"Why do you say that?"

"I think they agreed to Wednesday just so we wouldn't give them a hard time about leaving. But I'd be very surprised if they come back. Mrs. Springsted looked too good and if you'd just lost five months to this place, would you be anxious to return?"

Macey smiled. "Probably not."

"Mr. Springsted looked like he was ready to burst at the seams, yelling and practically pushing us out of the way to dance his wife down the halls."

Macey looked at her watch. It was 7:57 a.m. "Jerry, I have to be at the free clinic in a few minutes. Plan on me bothering you some more about this."

"It was a pleasure having you up here, Dr. Lewis. Don't be such a stranger in the future."

"I won't," Macey said, walking to the door before stopping to turn around. "Jerry, you said Mr. Springsted was yelling? After it was all over?"

Timmins grinned and held up his hands. "Yep."

"What was he yelling?"

"He kept saying that they didn't need to come back. That they didn't need doctors, nurses, medicines, and that they didn't even need the hospital. Mr. Springsted kept yelling that there was only one thing they needed to do—"

Macey could hear her name being called over the paging system at the same time Timmins finished speaking.

"That's me," she said. "I'm sorry, Jerry, I didn't catch what you said. What was the only thing Mr. Springsted said they needed to do?"

"Only believe," Timmins said.

Macey felt her throat close. The McDonald's cup slipped through her fingers. She felt her heart pounding at the walls of her chest.

All she could see was the carpenter's face.

"Are you all right?" Timmins asked, taking her by the elbow.

"I—I'm sorry," she said in a small, breathless voice, belatedly remembering she'd dropped her cup.

"Don't worry about it," Timmins said, patiently guiding her back to the chair.

She struggled to catch her breath and then leaned forward in the chair. She stood again and walked slowly over to the windowsill. Dr. Timmins was right.

There are things that are bigger than medicine.

"Macey?" Timmins said softly. "What is it?"

She turned the handle until the window was a little over halfway open and took in a deep breath of cold air before looking over at the new wing—and then slowly down at the parking lot. She knew he was out there somewhere. Right here at East Shore.

And as much as we doctors hate to admit, bigger than us.

Timmins brought her a Dixie cup of water. "Here you go."

She took the water and was leaning against the windowsill as she heard her name being called again over the paging system. She could feel the sock on her left foot, soaked in coffee, uncomfortably sliding around the inside of her brand-new tennis shoe, and glanced down. The Nike logo on the shoe was now stained a dull coffee-brown. She didn't care. She glanced at her watch again. It was five minutes past eight when she was paged a third time to the free clinic.

Brooke and Alex Thomas were waiting for her.

FIFTEEN

Alex liked the fact that he didn't refer to his mother as *mommy* anymore.

After all, *mommy* was little-kid talk, and he was almost six—almost big enough to play with the big kids. He knew because his mother had told him that next year, he'd not only be getting a lunch box with a thermos, but that the big yellow school bus would be coming to get him in front of the house to go to first grade every single day except Saturdays and Sundays. For the *whole* day.

As he got older, there were more and more things that Alex learned about his mother, including what not to talk about. He knew she didn't like to talk about the macaroni necklace her and her mother made when she was a little girl. She only told him about it two times and both times she cried a whole lot. Mom also said she never told anyone else about the necklace, not even Charlie, Pastor Jim, or Mrs. Lindy. He knew why. It was because they made the necklace out of something you eat and it was silly. Alex also knew that Mom's mom was his grandma and Grandma was wearing that macaroni necklace the day she and Grandpa went to heaven. So he always did his bestest to avoid using the words *grandma* and *grandpa* around her because they seemed to make her sad. Sometimes there were other words that put her in bad moods like *father, dad, money, laid off,* and *car payment.* But today he thought that there was a different one that was making her worry. The word was *list.*

Why would Mom worry about a list?

He knew it wasn't the shopping list Mrs. Lindy sometimes gave his mother when they went to the store and came back with food.

And it sure wasn't the Christmas list like the one they made when his mother asked him what he wanted from Santa (even though he figured Santa must not have read the whole list). He knew that the list that was worrying her was different. It was special. The list was special because Dr. Alisoni said that a *special list* was coming and for them to all wait in this room until the *special list* came.

He didn't like it when his mother worried—and he could tell she was *really* worried. Her feet were tapping on the ground, she was pinching at her forehead, she was eating the ends of her fingers, and she also was asking Mrs. Lindy lots of questions he didn't understand. He had a plan to make her feel better, though. He'd found something he thought was cool, and he was going to distract her from thinking about the special list by showing it to her and making her laugh.

"Look, Mom!" he said excitedly, pressing his foot down on a funny silver garbage-can pedal, making its lid open and close. "I can make it talk! 'Hi, Mrs. Lindy,'" he said, in a funny voice.

"Oh, you're good at that, Alexander," Mrs. Lindy said, sitting next to Mom.

"Hey, Mom," Alex said, holding the lid open and looking curiously into the can at the trash inside. "How long before we can go home?"

"I'm not sure, baby," Mom answered, biting on her fingers again. "I'm worried, Shirley. What do you think it is?"

Mrs. Lindy blinked real slow and shook her head at Mom. "I don't know. Let's just see what the special list says, honey."

Mom rested her chin on her hand. "I can't understand a word Dr. Alisoni says. How am I going to decipher what a special list has to say?"

"Brooke, honey, just trust. God sees us here. He'll help us."

"But why even bring in a special list?" Mom said. She was making that worried face again.

Alex's foot came off the foot lever, causing the lid to clank as it fell shut, and he moved over to a cool painting of a yellow-haired clown with big, square teeth that was getting lifted off the ground by a bunch of balloons. His eyes moved over to the next painting, taking two big steps sideways to stand beneath it. "What's this say, Mom?" Alex asked, pointing at the words.

Mom didn't answer, but Mrs. Lindy did. "It says Norman Rockwell."

Alex figured the painting had to be done in what Mom called the *olden days*. In the painting, he could see an old rocking chair with a blue seat. Next to the chair was a scale. Alex remembered that he weighed forty-six pounds now. In front of the scale, there was an old-fashioned shoe and a big mitten on the floor. He thought they really looked funny, and he wouldn't want to wear them. Then there was the boy he guessed was around ten, standing up on another chair and squinting at a piece of paper that was stuck on the wall. He didn't like the boy's T-shirt that didn't have sleeves on it, and he noticed that the boy's pants were pulled partly down and that he could see his—

"What the heck?" Alex said, laughing. "Hey, Mom! I see that kid's bare butt!"

"*Shh*," Mom said.

"It's right there in the picture! Look at it, Mom! His butt!"

"*Shh*, I see it, baby."

He knew why she didn't laugh; it was that list. He looked back at the rest of the painting, and his head swiveled back and forth as he studied it. There was a doctor in the painting who was tall, reminding him of Pastor Jim, but not as tall as Charlie—nobody was as tall as Charlie. The man was turned around and holding something in his hand. Alex looked closer at the man's hand. *What are you holding*? he thought. *A crayon? No, it's a pencil. No, it's—uh-oh . . .* Alex's eyes widened, and his stomach suddenly felt sickish.

"Are you okay, buddy?" Mom asked as Alex stutter-stepped back from the painting. He didn't answer. He pointed at the picture.

"Alex?"

"Alexander?" Mrs. Lindy said.

"He has a shot, Mom! This is a *shot room*!"

"No, it's not, buddy," Mom said.

He continued to point at the painting in terror. "Mrs. Lindy! It's right there!"

"That's just a painting, Alexander," Mrs. Lindy said.

He removed his Tigers ball cap and rubbed his head nervously. "Are you *sure*?"

Shadows appeared under the door, followed by grown-up voices.

"Someone is here," Mrs. Lindy said.

"Come here and sit on my lap, silly," Mom said.

Alex skipped to his mother, who picked him up and spun him around on her lap. She wrapped her arms around him, took his cap off, and lowered her chin softly to the top of his head.

"I want to go home," Alex said, looking back at the shot doctor in the painting.

"We have to wait for the doctor," Mom said as someone knocked and then opened the door.

Dr. Alisoni walked into the room, followed by Kaitlyn, and then Dr. Lewis. Alex wondered where the goldfish-with-pee-on-them eater was.

"Macey and Kaitlyn!" Mom said, tapping on Mrs. Lindy's arm. "Boy, am I glad to see your friendly faces." She nodded at Dr. Alisoni.

"Good morning, everybody," Dr. Lewis said, smiling in a way that Alex liked. "How did that cross look this morning? Still standing?"

"It looks perfect," Mom said. "Pastor Jim and I went out and touched it to do a reality check. It's hard to believe how good it looks."

"James can't wait for the congregation to see it," Mrs. Lindy added.

"It certainly is good news," Dr. Lewis said. Alex was looking at the doctor's feet, noticing that one shoe was a lot darker than the other. She kneeled in front of him and held out her hand for a high five. "And a special hello to you, Mr. Alex."

"Hi, Doc Lewis," Alex said, grinning bashfully and smacking the doctor's open hand. "Mom says you guys are coming to the party Saturday. I like sweet tarts if you want to bring some."

"I could maybe bring some," Dr. Lewis said.

Alex pointed at Kaitlyn. "Why did that man hit Charlie yesterday?"

"Let's not worry about that, Alex," Mrs. Lindy said.

"Okay," Alex said, wondering why nobody else was talking. He glanced over at Mom. She seemed worried again and was looking at Dr. Lewis. In fact, *all* the grown-ups were looking at each other. It got *real* quiet.

"It's you, isn't it?" Mom said. "You're the special list?"

Dr. Lewis ran her hand through Alex's hair and stood. "Yes, I am."

Now nobody was talking and it got *super-duper* quiet.

"But didn't you say yesterday that you worked with kids who have—"

"Brooke," Dr. Alisoni interrupted. "Maybe we should—"

"Alex has it?" Mom asked. Alex squirmed out of her arms and stood up to look at her. Her chin was shaking real fast.

"Yes," Dr. Lewis said.

"You okay, Mom?" Alex asked. He was beginning to think he might have to get a shot after all.

Mrs. Lindy grabbed Mom's hand. "It's okay, honey."

"No. No, it isn't, Shirley."

"Please, Brooke, let's just see what Dr. Lewis has to say."

"Why didn't you . . ." Mom stopped talking and wiped her lips. She looked back up at Dr. Lewis, then down at Alex. "Why didn't you tell me this yesterday?"

"It would not have been appropriate, Brooke. And for that, I am sorry."

"Shirley," Kaitlyn said, "I'm really glad you are with us today. Maybe you and Alex wouldn't mind stepping into the next room with me for a little bit?"

"Certainly," Mrs. Lindy said. She put her hand on Mom's shoulder. "Brooke—"

"Not Alex," Mom whispered, looking down and then burying her face in her hands.

"Not me, what?" Alex said, really scared now. "I feel good, Mom. I don't want a shot."

Kaitlyn smiled and leaned down in front of Alex. "Hey, buddy, why don't you and Shirley follow me?"

"Am I going to get a shot in there?" Alex asked. *Maybe if I run when they open the door—*

"No, sir," Kaitlyn said. "But let me tell you, there are some *really* fun things to do in there."

Alex looked at Kaitlyn and then back at Mom. "You okay, Mom?" he asked again, facing her and then plopping his hands on her knees when she just stared at the clown painting, her eyes wide and blank.

"Let's go," Mrs. Lindy said, gently taking his hand. "We'll be right next door, Brooke. It's okay, honey."

As Alex followed Mrs. Lindy and Kaitlyn out of the room, he watched his mother's mouth slowly move, but nothing was coming out. Her eyebrows looked funny and her bottom lip was starting to move real fast again like her chin. It *had to be* that special list. In fact, he knew it was, and he didn't like it. Not one bit.

● ● ●

Dr. Alisoni stepped forward to excuse himself in his best broken English. "Miss Thomas, Dr. Lewis tell me you meet her already before. I leave you now to let her discuss Alexander with you."

Brooke didn't say anything, and it seemed to her that Dr. Alisoni didn't walk out the door, but melted through the wall. She wanted out of the room too—out of the nightmare. This couldn't possibly be happening.

Macey sat in the chair next to Brooke, who immediately stood. Brooke's heartbeat became a dull *thud*, a foreign body in her chest, distant, not her own. Her mouth felt like it was coated with sand, and her legs wobbled like garden hoses, unable to support her weight. As she collapsed back into the chair, she felt stuck—a trapped animal—glued to this room, this awful place, this now-soundless box of panic and horror. She was suffocating, waiting to hear the actual words formally announcing that Alex had cancer.

"You said you worked with kids . . . who have . . . have cancer," she said, her words spilling out slowly. She already knew, but for some strange reason, she found herself needing to hear it again. "Does Alex . . . have cancer?"

Macey looked right at her. "Yes, he does, Brooke."

Brooke felt a cold finger tap lightly on her heart as she recoiled from the force of the answer. *Alex has cancer. My Alex. Alexander, my son, has cancer. Capricorn, Aquarius, Aries, and Cancer. Cancer. Please, God, not this . . . Cancer is for old people. Alex is only five. Five!*

"Brooke . . . ," Macey said.

Brooke grabbed at her own pants legs and squeezed tightly. *Wake up,* she thought. *Please wake up, Brooke. This is really not happening—it's one of those awful things that happen to other people's children—not Alex.* She lifted her hands to her ears and could feel herself starting to shake. "Please, please, not Alex. What am I supposed to do? Please help him. Please help us."

Macey put her hand on Brooke's shoulder. "We will, Brooke."

"I can't believe this is happening," Brooke said. "Why am I not crying right now?"

"Brooke," Macey said. "I don't have children, so I can't fully understand what you are feeling. What I can tell you, though, is that you are going to have a lot of different feelings. This is new to you. It's a lot at once—and I know it is scary."

"Where?" Brooke asked. "Where is the cancer?"

"Alex has leukemia."

"Leukemia?" Brooke repeated faintly.

"Brooke, I'm telling you right now. We are going to beat this."

Leukemia? Brooke asked herself.

"Brooke, leukemia is—"

"Hang on a second," Brooke said, rubbing her eyes. She started to think about Alex's costume for Saturday's harvest party. He knew what he was going to be, but he didn't have his costume yet. He also didn't have a bike without training wheels, his first baseball glove, or his first adult tooth. Alex did, however, have *leukemia.*

"Brooke, what are you thinking right now?"

Brooke looked at the doctor. "Is he going to die?"

"When I said we are going to beat this, I meant it."

"I don't even understand what leukemia is."

"And Alex doesn't either," Macey said. "And he won't. But what he *will* understand is that he doesn't feel well during many parts of his treatment. And the way he feels is going to get a lot worse before it gets better. I saw firsthand the wonderful support group Alex has, and he is going to need all of us. And when I say us, I mean you, me, Pastor Jim, Shirley, Charlie, and our whole pediatric oncology group here. Together, we *will* beat this."

Brooke stood and closed her eyes, turning away from Macey. *Why? Why? Why?*

What terrible thing could she have possibly done to deserve something like this? She couldn't stop herself from thinking about the last time she felt this way.

She was a little girl, a year younger than Alex. It was the night that *home* had changed forever. The night an intoxicated police officer drove south on northbound I-75 into oncoming traffic. He walked away from the accident physically unscathed.

Mommy, Daddy, and their 1979 Harley Davidson Roadster had not.

I can't do this, Lord. Not again. Not again!

"Why? Why us?" Brooke said, sitting down. "What in the world am I supposed to do now?"

"For starters, continue to be the great mother I saw yesterday," Macey answered. "And, Brooke, there are going to be *lots* of steps— lots of steps and lots of tests, then more steps and more tests. It's a complicated process, but I promise you, you'll know what we are doing every step of the way."

Brooke shook her head. "I'm so afraid."

"It's normal to be afraid. It's normal to be confused."

Brooke put her elbows back on her knees and leaned forward to rest her forehead on the heels of her palms. "This can't be happening. This can't really be happening. Please, God."

"Look at me, Brooke," Macey said, kneeling in front of her.

Brooke raised her head. She could feel the tears streaking down her cheeks. "Please, Macey. Please tell me this isn't really happening."

"I'm going to tell you again," Macey said confidently. "We're going to win. We will beat this. But we all have to do our parts."

"I will do anything for him," Brooke said through her tears.

"I know you will," Macey said. "Alex isn't the only one we're going to be doing tests on. We'll be starting Alex with something called a bone marrow aspiration to determine—"

"A what?"

"A bone marrow aspiration," Macey repeated. "Leukemia is a cancer of the blood cells, and the bone marrow is where the majority of our blood cells originate. We are going to need to remove a tiny sample from Alex to make a final diagnosis."

"Final diagnosis?" Brooke asked hopefully. "Is there any chance he doesn't have it?"

"I would say no."

"When do you want to do this aspiration thing?" Brooke sighed. "Is it going to *hurt* him?"

"Excellent question," Macey said, standing. "Most kids have a tendency to fight any invasive process such as shots or needles. I don't want to use the word *hurt*, and I will never mislead you. But I will tell you again that there will be times during the various parts of his treatment when he will be uncomfortable—extremely uncomfortable. But we'll do our best to minimize his discomfort."

"You said Alex won't be the only one you need to do tests on. What do you mean? Who else?"

"The most likely candidates for a bone-marrow match for Alex would be siblings, which he doesn't have, right? Even half siblings?"

"Right. As far as I know . . ."

"Then along with trying to find a marrow match through a donor registry, we are also going to want to run tests on you and Alex's father."

Brooke winced. "What does his father need to do?"

"Are you in contact with him?" Macey asked.

"No. Can't we test me first to see if I'm a match? Alex doesn't even know his father."

"We will certainly test you, Brooke. But is there a way to get in contact with Alex's father? We need *all* possible biological matches, as soon as possible. Time is a card we want to play well."

Brooke wondered how much bad news this windowless room had played host to in the past—this room with the clown paintings and the little boy who was about to get a shot. *If only Alex had been so lucky.*

"Alex's father . . . ," Brooke said, wiping her cheek and then looking around at the walls. They suddenly seemed so much closer together. "Doesn't know about Alex."

"That doesn't change the fact that he may be the marrow match we're looking for—that Alex is looking for. It's extremely rare for a parent to be a match, but I want to make sure we have all of our options on the table."

Though Pastor Jim had taught her that there was no such thing as fate, Brooke thought she could hear it knocking. It was loud, impatient, and pounding mercilessly on a door she had kept locked for over six years now. But it had to open. It needed to open for Alex.

"He was my boss at the plant," Brooke said. "There was a party for a big contract we had won. We were both drunk and it ended up happening. That was it. Just that one time. Not a single time before or after."

"That's all it takes," Macey said. "Regardless, you have a beautiful son."

"We both felt really stupid about what happened and never talked about it. When I realized I was pregnant, I was afraid to tell anybody who the father was."

"Even him?" Macey frowned.

"He was married," Brooke said. "He was a really nice guy and we both knew it was a mistake. I could only imagine the kind of problems it would cause with his wife, and I knew he'd get fired from the plant. I didn't know what to do."

"So you decided to go it alone?"

"Yeah," Brooke said. She hesitated. "I'm sorry for dumping this on you."

"I asked you about Alex's father and you're telling me. It's all right. You can tell me whatever you want."

Brooke crossed her arms and leaned to her side. She knew Macey meant it.

"I was living at my aunt's house when I found out I was pregnant. She and her third husband weren't doing too well at the time. She kept asking and asking who the father was and I would never say. A few months later, she and I were taking a walk at the park over near the church that runs along the lake. My aunt asked me if Frank was the baby's father."

"Was Frank your boss at the plant?"

"No," Brooke said. "My aunt's third husband."

"Oh," Macey said. "No wonder she kept asking you who the father was."

"I thought she was kidding and laughed at her."

"What happened?"

"She hit me with something," Brooke said. "I don't remember, but it was probably part of a branch. It broke my jaw and my nose, and I guess she hit me again in the back of the head after I was on the ground."

"That's awful," Macey said. "How far along were you?"

"Four or five months," Brooke said.

"What happened?"

"My aunt left me there."

"What?"

"Other than Alex, it's the best thing that ever happened to me."

"H-How is that?"

Brooke sighed and shook her head. "The only other thing I can remember about that day is that someone was carrying me, walking really fast, and he had blood all over his hand. I had no idea that it was my blood, *but that hand* . . . I can still see it, the way it crossed over the tops of *both* of my legs. I'd never seen a hand that *huge*. And then I saw the cross and blacked out again." She paused and looked at Macey. "It was the same cross you came to salvage at St. Thomas."

Macey squinted and then her eyes rounded sadly like she was

about to cry. She shook her head slowly back and forth as if to fight the tears, then she went still. "It was Charlie, wasn't it?"

"Yeah," Brooke said. "I'd lived in eleven different places by that time. I was twenty-one years old and I had finally made it home."

"That's beautiful."

"Yeah," Brooke said again. "But you're right, I decided to go it alone. Just me and Alex, Batman and Robin. I grew up without a father, and now five years later, I mean . . . what better father figure could you ask for than Pastor Jim?"

"He's an amazing man."

"The Lindys wanted us there and I wanted to be there. The five of us don't have much, but we have each other, and now this happens. Why?"

"It's going to be okay," Macey said.

"What do we do now?"

"We have Alex come back in here."

"Good," Brooke said, thinking about how Alex suddenly seemed so much younger than five. She wanted to hold him, cuddle him.

"And, Brooke, we are *not* going to explain to Alex that he is sick or even ever use the word *sick*. We are only going to focus on how everything we do is going to make him better. We keep it all positive."

"Okay," Brooke said.

"We'll do the bone-marrow aspiration on Alex tomorrow as an outpatient," Macey said. "But for now, I want you to go home and prepare some things for us."

"Okay," Brooke said again.

Macey put her hand on Brooke's shoulder. "I want to know everything about Alex's personal preferences. What he likes to eat, what television shows he likes, what books he enjoys, what makes him laugh, what makes him cry—everything."

"What am I gonna do?" Brooke whispered. "I'm so scared."

"Here's what you are going to do," Macey said. "Two things."

Brooke looked at her, and the doctor had a reassuring smile on her face.

"One. You are going to watch him get better. And two . . ."

Brooke knew what "two" was before the smile faded from Macey's lips.

Fate had quit knocking. That door she'd kept locked for six years had just been kicked open, and on the other side was a man named Ian Tobias Jr.

Alex's father.

SIXTEEN

M y sugar is feeling a little low right now," Jim said aloud. He casually crossed his arms and then patiently listened for someone's approval.

Nobody said a word.

"I had one at five this morning," he added boldly. "Another one won't hurt."

He put his hands on the edge of the kitchen sink, turned his head toward the pantry, and then began feeling a little embarrassed, realizing his voice held the pitch of a nine-year-old and the sincerity of a used-car salesman.

He dearly wanted another strawberry Pop-Tart and was having one heck of a time persuading anyone in the house that he should go against his doctor's recommended limit of only one per day. Truth be told, there was only one person he really needed to convince—himself.

He was home alone.

"Shirley?" he yelled, secretly hoping for no response. He got his wish. She had been gone for over two hours and apparently still wasn't home.

"Don't mind if I do," he said, reminding himself of Wile E. Coyote and quietly tiptoeing to the pantry door before coming to an abrupt halt.

"Charlie?" he said, turning his head cautiously toward the living room door. "You there, son?"

Once again, there was no reply. There weren't three taps on the kitchen table, three knocks on the living room or bedroom walls, or three tugs on his shirt sleeve, Charlie's way of answering him.

An hour earlier, he had heard the front door close and figured that his son was back up at the church, standing in front of the cross again. Like he'd apparently done five other times, through the night and early morning hours.

Jim timidly reached down to the second shelf of the pantry and was already feeling a little guilty by the time his fingers found the small cardboard Pop-Tart box. It seemed a little light. He shook it and laughed under his breath.

"Thank you, Alex," he said. "Thanks for looking out for Pastor Jim."

Alex had put the empty box back in the pantry.

Jim dropped the box in the trash and poured himself another cup of coffee before sitting back at the table. He ran his hand across the cover of the Bible in front of him.

He took a sip of his coffee, sat his cup back on the table, and then slowly opened the book. He dropped the heel of his palm to the base of the inside cover, then patiently began to guide the pad of his index finger over and across the series of tiny raised dots on the page.

He'd been impressed with Kenneth's ability to recall and quote Bible verses. What had impressed him more, though, was the young man's ability to seem even more convincing when he *misquoted* a verse.

Jim flipped anxiously through the braille pages, feeling his way to Luke 8:50.

He stopped and ran his finger across it.

"Do not be afraid; only believe and she will be made well."

Why would Kenneth say 'he'?

"And who am I supposed to tell?" Jim asked the empty house. He drummed his fingers on top of the kitchen table, shoving away the thought of Alex, back at the hospital.

And what did he mean when he said I'm not supposed to tell anyone about 7:16? The least he could have done was tell me the book.

He'd gotten as far as Isaiah 7:16, checking each book, when there were three knocks on the front door. *There's my boy.* "Hello, Charlie," he said in greeting. "I was wondering where you were, son." Charlie's big shoes pounded across the living room floor in deliberate steps. Jim could hear Charlie's labored breathing as his son's enormous hand landed on his shoulder. The three light tugs on the sleeve of his sweatshirt meant that Charlie wanted his father to follow him.

"What is it, son?"

Three harder tugs almost pulled him off the chair. Whatever it was, it was important to Charlie, so he stood and said, "I'll follow you, Charlie. Let's go."

Three light squeezes on his shoulder meant "okay."

As the two Lindy men made it out the door, Jim sensed that Charlie was anxious.

He also had a feeling it had something to do with the cross.

❋ ❋ ❋

Zach was back in the room.

He was trapped again. He had to save her. He slid across the cool white carpet and found her in the window. She couldn't breathe, and time was running short. He yelled for help, but nobody came. He kicked at the window. She clawed at the window. He kept kicking. She kept clawing in panic, leaving tiny strings of scratches on the smooth, frigid glass. He punched wildly with both fists.

Why wouldn't it break?

She stopped clawing and then stared at him. Her brown, curly hair flowed and feathered at the sides of her face—that beautiful face. He kicked one last time. She didn't move.

Don't stop trying. Please.

She fell back into the darkness behind the window and he could see the hands on her shoulders. They were wrinkled and weathered hands. Zach put his face against the cold window and looked back at her face. The panic in her eyes was gone now . . .

Behind her, an arm's length away, a face was becoming visible. An old man's face. With shining white hair and a majestic beard, accented by fiery red eyes . . . Zach couldn't look away as the face moved closer to him, shoving the girl behind him. The closer the face came, the younger it appeared. The glowing red eyes were developing an oval shape, and the color softening into a light green. The beard was gone, and the white hair darkened like dusk shadowing a snowy field.

The man slowly turned and wrapped his arms under the girl's limp body to pick her up. The hair on top of his head was now almost completely brown. The man put his hand over her face, that beautiful face, and closed her blue eyes. Her head dropped back and bobbed lifelessly as he held her in his arms. The man tilted his head and kissed her on her forehead before turning around to carry her off into the darkness.

No! Help her! Come back!

Zach pressed his face against the window one last time. Tears flooded his cheeks, which he frantically wiped with his bloody knuckles.

Please stop!

The man stopped and looked over his shoulder.

Please don't take her!

The man's stare drifted through the darkness, directly through the window, and into Zach's eyes.

It was then that he recognized the man.

It was that construction worker. It was Kenneth.

Zach yelled and sat up in his bed, the hair at the nape of his neck sweaty. He was trying to make sense of his dream, remember where he was, when the phone started ringing. He edged across the damp sheets and picked up the receiver. "Amy?" he said desperately.

There was a pause. "No, Zach, it's Macey. Who's Amy?"

Zach cradled the phone between his ear and his neck before rubbing his face, trying to wake completely.

His fingers and cheeks felt like they were freezing, even as he sweat.

The ice . . .

• • •

Charlie took Jim by the hand as they stood out in front of the church and carefully placed his fingers against the cross. Jim felt the smooth wood surface and could practically taste the lacquer that wafted in the breeze.

"The cross is like new, isn't it?" he said. "It was hit by lightning, and the carpenter fixed it yesterday. Remember? It's okay, son."

Charlie then lowered his father's hand down off the cross and placed what felt like three pieces of broken twig in it.

"What's this?" he asked, rolling the pieces across his open palm.

Charlie snatched the broken pieces away and quickly placed a single twig in Pastor Jim's hand.

"What is it, Charlie?"

Charlie tilted the twig straight upright in his hand.

"What are you doing?"

Charlie took the broken pieces and put them back in his father's hand, then quickly replaced them with the unbroken piece of twig.

"Yes, Charlie, he fixed it. He did a good job; I know."

He could feel Charlie shifting the twig in his open palm from flat to upright, flat to upright.

It was clear that Charlie was struggling to understand how the cross was now standing before them after being in ruins just the day before.

"Don't worry, Charlie, fixing the cross is a good thing. The carpenter—it's what he does, son. I'm not quite sure how he did it; I'm just glad he did."

Charlie kept lowering and tilting the twig in his hand.

Jim let out a little laugh, admiring Charlie's persistence. "I'm pretty sure you're trying to tell me they fixed it real fast, huh, Charlie?"

Behind them, he could hear the gravel stirring on Church Road.

Brooke and Shirley returning from their appointment at the hospital.

• • •

Macey was looking out her office window, her eyes continuing to bounce off the roofs and bumpers of each vehicle in the parking lot as she once again searched for the old Ford pickup. Her heart began racing in anticipation of spotting it, and she suddenly wondered if she really wanted to find it. The truth of the matter was that the idea of actually seeing the truck made her more than a little nervous. She was practically afraid.

Only believe.

"There's some weird stuff going on around here, Kait."

"You've been pretty quiet," Kaitlyn responded, sitting attentively on the couch, looking comfortable in the baby-blue scrubs, the third-floor nurses' assigned uniform of the day. "Is it Alex that's getting to you?"

"Among other things," Macey said, catching herself sounding apologetic. "It's just been a strange couple of days, that's all. The whole cross fixing thing and then that Tim guy at the bar. Why don't you want to talk to me about that?"

"I've already told you and Zach it was a fling from a long time ago. He's nuts and there's nothing else to it. What else do you want me to say?"

"I saw you drink a shot at the bar after he left. I've never seen you drink before."

"So what? Wouldn't you?"

"And then you had another one. Anything you need to talk about?"

"Nothing more than I've already told you. Thanks, *Mom*."

"Okay," Macey said. It's not like anything seemed to affect Kait's work. She really was the best. "Let's just write it all off as one strange day. At least we did what we set out to do. We got the cross fixed."

"Speaking of strange," Kaitlyn said, "I still can't believe Zach called in sick."

"He called in *late*," Macey said. "He'll be in around noon." Macey pictured the lost look on Zach's face at The Pilot Inn. She was certain that he'd always been able to make sense of everything around him—until yesterday. She knew how he felt.

"I couldn't imagine him ever missing a whole day," the nurse said.

"Kaitlyn?" Macey asked faintly. She glanced down at her coffee-stained Nike, took another cautious look out the window, and peeked back down into the parking lot. "Has Zach ever mentioned someone named Amy to you before?"

"Amy? Not that I can recall. Why?"

She turned around and crossed her arms. "Old girlfriend? Relative?"

Kaitlyn opened a manila folder labeled "Alexander R. Thomas" and placed it neatly on the coffee table in front of the sofa. "Not that I know of. Why are you asking?"

Macey dragged the chair from her desk over next to the couch and sat down. "Because I called him earlier, and he answered the phone expecting it to be someone named Amy. The way he sounded . . . it wasn't like him. It actually scared me a little."

"I don't ever remember Zach even saying that name before."

Macey looked at her and nodded at the folder. "Aspiration tomorrow morning for Alex at six forty-five."

"Wait a minute," Kaitlyn said, putting her pen down. She paused, then reached over and tapped Macey chidingly on the arm. "That's not fair."

"What's not fair?"

"Are you trying to tell me that you know who Amy is? Like it was someone he dated while he was seeing me or something?"

"I don't have the faintest idea who Amy is," Macey said, raising her hand and extending two fingers. "Scout's honor." She looked at Kaitlyn and couldn't tell if her friend was more disappointed in her for not knowing who Amy was or in herself for allowing anything to do with Zach to actually bother her.

"I'm sure it's nothing," Kaitlyn said, grabbing the folder and fidgeting with it before opening it up. "It looks like our little redheaded cutie may be missing the church harvest party on Saturday."

"Let's see how he responds to his first round of treatment," Macey said. "I told Brooke that if he feels up to it, he can go."

"He might," Kaitlyn said. "You can tell he's going to be a trouper."

"I think you're right."

"What about us?" Kaitlyn asked. "We still going? Or is it weird now?"

"We said we would, so let's," Macey answered.

Kaitlyn closed the folder and leaned back. "You know what, Macey?"

"What?'

"Amy couldn't be a relative. Zach is an only child, and I've met all his cousins."

Macey rolled her eyes and then grinned playfully at her friend. "Still not over him, are you? No matter how hard you protest."

"Oh, please," Kaitlyn said, laughing. "Over what?"

SEVENTEEN

Charlie turned around and waved at Alex. *It's now or never,* Alex thought. But he didn't like it.

Charlie was way down the dirt path that went from behind the church and into the haunted woods.

Alex had never been down the trail by himself, and walking any of it without Charlie protecting him didn't seem like too much fun.

Charlie lowered himself to one knee and opened his arms.

Alex lifted his left foot and stepped tentatively onto the crackly leaves and dirt that marked the beginning of the path. He quickly pulled it back as if he'd just stepped in burning hot lava. He put his hands in his pockets and began to wiggle his toes in his tennies. He noticed that his shoes were getting tighter and tighter, but that was okay, because Mom said he'd be getting new ones pretty soon.

As he continued to stare down the path at Charlie, he was beginning to feel more and more like a fraidy cat. Didn't he just take a vow of courage with Nurse Kaitlyn? He promised he'd try his best not to be afraid of things. Promised. What would Nurse Kaitlyn say if she saw him now?

'Course, she didn't know Looney Cooney was out here somewhere.

Mrs. Kipler had said.

Webster Cooney was a very scary man. Mrs. Kipler told Mom at church that Looney Cooney had *gone nuts* and was *off his rocker.* She also said that Looney Cooney drank water right out of the lake and that he also came out at night to kill animals with his bare hands to eat. But it all ended one night when Looney Cooney was *drunk off his butt.* That was the night when his house burned all the way to the ground with him still in it. And that was when she said the scariest thing of all!

Even though Looney Cooney died, Mrs. Kipler said that people walking on the shore at night still saw him sometimes, drinking from the lake and walking around in the woods. Alex knew it had to be true, because even though Looney Cooney's house and rocker may have burned to the ground, every once in a while, when it was real windy outside, he could still hear the rocker creaking back and forth in the woods.

Alex looked back up and noticed that Charlie had moved a few steps closer. He still wasn't close enough, but Alex thought about going for it.

But what if burned-up Looney Cooney is out there? What if he got up off his rocker and came and got me before Charlie could save me?

The longer he stared at the path, the more he thought that the leafless branches of all shapes and sizes leaning over the path were waiting—just *waiting* for him to move, *waiting* to reach down like bony little fingers to snatch him up and drag him into the darkness of the trees forever. He slowly lowered his head in despair, quietly hoping that Charlie wouldn't be too disappointed.

"Can you come get me, Charlie?" he pleaded, looking down at his tennies in defeat. "Please?"

He couldn't hear anything.

He was afraid to look back down the path.

And then he could hear the leaves moving. Charlie was coming.

"I'm sorry for being a fraidy cat," he said.

Charlie lifted him to his shoulders, and Alex wrapped his arms around his neck. Alex was a little mad that he had called himself a fraidy cat, but felt instantly brave with Charlie there. "Try to get me now, Looney Cooney!"

Charlie ran really fast for a super long time until they got to the spot in the woods that didn't have any trees in it. Pastor Jim said that God carved it out like that. There wasn't any wind there, and it was sunny. The grass was real long, and there was part of an old wooden picnic table that Pastor Jim started to make, but then he couldn't see anymore and had to stop. Now that Looney Cooney was behind them, Alex began to drum playfully on top of Charlie's head while telling Charlie about the hospital people.

"Hey, Charlie," he said. "Nurse Kaitlyn says that I'm going to be going to the hospital a lot." He noticed that his hand was almost the exact same length as Charlie's ear and smiled. "She showed me a cool trick where she can pull her finger off and put it back on."

Charlie stopped next to the old picnic table, lifted Alex off of his shoulders, and carefully set Alex on his feet on top of the lone bench.

"Hey, Charlie," Alex said. "Nurse Kaitlyn has puppets too. One of the puppets is called Mr. Brave. Nurse Kaitlyn says that I can be just like Mr. Brave if I want to be."

Charlie went into his pocket and pulled out his TicTac container.

"I asked Nurse Kaitlyn if I was going to get a shot, and she said that even if I do, that Mr. Brave will be there with me, and that it will only hurt for a second, and that sometimes shots are good and not bad." Alex paused and lifted his finger to his chin. "I think that's what she said."

Charlie tapped out two TicTacs.

"Hey, Charlie," Alex said, snickering. He jumped off the table into the soft grass. "Pull my finger."

Charlie tugged on Alex's index finger, and Alex farted, sending himself into a hysterical bout of laughter.

"Hey, Charlie," Alex said, still giggling. "You gotta try that one sometime."

• • •

Shirley could see the drawn expression on Brooke's face as they sat at the kitchen table. She hadn't worn any makeup that day, and she had a pair of light purple lines under her eyes. Shirley put her hand on top of Brooke's and said, "Why don't you try to rest for a little bit?"

"I can't," Brooke said.

"How long did Macey say it would be before she thought Alex would be better?" James asked, joining them at the table.

"They're going to start chemotherapy this week," Brooke explained, her hands still shaking a little. "And then test him weekly."

"For how long?"

"Until he goes into remission," Brooke said, covering her eyes with her hands. "Alex is going to get chemo. Can you believe this?"

James's silence let Shirley know that he was having difficulty absorbing the news. He'd always been able to offer the right words of comfort in times of trouble. But this was hitting too close to home. She watched him close his eyes and knew he was silently asking God to help him find the right words.

"Why is this happening to me, Pastor Jim?" Brooke asked, her voice without any trace of energy. "My parents—my life—now Alex. It's not fair."

Shirley edged her chair closer to Brooke and put her arm around her.

Brooke looked at Shirley, and Shirley saw the hopelessness in her eyes.

"Brooke," James said. "It's important that you understand something. God has a plan. And you and Alex are part of that plan. He will be there for you."

"Well," Brooke said dryly, "I need him now. Right here, right now. Tell me, Pastor Jim. Where is he?"

"We all need him," Shirley said. "And though you may not feel it, he is here."

"What do I do?" Brooke asked, her voice starting to quiver. "Please tell me what to do."

"Believe," Shirley said.

"Believe what?" Brooke shouted before shaking her head and getting up from the table. "That this, *this* is part of God's plan?" She looked to the window and shook her head again.

Shirley looked at James as if he was missing an unseen cue, but he had already risen to his feet. "You only need to trust in God."

"Trust in God?" Brooke mocked. She said it in a way that Shirley didn't like, but understood. "Why were my parents killed? Why would Alex have leukemia? And I don't want to hear about Peter, Paul, Job, or someone else right now. Tell me *why.*"

"Brooke," he said, reaching for her hand.

"What?" she snapped.

"Brooke," he repeated. "You know that God doesn't keep us from tests and trials."

"I never would have guessed, Pastor Jim," she said sarcastically. "Really?"

"No," James answered, giving Brooke's hand a little squeeze of encouragement. "He helps us get through them."

"Well, I don't feel his *help* right now," Brooke cried. "Where? Where is he?"

"Please," Shirley said, standing up and holding both palms toward the ceiling as if she were holding up an invisible tray. "Just trust him, Brooke. God loves you more than you can imagine."

"I have to go," Brooke said, crossing her arms and rolling her eyes. "I'll be back."

James lowered his voice. "Brooke, please. Shirley is right. Trust him, no matter how it *feels.*"

Brooke shook her head. "I want to believe in everything you two are saying," she said. "But this is a little much right now, okay?"

"Honey," Shirley said. "We know it's hard for you. It's hard for all of us."

"I have to go," Brooke said again, heading quickly out of the kitchen and toward the front door. "Can you keep an eye on Alex until I get back?"

"Of course," Shirley said.

"I'll be back in a couple of hours—unless, you know, my car blows up."

"Brooke," Shirley said. "That's not what you have learned."

"Not now," Brooke responded, her eyes starting to fill with tears.

"What can we do?" James asked. "Tell us."

"Looks like nothing," Brooke said, wiping her eyes and closing the door behind her.

James bowed his head and they were quiet for a moment. "I

didn't know what to say, Shirley. For the first time in my life, I couldn't find the words."

"Come here, James Lindy," Shirley said, sitting back down at the kitchen table. He walked up next to her, and she grabbed his sleeve and lowered the side of her face to his arm. "We're hurting too. It steals our breath, such news, let alone our words. And you know as well as anyone, James, all we can do is pray. Pray for Alex and pray for Brooke, and remind her to only believe that things will turn out."

James kissed Shirley on her cheek and walked out of the kitchen before making his way down the narrow hallway to the bedroom. Shirley walked slowly to the sink and turned the water on to rinse the morning dishes. She looked out the kitchen window and could see Brooke in her car, leaning against its steering wheel. She was sobbing. "Oh, you poor thing," she whispered.

She shut the water off and turned around to head outside. When she looked up, she found James standing in the doorway to the kitchen. The blood in his fingers seemed to have rushed to his nails as he squeezed his Bible with both hands. His face was flushed, and he was squinting, almost painfully. He was shaking.

"James?" Shirley said, rushing toward him and grabbing his arms. "Your sugar."

"Shirley," James said, his voice sounding weak and labored. "You just said it."

"James, get on the couch right now!" Shirley pleaded, grabbing the phone off the wall. "I'm calling 911."

James reached out and found her arm. He took the phone from her and hung it back up. "My blood sugar's fine."

"You're shaking!"

He turned around and ran haphazardly toward the front door and flung it open. "Brooke!" he shouted at the top of his lungs.

"She's in her car," Shirley said, frowning and coming up beside him.

James let go of the door and hurried outside. When he hit the end of the porch, he missed the top step and fell hard to the ground, landing facedown, square on his elbows.

"James!"

He raised his head and quickly got to his knees, and then slowly, to his feet. He was struggling to catch his breath when he yelled out, "Brooke, wait!"

"She's pulling out of the driveway!" Shirley yelled, helplessly watching James run across the lawn, falling again and bouncing right back up while protecting his Bible like a running back not wanting to fumble the ball. She'd not seen him run in over a decade.

"Brooke!" he screamed again.

"James, you're bleeding," Shirley said, walking as fast she could toward him on the lawn.

"Brooke Thomas!" he bellowed.

"What is it, James?" she asked.

He dropped back down to one knee to catch his breath. His pants had a tear at the other knee, and his elbow was bleeding. He lifted his head, wiped his mouth with his shirtsleeve, and then turned his head toward her.

"James?" Shirley said. "You're a mess. What are you *doing*?"

He slowly stood and held out his hand. Tentatively, Shirley took it. He inhaled deeply and leaned his head in the direction of the cross.

"Only believe, Brooke!" he yelled.

"She's gone, James," Shirley said. "She's halfway down the road."

"Only believe," he said again, letting go of her hand. He took a couple steps toward the driveway and stopped. Then he held his hands up in the air and turned around. He was smiling.

"Only believe . . . and *he* . . . will be made well."

EIGHTEEN

They were deep, deep, deep into the forest. Farther than they'd ever gone, when they reached an old, rusted barbed-wire fence. Alex's skin got the goose bumps all over, and he rubbed his arms as he walked beside his big friend.

He looked back down the path. "We better go home now, Charlie. Mom will be worried. But let's go out to Church Road and walk down that, 'kay? I don't wanna go back down the path."

Charlie nodded.

Alex picked up a big piece of bark off the ground and threw it as hard as he could at one of the rotting fence poles. It burst into a kajillion pieces. "Did you see that? Cool!"

Charlie nodded, smiling.

"I hope Mrs. Lindy went to the store and got some macaroni and cheese. Are you hungry too, Charlie?"

Charlie's big eyes lit up at the word *macaroni* and nodded his head.

"Look at this!" Alex yelled, pointing down into a bunch of mushrooms that were growing at the side of a dead tree. "It's ginormous!" The green and white cap was the size of a plate. Alex reached down to touch it, but a tan boot stepped in the way. Alex pulled his hand quickly to his side, then looked up in surprise.

Kenneth was standing there.

Charlie snatched up Alex and then took a few steps back, carefully cradling him in the crook of his massive left arm.

"It's okay, Charlie. It's just Kenneth!" Alex said, frowning at his big friend and wondering why he was acting like a fraidy cat. Alex looked around the woods and then back to Kenneth. "What are you doing out here?"

"Keeping you two away from those mushrooms," Kenneth said, taking a small step toward Charlie, who took a big step back.

Kenneth looked up at Charlie. "Hello, Charles Paul Lindy."

Charlie's head tilted back and forth. And then he smiled at the carpenter.

"Charlie likes hearing his name like that," Alex said. "Pastor Jim does that too."

"Hey, Alex," Kenneth said, taking another step closer to them. Charlie didn't move. "Mr. Cooney is a very nice man."

"No, he's bad," Alex said. "Looney Cooney killed animals and ate them and burned up in his rocker and died."

"Tell me something," Kenneth said, holding out his arms for Charlie to pass Alex to him.

"Tell you what?" Alex asked, reaching for Kenneth.

Charlie waited. His head teetered back and forth again.

"It's okay, Charlie," the carpenter said.

Charlie held Alex out and Kenneth took him. He tapped Alex lightly on the chin and said, "Tell me how those things make Mr. Cooney bad."

"I don't know," Alex said. "But he died."

"That doesn't make him bad, does it? Everyone dies, in time."

Alex looked at Charlie and then poked at Kenneth's chest. "But I dunno if he knew 'bout Jesus."

Kenneth squinted and lowered Alex to the ground, crouching beside him. "What do you mean?"

Alex looked at Charlie and back at him. Could Kenneth really not know? Didn't everyone?

The carpenter smiled. "Tell me," he said.

"Jesus died for us," he said.

Kenneth stared at Alex for a few seconds and then smiled. "How do you know, Alex?"

"Pastor Jim tol' me. That's how we get to heaven. Do you know Jesus, Kenneth?"

"Oh yes," he said, getting that warm look in his green eyes that

Alex liked. It made him just want to look and look at them. "He and I go way back."

"But I don't really get how he died and came back again."

"You will, in time," Kenneth said, standing and running his hand across the top of Alex's head. "Everyone will, in time. You guys want to race? I know a shortcut."

"Yeah!" Alex said. "You'll never beat me and Charlie!"

"You think so?" Kenneth said. "Why don't we find out?"

"Let's do piggy back," Alex said, pulling on Charlie's pant leg.

Charlie lifted Alex over his head, on top of his shoulders. Alex loved being up there. It was like he was on top of the world!

Alex reached his arms over to hang on to Charlie's thick neck. Charlie held his legs. Alex's big piggy was ready to go. "You ready?" Alex said to Kenneth.

"Ready when you are," Kenneth said, standing next to them.

Alex clicked his heels gently on Charlie's chest and yelled the magic words: "Giddy up, piggy!"

Fallen branches and dry acorns *pop, pop, popped* under Charlie's feet as he ran through the red and yellow leaves at the base of a narrow hill. Alex smiled as they moved through the woods, keeping a safe lead over Kenneth, who was behind them. As Kenneth came closer, Alex squealed and Charlie ran faster and faster. Alex laughed as they ran up the side and over the top of another small hill. Then Charlie began to slow down.

"Giddy up," Alex said. But instead of going fast again, Charlie came to a stop. "What's wrong, Charlie?"

Panting, Charlie lifted his left arm and pointed toward the fence.

Alex saw it. The woods suddenly seemed smaller and much quieter. The only noise in the woods was Charlie catching his breath and Kenneth walking up behind them.

"Oh man," Alex said softly. "What happened to it?"

But he could kinda see what happened. A deer had tried to leap over the barbed wire and one of its rear hooves got caught on the top of the fence. It hung upside down, with its tongue hanging out and its body twisted on the other side.

"Let me down, Charlie," Alex said. "I want to see it closer."

Charlie followed his instructions and carefully lowered Alex. They both stood and stared at the dead animal.

"Why did it have to die, Charlie?" Alex asked. "It doesn't seem fair to die like that."

Charlie was still. His arms were hanging straight down to his sides, and he bowed his head at a slight angle like a child who had just been yelled at. His eyes shifted back and forth between the deer's tongue and its lifeless eyes. He looked like he was going to cry.

"Something was eating at it," Alex said, noticing a patch of black blood on the deer's side, all dried up. "Its fur looks yucky."

Alex inched a few feet closer, shuffling slowly through the leaves. He stopped again, wishing the deer would wake up and run away. He turned around and looked back at Charlie and Kenneth.

"C'mon, guys! Let's go closer," Alex said, going back to Charlie and tugging on his pant leg so he'd lift him up. He wanted to see the deer. But he'd feel better if Charlie was holding him.

Charlie remained still. Alex looked up and saw he was about to cry. "It's okay, Charlie. Don't cry."

"He'll be all right," Kenneth said.

Charlie's eyes never left the deer as he lifted Alex and moved them a little closer. The closer they got, the faster Alex's heart raced and the tighter he clung to Charlie. Alex didn't like the way the deer's eyes were, open but not seeing.

"I feel bad for that deer," Alex said, lifting his head to see little puffs of light dust that were coming off of Church Road as a black car approached from the distance.

"Its foot got broken on the fence," Alex said, noticing a tiny broken bone sticking out of the deer's hoof. He turned back up at Kenneth. "There's a bone; you can see it."

"I know," Kenneth said.

Charlie still didn't move.

"Can we get it off the fence?"

They all looked up at the road as the fancy, black car hummed by them. It caused a small tornado of leaves to swirl off the ground in tiny circles behind it as it made its way toward St. Thomas. Alex thought the driver was the man who ate the crackers with pee on them yesterday. Doctor Something. But he was more interested in the dead deer.

Still holding Alex, Charlie snapped a branch off of a nearby tree and then slowly approached the dead deer as if he would protect them. He tapped at the deer with the branch, and Alex didn't like the hollow way it sounded. Charlie poked it again as if he were making sure the animal was dead. He put Alex down and then carefully lined up the end of the branch with the deer's trapped hoof. He gave it a firm shove, ripping its skin from the rusty brown wire. It tumbled over and into a bunch of tall, dry grass.

Alex took another look into the deer's lifeless eyes. Charlie scratched at his chin, wiped a tear, and then leaned over and picked up Alex to place him over the fence.

"Don't cry, Charlie," Alex said again. "Maybe that deer went to heaven. Maybe she is okay."

Charlie straddled and then pulled one leg carefully over the fence.

"She sure is stinky," Alex said, holding his nose. He backed away and reached up for Charlie to lift him again. He stared down at the deer. She looked smaller, now that she was off the fence. "I wish she didn't have to die, hangin' up like that."

"Me too," Kenneth said. "But she's fine now. Better than you can imagine."

She did look more peaceful now that she was down in the tall grass.

"I'm tired, Charlie." A nap on the couch right now sounded really good to him. Right after a bowl of macaroni and cheese.

• • •

James's leg twitched as if someone were holding the open flame of a lighter against his bare knee. "I'm telling you, Kenneth was talking about Brooke and Alex."

"How could he know?" Shirley asked, patting James's wound with a cotton ball soaked with antiseptic.

"I don't know. Maybe he heard Brooke talking about the hospital visits. But that's why he switched the Bible verse to *he*."

"Sit still, James Lindy," Shirley said sternly, taking another bandage out and tearing off its paper cover.

James briefly held his hands up in surrender before dropping them to his lap. He rubbed the top of an oval-shaped bandage that she had just applied to his elbow, making sure the edges would stick. "It's too much of a coincidence."

"Why don't you ask him when he comes to the harvest party on Saturday?"

"I will. You know I will."

Shirley looked out the kitchen window. "That same fancy black car that was here yesterday is parked out in front of the church."

"Fancy black car?"

"I'm pretty sure that it's that doctor." Shirley hesitated before putting her glasses on to look again. "Zach Norman. He's going up the walkway to the church."

"Maybe he's looking for me," James said, getting to his feet. "I better go over there."

Shirley's palms were on the edge of the sink, and she went up on tiptoe. "Now he's walking across the lawn."

"Coming here?" James asked. "Why didn't he drive over?"

"I don't think he is coming here," Shirley said. "He just stopped."

"What's he doing?"

"Nothing." Shirley shrugged. She stepped back and then turned to James. "He is just standing in front of the cross, looking at it."

* * *

Zach turned around and acknowledged Charlie and Alex as they approached him from behind. "Hey, guys," he said distantly. He turned back to the cross.

"What are you looking at?" Alex asked, the tiny freckles beneath his eyes huddling together as he squinted up past the cross and into the sky, as if he were missing something flying overhead.

"It's awesome," Zach said.

"What is?" Alex asked.

"The cross," Zach said, placing his palm firmly on it and feeling as if it were alive in some way. "It's a miracle."

"Yes, it is," Pastor Jim said as he arrived on the doctor's left. His arms were crossed in defense of the breeze, and the bandage on his elbow had come undone, flapping with each step he took.

Zach didn't respond.

"Yes, a miracle," Pastor Jim repeated. "The Lord blessed us with the work of our friends' hands."

"Yeah," Zach said politely, knowing there was a little more to the cross's resurrection than what the good minister believed. He didn't really expect Pastor Jim to be able to explain what had happened—mostly because he himself couldn't explain it. In fact, looking at the cross again today convinced him of what was spooking him the most, and that was his high degree of certainty that *nobody* could explain it.

"Is there something I can help you with, Dr. Norman?" Pastor Jim asked.

"I guess I just wanted to see it again," he said as Beethoven's Symphony No. 9 flowed through the half-opened driver's side window of the Mercedes. "That's all I really needed, Pastor Jim." What he really needed was what no one could give, and that was the answer to exactly how the carpenter did it, because what he did was, by a strict definition, impossible. It was, in fact a miracle.

"See what?" Pastor Jim asked. "The cross?"

Zach nodded again. "It really happened, didn't it?" He slid his hand a little higher on the vertical beam. "He really did this."

"What really happened?" Pastor Jim asked, his forehead creasing.

Zach had no answer. That was part of the problem. There were no words to explain it.

Charlie stepped closer and placed his hand above Zach's on the cross. They looked at each other and exchanged what Zach felt was a mutual understanding.

"You—" he said to Charlie. "You saw it, didn't you, big fella?"

Charlie looked into Zach's eyes.

"Are you all right, Dr. Norman?" Pastor Jim asked.

"I'm not sure." Zach kept his right hand on the cross while lightly rubbing his forehead with his left. "To be honest with you, sir, I really don't know."

Alex stepped between Zach and the cross and poked at the doctor's leg before looking up at him. "I was at the hospital today. Nurse Kaitlyn was there."

Zach didn't even acknowledge Alex. He didn't mean to ignore him; he just couldn't look away from Charlie.

"Would you like to go inside the church and talk?" Pastor Jim asked. "Maybe I can help. I don't see real well, but I think I'm a pretty good listener."

"I appreciate it, Pastor Jim," Zach said, his hand lifting off the cross before turning to the minister. "I may take you up on that sometime—sometime soon. But I'm running late as it is, and I need to make another stop before I get to work."

"I understand," Pastor Jim said. "Just remember that I'm always here."

"I like Nurse Kaitlyn," Alex said.

"She is a very nice lady, Alexander," Zach said. "I like her too."

Even though she won't tell me anything about that Tim character. Old fling. Yeah, right.

"We found a dead deer on the fence back in the woods," Alex said, somber and earnest in his reporting. "Its toe got stuck, and it stinks, and something ate its stomach."

Zach didn't say anything, smiling at the redhead. *Poor kid. Rough go for him ahead.*

"It went to heaven," Alex said while lifting his chin.

"Heaven, huh?" Zach's smile melted. *Did dead deer go to heaven? Did anyone?* "I have to go, you guys. I'm really sorry to have bothered you today."

He took a hand out of his pocket and placed it back up on the cross one more time, only a few inches below Charlie's hand, which was still resting there. Something about touching the cross made him feel good. A tangible reminder that he wasn't losing it—it had really happened.

Charlie suddenly dropped his hand over Zach's, and Zach startled. Charlie looked like he wanted to say something.

"I'm tired, Pastor Jim," Alex said. The pastor picked him up and kissed him. Alex rested his head on his shoulder.

Zach took his hand off the cross, patted Charlie on the shoulder, and then buttoned up his jacket. At least he wasn't alone. Charlie knew something really bizarre had happened here too. "See you later, guys."

"You're welcome here anytime you like, Dr. Norman," Pastor Jim said. "Anytime you like."

"I appreciate it, Pastor Jim." Zach turned and offered his hand to Charlie. Slowly, they shook, and Zach looked into his eyes. "I know you can't do it, so I'll say it for you, big fella. It's a miracle. A true-blue miracle. You know it and I know it, and somehow, that makes me feel better."

NINETEEN

Zach double-clicked his key holder, the chirp confirming that the Mercedes was locked behind him. He dropped his hands to his sides and then looked up to read the copper block letters that arched above the wrought-iron gate—the sole entrance to St. Victor's Cemetery.

He'd heard that the last of the 150-year-old cemetery's 6,500-plus plots had all been claimed twenty years ago, which was one of several reasons its upkeep was no longer on the top of anyone's to-do list.

"Here goes nothing," he said, shoving the rusty gate, which swung open with a creak that felt like an invitation to proceed onto the gravel walkway within the cemetery grounds.

Zach closed the gate behind him and then looked around. None of it was familiar anymore. He hadn't been to the cemetery in at least fifteen years, and the lack of maintenance had left it looking like an abandoned set from a low-budget horror film. Tumbleweeds piled against the highest gravestones. Weeds were overtaking everything. Half the grass was dead and gone, and not coming back with spring.

He buttoned up his coat, lifted his shoulders, hid his hands in his pockets, and walked slowly down the first of countless rows of tombstones, his head moving back and forth, trying to remember any visual clues about where it was. His confidence in just happening upon the tiny headstone was pretty low. Were there two trees?

A hedge? A huge angel tombstone somewhere close? He shook his head. He couldn't be sure of anything.

He stopped abruptly and glanced at his watch. He was supposed to have been at East Shore fifteen minutes ago. He had already called in late for the second time that day, which would make it the second time in his entire career as a medical doctor.

His cell phone rang, and he took it out of his pocket. Kaitlyn. She hadn't called him in over three months, and as surprised as he was—as much as he really needed to talk to her about everything that happened the previous day—he couldn't. Nothing could interrupt him now. He had to find the grave.

The phone quit ringing, and he put his hands back in his pockets while quickening his pace down another row, and then another, scanning names on what had to have been over a hundred headstones.

Maybe he'd purposefully forgotten where it was, part of his effort to banish the memories of that tortuous winter . . .

Zach's eyes swept over the balance of the cemetery. An overwhelming sea of headstones, dead grass, and patches of dirt sprawled in all directions.

"Needle in a haystack," he muttered, shaking his head.

He sat down on the cleanest half of what looked like one of the cemetery's original cement benches. Part of the seat back had crumbled to the ground, and the rest of the bench was nothing more than a nasty collection of bird droppings and stress cracks.

He could hear someone talking.

To his left, halfway up a shaggy hillside, an elderly man with flowing white hair was on one knee, removing dead flowers from a pot at the head of a tombstone. The grave appeared to be one of only a few receiving any form of regular maintenance. *Probably because he's doing it himself.*

The old man seemed familiar and Zach watched him gently tilt the flowerpot upside down, remove a handkerchief from his breast pocket, and wipe the outside of the pot clean. The man then opened a cardboard floral box and arranged an assortment of flowers in the pot before centering it back at the head of the tombstone.

Zach scanned the grounds again and took note that only two other people were in the entire cemetery. He looked back at the man, who now appeared to be talking to the grave. *I wonder if anyone is listening,* Zach thought.

He glanced again at his watch, conceded defeat, and decided to head back to the car. There were simply too many graves. He brushed off the seat of his pants and turned around when something caught his eye—a cross.

About five hundred feet away, the top portion of a metal cross jutted up over the edge of one of the cemetery's many small and unkempt hills. Zach quickly stood on top of the bench, causing a softball-sized chunk of its edge to collapse, but it didn't matter. He had to get a better look at the cross. He shaded his eyes as the early afternoon sun glistened off it.

He wanted to touch it, be near it, just like the one at St. Thomas. Not later, but now.

Zach jumped off the bench and walked quickly, trampling directly across the tops of several graves as his eyes never left the cross. *Hurry,* he thought. *Get there.*

He picked up his pace, becoming filled with a new sense of energy and purpose as to why he had come here in the first place. The answer was straight ahead.

The more he focused on the cross, the more he was drawn to it. The more he was drawn to it, the faster he went—faster and faster, closer and closer—until he was running.

His coat was restricting his arms, and he unbuttoned it as he ran. He freed his right arm and lowered his head like a halfback, picking up more speed as his coat waved off his back and left arm like a thick cape. The cross was getting closer.

Zach dropped his coat behind him, free, faster now.

He cut into the next row of headstones, hoping to shorten the distance, when his left foot banked awkwardly off the edge of a partially buried flowerpot. A bolt of pain shot up his leg, throwing him flat on his chest, directly on top of a grave. He bit his tongue, and the wind was knocked out of him.

You have to be kidding me. He turned over, struggling for air. He managed a small breath, followed by a deeper one. Slowly, he sat up, doing a mental body check. Nothing broken. Just bruised.

This is insane. Running? Why?

He thought about the word *insane* and how well it described his thoughts and feelings over the last couple of days. Very little of it made sense to him. He shivered, glanced back to see where his coat had landed, and saw it spread out across the top of a grave several rows down. He looked over his shoulder at the cross, still strangely distant. What religious taboo had he committed by running across the tops of all those graves?

He leaned back again on his elbow, took another deep breath, and caught the name on the tombstone only a foot or so from his face.

"Pardon the intrusion, Andrew Hood," he said.

He brushed his hair back from his eyes with the heel of his hand. "And hello there, Robert and Karen Thomas," he added, reading the two names that shared a single headstone directly across from him. What had happened to them? They'd died the same day.

"Needle in a haystack," he said again, looking around. "I'm sorry, Amy. Please forgive me for not being able to find you."

Somewhere within these grounds was the body of his dead sister. Not that her body would look the way he remembered. After all of these years, he imagined she was nothing more than bones and dust inside the pink dress she was buried in.

The funeral.

He could still see the emotionless expression on his father's face as Drake Norman looked at his dead daughter, too young to be wearing makeup. Her curly brown hair splayed out across a small satin pillow.

And then there was the stare.

He remembered his father's arms crossed and the peculiar tilt of his head. That stare stayed on Zach long after Amy's casket was closed for the last time. And it said many terrible things that words could never convey. *You failed. She was your responsibility, Zachary. How could you let it happen?*

He'd never forget it.

Zach swallowed hard and rose, brushing off the grass. He put his head in his hands and closed his eyes.

"I am so sorry, Dad," he said. "I am so sorry, Amy. Please, please forgive me."

"It wasn't your fault, Zach."

He instantly recognized the voice. He opened his eyes, and the carpenter was standing four graves down, the tip of the cross glimmering behind him in the distance.

Zach nodded. "I knew it. I knew you would be here."

Kenneth stepped closer, walking around the back of the headstones before cutting back to the side of the grave he sat on.

Zach crossed his arms and looked into his eyes. "I've been thinking quite a bit about you. That was some nifty work with that cross yesterday."

Kenneth nodded.

Zach looked away. "I have a feeling that one was just for me."

"Maybe it was, Zach."

Zach lowered his chin. "I tried to find out who you are. I called your employer to get some background on you. They wouldn't give out any information."

"That's not important," Kenneth said. "But, Zach, you need to know that what happened to Amy wasn't your fault."

"What do you mean?"

"You know exactly what I mean."

Zach stared at him for a long moment. "Who are you, man?" he whispered.

"I am—"

"It *was* my fault," Zach said. "It was *all* my fault."

"Says who?" Kenneth asked. "Your father? Don't you think it's time to let it go?"

Zach's hands clenched. He could see Amy's flowing hair behind that window—outside that room. It was his fault. Hadn't he relived it over and over in his dreams? "She wanted in so badly. I couldn't open that window."

The carpenter remained quiet.

Zach's voice weakened and his fists starting to shake. "I kicked it, I punched it . . . and she scratched at it and scratched at it. She wanted in. I tried. I did my best."

Kenneth was perfectly still. "Yes, you did."

"How do you even know what I'm talking about?" Zach asked. "How did you know my sister's name? Tell me. Please."

Kenneth didn't respond.

I'm totally losing it. Here I am, spilling my guts to a carpenter . . . But that wasn't true. There was something special about the man. Something that let him see everything, know everything. You could see it in his eyes. Zach combed his hair back with his fingers and crossed his arms. "I just want the nightmares to stop."

"I know it hurts," Kenneth said, stepping to the foot of the grave to face the headstone. "But we both know it's not only a dream but a memory—an instant replay that has been torturing you for a long time."

"It isn't fair," Zach said. He could still see her small hands pressed against the window. "I was supposed to be watching her. It should have been me."

"It wasn't your fault, Zach."

"The carpet—it was so cold."

"It wasn't carpet. It was snow."

"I was trapped."

"No, you weren't, Zach. *She* was trapped."

"No!" Zach yelled. "I couldn't open the window!"

"It was ice you couldn't break."

Zach looked quickly at the carpenter.

"Do you remember the ice?" Kenneth asked.

"Yes! It wouldn't break!"

"It was a foot thick, Zach."

"I couldn't break it!"

"You were a boy, Zach. Twelve."

"I should be here, not her," he said, his finger pointing in a circle around the cemetery. "Why couldn't it have been me? Amy never hurt anyone."

"It wasn't your time, Zach. It was Amy's time."

Amy's time?

Zach covered his face with his hands. The carpenter's answer was too cliché. It made Amy's life sound like an expiring gallon of milk, like some predetermined date stamp that couldn't be negotiated.

"You're wrong," Zach said, pressing the heel of his palm against his forehead. "Amy had on brand-new skates. It was the first time she'd worn them . . ." He closed his eyes and shook his head.

"Take your time," Kenneth said.

"I saved from my paper route to buy her white figure skates for Christmas. She had always worn my old black hockey skates. She never complained about them; it's just that all of her friends had the white ones—the pretty ones. I was so excited, I gave them to her early, and we went out to the lake. You should have seen her. She was so happy."

"Yes, she was," Kenneth whispered.

He paused over the carpenter's strange remark, but by now he was too immersed in the story to stop. He had to get it out. "I heard the ice break, the only place it was so thin—the *only* place. Every other place it was rock solid. She fell straight through the ice—and the current . . . it took her farther, and then . . ."

"Zach," Kenneth said.

Zach's breath was rapid. He wanted to cry, but he didn't remember the last time he had—maybe he'd forgotten how. "Her face—I could see it under there, under the ice. I tried so hard. She was looking up at me, clawing at the ice. I couldn't—I tried everything—I just couldn't break it." He lowered his head, staring down at his hands, shaking violently.

"Do you think everything happens for a reason, Zach?"

"Reason?" Zach said. He was suddenly welling with hate, and

he fixed his resentment on Kenneth. "What reason could there possibly be for Amy to die? Tell me why an innocent, ten-year-old girl falls through the ice and drowns. Please tell me that."

Kenneth stepped around the grave, but remained silent.

"Tell me!" the doctor yelled at the top of his lungs, the sound echoing through the cemetery.

"Why don't you tell me something?" Kenneth whispered, touching Zach's shoulder and pointing in the direction of the cross with his other hand. "Tell me what you feel when you look at that."

"The cross?" he asked. The hate seemed to drain out of him, leaving him hollow, weak.

"Tell me what you think about when you look at it. Tell me what you feel."

Zach hesitated for a moment, needing to examine what exactly he was feeling. He thought about the carpenter's question and then said, "Oddly calm. But I'm so confused. No, more like bewildered. It makes me think about the cross yesterday, at the Lindys' church, and *you*. I've gone over it dozens of times in my mind, man. It's insanity. I went back to St. Thomas this morning. Just to look at it. It's impossible, any which way I try to explain it."

Kenneth lowered his hand from the doctor's shoulder and said, "You know what, Zach? You don't have to understand everything, and you don't have to be the one who is always in control."

"Yeah, I do."

"Listen for a second," Kenneth said. "Truly listen. You don't have to understand everything, and you don't always have to be the one who is in control."

"Why not?"

"Because, regardless of how you feel, and what you think you've experienced, you can't—and you aren't."

Zach shook his head. "I don't understand you, man. I'm not even close to understanding."

The carpenter grinned in a way Zach wasn't sure he liked—but maybe it didn't really matter, because this was just another weird day in a series of weird days.

"What are you looking for here at the cemetery, Zach?" Kenneth asked. "Why are you here?"

"I guess I'm looking for Amy's grave."

"Why?"

He started to say something and then stopped. He finally looked at Kenneth. "I'm not sure. I can't find the grave anyhow and I have—"

"How would you feel if I told you Mr. Hood isn't dead?" Kenneth pointed to the grave beside them.

"What?" Zach read the man's name on the granite headstone again. "That's his grave."

"Let me try that again," the carpenter said. "Would you understand or believe me if I told you that Amy was more alive than ever?"

"No," Zach said, unable to block the memories—the police yelling and pointing, ordering people to stand back; the whining, whirring sound of the chainsaw opening up a square in the ice; the frog men pushing Amy's lifeless body out through the hole in the ice and onto the frozen lake like a stillborn baby.

"No?" Kenneth asked. "Why not?"

"No," he repeated, trying to block out the figure skates, the wet clothes, the matted hair, and the light-blue color of his sister's face. "It's impossible. I *saw* her." He shook his head and pressed on his temples. "Much as I wish I hadn't."

"Let me try another one, then," Kenneth said, squatting down into a catcher's position and tugging out a few blades of dead grass from the grave. "Would you believe it if someone told you that a cross cut in half by a bolt of lightning could look like new in a matter of moments?"

Zach studied the carpenter suspiciously from the corner of his eye. "That's not fair."

"Why not? Did it happen, or did it not?"

"Normally I would say that it's impossible, but in this case, I *know* it happened. I was there."

"But Amy being more alive than ever is impossible? What's the difference?"

"I just told you," Zach said. "I *saw* it. I saw the cross only a few minutes before *and* after it happened. Seeing is believing."

"Zach," Kenneth said quickly, "if you told someone what happened yesterday with the cross, what would they say to you?"

"They probably wouldn't believe me. They'd think I was nuts."

"But you understand why they'd think your story was a little tough to swallow?"

"Of course," Zach said. "But that doesn't change the fact that it happened. I saw it with my own two eyes."

"Tell me, then," Kenneth said, putting his hand on Zach's shoulder again and giving it a little squeeze, "how would you tell someone they should trust what you say—to believe—to believe *without* seeing?"

"I don't know," Zach said. "I guess I'd tell them that they have to take my word for it. They'd just have to believe what I say."

"They'd have to believe you?"

"I guess they wouldn't have to. I'd hope that they chose to."

"There you go!" Kenneth said, taking his hand off Zach's shoulder and stepping around the back of the grave as if to leave.

"W-what?" Zach said, wishing he had never come to the cemetery, but feeling, somehow, like the carpenter was abandoning him. "Where are you going?"

Kenneth let out a little laugh. "I have some errands to run. I still have to get my costume for Saturday."

"Saturday?"

"The harvest party at the church," Kenneth said cheerfully. He clapped his hands together and leaned over slightly to put his hands on the top edge of Andrew Hood's headstone. "Believing is a choice, Zach. You can't force somebody to do it. Does that make sense?"

Zach nodded.

"Amy is more alive than you could ever imagine."

Zach stared into his eyes. There was no shade of dishonesty in the man. No sense of ego or malice he could identify. He swallowed hard. "I want to believe that, Kenneth. I really do."

The carpenter smiled. "Tough to swallow? Kind of like how people might respond if you tell them about the cross?"

Zach looked around the cemetery again. "Something like that. Yes."

"I have a quick question," Kenneth said, holding his hands out. "What do you call believing without seeing? What do you call it when you make the choice to believe—the choice to let everything else go that you thought you knew and just believe?"

"I'm not sure," Zach said. "What do you call it?"

The carpenter slowly walked toward him. Zach kept waiting for him to stop, but he didn't until their faces were only a foot away from each other. He felt a slight chill flit across his neck but also felt steadied, strong, assured. He looked into the man's eyes and waited for the answer.

"It's called faith, Zach."

Zach couldn't look away. The chill ran down his back, and what he tried to ask only came out as a whisper. "Who are you?"

"You know who I am."

Zach froze, and the carpenter's face was now within inches of his.

"Zach, I know it scares you, because it goes against everything you always believed."

The chill was gone. A warmth passed through him, as if he'd just wrapped up in a down blanket. He stood speechless as Kenneth took a few steps backward and then turned to walk slowly up the hill. The carpenter finally stopped at the top and turned around. He held his hands up in the air and shouted, "Only believe, Zach! Amy is more alive than ever!"

"Only believe," Zach whispered, his ankles and feet still feeling as if they were buried in wet cement. "I want to. But I can't."

The carpenter disappeared over the other side of the hill toward the cross, and Zach looked at his watch. He was now over an hour late. "Only believe," he muttered again.

He turned around and limped back toward the entrance.

"Don't forget your coat!" he heard. "You dropped it while you were running." It was the old man who'd been fiddling with the flowers, who was now sitting on the crumbled bench, pointing behind him.

"Thanks!" Zach yelled, waving to the old man before rotating gingerly on his slightly twisted knee. He walked toward the coat, and when he finally reached it, he said to the back of the headstone, "I'll bet this is the first time you ever had on a twelve-hundred-dollar coat. Thanks for keeping an eye on it for me."

He stepped on top of the grave, picked the coat up, and folded it across his arm. "And I guess I probably owe you an apology too," he said, turning to face the tombstone. "I certainly didn't mean any—"

Amy Elizabeth Norman
Beloved Daughter and Sister
September 22, 1971–December 18, 1981

Zach dropped the coat and blinked hard before quickly stepping to the side of the grave. He tried swallowing and couldn't. His cheeks felt paralyzed, and his mouth gaped open as he stared at the headstone.

"Amy," he finally said breathlessly, the faded black letters on the tombstone blurring and then slowly coming back into focus. "There you are."

He licked his lips and ran his hand across his forehead. He looked back to the old man on the bench. He was gone.

But then he felt it. Knew it. Knew it before he even looked.

The carpenter was back on top of the hill, arms at his sides, looking down the hill and straight across Amy Norman's grave into the eyes of her big brother.

Zach felt something creeping down his cheek. He wiped it away and could feel the wind cooling it on the back of his hand. It was a teardrop. There was another one, and then another. He lifted his hand to his face, choking on sobs long buried, and looked back up on the hill.

The carpenter was gone.

"Only believe," Zach whispered again, this time to the tip of the cross that glistened beyond the hill.

His legs gave out and he dropped to his knees on top of the grave.

Then Zach leaned his head against his sister's headstone and cried—for the first time in twenty-eight years.

TWENTY

Despite the brief nap she had taken, Brooke couldn't remember ever being so tired. She tugged the sleeve of her sweatshirt down into her palm and gripped it tightly to wipe the side of her face. She sat up on the couch and looked out the window at three doves that had settled on the front porch's wooden railing.

"You feeling better?" Shirley asked, crossing the living room to lean over and kiss Brooke on the cheek.

Six years ago, it wasn't really that difficult to explain to the Lindys the chain of events that led to her getting pregnant. But what was coming would be tough—the thought of finally chasing that skeleton out of its closet took her from euphoric relief to absolute terror and back again, banging off two imaginary borders like a tiny metal pinball.

"So," Pastor Jim said, sitting back in the aged recliner. "I hear you'll be meeting with Alex's father? That was quick."

"Yeah," Brooke said. "He has the same cell phone number as before."

"When was the last time you saw him?" Shirley asked, perching on a rocker, coffee cup between her hands.

"I ran into him a few years ago at the movies," Brooke said, sitting up. "I'm lucky I got hold of him. Other than the movies, I haven't seen him since I worked at the plant. I don't even know what I'm going to say." *Hey there. Funny thing. I forgot to tell you that you're a daddy . . .*

"What'd you tell him?" Pastor Jim asked.

"Just that we needed to talk and that it's important," Brooke answered. "He said he'll be back in town Thursday." She looked at the ceiling and shook her head. "Seriously. How do you tell someone something like this?"

"Just tell him the truth," Pastor Jim said. "And God will take care of the rest."

"Tell him Alexander is a gift from God," Shirley said. "He'll know that when they meet."

"And tell him he may lose a son he hasn't met?" Brooke whispered. "Isn't it . . . I don't know, sort of cruel?"

"That's not going to happen," Shirley said, walking into the kitchen, leaving a silence in the living room that seemed to hum.

"Leukemia," Brooke said. The word detonated like a bomb, flooding the room with an invisible threat.

"It's not going to happen," Shirley repeated from the kitchen.

Pastor Jim slowly leaned forward in the La-Z-Boy and laced his fingers tightly together. "Let's take a walk, Brooke, shall we?"

"Okay," she said. "Let me check on Alex real quick."

"They're out cold," Shirley said, walking back into the living room. "Down in the basement."

Brooke opened the basement door and tiptoed down the steps to peek around the corner.

Charlie was flat on his back on the small couch, his legs folded over the end at a ninety-degree angle, his feet flat on the floor. He was wearing a white T-shirt, his gray cotton sweatpants, and the big toe of his right foot was sticking out through a hole in his sock.

Alex was sprawled out across Charlie's chest. He was snoring lightly and appeared to be wrapped in a gray sleeping bag that was actually the matching top to Charlie's sweatpants. He had a piece of popcorn in his hair, and tiny beads of sweat dotted his forehead. His small body rose with each of Charlie's inhaled snores, and then slowly lowered as Charlie exhaled.

Brooke lightly touched the side of Alex's cheek, and then his forehead, noticing that the sweat which had dewed on her son's head was alarmingly cool. Alex lifted his head, mumbled something in his sleep, and then plopped his cheek back on Charlie's chest.

Brooke picked up a half-empty glass of cherry Kool-Aid, grabbed a pair of macaroni-and-cheese-stained plastic bowls off the coffee table, and headed back upstairs.

Pastor Jim was pulling a faded navy blue sweatshirt over his head that had *Carlson Rotary* emblazoned across his chest. "We'll be back in about an hour," he said to Shirley. He leaned his head toward Brooke. "Let's go, kiddo."

Brooke put the dishes in the kitchen sink and then returned to the living room to grab a rarely worn jean jacket out of the closet. She followed Pastor Jim out the front door into a light breeze and unusually bright autumn sun.

Both of them were quietly absorbing the news of the day, and neither of them said anything until they had reached the gravel of Church Road.

"Why don't you ever worry about anything, Pastor Jim?" Brooke asked. "Why doesn't anything ever seem to bother you?"

Pastor Jim continued to walk while pulling lightly at his ear. "My father once told me something when I was quite young. He told me that worry is disbelief in disguise."

Brooke crossed her arms and cupped her elbows with her palms. "So if you worry, that means you don't believe?"

"I'm really not sure," he said. "I think what my father meant was to give up control to God."

"I can't help it, though," Brooke said. "I still don't see how you never worry."

"Oh, I have my moments of worry," he said with a frown.

"What do you worry about?"

"Charlie," Pastor Jim said without hesitating. "I worry about Charlie."

"Charlie?" Brooke asked. "Charlie always seems so happy."

He nodded. "That may be true, but . . ."

Brooke took his arm and they stopped. "But what?"

He turned his head away and then back to Brooke. "What is going to happen to him when Shirley and I are gone?"

Brooke didn't say anything, painfully imagining life without

Pastor Jim and Shirley. "Don't worry about Charlie, Pastor Jim. I'll take care of him. He'll always have a home with me."

Pastor Jim held out his arm, which Brooke stepped under. He pulled her next to him as they continued to stroll. "You're wonderful, Brooke. But your whole life is in front of you—and Charlie isn't your responsibility."

"We are all each other's responsibility," Brooke said. "We're a family, and Charlie will always be part of the life that's in front of me."

"Yes, we are a family," he said, smiling. "Thank you, Brooke. Thank you for reminding me. And, honey . . . Alex is going to be fine."

"You seem so sure," Brooke said, looking at three doves on the side of the road in front of them. The same three from the porch rail? *Strange . . .*

"Do you believe that the Lord sometimes works in unusual ways, Brooke?"

Brooke stopped walking. "I guess so."

"I've been meaning to tell you this since you got back. I think our construction worker friend may be blessed. And I also think he may have given me a word, intended for you."

"You're talking about Kenneth."

"Yes." He took her by the arm. "Listen, he told me something that I want to share with you."

Brooke hesitated. "What is it?"

Pastor Jim looked like he was mulling it over. "Brooke, I have complete faith in God's ability to heal Alexander."

"What did Kenneth say?" Brooke said, narrowing her eyes. "Tell me."

"He quoted a Bible verse at the diner, but changed it slightly. I can't really explain it, but I just know that he was talking about Alex. It was as if he knew Alex was sick, before any of us did."

"He couldn't possibly know," Brooke said. "What Scripture did he quote?"

"He said 'tell her to only believe and *he* will be made well.' What else could he possibly have been talking about?"

"It's obviously some kind of coincidence, Pastor Jim."

"Maybe," he said. "Regardless, we already believe with all our hearts and our souls that God can heal Alex. Right?"

"I believe that," Brooke said.

"That's all you can do."

They walked for a time in silence, each deep in thought. Brooke looked over her shoulder, thinking about Alex sweating, but cold. And sleeping again. "Maybe we should get back, Pastor Jim."

"Of course, of course." They turned and went back the way they came. When they reached the edge of the driveway that separated the house from St. Thomas, Brooke stopped again. She crossed her arms and glanced up at the cross.

"Pastor Jim, do you really believe that people can know things? That there are people that can give—I mean, really give—'a word' from the Lord?"

"I do," he said. "But I'm not sure I ever really witnessed it until I met Kenneth." He smiled. "Take a look at that cross. Doesn't seeing that burned and broken, then whole, all within an hour make you a tiny bit more open to what he had to say?"

"Open to what he has to say . . . or just willing to accept amazing carpentry skills. He didn't claim it was an act of God. Why should we?"

Pastor Jim just smiled and turned toward the cross as if he could see it too. "Truly, Brooke. How can we not? Sure, God used a man. But he used him mightily—all we can ever pray that he would do with each of us. I would say the Almighty has placed someone special in our path, and we'd be wise to pay attention when he has a word for us."

Brooke took a deep breath and saw them again out of the corner of her eye—the three doves. They were about thirty feet in the air and banking hard off the tree line on the other side of the church. She held her breath as they cut across the church lawn and then pulled up, gracefully lifting their wings to softly land.

They landed on the cross.

She slowly tilted her head to the side and said, "What'd Kenneth say again?"

"Only believe," Pastor Jim said. "And he will be made well."

TWENTY-ONE

It's the salsa that makes this place famous," Kaitlyn said, dipping a warm tortilla chip into a bowl of Dos Hermanos's super hot salsa.

"Mm-hmm," Macey said, taking a sip of her margarita.

"You sure seem quiet," Kaitlyn said, eyeing the doctor's drink. It looked good, and despite Macey busting her doing the shots at The Pilot, Kaitlyn never drank around anyone from the hospital, even Zach, the entire time they dated.

"Seems like we are taking turns asking each other what's wrong." Macey broke a chip in two. "I'm just thinking, that's all."

"A quiet Dr. Lewis is like a Sasquatch or Nessie sighting," Kaitlyn added. "It's more than a little rare. I'm guessing it's my turn to ask. What's wrong?"

Macey seemed to force a smile. "I don't know. You're going to think I'm losing my mind."

A pair of elderly mariachis began serenading three women a couple booths down, and Kaitlyn hoped they wouldn't come their way. "For me to think you're losing your mind, it must be good. Lay it on me."

"Do you believe in God?"

"Wow," Kaitlyn said, surprised. Something about the way Macey asked it made Kaitlyn uncomfortable, as if a stranger had guessed her age or weight. But this was no stranger—this was Macey Lewis.

"Wow? I get a wow?"

"Yeah," Kaitlyn said, squinting suspiciously. "One trip to church, and you're asking the ultimate question?"

"I'm sorry," Macey said. "You asked me what was wrong, and I'm telling you."

"What are you sorry for?" Kaitlyn said, noting that her friend was being way too serious.

"The God talk. I guess there's a reason people don't talk about politics and religion. The topics can obviously create some discomfort."

"I'm perfectly comfortable discussing it," Kaitlyn said. "Even though I may not know what I'm talking about when the subject comes up, I'm still comfortable with it."

"Answer the question, then," Macey said, tapping her finger on the table.

Kaitlyn rushed to drink some ice water. Her mouth burned from the salsa, and she tongue-parked a piece of ice against the inside of her cheek. "I guess I want to believe in God—that there is something more."

Macey ran her finger around the rim of her sweating glass. "What would it take for you to actually believe?"

"I'm not really sure." Kaitlyn wasn't dodging the question; she kind of liked the idea that they were talking about God. "Is it safe for me to assume that going to church inspired this?"

"Of course," Macey said. "But it had a little more to do with the people we were *with* at the church."

"I agree." Kaitlyn adjusted the napkin on her lap. "It felt good just being there, like I was doing something right. It was like I was actually where I was supposed to be on Sunday mornings."

"Yes," Macey said, "but I'm not sure it was just being in church, per se; I think there are some strange things happening around us. It's hard for me to explain. Some of it just doesn't make sense."

"Like what?"

"You saw that cross before they fixed it," Macey said, scraping the tomatoes off a pair of tacos on the plate in front of her.

"I'll take those if you don't want 'em," Kaitlyn said.

"Sure." Macey picked up her plate and slid the tomatoes onto Kaitlyn's. She paused. "Kait, something's going on, and I think Zach knows it too. Have you ever seen him as quiet as he was at that Pilot Inn?"

"I thought he was sulking about me."

"Sorry to burst your bubble," Macey said. "But I think it's because he was totally overwhelmed. Zach *just* missed seeing whatever happened to that cross because he conveniently got that splinter in his hand. And that big guy, Charlie, saw it happen and peed his pants. He was terrified! Kait, I'm telling you that the construction worker did his thing to the cross in front of the minister who couldn't see it, and the big guy who couldn't *talk* about it, while the doctor was away."

Kaitlyn took a sip of her water. "So you're saying the carpenter made Zach get a splinter? Don't you think that's a stretch, Macey?"

Macey sighed and sat back, crossing her arms. "Any way you dice it up, something bizarre happened."

"Because the carpenter fixed the cross. Like he was supposed to."

"Kaitlyn. He. Fixed. It. Too. Fast."

"We don't know that. He does that stuff for a living."

"C'mon, Kait!" Macey said, smacking the table with her hand and turning a few heads. "The cross was totally destroyed. You don't have to know anything about construction to recognize that. Even if he had a brand-new cross sitting there, he couldn't have planted it that fast!"

"But he did," Kaitlyn said, squinting at her friend. It made Kaitlyn feel a little bit saner knowing her own head wasn't the only one Kenneth had spinning. Him and his magic apple. Still, she had never seen Macey so worked up over anything but a patient. "You said strange things were happening. What else?"

"How about Zach yelling 'Amy' in the phone when I called? I wonder if that had anything to do with why he was late for work today."

"Late?" Kaitlyn said. "He never came in."

"Yes, he did. He ended up coming in around two."

"Hmm. I didn't see him," Kaitlyn said. *He came in and didn't talk to me? He's still mad that I never gave him the full story on Tim*

Shempner. Everyone is going to find out about the real me. And then what?

"He made his rounds and left. In fact, I heard he spent more time with the kids today than ever."

"That must explain why I didn't see him then," Kaitlyn said.

Macey took a bite of her taco and stared at Kaitlyn. "Someone sounds miffed. Weird, for a girl who doesn't care anymore."

"Please," Kaitlyn said. "Now you are really talking bizarre."

Macey bit her lip and then paused. "You want to hear something really weird?"

"Go for it," Kaitlyn said.

"I also think Kenneth may have had something to do with Mary Springsted's recovery."

"How?"

"Before he came to see us at my office, when I was getting on the elevator, all of the elevators were stuck on Five. And then, when I apologized to him for being late, I could have sworn he said it gave him a chance to visit an old friend *on the fifth floor*. I believe that friend was Mary Springsted."

The mariachis came to their table, and Kaitlyn politely waved them off.

Macey took another sip of her drink. "Not to mention that phrase I've heard Kenneth say on more than one occasion."

"What phrase?"

"*Only believe*," Macey said. "He said it a couple times to me, and then Dr. Timmins said Mr. Springsted was shouting it."

"Check with the staff on Five and see if he was up there."

"I did."

"And?"

"They said the only visitor she ever had was her husband."

"I think that about closes the case, then," Kaitlyn said with a wink. "Unless Kenneth had his magic carpet parked outside the fifth-floor window. Maybe he is a genie."

"Zip it."

"Or maybe he is God."

"Maybe he is."

"What?"

"I'm being totally serious," Macey said. "He was there. I know it. And quit looking at me like I'm crazy."

"What are you trying to say then?"

She gave her a little shrug, fiddling with a chip. "I don't know. Only this . . . regardless of who he is, I can't wait to see what happens next."

• • •

Jim used his left thumb as a bookmark and gently closed the Bible. He lowered the book to his lap and took a long, slow breath, struggling to digest what he'd just read. He pulled up on the lever on the side of the chair to lift the leg rest and laid back, closing his eyes, thinking on it.

He imagined the ancient prophets and their remarkable God-given abilities. He wondered about the possible existence of modern-day prophets, or those capable of "signs and wonders."

He wasn't quite sure who Kenneth was, but he knew for certain that he had never met anyone like him. And the more he thought about the carpenter's indirect quote of Luke 8:50, the more he was convinced that Kenneth's words directly related to Brooke and Alex. He opened the Bible back up, thumbed his way to Deuteronomy 18, and then ran his finger across a half page of braille until he reached verse 21. "And if you say in your heart, 'How shall we know the word which the LORD has not spoken?'—when a prophet speaks in the name of the LORD, if the thing does not happen or come to pass, that is the thing which the LORD has not spoken."

Jim took a sip of tea that had cooled off too much. *Who are you, Kenneth? You didn't speak in the name of the Lord like the Bible says, but you quoted Luke 8:50 almost perfectly. Why would you say it if it didn't have anything to do with Alex? What else could you possibly have meant?*

Shirley walked into the living room from the kitchen. "Are you coming to bed?"

"I'll be there in a minute," he answered, closing his eyes.

185

"You are going to fall asleep right there in that chair, James Lindy."

"No, I won't," he said, opening his eyes dutifully.

"Yes, you will."

He smiled and picked the Bible off his lap to set it on the side table. "What time is it?"

"Quarter past eleven."

"Okay. You're right. I'm coming." Jim pushed the side lever down and lowered his leg rest. But he didn't rise. "What time are you guys going to the hospital in the morning?"

"They are doing the procedure at six forty-five," Shirley said, walking into the kitchen. He could hear her setting cups down in the sink. "I'm guessing we will leave here around six."

Shirley came back in and kissed him goodnight, leaving Jim to the silence of the living room and his big, comfy chair. He lay back again and closed his eyes. He raised the leg rest again. *Just five more minutes.*

Jim could feel someone tapping on his arm. "Charlie, is that you, son?"

"No, Pastor Jim. It's me, Alex."

Jim turned his head, realizing he'd fallen asleep in the chair. "Alexander? What are you doing up?"

"Mom and Charlie are sleeping," Alex said. "I had a bad dream."

"Come here," Jim said, lifting Alex up into his lap. By the chill and quiet of the house, he knew it was very early morning.

Alex was fully aware that he had two dead grandparents, two unknown grandparents, and an unknown father. He also suspected that Alex had him pegged as all five wrapped up in one, and on more than one occasion had confided in him certain fears he didn't want anyone to know about. Jim had a feeling one of those was coming right now.

"I was getting chased by the shot doctor from the hospital. He was in a painting. He was laughing and chasing me around the hospital with a *ginormous* shot in his hand."

"Then what happened?"

"I woke up," Alex said. "Can I tell you something else—and promise not to tell Mom?"

"I'll try."

Alex put his mouth next to Jim's ear and then surrounded it with his hands to whisper, "I'm afraid about tomorrow."

"Why is that?" Jim whispered back.

"I'm getting a shot. Don't tell Mom or Nurse Kaitlyn I'm afraid, okay?"

"Your secret's safe with me. I don't like shots either."

"Really? But you give yourself shots all the time for your sugar."

"That's right," Jim said. "For my diabetes. But I still don't like the shots, even though they only hurt for a second."

"I know," Alex said.

"You're a big kid now, and you know they only hurt for a second."

"Yeah," Alex said. Jim could feel him stretching out on the chair next to him. "Why was my mom crying today?"

"Don't you worry about your mother. She is just fine."

"Why was she crying, then? Was it because of me?"

"People cry for all sorts of reasons," Jim said. "The important thing to know is that she's okay." He gave the boy a hug. "When was the last time you cried, Alex?"

"I don't cry as much as I used to," Alex said, sounding more like eight than five. "I'm growing up."

Jim chuckled. "Yes, you are, Alex. Yes, you are. But you still fit when you're cuddling with me." He leaned the chair all the way back and could feel Alex's head rest on his chest. "How about a story?"

"Can you tell me about the man in the fish?"

Jim smiled. "There was a man who lived a long, long time ago."

"How long ago?" Alex asked sleepily.

"A long, long time ago," Jim repeated.

Alex was asleep by the time Jonah boarded the ship.

With one hand, Jim ran his fingers over the cover of the Bible. The longer he thought about what Kenneth had said, the more convinced he had become.

Tell her to only believe, and he will be made well.

He closed his eyes and looked forward to talking with Kenneth at the harvest party on Saturday to confirm it. *Now to figure out what the 7:16 thing is all about . . .*

TWENTY-TWO

Brooke and Shirley were sitting alone in the small waiting room. Alex had just been taken away by both Kaitlyn and Dr. Lewis for a bone marrow aspiration, where they'd take a sample of marrow from either his leg or hip. Even though he was only in the next room and the procedure wouldn't take long, Brooke had never felt so far away from her son.

She stared at the small pamphlet on the table in front of her without really seeing it.

"Why can't I be in there with him?" she asked. "He probably wants me in there."

"Brooke," Shirley said. "You are going to have to trust Dr. Lewis and her team. They certainly seem to know what they are doing."

Brooke picked the pamphlet up and read it. *What to Know When Your Child Has Leukemia.* Her eyes couldn't leave the last word.

Brooke dropped the pamphlet to her lap.

"You need to be strong," Shirley said. "Open that back up and read it, Brooke Thomas. I think you should know everything and do your best to understand what they are doing at all times."

Brooke closed her eyes and took a deep breath. She was stretched in a three-way tug-of-war between disbelief, denial, and reality. She struggled to hide the panic in her voice. "I don't know what to do, Shirley."

"Remember what you told me about the doves?" Shirley asked. "And do you remember the words on the train car?"

"I know," Brooke said. "If I only believe, Alex will get better."

She flipped the pamphlet open. Inside was an illustration of a little girl. Brooke guessed that she was maybe a year older than Alex, lying on her side with her bare hip exposed. She was smiling eagerly as if she were enjoying what was happening to her. Next to her was a doctor, who looked considerably older and much more experienced than Macey, preparing to draw bone marrow from the little girl's hip with a long needle.

But Brooke knew her son. And if they were about to insert a needle like that in him, he wasn't smiling.

• • •

In the next room, Macey glanced over the edge of the small surgical theater that Kaitlyn had created. The three-foot-wide, two-foot-high curtained display spread across Alex's midsection, with bright red drapes that closed around his belly button and lower back, making it impossible for him to see his lower body—or what was being done to him. Alex was smiling from ear to ear and seemed to be fully distracted by Mr. Brave, Kaitlyn's hand puppet. Mr. Brave's head bobbed back and forth over the top of the theater, and his shiny, black button eyes and sing-song "voice" were clearly making Alex less nervous.

Alex rested on his side, wearing a purple hospital gown and his SpongeBob underwear. Macey settled a warm blanket across his legs.

"You're going to like this part!" Mr. Brave said, as Kaitlyn performed the dual roles of nurse and puppeteer while applying more EMLA cream to Alex's hip to further numb his skin.

"Hey, Mr. Brave," Kaitlyn said calmly. "Ask Alex if he can feel that."

"I heard what she said, Mr. Brave," Alex said. "Tell her it feels warm. Tell her I like it."

"He says it feels warm. He says he likes it," Mr. Brave reported back to the nurse in his high-pitched voice, bringing another grin to Alex's face.

"Isn't Alex doing well?" Kaitlyn asked the puppet as she continued to massage the cream into Alex's hip.

"Well? He's amazing!" the puppet squeaked as the nurse tapped on Alex's leg.

Alex giggled.

"Can you feel that?" Kaitlyn asked, pinching on the loose skin of his tiny hip.

"Feel what?" Alex asked.

"Nothing," Kaitlyn said. "Nothing at all." It looked like he never felt the quick pierce of the needle numbing him further, and she gave Macey a quick nod.

Mr. Brave peered back over the curtain, and his fist-sized head teetered slowly back and forth. The puppet whispered, "Hey, Alex . . ."

"What, Mr. Brave?" Alex said, his eyebrows lifting.

"It's time to be brave—real brave."

"Okay," Alex said, his eyes round in anticipation.

Macey winked at him and had a feeling he really wasn't interested in being any braver than he already was. But she was sure that he didn't want to let Mr. Brave or Nurse Kaitlyn down.

Kaitlyn looked over the edge of the curtain. "There is going to be a little pinch here, Alex."

"Are you ready?" Mr. Brave said loudly, soliciting a bolt of enthusiasm from the boy.

"Yeah!" Alex said.

Macey lowered the aspiration needle to his hip and could see Alex swallow hard.

Then his cheeks puffed.

Then he asked where Charlie was.

Then he wanted his mother again.

Then she removed the needle.

"Man, you did good!" Mr. Brave said, sliding across the top of the theater.

"Great job, Alexander," Macey said. "You were terrific!"

"Wow," Kaitlyn said, lowering her head next to Mr. Brave's. "You are so brave, Alex."

Alex laughed and took a quick wipe at his eyes. "I did do good, didn't I?"

"Yes, you did!" Mr. Brave affirmed. "Really good!"

"Am I done?" Alex asked, sounding not even remotely open to the possibility of the answer being a no.

"That's it for now," Kaitlyn answered, pushing Mr. Brave all the way over the curtain rod so the puppet could request a congratulatory high five from the boy. "Sit tight, and I'll grab your mom for you."

• • •

Jim poured the dregs of his coffee over the edge of the front porch and took in a deep breath of early morning air. It was cold outside. He recognized the remaining hints of lacquer that the breeze had continued to pull off the cross. Birds were chirping their good mornings, and a car's horn beeped impatiently somewhere miles away. He thought about Alex and Brooke and closed his eyes for a quick prayer to give both of them strength.

The front door of the church opened and then banged shut. Charlie had gotten an early start on his chores and had ambled up the hill when Shirley, Brooke, and Alex had left for the hospital. By the sound of it, he was ruthlessly pounding on a rug with a broom handle, knocking the dust out of it and into tomorrow.

"About fifteen minutes, Charlie!" he yelled, letting his son know when it would be time to eat breakfast. In response, the church door opened and closed again. Jim rubbed the tops of his arms, took another breath of the cool fall air, and went back in the house.

Inside the kitchen, Jim unwrapped two double-packs of blueberry Pop-Tarts and dropped them into the spring-loaded slots of the old toaster. He felt for the electrical outlet, plugged the toaster in, and pressed firmly down on the plastic lever. He rinsed out his coffee cup, put it in the sink, and breathed in a lungful of toasting Pop-Tarts. "Yes, my boy," he said, as if Charlie were already with him. "The finest breakfast known to man. And no ladies here to refuse me my double portion!" He rubbed his hands together in excitement.

Jim turned and reached up in the cupboard, feeling for and then retrieving two glasses. He lowered them to the counter and then filled each with tap water. He quickly set the last one down, overcome by a sudden need to sneeze. He pulled out his handkerchief just before he let go of the biggest sneeze he could remember.

"Bless you, Lindy," he said with a little laugh, lifting the handkerchief to cover his nose before sneezing uncontrollably three more times.

"Wow." He wiped his nose, his chest expanding before sneezing again. "Good grief," he said, putting a hand to his chest, actually feeling winded from the episode.

He blinked rapidly, clearing the tears from his eyes. He dabbed at the sides of his face and then the corners of his eyes with the handkerchief. His body rocked as he sneezed yet another time. He chuckled. "Here we go again."

He covered his eyes with the handkerchief and sneezed twice more.

Jim braced himself against the counter. "What in creation?" he said to the empty kitchen, wiping his eyes again with the handkerchief. "I must be getting allergies in my old age."

He began to take the handkerchief away from his eyes and suddenly froze.

It can't be.

He spun in a slow circle. *Lord? Is it possible?*

He'd prayed for it, in the early years. But there'd always been bigger items on the prayer agenda. Prayers for provision. For his people. For Brooke. And lately, for Alex.

He'd thought he'd become content with the memories over the last twenty years.

Memories of Shirley's face. Charlie's.

He thought he'd become content with the sound of Shirley's voice and Charlie's laugh.

He thought he'd become settled with the mental snapshots of

faces that he alone had personally assigned to Brooke and Alex. Faces he loved, but faces he'd never actually seen.

But right now, the thing he wanted most was . . . to truly see Shirley, Charlie, Brooke, and Alex. The people that made up his personal fortune, making him the happiest man in the world.

Until he did, he wasn't sure he could trust this.

"Charlie!" he yelled. "Charlie!"

He continued to pull the handkerchief away from his face, watching it wave. He didn't need his son to know it had really happened. This was no dream.

He could see.

The handkerchief was white. It fell away from his hand like a parachute falling out of a navy bomber toward his feet.

His feet were covered by a pair of faded black slippers. He knew about the hole in the side of his left slipper. He had felt it for a long time. Its torn edge was drooping pathetically against the floor.

The floor was the same light brown linoleum he and Shirley had put in close to thirty years ago. It looked awful. It was beautiful.

The table.

The finger paintings posted on the refrigerator that had obviously been done by a child. Alex.

The toaster.

The steam coming off the Pop-Tarts.

The cookie jar.

The digital clock next to the stove.

Jim walked dreamily to the sink and looked out the window.

The cross.

The church.

Please don't be a dream. Please—not this time. He'd had plenty of those over the years. Dreams where he could see but then woke to blindness.

The toaster again.

The clock next to the stove.

The numbers.

The clock.

Lord? Lord! The numbers on the clock.

Kenneth knew.

Jim let go of the counter and crept over to the stove. He fell to his knees for the second time that morning, bowing low. *It's impossible! Isn't it?*

"Praise be to God," he said, knowing the full measure of possibility. "Thank you, Lord."

He gently rubbed his eyes with his fingertips, then slowly pulled himself up to peek over the front edge of the stove at the clock again.

Kenneth knew this was going to happen.

Chills ran across the minister's back and arms, and his heart raced. And then he began to weep uncontrollably as he stared at the three black numbers on the clock.

7:16

TWENTY-THREE

Jim immediately recognized the man, even though he hadn't seen him in over twenty years. The hair was certainly grayer. The skin under the chin and along the neck seemed to have loosened a bit. He had a late-fall tan, making the distinct creases coming off the corners of his mouth look like thin cracks on sun-baked mud. The lines across the forehead were more pronounced and obviously permanent. The nose was the same, but he couldn't stop staring at the man's ears. They seemed like they had gotten bigger.

He smiled easily—loving it all—and leaned closer to the mirror for a better look. There was no doubt about it. His ears *had* gotten bigger.

Jim continued to stare. His Indian-brown eyes were shining, as if made of glass. Unwavering, fearless, unblinking. *My eyes.* They looked exactly as they had in his youth. *A young man's eyes in an old guy's face.* He grinned at his reflection.

"Lindy, you look a hundred," he said. He ran his hands down the sides of his cheeks, and they met at his chin in prayer pose. "But it's great to see you."

Jim headed down the hallway, looking curiously at the tops of his hands, noticing the wrinkles and spots, the puffy, age-thickened knuckles. Even the sight of them made him glad. Because they screamed of his miracle.

He knew that miracles took place all the time, and that every one of them—without exception—was from the hand of God.

There were big ones. There were small ones. There were those everyone noticed, like surviving life-threatening illnesses and accidents. Then there were the many more that went unnoticed, like healthy children, something to eat, a roof, someone to love, birth, and sometimes, even death.

Jim walked into the kitchen and ran his finger along the tiny knit cross that hung like mistletoe directly above him. He wasn't Lazarus from the book of John. He wasn't the lame beggar from Acts, and he wasn't the risen son of the widow of Nain. He was the blind man. He was the minister, James Lindy, from the small town of Carlson, Michigan. He once was blind, but now could see. "Oh, can I see, Lord!" he shouted to the ceiling, grinning. "How I can see! Thank you, Father. Thank you!"

Though he had always known, he now knew more than ever how truly amazing grace really was. He put his hand to his heart, overcome with the knowledge that God had chosen him, *him*, to touch. It made him feel as tiny as an ant, and as big as the earth, all at once.

What a better witness he would become. He had places to go. People to see.

"To *see*," he said aloud. "Praise God!"

He picked up the phone and dialed Brooke's cell. It went straight to voice mail. He didn't leave a message and was glancing back at the digital clock next to the stove when the carpenter's words flitted through his mind again. *And when it happens, promise me that you will never tell anyone about it.*

"Don't tell them, Kenneth?" Jim asked the clock, expecting it to answer. "It won't take a detective to know I'm not blind anymore." He lifted the phone receiver and paused. "I'm not supposed to tell anyone that you *knew* it was going to happen?"

The front door closed in the living room, and Jim froze in anticipation. He couldn't move. He held the phone to his ear and leaned against the wall like he had stage fright, his heart racing triple-time.

Someone grabbed his shoulder lightly and stomped past him to the kitchen table, snatching up one of the glasses of water before stepping to the window to look outside.

Charlie turned sideways, not having any idea he was being watched.

Jim felt breathless as he studied his son. He didn't know what to say, where to start. Charlie was the most beautiful sight he had ever seen—the tight crew cut; the high Lindy forehead; the slow motion blinks of his eyes; the innocent, trusting, and youthful face.

Jim had not forgotten about his son's enormous size. His seven-foot height and bulk created a presence that was felt as well as seen.

Charlie sipped at his water, and Jim noticed that the glass had completely disappeared into a rounded hand that looked to be the size of a catcher's glove. Charlie held the glass to his mouth and looked right at him. Jim lifted his head off the wall and hung up the phone. Charlie grabbed the Pop-Tarts out of the toaster and put two each on the plates that had been set out earlier. Charlie then approached and tugged at Jim's sweatshirt sleeve, prodding him to the table to join him for breakfast.

Jim didn't move. Charlie tugged again, and he grabbed Charlie's arm, prompting him to turn around and look at him.

"Hello, Charles Paul Lindy," Jim said. "Hello, my son."

Charlie smiled. He always did whenever he heard his middle name. Charlie then took a giant step toward the table. He stopped, slowly turned around again, and looked at his father in a peculiar way. Charlie looked at his face—and then his eyes. He stepped back next to Jim and hunched over, lowering his face within inches of his father's. His head slowly swiveled back and forth, examining closely the face before him.

He lifted his hand and waved a thick finger in front of his father's face.

Jim put his hand around Charlie's finger, which felt like the handle of a baseball bat. "I can see you, Charlie," he said, nodding. "I can see you."

Charlie squinted, as if confused, and Jim grinned.

He heard a car door close. Jim patted Charlie on the arm and went quickly to the living room and looked out the window. He held his hand against the glass as an attractive young woman lifted a young, redheaded boy out of the backseat of a small sedan.

"Hello, Brooke and Alex," he whispered, lowering his hand from the window.

There was an older woman closing the dented passenger door. She was saying something to the woman and the boy. She threw a floral-designed purse over her shoulder. She wore jeans that were pulled up a little too high, a hooded sweatshirt with the sleeves rolled to her elbows, and small, gold-rimmed glasses that formed perfect circles around her eyes. The top of her back was arched slightly forward, and she walked slowly, as if in pain. Her arthritis.

"Hello, beautiful wife," he said, his mouth hanging slightly in amazement.

The front door opened, and he faced the two strangers who walked in. Alex had his head on Brooke's shoulder, and he opened his eyes to glance sleepily at Jim. Brooke carefully put Alex on the couch and covered him with the green and white knit quilt that was folded over the top of the recliner. The boy promptly fell asleep.

"What happened?" Jim asked, watching Shirley through the glass, climbing the steps to the porch. "What did they say?"

"They did the bone marrow aspiration," Brooke said in a tone that Jim found surprisingly upbeat. Brooke walked into the kitchen. "Everything went well, and we go back tomorrow."

"Praise God," Jim said.

Shirley walked in, and he looked down and away shyly. He wasn't sure why.

Charlie was ducking under the kitchen doorway. He waved at his mother and pointed excitedly at Jim.

"Are you men having a good morning?" Shirley asked, looking to Jim to see what was up.

"I guess you could say that," Jim answered, slowly meeting her gaze. "It has certainly been a rare one."

Charlie took hold of Shirley's hand and pointed at Jim again.

"What is it, Charlie?" Shirley asked, looking over the edges of her glasses. "Something on your mind?"

Charlie poked toward Jim.

"Okay," Shirley said playfully. "What are you two up to?"

Charlie's head bobbled, and he waved toward Jim again.

But Jim paused, no words seeming right to him. No words were magnificent enough to capture what had happened! So he just grinned.

"What's going on?" Shirley asked, turning to Jim. "What's Charlie trying to tell me?"

Jim raised both of his hands to the window and looked up at the ceiling. He slowly outlined a handprint on the window with his left index finger. "Sorry about messing up your clean window, Shirl."

Shirley's head pulled slightly back. "What did you just do, James Lindy? You know how I feel about people putting their hands on my clean windows!"

"I apologized to you," he answered. "I apologized for putting handprints on your window. It was so clean."

Shirley let go of Charlie's hand and took a couple of steps toward Jim. Her tone was trusting, but suspicious. "What are you trying to say, James? Out with it already."

He cleared his throat and continued to stare at the smudged window.

"Your sweatshirt," he said. He had never forgotten about colors. "It's purple."

"How did you know that?" Shirley asked, looking down as if she'd forgotten what she'd put on. "Who told you?"

"Brooke's car," he said, lifting his hand back up against the glass. He tapped on the window and pointed right at the vehicle. "It's white, and there is a dent in the passenger-side door."

"You knew that."

"And over there," he said, nodding out the window to his left at a deer that meandered down the driveway from St. Thomas toward Church Road. "There is a doe."

"How in the world do you know that?" Shirley asked, crossing her arms and looking out the window at the deer. She stepped to his side, and he looked away. "How do you know that, James?"

"Because God healed me."

"What?"

"Because I can *see*," Jim said, facing her. "I see *you*, Shirley Lindy. And you're more beautiful than ever."

Shirley looked into her husband's eyes, frowning in confusion and wonder, and her arms dropped to her sides like dead weights. Jim smiled boyishly and hoped his eyes were sparkling. He hoped they shouted his love for her.

"James?" Shirley said faintly, still staring at him. He kept looking back, knowing what she was seeing. No longer were there milky patches of scar tissue that clouded the surface. No longer were there frayed and jagged edges of detaching retinas. His eyes were clear and brown. The way they used to be. They were the way God had made them before. They were the way God had made them *again*.

"James?" she whispered, completely absorbed in the gaze of a long-lost friend. Her eyes began to well with tears.

"It's a miracle," he whispered back. "Something happened."

"What's everybody mumbling about in here?" Brooke asked, returning from the kitchen to find Shirley falling into Jim's embrace.

"Something wonderful has happened," Shirley said, her face nestled against Jim's chest.

"What?" Brooke asked.

Shirley wiped away her tears and grinned up at him.

"What is it?" Brooke asked again. But she wasn't looking at them; she was looking at Charlie, who was standing by the window. He wore a frozen grin, his small lower teeth exposed in pure joy.

Brooke inched next to him and looked out to the front yard. "He's looking at that deer like he's never seen one before. You all right, Charlie?"

Charlie's head bobbed and his smile broadened. He lifted his hands and began to clap ecstatically.

"Shh, Charlie, shh," Brooke whispered. "You'll wake Alex."

"What is it?" Jim asked.

Charlie clapped harder. His hands thundered together joyfully.

"Something sure has him going," Brooke said to Jim, then slowly did a double-take. "Pastor Jim?" She grabbed his arm and half squinted in apparent disbelief. "Your eyes."

Jim smiled at her, and Charlie shot out the front door, letting it slam shut behind him. He took an enormous leap over the porch steps and ran to the center of the front yard. He turned back toward the living room window and started clapping again, jumping up and down and pointing at the deer, which had turned around and was making its way toward him.

Alex stirred and then sat up, and Brooke pulled him into her arms.

"Crazy deer," Shirley said. "She's coming right at him! She better look out, because Charlie looks like he's fixin' to try and claim her as a pet or something."

"He looks like he has gone crazy," Brooke said.

Jim put his hand lightly around the back of Shirley's neck. "Heck. I'm starting to think I've gone crazy too."

"Poor thing," Shirley said, looking at the deer as it got closer. "What do you suppose happened to it?"

"I have no idea," Jim said, wincing. "Whatever happened, it sure doesn't seem to be bothering it much."

The doe had stopped and turned its head toward the house. Jim could see what looked like a thick, reddish-brown patch of dried blood that had clotted around a nasty wound across the edges of the doe's rib line.

Alex leaned out of his mother's arms. "Put me down!" he cried. "Put me down!"

"Be still! Your hip is gonna be sore!" Brooke tried to set him down, but he was squirming so much, he fell heavily to his feet. He was out the door as fast as Charlie had been.

Brooke, Shirley, and Jim moved closer to the window, watching as Alex joined Charlie on the lawn. The big man took the little boy's hand, and the sight of it made Jim start to cry.

Charlie and Alex took three slow steps toward the deer and paused. They turned back to the living room window and smiled, pointing at the deer again like they were trying to tell them something.

Alex was shouting and lifting his hands.

"It's the deer," Jim said. "C'mon." He took Shirley's hand and led her out to the porch, Brooke right behind them.

They couldn't hear what Alex was screaming at first. But then he turned around and ran toward them.

"Don't you see?" Alex asked, clenching his bright red hair as if he wanted to pull it out. "Don't you see? The deer was dead! But now she's alive! She's alive!"

. . .

Macey dropped the folded copy of the *Carlson Herald* on the coffee table in front of Kaitlyn. "Check it out," she said, sitting at her desk and grabbing a handful of manila folders. "Zach brought it by earlier."

"Already saw it," Kaitlyn said, leaning back on the couch. "Carrie Armstrong showed it to me down at the cafeteria. A lot of people down there were talking about it." She picked up the paper for another look and read the headline above the photo: "East Shore Professionals Nurse Cross Back to Health."

"It's a good picture." Macey opened one of the folders and pulled a red pen out of her desk drawer. "Zach must be eating it up."

Kaitlyn glanced at the photo again. She tried not to look at Zach and instead checked out Kenneth. The photo made her stomach turn, reminding her of that day's events, mostly those at The Pilot Inn. She played it off with a fake grin. "I don't think God would ever look bad in a picture."

"Very funny," Macey said, pulling a sheet of yellow legal paper out of the folder. She crumpled it up and tossed it at Kaitlyn, missing horribly.

Kaitlyn tapped on the photo, feeling slightly bothered that Zach hadn't dropped the paper off to her. Thank God she had the following day off. *I may even hit my four-drink limit tonight and blow off a little stress.* "It is interesting that Zach and Kenneth are standing next to each other in the same picture, don't you think?"

"Why is that?" Macey asked, rising.

"One guy thinks *he* is God. The other guy, *you* think is God."

"I never said that," Macey said, snatching the newspaper out of Kaitlyn's hand and plopping down on the far end of the couch. "Why can't I ever be serious with you about things that aren't work related?"

"Lighten up," Kaitlyn said, leaning her head apologetically toward the doctor. "I thought you were suggesting that he was—"

"I didn't say that. I was just—I don't know—theorizing."

"Theorizing?" Kaitlyn asked, tilting her head and knowing full well that her friend had been doing more than just *theorizing*. "You were dead serious."

"Okay," Macey said. "So what if I was?"

"Well, it's not every day that one of your best friends *theorizes* about a higher power hanging drywall," Kaitlyn said, thinking about how Kenneth somehow reminded her of every mistake she had ever made. But it was impossible for him to know. He was just in the right place, at the right time . . . at The Pilot, where it was easy for her to rehash bad memories and then drink them away.

Macey crossed her arms. "Like it or not, and as weird as it sounds, I'm standing by what I said."

"Okay," Kaitlyn said, raising her eyebrows and hands. She sat up straight. "Subject change. I'm putting in an admin supply order. Need anything?"

"We don't have to change the subject."

"I didn't mean to hit a nerve," Kaitlyn said. "I'm sorry, okay?"

"You didn't hit a nerve," Macey said and paused. "Okay, maybe you did hit a nerve. I'm probably being too sensitive about all of this, but it has been a bizarre couple of days. It's not like me to talk religion. It's embarrassing."

"Sorry," Kaitlyn said again. She meant it.

"No, *I'm* sorry," Macey said. "I need some black pens. And some rubber bands."

"You've got it," Kaitlyn said.

Macey picked up the paper again. "Kenneth certainly seems like a good guy, though, doesn't he?"

Kaitlyn grinned. "Oh, I would say almost . . ." She stopped at the risk of going overboard.

"Almost what?" Macey said, with a hint of smile. "Say it, smart aleck."

"Heavenly."

"I knew it." Macey shook her head.

"By the way," Kaitlyn said. "Other than him dropping off the newspaper, have you seen much of Zach today?"

"No," the doctor answered.

The office phone rang, and Macey grabbed it on the second ring.

"Hello, this is Dr. Lewis."

Kaitlyn crossed her arms and looked back at the paper—mostly at the image of Zach.

Macey snapped her fingers and pointed at the paper, wanting Kaitlyn to hand it to her.

"She called the paper ten times?" Macey asked. "The man of her dreams? Oh, man in her dreams. Which one was he?"

Kaitlyn watched as the doctor ran her finger across the page.

"On the far right?" Macey asked, squinting at the picture. "I, uh . . . I can't make any promises . . . Well, yes, I suppose I could try. What's her phone number?"

The doctor grabbed the pen off the desk.

"Go ahead and give me her number, Shannon. Got it. And her name is? *What?* You're kidding me . . ."

Kaitlyn watched the color drain from Macey's face.

"Okay," the doctor said, gripping the phone, her eyebrows huddling as if she was confused. "Thank you, Shannon." She promised to have Zach call her back and hung up.

"What's wrong?" Kaitlyn asked.

Macey was still staring at the phone. "That was Shannon from the *Carlson Herald*. You know . . . the one who came and took our picture?"

"Yeah," Kaitlyn said.

"She tried to call Zach a couple of times today." Macey's eyes were wide and staring.

"Macey. What'd she want?"

"She said there's a woman who keeps calling, demanding to know the name of the man in the photo. She said he's the 'man in her dreams.' It's Kenneth."

"So? Maybe she thinks he's cute."

"She wants Kenneth to call her."

"Well, there you go. Some girls just can't give in to eHarmony."

"Kait," Macey said, meeting her gaze. Her face had gone pale. "The woman's name is Mary Springsted."

Kaitlyn's throat suddenly tightened, dry like she had a mouthful of chalk. She was desperate for her shift to end. To put on that makeup. To get to The Pilot.

If Macey was right about Kenneth, then Kenneth knew everything.

Every. Thing.

TWENTY-FOUR

K aitlyn's head was pounding.
She turned over on the couch and opened her eyes. The living room in her small apartment was dark and silent. She could smell rum and the ashtray on the coffee table only a few feet away. *Please tell me I didn't start smoking again. I was doing so good.* That failure was quickly drowned out by a rush of memories that replayed in her head.

Tim Shempner.

Charlie getting hit.

The carpenter.

Her father.

The booze was wearing off, and she vaguely remembered spilling what had been left in the bottle. Kaitlyn pulled her T-shirt up over her face, trying to forget what she'd been drinking to forget. The anger. The doubt. The shame.

She lowered the shirt, then gripped it again to pull it back up to her nose. It had a funny smell to it. Smoke, sweat, a man's cologne? Worse, it was the only thing she had on.

Was I with somebody last night? What am I doing on the couch?

Kaitlyn sat up—light-headed. Her throat was dry and she swallowed, licking her lips with a thick tongue that tasted like she may have gotten sick. She couldn't remember the apartment ever being this warm—what was the thermostat set at, ninety?—and she wiped the sweat off her neck. She heard a clanking sound, followed by a toilet flushing.

Her mind raced, trying to remember. She wanted a cigarette.

Maybe there were some in her purse. She reached over on the table but felt nothing. No purse, no table. She squinted in the darkness. She sat up and put her feet on the floor. Something was different about the carpet.

Why is it so hot in here?

She stood and made her way across the floor, holding out her arms in front of her to protect herself, feeling for a wall, for anything. She angled toward the moonlight that was coming in from a window and stopped.

This isn't my apartment.

A light came on behind her and she turned around, startled. A skinny little girl, maybe six or seven, was standing there. She was wearing a Hello Kitty nightie and had straight blond hair.

"You need to go home. This is not your house."

"Sweetie," Kaitlyn said, staring in disbelief. She didn't have any idea where she was or who she came here with. "Who else is here?"

The little girl pointed behind her to the hallway. "Just Daddy."

Daddy. Something about the way the girl said it stabbed Kaitlyn.

The little girl frowned. "Why are you wearing Daddy's shirt?"

Kaitlyn looked at the T-shirt she was wearing, then glanced over at the couch. It looked like she had used her coat as a pillow, and in the light cast from the bathroom, she could see that she had thrown up all over the armrest. Her jeans and underwear were on the floor.

"Mommy comes home from work right before I go to school. I'm telling her that you puked on the couch. That's bad."

"Your mommy lives here?" Kaitlyn asked. She felt like she was going to be sick again.

"You aren't supposed to kiss Daddy. I saw you. That's bad and I'm telling Mommy that too."

Kaitlyn closed her eyes and thought about the carpenter. *He knows it all.* She leaned toward the little girl and whispered, "Honey, please don't ever say—"

"You're not supposed to," the little girl repeated. "Only Mommy is supposed to kiss Daddy."

I know, Kaitlyn thought. *You're right.*

"You are bad," the little girl said. "Go away."

Kaitlyn smiled at her and nodded. Her smile faded. This was it. It all had to end. The little girl was right.

I am bad.

And I need to go away.

* * *

"Good morning, everyone," Macey said, entering through the staff door of the examination room, and was greeted by a big smile from Alex. He was in Spider-Man pajamas and new Winnie the Pooh slippers, just a little too big for him, and sat between Brooke and Shirley. "Five-thirty in the morning sure comes early doesn't it?"

"Sure does," Brooke said. "Dr. Lewis? Alex has a question for you. He's asked me it about three hundred times this morning."

She bent down in front of him. "What is it, Superboy?"

"When do I get to take my sleepy medicine?" he asked, resting his chin on his knee.

"Can you wait a little bit longer?" she asked, surprised at how anxious Alex was to reap the benefits of the sedative.

"Okay," Alex said, standing up and shuffling his feet. His new slippers swooshed on the carpet, and one slid partially off his heel. He bent over and pulled it back on. "Nurse Kaitlyn told me about it. Why isn't she here today? Did she not want to get up early like us?"

"Today is her day off," Macey said with a little laugh. "How's your hip feeling today? I'm guessing a little sore, maybe?"

"A little," Alex said, holding his thumb and index finger a half inch apart. "That much." He tapped Brooke's leg for her to lift him to her lap. "Will it hurt, getting a pote put in me?"

Brooke kissed the top of his head. "It's called a *port,* little man," she said. She looked to Macey to answer him.

"That port is going to help us give you your medicine. And no, it won't hurt going in. That's why you're getting the sleepy medicine. You'll wake up and wham! It'll be in place."

"Okay. But where is Mr. Brave?"

"Mr. Brave took his sleepy medicine *already*," Macey said quickly. "He'll be asleep for a little while too."

"Okay," he said.

"Alex," Macey said, pushing a wheelchair to the center of the room and then sitting in it. She grabbed the tops of the rubber wheels. "I want you to know what a great job you are doing so far. I'm super impressed."

"Thank you," he said, then leaned to whisper in his mom's ear.

"Ask her," Brooke said to him, nodding at Macey. "Go ahead."

Alex seemed hesitant to ask, as if he liked being the kid who had all the answers.

"He wants to know how long he will be asleep," Brooke said. Alex looked thankfully to his mother and then quickly at Macey.

"Not long," Macey said. "When you wake up, don't forget you may feel a little sore and a little sleepy, but both your mom and I will be with you, all right?"

"All right," Alex said. "Can I have that sleepy medicine now?"

"When you leave here, the anesthetist will give it to you," Macey said, getting out of the wheelchair. "Can you say anesthetist?"

"Yeah," Alex said confidently. "Anesterrist." He looked around the room, as if proud of himself.

"You ready, Alexander?" Macey asked, standing. She stepped behind the wheelchair and grabbed the handles. "You want to walk or ride?"

"Ride!" Alex blurted, sliding off his mother's leg.

Macey gestured toward the chair, and he hopped on. She put down the foot pedals, but his feet didn't reach.

"Don't I get a hug, mister?" Brooke asked.

"I'll take one too," Shirley said. "Charlie is going to be wondering where you are all day."

"Tell Charlie I got a wheelchair ride, Mrs. Lindy!" Alex said excitedly, shimmying off the wheelchair. He gave his mother a quick hug and then wrapped his arms around Shirley's leg.

"We love you," Shirley said. "We'll see you in a little bit."

Alex climbed into the chair again. "Hey, Mrs. Lindy, are you gonna tell them about Pastor Jim's eyes?"

Shirley smiled. "At some point, Alex."

Alex's left slipper fell off, and Macey picked it up and put it back on for him. She patted his head, winked at Brooke, and then looked down at Alex. "Tell Mom and Mrs. Lindy good-bye."

"See you later, alligators," Alex said. Macey popped the metal square on the wall that automatically opened the door, and Alex dropped his elbows on the armrests as she pulled him backward out of the room.

Tony, the orderly, was on the spot to take the handles from Macey.

"Mr. Tony is going to push you where you need to go," Macey said. "I'll see you in a few minutes, okay Alex?"

"Okay," he said, giggling as Tony took him away.

"He is so cute," Macey said, stepping back in the room and closing the door. She walked over, sat next to Shirley, and then laced her fingers together and leaned forward. "Do either of you have any questions? About anything at all?"

"I don't," Brooke said. "Can you think of anything we should be asking, Shirley?"

"I think they have done a wonderful job of explaining things," Shirley said.

"I know this is a lot," Macey added. Brooke had been dealing with the situation as well as any parent the doctor had seen. "Alex is off to a great start. Most kids constantly fight any type of process, and he has done incredible. Believe me."

"I believe Alex is going to be all right," Brooke said. "Just keep telling me what I need to do and I'll do it."

"All right," Macey said, standing back up. "Dr. Norman will be done with the procedure in about an hour, and then I will take you back there. Remember, you will see him with two bandages. There will be one on his neck and a larger one where the incision is on his chest. And plan on seeing a small amount of blood under or around the dressing on his chest. Don't let that alarm you."

"Okay," Brooke said.

"And you'll start his chemotherapy this afternoon?" Shirley asked.

"Most likely," Macey said, the doctor tone fading from her voice. "Mrs. Lindy, I know I'm going to be seeing a lot of you guys in the weeks to come, but I was wondering if I could somehow speak with Pastor Jim before Saturday's harvest party? On a personal matter?"

"Of course," Shirley said. "He'd love it. Come by anytime you wish."

"I could maybe stop by tomorrow evening, if that's convenient."

"I'll tell him you're coming," Shirley said. "And I actually had a question for you about James."

Macey sat back down. "Sure."

"An amazing thing has happened. James sight has returned, and I was wondering what the medical explanation might be. We were out and about and when we came—"

"I-I'm sorry," Macey interrupted. "Did you say Pastor Jim can see?"

Shirley's smile widened. "Yesterday morning, when we arrived back home from here, his eyes—all of the damage to his eyes—it was all gone. They look brand-new."

"What do you mean, brand-new?" Macey asked slowly, waiting for a punch line.

"James said that he was in the kitchen and that he had a sneezing fit. When he opened his eyes, he could see."

"From sneezing?" Macey asked, wondering how Shirley and Brooke could be so calm. They acted as if a scab had fallen off the minister's elbow. Regardless, something key was obviously missing from the story.

"That's what happened," Shirley said. "He's been healed. You can see it tomorrow for yourself."

Dumbfounded, Macey watched Brooke nod and grin. "That's what happened," Brooke said. "I'm guessing you don't hear *that* every day."

Macey stared at Brooke and then shook her head, not in disagreement, but to clear it. "Mrs. Lindy, maybe I should come by tonight, instead of tomorrow. Would that work?"

"Of course," Shirley said.

Macey stood and crossed her arms. Her stomach was churning in a tightly bound ball of anxiety for the third straight day. *Things keep getting weirder . . .*

She brushed her palm nervously against the end of her ponytail and faked a smile.

Wait 'til Kaitlyn hears this one.

• • •

It was before dawn and it had been a couple of years since Kaitlyn had been this drunk, for this long. But no matter how much she drank, she couldn't find the freedom she was looking for . . . only emptiness.

She sat on the edge of the Big Island Toll Bridge in the dark, her feet dangling over a hundred feet of emptiness. *An empty girl, in an empty space. If I just let go, I might disappear. Maybe then I'll find freedom.* She stared down at the dark, swirling waters, catching the reflection of the moon on the crests of the small waves.

Cars passed by her, but with a support beam directly at her back, she doubted any of them could see her. She adjusted her earbuds. Seals and Crofts' "Summer Breeze" ended, then Phil Collins' "In the Air Tonight" started. She looked down, and the frigid wind that bounced off the Detroit River hit her arms in a way that felt everything but summery.

Dark forms swept from the sky, and she was so startled by the movement, she almost slipped from the rail. Wings came so close to her face, she could swear she felt feathers. Ten feet away, three small owls landed and drew in their wings. The one closest to her stared at her with a wide, slow blink.

She stared back at them in amazement, wondering if that last rum and Coke was now giving her hallucinations. "Go! Shoo!" she said, waving her hand.

The closest one only blinked again and rotated his head to look at the passing traffic, then over to his two friends, then back to her.

Kaitlyn had never seen anything like them. She'd only heard

owls at night, never laid eyes on one. And now, here was a family of them. She frowned. The closest acted like a sea gull, begging for scraps.

"Go on, now!" she shouted, moving as if she intended to jump up and grab him. "I don't have anything for you! Can't you see? I'm nothing. Worthless. Hopeless. A dirty drunk! Go! Shoo!"

But the owl remained where it was, with the two behind it nothing more than a pair of shadows, closing their eyes as if to rest. *Maybe this is their home*, Kaitlyn thought.

Her cell phone vibrated against her hip through her coat pocket. It buzzed three times, and she took it out and looked at it. It was a text from Macey.

Call me when you get up. I have to tell you something about Pastor Jim at St. Thomas.

Kaitlyn started to text Macey back, but decided to call her. It was time to say good-bye.

She hit Send and when Macey answered, Kaitlyn listened without saying anything.

"Kaitlyn?" There was a brief pause. "Hello?"

Kaitlyn didn't know what to say. There were a lot of things she wanted to tell Macey. She wanted to tell her the real reason why she was at the bridge, after all this time. She had always wanted to tell her, to tell everyone, why she led a double life, but never could.

Kaitlyn ended the call and rubbed the smooth surface of the phone with her thumb. She could almost see Macey's face in it, little Alex's, and so many other kids she had worked with. Then there was Tim Shempner's face. Her father's.

"I'm sorry," she whispered. She held the phone straight out in front of her and let it drop, watching it fall away from her, then disappear into the water with a little splash.

She carefully wrapped her earbud cord around her smartphone, still playing, and sent that to the depths too.

Just a little splash and they're gone. Like me.

The owl shifted, partially opening and closing his wings, startling her. In her drunken haze, she'd kind of forgotten he was there.

Hoo-hoo. The sound was oddly comforting.

She lit another Marlboro Light, took a deep drag off it, then looked straight up the river toward Detroit. In the distance, to the right of the Detroit skyline, she could see the Ambassador Bridge connecting Detroit to Canada. The upper supports of the bridge were lit up, making it look like the hills of a roller coaster that took people to another country.

Anywhere away from the way she felt sounded good to her.

She rubbed her cheeks, numbed by the cold breeze. She looked off the north edge of Big Island into Canada and could see little fingers of lightning flickering miles away. She thought about where she would be when the storm finally came. *Where my body will be.*

Sometime between bar three and bar four, Kaitlyn had quit wondering why her life had turned out this way. *It's not unfair—it's my fault. Every rotten thing. I'm a curse on people, always have been, always will be.* Except for the kids at the hospital. They were her sole bright spots. Everything else? Superficial. False.

Even Daddy . . . he didn't really love me. If he had, he wouldn't have—

Hoo-hoo.

"Who?" she said, with a humorless laugh. "Well, my dad, for starters." *I hate him, for what he did. For all of it. For coming to my bedroom all of those nights. For blowing out his brains when I told Mama.* She blew out a long stream of cigarette smoke. Guilt washed through her. Familiar confusion. Doubt. Love.

She thought about her mother, starving and drinking herself to death after Daddy died.

My fault too. But that's okay. I'm about to make it right.

And then she thought again about everyone at the hospital, and how she never really disappointed them. But it was just a matter of time, wasn't it?

She thought about Tim and how he'd hit Charlie at the diner, and how he used to hit her. As much as she tried, she was always screwing up whatever relationship she was in. Making bad choices. Finding another bad seed.

But that's okay. It's over. No man will ever touch me again.

Kaitlyn took one last, deep drag on her cigarette and scooted closer to the edge of the wide rail. She leaned over and looked straight down. The river seemed so close.

She thought about the little girl she'd met in the apartment last night. *This morning*, she corrected herself. It seemed like so long ago. And then she thought of herself as a little girl. It seemed like yesterday.

Then she thought about Kenneth one last time and how he knew everything about her.

All of it.

That's . . . not okay.

And then she jumped.

TWENTY-FIVE

Kaitlyn opened her eyes.

She felt like that time Tim had shoved her against a wall as hard as he could. But this time, she could smell the river all over herself. She could see the undergirding of the bridge and the glow of headlights that spilled over the edge of the rails, but here, far below, she was in total darkness. She blinked, wondering if she could trust her eyes.

What am I doing here?

She took a deep breath and sat up, looking down the shoreline to her left, into the darkness. She thought she heard something behind her and looked over her shoulder.

Nothing.

Kaitlyn stood on shaking legs and brushed the sand and pebbles off the bottom of her left arm and hip. She was cold, and the uncomfortable cling of wet jeans made her look up at the bridge again.

Way to go, loser. You've even managed to screw up your own suicide.

She brought her hands up to her ears and shook her head.

She felt the full effect of the wind off the river as if it were bent on making her pay for her sins. Kaitlyn turned her back to it and wrapped her arms around herself, trying to keep warm. She started walking down the shore, wondering if a good cold night might finish what she couldn't manage to complete, when she heard the voice behind her.

"Things are that bad, eh?"

Kaitlyn stopped immediately. The wind was gone and the side

of her face warmed. She recognized the voice and that *feeling* on her neck. She turned around and could see Kenneth's silhouette against the lights of the city.

"Why are you here?" she asked.

"You can be forgiven, Kaitlyn," he said in that calm voice of his. He started walking toward her, and Kaitlyn noticed that with each step he took, that warm feeling spread a little more throughout her body.

"No, I can't," Kaitlyn said. "What are you doing here?"

"Saving you."

Kaitlyn glanced out at the river and then at the carpenter. She lifted her arm and gripped her wet sweatshirt just below her elbow. Then she reached out to touch his arm. But his sweatshirt was bone dry. She jerked her hand away.

Did you think he dived in? Hauled you to shore?

"Why are you really here?" she asked.

"I already told you," he said, stepping closer. "Kaitlyn, there's an easier way. And it begins with forgiving your father."

Kaitlyn took a step back, gaping at him. "I knew it," she muttered. "You really do know everything about me."

"Some might say that."

"Then you know you shouldn't be hanging out with a girl like me. A drunk. A loser nobody wants. I just want it *over*." She pointed up at the bridge. "But I—I can't even kill myself without screwing up!"

"It can be over, Kaitlyn."

She gaped at him. "It can?"

"Just not in the way you are thinking. You can have a new beginning."

"What?"

"Tell me why you were up there, Kaitlyn," he said.

"You know exactly why I was up there. The night I met you, when you told me to forgive, I know you were talking about my dad. But I can't forgive him. I can't!"

"You must. It's the key to your own freedom. Let him off the hook, Kaitlyn. Forgive him."

"No. I can't. It's not fair."

"Does forgiveness have to be fair?"

"Please go away. Just leave me alone."

"No," he said. "I'm staying. Right here, until this is done."

She resisted the urge to strike him. "I can't be forgiven! Not for what I've done! And neither should my father!" Hot tears came then, choking her. She swallowed hard and angrily wiped them away. "Some things, some decisions . . . make us who we are. You can't take the stripes off a tiger."

He was perfectly still in the dark. "Yes. Yes, you can."

"You're impossible!" she yelled, quickly turning and walking away. He came up beside her, easily matching her stride.

"I know you can forgive him," he said. "And you can be forgiven too."

"No, I can't! What I've done is terrible! And I can't forgive my father! Get it through your head!"

"Why can't you forgive your father?"

She stopped, turned to him, and crossed her arms and cupped her elbows as the wind blew against her. "Look, I've been to a counselor or two in my time. I know my dad's a big problem in here," she said, pointing to her head.

"No," he said. He reached out and laid a gentle hand over her heart. "It's a problem in here."

Warmth spread out from where he touched her, and she resisted the urge to lean into him, to ask him to hold her, comfort her. Instead, she pulled away, as if breaking a magnetic force. She took two steps back and shook her head. "You don't understand. I can still see my dad standing in my bedroom doorway the night before he died. The day before he did that to himself. I see it, every day. It's why I drink. To block it out."

"To block what out?"

"To block out what he did to himself. What he did to *me*."

"Forgive him, Kaitlyn. Forgive him now."

"I said no. What he did was too terrible."

"Answer this for me," he said. Kenneth paused and the silence grew between them. "Is one sin greater than another?"

"Yes."

"You're wrong. Sin is sin. If you can be forgiven for doing what you think is terrible, why can't he?"

She paused, his words playing over in her head. "But who would forgive me?"

"Him," Kenneth said, pointing toward the sky. "That's all the forgiveness you'll ever need."

Kaitlyn thought about it and it made no sense. "How can God forgive me after the things I've done?"

"That is up to him, not you. I want you to forgive your father."

"No!" she yelled, the word echoing under the bridge. "It wouldn't be fair to forgive him! I'm glad my dad killed himself!"

Kenneth didn't say anything, and Kaitlyn closed her eyes. She remembered getting off the bus that day and tiptoeing into the house, hoping. . . *praying* her father wouldn't hear her come in. The empty beer cans that normally littered the kitchen counter weren't there. Neither were the ashtrays that were always overflowing.

The only thing on the counter was the case to her father's shotgun.

"Forgive him," Kenneth whispered. "The time is now."

I love you, baby girl.

Why did her father have to say that the night before he killed himself? It was the only time she could remember him saying it. And he said it on the very last night, of all the nights he stood in her bedroom doorway.

Nights.

Kaitlyn wrapped her arms around herself, desperately trying to hold on to the flood of shame that had eaten away at her for so long, to keep it from overflowing onto the carpenter.

She couldn't hold it any longer. It was like he was *pulling* it from her.

"I can't be forgiven for the things I did with my dad."

"Yes, you can."

Kaitlyn couldn't look at Kenneth. Though she was sure he already knew, she still had to say it. What she wanted to yell was nothing more than a whisper. "I was only a kid. Only a little girl. He made me do those things."

Her shoulders dipped and she lowered her head. All she could hear was the water and a few cars passing over the bridge. And then Kenneth gently pulled her into his arms, his embrace nothing but brotherly, warm, protective.

"I know," he said.

I know. The only words she'd longed to hear. Understanding. Acknowledgment. And yet acceptance too.

"But how?" she asked, feeling the beat of his heart under her cheek, even as doubt began to creep into her own. "How could God possibly forgive someone like me?"

"You know how," he said.

Kaitlyn heard Pastor Jim talk about it at the service. She opened her eyes and gave Kenneth her answer.

"The cross."

The carpenter nodded.

Kaitlyn thought about Christ on the cross for her. "Why would he die for the sins of people like me and my dad? I still don't get it. It doesn't seem . . . it just doesn't seem—"

"Fair?"

"Yes," Kaitlyn said as the word she used earlier took a little bite at her. "Why would he do it, then? Why such a sacrifice for people like us? What is the reason?"

Kenneth released her and stepped slightly away, but he still held her hands. She could feel the heat of his gaze. "Because God wanted this. Relationship. Unbroken relationship."

Was it possible that she might be not only forgiven, but sought after?

"He wants your heart, Kaitlyn," Kenneth said. "He loves you already. More than anyone will love you. More than all the people who've ever loved you, combined. And he will never fail you. Never leave you." He paused. "Close your eyes."

When she did, she remembered the first time he took her wrist, and how everything seemed all right. And then that overwhelming feeling that if she did just one thing, her mistakes would be erased.

"Tell me something," Kenneth said, dropping her hands. Kaitlyn could feel the warmth in his palms as they met the sides of her face. "Do you really believe that Christ died for you?"

"Yes," Kaitlyn said. She really did.

"Kaitlyn, did he die for your dad too?"

She hesitated. Swallowed. She didn't want to say it, but had to. It was the truth. "Yes," she whispered.

"Was his sacrifice in vain?"

"No," she said reluctantly. But clarity strengthened her. "No!"

"Why?"

"Because he saved me."

"Yes, he did," Kenneth said. "Just as he saved your dad. Because he loves you both. Completely. Forever." He paused. "Open your eyes, Kaitlyn."

She immediately knew that this was different from the first time they had met at The Pilot Inn. There was no more shame, guilt, or fear as she stood under his gaze. She now understood with absolute clarity what his eyes were telling her. She'd figured it out. She knew she was loved unconditionally in a way that represented pure acceptance, regardless of what she had done. *Or whatever I do next.*

Kaitlyn began to sense a limitless form of strength building inside of her. It was building out of that perfect love she felt, and she knew it would allow her to do things beyond anything she ever imagined.

"You know what to do," the carpenter said.

"Forgive him," she whispered. "Forgive him as I've been forgiven."

"Do it now, Kaitlyn, as if your father were standing here, before you." Kenneth continued to hold on to her, as if pouring his strength into her. And for the first time, Kaitlyn felt hope. A possibility . . .

She closed her eyes again, seeing her dad stumbling toward her, close enough to see the lines on his face.

Drunk. Crying. Broken.

Broken, like me.

"Say it," Kenneth whispered, still holding on to her face.

In her mind, she reached out to touch her father's face just like Kenneth held hers. Seeing him. Acknowledging him for all he was . . . and all he was not. But loved, regardless.

"I forgive you, Daddy. I'm sorry—so sorry you were hurt and broken too. I forgive you."

Kenneth's hands fell away from her face, but she could still feel a measure of what he'd given her.

Power, through love. Never had she felt stronger.

Freedom. She felt ten pounds lighter.

And *hope*. A conviction that things really were going to turn out all right.

Kaitlyn opened her eyes and blinked.

The carpenter wasn't there.

She smiled and glanced back up at the bridge, never more certain of just one thing.

I'm not alone.

TWENTY-SIX

Macey dropped a handful of manila folders behind the desk at the nurses' station. It had been a long day and she was about ready to head out to the minister's house. The guy who could now supposedly see.

From sneezing? she thought. *Gimme a break.*

She drummed a pen across the top of the counter and turned her head in the direction of Zach's office, down the hall. He was still there. Not that she'd seen him. Was he avoiding her now too?

The third floor had seemed quiet over the past couple of days, almost too quiet. Down the hall, she could hear a vending machine buzzing steadily from the waiting room. And then she heard a fresh batch of ice fall and crash in the ice machine before giving back into the dull silence. A closet door closed in the A wing, immediately followed by the stuttering laughter of one of the kids. And then there was nothing—nothing but the steady hum of the vending machine in the waiting room again.

But there was also something else.

Something other than the vending machine was humming. It wasn't a buzz or hum she could hear, but one she could *feel*. Almost like a glow you could touch. Macey held her hand out in front of her face and pinched dreamily at the air, as if she were trying to capture a piece of it.

"What are you doing, Dr. Lewis?" Harriet Jasper asked.

Macey snapped out of it and blushed as she looked at the nurse. "Oh! Nothing . . ." She shook her head and yawned. "I'm obviously working too much. I'm practically seeing things."

Harriet laughed. Layers of fat jiggled at the bottom of her arm like tiny water balloons as she imitated Macey pinching at the air. "You looked like Mr. Miyagi from *The Karate Kid* trying to catch a fly with chopsticks, except there was no fly and no chopsticks."

Macey wasn't all that amused, but couldn't summon the strength to fake it. "Does it seem quiet to you around here lately, Harriet?"

"Lesia and I were talking about that earlier." Harriet sipped the third mineral water that Macey had seen her with today, a critical element of yet another diet. "Quiet and low maintenance. The kids all seem to be doing great."

"It's strange, isn't it?"

"You know how it goes. It'll be chaos before you know it," Harriet said.

Macey nodded and picked up her coat. "I'm outta here, Harriet. See you tomorrow."

"Have a good one," Harriet said.

Macey put her coat on and took a few steps before turning around. "Have you heard from Kaitlyn today?"

"I never hear from her on her days off," Harriet answered.

"Just curious," Macey said, pulling out her phone to see if Kaitlyn had called. "See ya."

"You too," Harriet said.

Macey headed down the hallway toward the elevators and past the waiting room, thinking about Wendy's or Taco Bell. *Dinner, then a long bath, and then a good night's sleep. That's what I need.*

Her pace slowed until she finally stopped about fifteen feet from the elevators. She turned around and looked suspiciously back at the waiting room door. The buzz—that *presence.* It was coming from there.

She turned, went back to the waiting room, and peeked in. A young couple watched their two-year-old play with wooden blocks on the floor in front of them. The dad looked indifferent, sprawled out in his chair, his eyes on his smartphone. The boy's left arm was in a cast, and the woman seemed to have the dark yellow remnants of a black eye that didn't exactly match the fresher and darker string of bruises at the base of her neck. She quickly looked away in what

Macey recognized as shame. Macey felt a shiver of rage and studied the man again.

On the far side, a bearded old man stood in front of the aquarium. He turned around and offered a pleasant smile—one she found familiar—and stroked the whitest beard she'd ever seen. He had a folded newspaper tucked under his left arm, and the long, thin fingers of his wrinkly right hand seemed to be wrapped around what looked like—she studied it for a second—like an apple.

"I'm heading home for the night," she said, not that they would have a reason to care. "You folks need anything?" Macey looked directly at the young woman, but she didn't meet her gaze. Then she looked at the young man and gave him a threatening look that she hoped said, *I'm on to you.*

He yawned at her and waved at the woman and child, muttering "car accident" with an innocent face that sickened her. He smirked, and she made herself turn and leave the room.

She made it to the elevator doors, pressed 1, and waited. She leaned back and glanced down the length of the empty hallway again.

So quiet.

Admissions were down. Remissions were up. The kids had been less irritable and more cooperative with treatments and medications. Johnny Lawson had actually gone three days without kicking any of the nurses, and the new kid on the block, little Alexander Thomas, took his first round of chemo like it was nothing and happily made his way home.

Macey wasn't sure what was going on—not only with the kids, but also with some of the grown-ups around her. The elevator arrived, she got in.

Religion—the great unknown.

When Macey thought about religion, she thought about going to church as a kid. It made her remember how she and her older sister, Connie, used to hold back laughter as Mrs. Trotter sang brazenly off-key. She thought about all those boring sermons and constantly looking at her watch, praying for twelve o'clock to come and the service to end so they could eat overcooked brownies and drink watered-down punch.

And then gradually, over time, other things seemed to become more important. Church became every other weekend, then once a month, then hardly ever.

Religion—the great unknown. She never liked that word. Religion seemed like a man-made thing, made to control other men. Now, however, religion—or something spiritual—appeared to be trying to nose its way back into her life.

I'll go visit the blind minister to see for myself. If it's true, she'd share the news with Zach.

Zach.

The elevator doors opened, and Macey didn't move. The five other people on the elevator each gave Macey a look that seemed to ask, *Are you going to get out? This is the ground floor.*

"I'm sorry," she said, stepping toward the rear. She knew, then, that she had to go back up and talk to Zach. She had no idea what she was going to say.

She got off the elevator and passed the waiting room. The old man was sitting and talking with the young couple.

She passed the nurses' station. Harriet had managed to find a twin pack of Twinkies to go with her mineral water and never even noticed Macey as she walked by and continued down the hall.

The door to Zach's office was open, and it was a little darker than usual. She saw only a spill of light from a desk lamp. Zach was sitting at his desk, eyes closed; his hands were together at the palms, and his index fingers formed a steeple directly under his chin.

Is Zach praying?

Macey tapped lightly on the door. "Knock, knock."

Zach's eyes opened, and he slowly turned toward her without saying anything.

"Hey, Zach," she said, in the least threatening tone she had used with him in months. "I didn't mean to interrupt. I was just stopping by to say hi."

"Well, hello back," Zach said kindly—almost too kindly for her. "What's up, Macey?"

"I guess I wanted to say great job with Alexander Thomas today."

Zach cocked his head and squinted, in a way that suggested he knew the Thomas boy had nothing to do with her visit. "Come in, if you want."

"Oh, I was just taking off for the day." Macey spotted a Bible on Zach's desk. *A Bible*? "Just wanted to tell you that."

"Oh, right," he said, shifting to the side of his chair. "Though I don't blame you, Macey, you haven't complimented me or just stopped by my office to say hi in over a year. What's going on?"

She half frowned and took a small step toward him. "Zach, I was going to ask you the same thing."

"Why is that?"

"I don't know," she said. She knew. "You haven't been yourself the last couple of days."

Zach nodded and rose. He came around the front of the desk and leaned against it, as if he were trying to keep a respectful distance. "Hopefully I can keep it up."

Macey just stared at him. He was more reserved than he usually was. "Keep it up?"

"Yeah," he said. "Keep from acting like my old self."

She squinted in confusion. "What's really going on, Zach?"

"What's going on is that I owe you and Kaitlyn, and everybody else around here, an apology."

"Apology? For what?"

He looked embarrassed. He waited, and then he looked back at her and said, "I'm sorry for the way I treated you. I'm particularly sorry for the way I treated Kaitlyn. I really am. I'm sorry for the way I treated a lot of people. I guess I was focused on the wrong things."

"Like what?" she asked.

"Like everything." He slowly shook his head, as if he was a little confused. "But more importantly—"

"Are you all right, Zach?"

"More importantly," he continued. He quit shaking his head and stared at her. "I think I may have been wrong about something."

Macey could feel that buzz again. She could also see something.

It was in Zach's eyes. He looked like a man who was close to finding something valuable.

"Wrong about what?" she asked.

Zach brought his hands to the sides of his face and closed his eyes. He shook his head again, then reached behind him and grabbed the Bible off the desk, and lifted it toward her.

"About this, Macey. About this."

TWENTY-SEVEN

Jim heard the front door to the church open. He lifted his head up from the Bible he was reading at the pulpit and watched as Charlie led a woman toward him. She had straight brown hair pulled back into a simple ponytail and a youthful, healthy glow that belonged, at tops, to a twenty-year-old.

Wait a minute. That's no twenty-year-old. I know who that is.

Charlie stopped at the fifth pew and turned around to head back out the door.

"Thank you for walking me up here, Charlie," the woman said.

Jim closed the Bible. He went down the carpeted steps from the altar and held out his hand. "I am certainly no Henry Morton Stanley, but—Dr. Lewis, I presume?"

"You presumed correctly," Macey said, shaking his hand and studying his eyes.

"Please, have a seat," he said, pointing to the first pew. "It's certainly nice to see you, Dr. Lewis. Pun intended, I guess."

"Pastor Jim," Macey said, "when I heard the news, I didn't know what to think. But it's true, isn't it? I don't know what to say. You . . . you can see."

"Yes, I can," he said. "It's remarkable, isn't it?" He helped her take her coat off and folded it over the back of the pew. He caught her looking at—*examining*—his eyes.

"I am sorry for staring," the doctor said. "It's just . . . I mean, I'm no ophthalmologist, but I guarantee there is no medical explanation. And then there's the *look* of them—Mrs. Lindy was right. Your eyes really do look brand-new."

"Only by the grace of God."

"Pastor Jim," she said. "I was going to see if I could come by this week and talk to you anyhow, but when I heard about your eyes, I just had to come today."

"You're welcome here anytime."

Her face went from amazement to confusion. "I guess I'm not really sure where to start."

"I suppose you want to know what happened to my eyes? How I can see?"

"It's not only your eyes," she said. "There are other things—several things—happening around here lately that flat out don't make sense to me. To be honest, I'm not that well-versed on matters of religion, and I guess what I'm looking for is your help in understanding it all."

"Interesting," Jim said, smiling. "Why don't you tell me about some of the other things you've noticed."

"We recently had a patient come out of a twenty-two-week coma."

"Praise God."

"And then walk right out the door a few *minutes* after waking up. Her doctor described her as being in the best physical shape she'd been in for years."

"That certainly sounds unusual."

"It's more than unusual. It's impossible!"

"Improbable, apparently. But not *impossible*. Her family must be thankful."

Macey sighed. "And then there's your cross. If you'd *seen* it . . . It was unfixable. When we got here, we looked at it and knew there was no way anybody could do anything with it other than haul it to the dump and get a new one. But *he* did. He fixed it."

She started to ramble, and Jim wanted to slow her down. He held up his hand as if he were stopping traffic and said, "You are talking about the carpenter?"

"Yes!" she blurted. "He fixed it, and your son saw him do it."

"He was right there," Jim said. "I know he saw it."

"Pastor Jim," she said, "feel free not to answer this, but does Charlie have any history of incontinence?"

"What?" Jim was a little taken aback and then understood where Macey was going. "You're referring to Charlie's accident that day."

"I'm sorry for asking," she said. "But yes."

"No," Jim said. "I don't remember him doing that since he was little. Are you concerned that something may be physically wrong with Charlie?"

"Not at all," she answered. "I believe he saw what happened, and I think it scared him enough that he wet himself."

"Saw what, though?" he asked. "Kenneth fixing the cross?"

"I'm not really sure. But I think what scared him wasn't the cross itself, but rather how it got fixed."

"Charlie was clearly afraid," Jim said. "The carpenter even told us to step back for a second. I could hear some peculiar sounds, like wood bending and snapping. Charlie panicked, picked me up, and carried me away from the site. And then it was over and the cross was complete."

"How long did it take him?"

"I'm not sure how much was done before Dr. Norman left, but the noise only lasted a matter of seconds."

"A matter of seconds," she repeated. "To do the job. *The whole job.*"

Jim paused, remembering. "I think Kenneth said it'd be done quickly."

Macey brought her hands to her cheeks and exhaled in agitation. "Pastor Jim, hardly anything was done when Zach left. I'm telling you that something quite unusual happened—something that most people would consider impossible. Why don't you tell me how anything he did on a cross could possibly scare Charlie that badly?"

"Good question."

She shook her head and frowned. "It just seems like the carpenter is at the center of all these things that are happening."

"What'd he have to do with your coma patient?"

"I think he was in her room before she woke up."

"Why is that?"

"The woman called the paper because she saw his picture. She wanted to know who Kenneth was—said he was the man from her dreams." Macey took a deep breath and covered her eyes like she was counting for hide-and-seek. Then she lowered her hands and glanced back at Jim. "Something is going on around here, Pastor Jim, something big. Bigger than some children's story of Noah's Ark."

Jim grinned. "Why would you call it a children's story?"

"I'm sorry," she said, looking contrite. "I hope that wasn't offensive."

"Not at all," he said. "I was just curious."

"I don't know," Macey said. "I always thought a four-hundred-foot ark with two of every animal on it was a bit of a stretch."

"A bit of a stretch?" Jim repeated. He put his hand on her shoulder. "Just remember that we're talking about *God* here. He made the world. He made you. He made me. When you can do that, you can do things that may appear a stretch. You can do things like help with the ark, help with a woman coming out of a coma, heal a blind man, or even help fix a cross. And I'm using the word *help* a little loosely."

She stared at him for a long moment. "I came here thinking that Shirley and Brooke were confused—traumatized by all that's going on with Alex." She tossed him a rueful look. "I didn't expect it to be real."

He simply smiled back at her.

"This should all be documented," Macey said. "I am an oncologist, not an eye doctor. But I know the body, and I know medicine." Her head dropped, shook, and then she rose suddenly and pointed at him, as if frightened. "What has happened to your eyes . . . *It just does not happen.*"

He pointed an index finger at each eye. "It just did, Macey. I asked the Lord to heal me, and he healed me. It's that simple."

Macey laced her fingers together and then lifted them, bouncing them lightly off her forehead. "It can't be that simple. I saw the damage to your eyes the other day. And now it's gone."

"I don't know what else to tell you. The Lord did it. Let's call it a stretch, shall we?"

"So you just woke up yesterday morning, asked God to heal your eyes, and *poof*—they were brand-new?"

"Not exactly," he said. "I haven't prayed for my sight in a good ten years."

"Ten years? And it happens now? I'm sorry. Now I'm prying."

"Yes," he said. "It 'just' happened now. In his perfect timing. When he has your attention."

Macey smiled. "You seem too nonchalant about it. You can see, for Pete's sake!"

"I am a man of faith," Jim said, shrugging. "It's not a stretch. Regardless of what you believe, Macey, once again, look at me. It happened."

"So if God heard your prayer, isn't he answering it a little late?" Macey asked, shifting her head closer to Jim.

"All prayers are answered," he said. "People just sometimes get confused because they just don't get the answers they want. I figured he'd heal my sight in heaven, if nothing else. It boils down to trusting in our maker and his ways, even if his ways don't appear to match up with ours. Make sense?"

"I guess." But she didn't look sure at all.

"Let me give you an example," he said, tugging down on his maize and blue sweatshirt. "Three Saturdays from now, Michigan will be playing football against Ohio State."

"Biggest game of the year," she said.

"Only if Michigan wins," he added with a perfectly straight face. "Regardless, I am confident that before the game, players and fans from both sides will pray for a victory. Right?"

"Sure."

"Well," he said, "both prayers will be answered."

Macey looked at him and said, "Even if the answer is no, it is still an answer."

"Right," Jim said, tapping her on the shoulder. "What we need to understand is that it isn't about what *we* want. It's about what *God* wants for us. It's about God's plan and God's will. And if we want something and pray for it, we will get it if . . ." He tilted his head toward the doctor, inviting her to answer.

Macey's eyebrows arched. "If it is God's will?"

"That's what I believe," he said. "And I believe it was God's will for me to see again."

"I think I understand," Macey said. She paused again and looked up toward the altar and cross. "I like it here. I think I'm going to start coming on Sundays."

"Praise God," he said.

"Now the other reason I came," Macey said. "That's if you haven't had enough of me today . . ."

"I've got all the time you need," he said. "Let me have it."

She stared at the cross. "This might sound really strange to you, Pastor Jim."

Jim waited patiently as she searched for the right words.

"He's here," she said calmly. "I think God is here."

"Yes, he is," Jim said with a smile. "This is his house."

"No, Pastor Jim. I mean here in Carlson."

"He is everywhere, Macey."

She looked back at the cross, and her voice sounded like it went up an octave as she whispered, "He brought that woman out of her coma. He fixed the cross. And he made you see."

"Yes, he did," Jim said, a warm glow filling him. "And praise be to him."

Macey turned her head and faced him. "I don't think you understand what I'm saying. He is here. He is *literally* here."

"I understand," he said. "And when we learn to—"

The front door opened behind them and they both turned around. A woman was standing there—tall, sharp features, very pretty, and a little rough around the edges. Jim guessed that she was having a bad day. The woman smiled, but he didn't recognize her.

"Can I help you?" he asked, his voice resonating throughout the small church.

The woman began walking slowly up the aisle. "I'm pretty sure you can."

Jim stood. He thought he recognized the voice.

Macey also stood and crossed her arms. "Kaitlyn, where on earth have you been?"

• • •

"It's good to see you," Jim said, returning an unexpected hug from Kaitlyn.

"I need to talk to you when you can," Kaitlyn said. She glanced apologetically at Macey. "I'm sorry for interrupting you guys."

"What are you talking about?" Macey said. "No problem."

Kaitlyn hugged Jim again. She backed up, but her hands still rested on his shoulders. She stared at him with a troubled look. "Your eyes."

"It's okay," Macey said.

Jim smiled and wasn't sure what to say. "God is good. I'm guessing it's not every day that someone gets their eyesight back."

"That's for certain," Macey said, taking her turn at hugging Kaitlyn. "Pastor Jim is the *miracle man*. I know *I* certainly can't explain it. Where have you been all day?"

"I've probably had the most unusual day of my life," Kaitlyn said. "But at the same time, I'm not sure if I've ever been better."

"Never been better?" Jim asked.

"Yes," Kaitlyn answered. "And I just left your house. I stopped over there first, looking for you. Shirley's making peanut-butter fudge, and she wants you both to come get some when you're done talking."

"Oh, I really should be going," Macey said. She sounded like she didn't want to go anywhere, and Jim had a feeling she had more to talk about. "I've taken up enough of your time."

"You have to hang on, Macey," Jim said. "For two reasons."

"Oh?" the doctor said.

"One," he said, holding up his index finger. "You haven't truly lived until you've tried Shirley's peanut-butter fudge. Even though I shouldn't, given my diabetes, I always have a little."

Macey shrugged. "Well then. How could I possibly turn down the opportunity to truly *live*?"

"And two," he continued, "I think there is something that you still want to discuss?"

"Yes," Macey said. "More like *someone* I want to discuss. I want to talk about Kenneth."

"That's strange," Kaitlyn said. "That's exactly who I wanted to talk about."

"Now isn't that *another* coincidence?" Macey said, her tone playfully sarcastic.

"Could be, could be," Jim said, winking at the doctor. "Since Kenneth is on both of your minds, let's head over to the house and talk some more." He rose and rubbed his hands together in anticipation. "Nothing greases the conversation wheels like peanut butter and chocolate."

• • •

Brooke and Macey walked back in the kitchen after checking on Alex, who was sleeping.

Jim set the pan of Shirley's fudge on the table and looked at Kaitlyn. "So Kenneth just showed up out of nowhere?"

"Yes," Kaitlyn said. "I know it seems weird, but he said he is there all the time."

"Under the Big Island Toll Bridge?" Jim asked. "That early in the morning? At the exact same time you happened to be there?"

"Yeah," Kaitlyn said. "What are the odds?"

"Kaitlyn," Jim said. "Do you mind if I ask you what in the world were you doing out near that bridge at that hour?"

Macey looked bewildered. "I was going to ask the exact same thing."

"I used to go to the bridge a lot when I was a teenager. You know, to think about things. I went there today to think about my dad. I lost him when I was young."

"There is something up with Kenneth," Macey said. "It's one thing after another with that guy."

"Something is definitely up with him," Kaitlyn said.

Macey picked up a piece of fudge and nodded. "I really *hadn't* lived yet, Mrs. Lindy. This fudge is addictive."

"Oh, aren't you kind!" Shirley said.

Charlie took five individual pieces of fudge and stacked them one by one on top of each other on his plate. He grabbed them all between his index finger and thumb and shoved them in his mouth like a tiny burger. His cheeks puffed, and he looked at Macey. He covered his mouth and smiled at her.

Macey grinned and then looked back at Kaitlyn. "Other than the things we talked about at the hospital, why do you say that something is up with Kenneth?"

"Because," Kaitlyn said, "from the time we met him, he has said a lot of interesting things."

"Like what?" she asked.

While Kaitlyn seemed to mull over her answer, Brooke jumped in. "Kenneth knew Alex was sick. Tell her, Pastor Jim."

Jim paused, worried that they were all taking this too far. But there was a lot of truth to what they were saying. "Kenneth made a biblical reference that was quite timely in relation to Alex's illness. It was from Luke 8:50."

"He knows the Bible well, does he?" Macey asked, arching a brow.

"You might say that," Jim said, pausing to glance at the clock near the stove.

"What else?" Macey asked. "What else has he said?"

"The first day I met him," Kaitlyn said, "he pulled out this apple and asked me what would happen to it if it had a worm inside of it. And then he told me to learn to forgive."

"Kenneth did that?" Macey asked. "At the hospital?"

"No." Kaitlyn looked straight at Macey. "I'd seen him once before, but that's not important now."

"Why didn't you tell me you already met him?" Macey asked.

"And he told you to learn to forgive? Pretty intriguing stuff from a man you just met. A carpenter."

Jim wrapped his hands around a glass of milk. "Want to tell us more about that, Kaitlyn?"

"Not everything," Kaitlyn said. "In time. But I've turned everything over to God and now I'm going to let things fall in place. Kenneth taught me that part of being human is making mistakes, but living in those mistakes is an even bigger mistake. We can all be forgiven and should quit living in our pasts, because the past has nothing new for us."

"I've never heard you talk like this, Kait," Macey said. "It's awesome. I like the forgiveness stuff."

"Yeah," Kaitlyn said matter-of-factly. "And we talked about forgiveness again near the bridge. Actually, it was near the shore."

They all stared at her.

"He told me that I was forgiven."

"Oh, honey. Did you accept it, then?" Shirley asked.

"I did," she said. "Right after that, Kenneth left, then I walked home and slept practically all day." Kaitlyn turned her head toward Jim and suddenly seemed distracted. "Pastor Jim, I'm pretty sure Kenneth knows God. In fact, I know he does."

"He always seems so calm," Brooke added. "So confident, like he's got it all under control."

"He certainly seems to have a relationship with the Lord," Jim said.

"I don't think you know what I mean," Kaitlyn said. "This is why I came to see you, Pastor Jim. This may sound a little crazy, but when I say I think he knows God, I mean he knows knows him. Like he has personal access to him."

"You're not the only one that thinks that," Macey said, reaching out to put her hand over Kaitlyn's before repeating herself. "You're not the only one."

TWENTY-EIGHT

Ian Tobias sat in the back corner booth of Kamren's Grove, sipping at the last couple ounces of a draft beer. He was staring at the second page of the fall dessert menu as different thoughts of Brooke came to mind. His mind registered listings such as Obscene Chocolate Cake, The Monster Vanilla Cookie, and Granny's Apple Crisp Surprise, but all he could imagine was her. He hoped she was all right. She sounded pretty serious on the phone, so he agreed to meet her as soon as he got back in town from Milwaukee.

It'd been just about forever since he'd talked to her, but he'd immediately recognized the number on caller ID. It was good to hear her voice again. She always seemed like such a nice person, and they'd become pretty decent friends before that night . . . when they'd made a really bad decision and ruined it all. She'd been a great employee. It practically broke his heart when the cutbacks came and he had to lay her off from the plant, particularly after she had her little boy. Just about everybody at the plant missed her after she left. Especially him.

"Sweetheart, would you like another?" the waitress asked. She had to be almost eighty years old, and her smile showed off what seemed like a brand-new pair of flawless dentures. He glanced at her name tag and pushed the glass in her direction.

"Ruth, darling, I'll bet you run around here and call all the guys *sweetheart*, don't you?"

"Only the handsome ones," she answered.

"You made my day, Ruth," he said. "If I were ten years younger, you would be in a heap of trouble. Let's have another Budweiser."

"You better cut him off after that one."

He knew the voice. He turned around and there she was.

"Hello, Brooke," he said, standing.

"Hey, Ian." She didn't sound quite as enthused as he was.

"You want something to drink, sweetie?" Ruth asked.

"A Coke, please," Brooke said.

Ian gave her a hug, and it seemed like she was having a hard time hugging back. She sat down across from him in the booth and started fiddling with the salt shaker, like she was afraid to look at him.

"So what've you been up to?" he asked. Not the most original line to break a few years of ice with. "Where you working?"

"I'm doing nails at the mall," she said.

"I missed you after you left," he said. "We had a great crew when you were there."

"Yeah," she said distantly. Ian thought an *I missed you too* would have kind of been nice, but she seemed preoccupied.

Ruth was already back with the Coke and the Budweiser. She called him "sweetheart" again and wanted to know if they wanted an appetizer, which they declined.

"I've got you figured out, Ruth," Ian said, grinning. "You keep calling me sweetheart, thinking I'm going to fatten your tip, don't you?"

"Am I that obvious?" she said with a laugh.

"Shameless," Ian said.

"You always were such a flirt," Brooke said.

Was she really taking him to task for teasing an old waitress? He could flirt with anyone he wanted to—he was a free man. Divorced. Single. Somehow he had to let her know. Part of him had wondered if she'd heard and that's why she'd called.

He cast about for another topic to discuss, waiting for the opportunity to work it in. "Remember that one girl who got drunk and fell off the stage singing karaoke at the Best Western over in Woodhaven?"

"I can't remember her name," Brooke said. "I think it started with a *P* though."

Ian smiled. "She was halfway through 'Summer in the City' and did a back dive into the speakers. But she was so far gone, I don't think she felt a thing."

"It's hard to believe that was six years ago," Brooke said, shaking her head and now tapping her finger on the ketchup bottle. "Unreal."

Ian nodded and took a sip of his beer. "How is your little boy? He's gotta be about five or six by now, isn't he?"

"Almost six," she said. "His name is Alex."

"Growing like a weed?"

"Yeah."

Brooke still hadn't looked at him and hadn't touched her Coke either. He figured the emergency that prompted their get-together either got her tongue or had been falsely categorized.

He waved his hand to get her attention. She finally looked at him with those pretty green eyes.

"What's on your mind, Brooke? Why the call, after so long? You said it was an emergency."

"Alex has leukemia," she said quickly. "I just found out."

It was only two sentences, but Ian wasn't about to complain. He suddenly felt like taking his turn playing with condiments, but he couldn't look away. He could see the lost look in her eyes and wanted to help her. What'd she need? Money?

"What's going to happen?"

"A lot of stuff," Brooke said. "He's started chemotherapy and they are running lots of tests. It's gonna be a tough road, but I know we're going to make it."

"Of course you will," he said. "You have insurance?"

"Yeah. Thankfully."

He breathed a sigh of relief. Lots of people, once they got laid off, had insurance for a while, but after COBRA ran out, they did without.

Brooke took a sip of her Coke and her cell phone rang. She reached in her purse and instead of answering it, silenced the call. Ian suspected he was about to find out what she really wanted.

"You know, Ian," she said. "It's kind of a coincidence that you brought up the night that woman fell off the stage at the Best Western. The second I saw you, I was already thinking about that night."

Ian didn't need the funny look she was giving him to remind him of what else happened that night. He'd had a hard time thinking about anything *but* that since she called.

"She wasn't the only one that was bombed," Brooke said. "So were we."

"Everybody was," he said with a shrug. "It kinda ended up being an interesting night."

"You can say that again," she said, pausing. "You know something, Ian?"

"What's that?"

"We never once talked about what happened between us that night."

"I know," Ian said, realizing how uncomfortable she seemed. "I'm sorry I even brought it up. I wasn't thinking."

"It's all right," she said.

"You should know," he said, "that I'm divorced." He lifted a hand. "I don't want you to think I'm running around behind my wife's back."

"Oh," she said, her eyes widening a bit.

"I mean . . . because we . . . That was a one-time thing for me."

"For me too," she said, looking miserable at the memory.

"I don't want you to think . . ." He sighed. "Whatever. I was drunk. You were drunk. We made a mistake. But other than that, I was a stand-up guy. Unfortunately, my wife went looking for greener pastures."

"I'm sorry," Brooke said.

He was screwing this up. It wasn't going at all the way he'd hoped. He leaned forward. "I've wanted to call you, Brooke. I've thought about you a lot."

"W-wait," she said, lifting both her hands slightly off the table. "You think . . . ? Look. I actually came here to talk about Alex."

"Oh, right," Ian said. "Of course." He felt the slow burn of a blush at his jaw and hoped she wouldn't notice in the dim light. He searched his mind, wondering why the hundred hours of useless

HR training at the plant hadn't covered how to ease the minds of former employees who'd just found out their kids had a life-threatening disease.

"You know how I told you they were going to be doing a lot of tests on him?"

"Yeah."

"They're also gonna be testing me and Alex's father to see if either of us are a bone marrow match for him. I guess it's a long shot, but we're potential candidates for a match."

"You never know," Ian said. "Long shots can happen."

"I need your help with something, Ian."

"Sure. Anything."

"And it's the only thing I'll ever want from you, Ian. I swear."

He stared at her. What was she trying to ask him? "Go on, Brooke," he said, frowning. "Ask me. I'll do whatever I can."

"I hope you can. I hope you're a match for Alex. And that you'd be willing to do whatever it takes to save him."

His mouth went dry. "Ex-excuse me?"

"Ian," she said. "Alex is your son."

• • •

"Shh," Brooke said as she and Alex watched Charlie. They were hiding near the foot pedals of the piano, both of them peeking out, desperate not to be noticed. Alex was totally into the game, but Brooke's mind kept wandering back to Ian, and the expression on his face last night.

Charlie was "it" and Alex was struggling not to laugh as he peeked over each of the individual pews in an effort to find someone. They turned on every light possible to get Charlie to play with them—convincing him that it wouldn't be nearly as dark as during the storm.

He started toward the fellowship hall when Alex yelled out, "Charlie!"

Charlie spun around. His eyes widened and his mouth rounded as he ducked back under the door. He laughed, covered his mouth, and then tiptoed halfway up the center aisle. His head tilted to the front and then to the back of the church before he resumed his walk back toward the altar. Something bumped near the front door. It was Shirley. Charlie stopped and turned his head back toward the main entrance as if he suspected she was kneeling behind the stack of folding chairs in the corner.

"Go save Shirley, she's toast," Brooke whispered. "He's gonna get her."

"I'm gonna scare him," Alex whispered back, crawling out and crouching out of Charlie's view.

"Don't get him too bad," Brooke warned. "Be sweet."

Charlie reached the edge of the stack of chairs and was leaning slowly over the top to peek down at Shirley, who was standing behind them. He began to smile.

"Boo!" Alex yelled, hurtling himself toward his friend and wrapping his arms around Charlie's leg.

Charlie had gasped and jumped, sending Alex into a bout of hysterics. Charlie bent over and quickly picked him up, tickling him.

"Careful with the port, Charlie!" Brooke yelled, walking toward them.

"Aww, it's okay, Mom!" Alex said. "He's not hurting it. I got you, Charlie! I scared you!"

"Is it safe to assume that I am found?" Shirley asked from behind the chairs.

"Yeah. Come on out, Mrs. Lindy!" Alex said, taking notice of the odd way in which Charlie was looking at him. "He's worried about me now, Mom. You got him all afraid."

Charlie squinted and then lowered his chin to the top of Alex's head. He cradled him and then rocked him back and forth.

"You're so sweet, Charlie," Brooke said, leaning her head on his massive arm.

"What are you doing, Charlie?" Alex asked, sounding embarrassed at his mother's sentiment. "I'm not that sick. I'm okay."

Brooke's head lifted off Charlie's arm. She looked up toward the front of the church. "I think my cell phone is ringing."

"I think you're right," Shirley said.

Brooke ran up to the first pew and pulled the phone out of her purse. "Hello." She glanced back at Shirley and held up her hand.

It was the call she had been waiting for.

Ian.

● ● ●

Ian sat in his gray Ford Explorer in the parking lot of St. Thomas. He stared up the hill at the light pouring through the glass of the church's front doors.

He looked at his watch for the fifteenth time. Six thirty.

Time to head up.

He stepped out of the Explorer, buttoned up his coat, put his hands in his pockets, and started slowly up the stairs, deciding to abandon all of the lines he had just rehearsed.

He stopped in front of the church doors. The last time he'd been here, he was with David Mills for sixth-grade Vacation Bible School. He had memorized all of the books of the New Testament and had won a fancy Bible. He remembered taking the Bible home and reading it for three hours until the novelty of it wore off in the middle of a blockade of Old Testament names.

He opened one of the doors and stepped inside. The door shut behind him with a loud click that seemed to echo in the mostly empty hall. Four people turned around to stare at him from the first pew.

Brooke and an older woman both stood. And then there was the big guy he remembered from Vacation Bible School. But his eyes were on the small boy, kneeling on the pew with his elbows on top of the backrest, looking back at him. He realized that he'd been thinking about Alex like something he'd forgotten and had to go and collect. But the little kid wasn't a pair of gloves he'd accidentally left at the airport. This kid was his son.

But I didn't know.

Brooke and the older woman walked down the aisle, and

Brooke gave him a hug. He was introduced to Shirley, but his eyes were on his son. *My son.*

"Did you tell him?" Ian asked, pointing up at Alex.

"Not yet," Brooke answered.

"And what's the big guy's name? I remember him from when I was a kid."

"Charlie," Brooke said. "He and Alex are best friends."

"If you don't mind, I would like to tell Alex myself," Ian said, unbuttoning his coat. He took a deep breath and ran his hand across his forehead. "Wow. This is crazy."

"Everything is going to work out," Brooke said, taking Ian's arm. She sounded more confident than he felt.

"It has to work out," he said.

"It will," Brooke said.

The three walked up to the front of the church and stopped at the first pew, where Alex and Charlie were sitting. They both looked up at Ian.

"Charlie, this is Ian," Brooke said. Charlie stood, and the awe was no less for Ian than it had been twenty-five years ago. The only difference was that Charlie had gone from maybe six foot six to nearly seven feet tall.

"It's good to see you, Charlie," Ian said, smiling and holding out his hand. He suddenly remembered from VBS that a response wasn't likely to come. *He's only fifteen? Look how tall he is. Hey, guys—the big kid can't talk.*

Charlie took his hand gently and then let it go.

Brooke gestured toward Alex. "And this is Alex."

Alex looked up at him, and Ian's first instinct was to hug him. But he couldn't. He recognized the boy's hair. He'd also seen the button nose and the oversized Tobias ears. He had seen this child before, because he was looking at a five-year-old version of himself. He remembered one of his mother's favorite photographs, the one where he was sitting on Santa's lap at the Kiwanis Christmas party. He looked at Brooke and then back to Alex—back to his son. Ian squinted, and his mouth slowly opened and closed like he was a fish out of water. The resemblance was uncanny. That little boy had jumped out of his mother's favorite photo and onto the first pew of St. Thomas's sanctuary.

He turned to Brooke, who looked like she wanted to cry, but Shirley beat her to it. Brooke kneeled in front of Alex and said, "This man wants to talk to you, Alex."

"About what?" Alex asked. "Is he a doctor too?"

"No, baby," Brooke said.

"Why is Mrs. Lindy crying?" Alex asked. Shirley edged away.

Brooke took Charlie's hand. "Shirley, Charlie and I are going to go sit in the back so you two can talk. Okay, buddy?"

"Why?" Alex asked.

"Ian has something to tell you, Alex."

Alex shrugged and looked at Ian. "Okay."

Ian took his coat off and sat down next to Alex as the others moved off. "I'm really not sure what to say to you, Alex."

Alex stared back at him. "Who are you?" he demanded, looking suspicious.

Ian found it interesting that Alex's question seemed to pierce the heart of the matter. He leaned closer to his son and tried to answer. "I am friends with your mom." He lifted his hand and held it out. "Let's start with a handshake, okay? My name is Ian Tobias."

Alex shook his hand and looked up at him. "That's a funny name."

"I agree with you," he said. "I don't want you calling me that, though."

"Okay," Alex said in a way that Ian felt was a bit indifferent, as if the boy was already losing interest in him. Alex looked back at his mother and then to Ian. "What do you want me to call you?"

"How about *Dad*?"

"I don't have a dad," Alex said, turning quickly back to his mother again. "I don't have a grandma and grandpa either."

Reading bedtime stories, playing catch, playing baseball, teaching a child how to ride a bike—things a father was supposed to do—danced through Ian's mind like single frames of a black-and-white movie. He put his hand on Alex's shoulder. "Yes, you do."

"I do?"

"It's me, Alex. I'm your dad."

Alex propped himself up on the heels of his palms. "Really?"

"Really."

Ian noticed the peculiar way Alex stared at him. The boy's eyes suddenly rounded as if a five-dollar bill had just dropped out of a birthday card. Alex stood up on the pew cushion and yelled, "Hey, Mom! He's my dad!"

"Yes, he is, buddy," Brooke said, patting her hands on top of the pew in front of her and rising to join them again.

Alex pulled down the top of his shirt and pointed to his port. "I have this for my medicine."

Ian smiled at Brooke as she approached and then at their son. "Yes, you do, Alex."

"I have leukemia and get chemo syrupy."

Ian dared to put his arm around Alex, pulling him a little closer. He wished he could pull him into his arms.

"Are you all right?" Brooke asked.

"Yeah!" Alex said excitedly, clearly not realizing Brooke was talking to Ian.

"How about you?" Brooke asked, nodding at Ian.

Ian looked up at her and then over to Alex. "Never better," he said. And deep down, he meant it.

TWENTY-NINE

Y ou are Jesus." There was no doubt in Jim's mind. He knew exactly who Kenneth was and wasn't the least bit shy about telling him.

Kenneth stared at him for a few long seconds, then finally nodded. "I didn't think it would take you long to figure it out, James."

Jim smiled. "Shirley had you pegged too."

The carpenter grinned and then gave a little tug on Jim's tie. "And you make a good Fred Flintstone. Better lay off Shirley's fudge."

"Can't. Wilma makes the best in the county," Jim said.

The two had just sat down in the last pew of the church, and Jim could hear Bobby Boris Pickett's "Monster Mash" entertaining the partygoers over in the fellowship hall. The second he had spotted the man wearing the cheap, brown cotton beard, T-shirt, blue jeans, terrycloth bathrobe, and sandals, he couldn't wait to invite the carpenter over for a little chat.

"Best costume goes to Charlie, though," Kenneth said. "It's kind of hard not to vote for a seven-foot tin man."

"I don't know. I kind of liked Dr. Norman's Elvis," Jim said, "but I'm a little partial, so I'll make mine a swing vote."

Jim thought about how Alex had laughed when Charlie had his turn at "Pin the Tail on the Donkey." It had become "Pin the Tail on the Donkey Eight Feet to the Right of the Donkey." Just remembering his giggles made Jim smile; he was thankful they could have this party and bring so many people together for good family fun. But he had bigger things on his mind.

"You know, Kenneth," Jim said, "you have some people around here, myself included, thinking some pretty unconventional things."

"Unconventional, huh?" Kenneth asked, pulling the beard down below his chin and scratching his upper lip. "I personally like the unconventional."

"Me too," Jim said. "More and more."

Kenneth narrowed his eyes and smiled. "Something specific on your mind, James?"

Jim shrugged, then fidgeted with his tie. "I think you are blessed. I believe you have a gift."

Kenneth picked up a hymnal and leafed through the pages. "Everyone's blessed, James. Everyone has gifts."

"You know what I'm speaking of," Jim said, his tone slightly chiding. "7:16? How could you possibly know when I would see?"

Kenneth's smile grew.

"It was no accident. And I believe that you were talking about Alex and Brooke with Luke 8:50. Correct?"

"Time will tell, right?"

Jim studied him, a little disappointed he couldn't get the man to give him a direct answer. "Macey said there was a woman at the hospital who came out of a coma, and she seems to think you were somehow involved. Then, both she and Zach, two very smart people, think that the cross couldn't possibly be fixed . . . and I think that maybe Charlie was trying to tell me the same thing. Then last night, even Kaitlyn . . ." He paused. "I'm sorry, I'm blabbering."

"No, not at all," Kenneth said. "Please go on."

"Look. I am a man of God," Jim said after taking a deep breath. "And I'm not sure what to say to these people when they ask me about the things that have been happening. Christ himself said, 'Unless you people see signs and wonders, you will by no means believe.'"

"Not you," Kenneth said quickly. "Not you."

Jim shook his head. "I'm surprised you didn't tell me which verse that was."

"John 4, verse—"

"I know you know the verse," Jim said, shaking his head in humility. "Why do you think the Lord allowed me to see? I mean, kids are sick. Kids are dying. There is a war going on somewhere all the time. There are so many things happening that are more important than my sight."

"Says who?" Kenneth asked, leaning forward to rest his elbows on his knees, hands clasped.

"Says me," Jim answered. The sounds of the party seemed to fade as Kenneth stared over at him, connecting with him.

Kenneth tugged at the beard again, exposing the thin rubber band that ran up his cheek into his thick brown hair. "You are an incredible witness, James—with or without your sight. You are and always have been."

"Who are you?" Jim asked, wanting—*needing*—to know how the carpenter seemed to be at the center of all these happenings. "How do you get the visions? How do you know what's going to happen? Does it come straight from the Lord?"

"I guess you could say that," Kenneth said calmly.

"Why didn't you want me to tell anyone that you knew what time I would be able to see?"

"Because that isn't important."

"But I want to tell the whole world about God's glory. I want to talk about the Lord's incredible works."

"You already do," Kenneth said.

The earnest look in his eyes took Jim's breath away for a second. *It's like I'm really staring into the eyes of Jesus. The man is touched. Gifted by God. I can see it in his eyes!*

"I would give up my sight right now for Alex's health," Jim said. "Right now, this very second."

"I believe that," Kenneth said, leaning toward Jim and lowering his voice. "But you don't have to do that. Tell her—tell Brooke to only believe, and Alex will be made well."

"She does believe. I know it, Kenneth, I know it."

"Yes, she does," Kenneth said.

"How do you know?" Jim asked.

Kenneth smiled. "I just do."

"Praise God," Jim whispered.

Kenneth nodded. "Praise him, indeed." He smiled again. "Should we get back to the party? I saw some Special Dark chocolate bars in there."

Jim laughed under his breath. "I'm talking with a man who knows everything about everyone, past, present, and future, and all he wants is some dark chocolate?"

"Best thing on earth," Kenneth said, standing.

"Not better than a good Reese's cup," Jim said, standing too. "But can I ask you one more question?"

"Of course," Kenneth said.

"You sure seem to be taking quite an interest in a lot of people around here."

"Yes," Kenneth said. "And?"

Jim opened one of the fellowship hall doors, and the noise from the party seemed to bounce off them. He raised his voice so the carpenter could hear. "Kaitlyn said you were there at the bridge. In the dark. I don't like talking out of school, but my gut tells me you somehow saved her."

"Something like that," Kenneth said.

"And Macey . . . well, she actually thinks that you—"

"Macey Lewis," Kenneth interrupted, scanning the crowd for her. "She sees things as they are. She is very intuitive, very perceptive. Maybe even more perceptive than you are, James."

Jim wasn't offended by his words. It gave him hope for the doctor. "I think it's great that you're using your gift to be a witness for the Lord. That you're establishing personal relationships with all of these people, myself included. We're really glad you're here." Jim felt something strange race through his chest as the carpenter looked at him with his warm, green eyes.

"That's all I've ever wanted, James," he said, pulling his beard back into place and smiling. He rested a hand on his chest. "It's all I'll *ever* want."

THIRTY

B rooke sat next to Shirley on the couch, only partially listening to her chat with Ian, as everyone else in the house slept.

It had been a draining, strange couple weeks since the harvest party, with Ian coming by every day, sometimes twice a day, to be with Alex and go to chemo treatments and other appointments.

Ian hadn't been shy about letting everyone know he didn't have the faintest idea how to be a father. But the general consensus was that he was doing a pretty good job, and Brooke found herself wondering if maybe Ian was a little *too* good at it.

All she heard lately was "Dad this" and "Dad that."

Last week when her son, *their* son, had refused to let her tuck him in for the night and insisted that Ian do it, the only thing that eased the hurt was the look on Alex's face when Ian came into the bedroom. Stubborn as she was, nothing melted her heart like Alex's joy. Especially now.

But that didn't keep her from secretly hoping that Ian would do something that Alex didn't like. Maybe it would bring the hero worship down a notch or two. Make a little room for her again.

She thought about the questions that kept her on guard. How could she possibly let Alex be around a man whose morals were loose enough to allow him to have an affair on his wife? But she was as much to blame as he was. And if she was a different woman now, couldn't he be different too?

She looked at Ian as he sat in Pastor Jim's La-Z-Boy. They had agreed that they didn't want to be a couple, but they both wanted to be good parents.

Parents, Brooke. As in plural.

Alex now had two. It was harder to get used to than she thought it would be. Half of her had expected him to give his marrow sample to see if he was a match and then run. Becoming a dad? An involved dad? That really hadn't entered her mind. And as much as she was struggling with it, she knew it was good—really good—for Alex.

My issue. Not his. Don't make it his.

"Thanks for being here, Ian," Brooke said softly, interrupting the conversation.

"Will you quit saying that?" Ian said, giving her a playful frown. "I want to be here."

"I know you do," Brooke said, trying to hide a small sigh with a fake yawn.

"So, let me get this right," Shirley said. She tossed a kernel of popcorn in her mouth and passed the bowl to Brooke. "They're gonna do a platelet transfusion if the chemo lowers Alex's white blood cell count too much?"

"Yes," Ian said. That was another good thing about him being here. Ian asked lots of questions, and he seemed to understand practically everything Macey talked about, even when the doctor was going a million miles an hour.

"So we should be concerned if they have to do that?" Shirley said, pulling her feet up on the couch and wrapping them in a quilt.

"No, not at all," Ian said. "Macey says it happens all the time."

Brooke heard the bathroom door click shut, back in the hallway.

"I guess I don't understand all of it," Shirley said. "But either way, from what everyone says, it sounds like Macey is the perfect doctor for Alex."

Brooke leaned forward and listened for the bathroom. She had a feeling it was Alex.

"I just wish they could get his white blood cell count down to where they want it."

"What did Macey say about that?" Shirley asked.

"She said it wasn't that unusual," Brooke said.

"Okay," Shirley said. "So what's next?"

"They're changing up his regimen slightly."

"His regimen?"

"Yeah," Ian said. "They changed the combination of drugs they're giving him to lower his white blood cell count, and if it knocks it down too much, that's when they will give him the platelet transfusion."

"I think I understand," Shirley said. "How long are they going to keep doing all the chemo and testing?"

"That's what we're still not sure about," Brooke said.

Ian looked over his shoulder. "Is that Alex in the bathroom?"

"I think so," Brooke said. "I'll give him another couple minutes."

Shirley turned to Brooke. "Didn't you say you guys are both getting tested for something Friday?"

"To see if either of us are a marrow match," Brooke answered. "That's what Kaitlyn told me. But I guess the odds of me or Ian being a match for Alex are like a gazillion to one." Brooke glanced back at the empty hallway.

"Want me to check on him?" Ian asked, following her gaze.

"I got it." Brooke pushed back a wave of irritation. *He's just trying to help.* She went down the hallway to the bathroom door. "Is everything okay in there, Alex?"

There was no answer. She knocked lightly on the door. "Alex, are you in there?"

"Yeah," a small voice said, muffled behind the door.

"What are you doing, buddy?" Brooke asked. "Are you okay?"

"Yeah," Alex said faintly. "I'm trying to go potty."

"You sure have been in there awhile. You want me to come in?"

"I'm okay," he said. "Is my dad still here?"

"He is," Brooke said, pressing her ear to the door. "Are you sure you're okay?"

"Yeah."

"Yell if you need me. Okay?"

"All right."

Brooke walked back into the living room and dropped on the couch. "It's Alex."

"Is he okay?" Ian asked.

"I think so. I'll give him a few more minutes and then check on him again."

Ian looked at his watch. "I should probably get going in a bit."

Shirley grabbed the bowl and scooped up the popcorn that had spilled onto the couch. "I better get to bed. Before I know it, James will be doing his 5:00 a.m. rattling thing in the kitchen, waking the whole house up."

"You're probably right," Brooke said, smiling.

Shirley gave Brooke a quick squeeze and smiled over at Ian. "Everything's going to be all right, you guys. Remember what James said?"

"Only believe," Brooke said.

"I like that," Ian said.

Brooke hugged Shirley tightly, stood, then headed back down the hall. The bathroom door was still closed. She tapped on the door. "Alex?"

"Yeah," he answered. He sounded younger this time.

"What are you doing, buddy?"

He didn't say anything.

"Alex, I'm coming in." She tried the door, but it was locked.

"Are they still here?"

"Yes, honey. Unlock the door."

"Are they with you or in the living room?"

"In the living room. Unlock the door."

He fumbled briefly with the doorknob, and then she could hear the lock turn. Brooke slowly opened the door and noticed that the only light was the soft glow of a nightlight that was plugged in near the bottom of the wall.

Alex was by the bathtub with his head down and his hands at his sides.

"What's wrong, buddy?" she asked, still not approaching him. "You don't feel good?"

"It feels like I sunburned my head and . . ." He stopped and covered his face as if he were ashamed. She noticed his shoulders had started to bob. He was crying.

"Alex," Brooke said, kneeling down and hugging him. This was the first time she had seen him cry since he had begun his treatment. The needles, the port, the prodding, the constant orders to be still, the chemo . . .

Everyone had marveled at how well he was taking things. How well he was doing. How brave he was. But he was still only five.

"What, baby? Tell me what's wrong."

"Close the door," he whispered into her shoulder.

"Okay," she said, swinging the door shut behind her.

"It's happening," he whispered.

"What, buddy? What's happening? Tell me."

"Turn the . . ." He paused and lifted his head. "Turn the light on."

Brooke flipped the switch, and they both squinted against the light.

"See it?" Alex asked, climbing the step stool in front of the sink.

Brooke looked in the mirror at their reflection. She couldn't see anything out of the ordinary. "I don't know what you're talking about, Alex. What is it?"

"Really?" he asked, sounding hopeful.

She rose and glanced back in the mirror. There it was. Now she could see it. She looked down at her chest, where Alex's head had been.

"Look," he said, pointing up at her. She could see the hopelessness in his eyes. "See it?"

"I do, baby," she whispered.

Tiny shreds of reddish-orange hair clung to her shirt. She glanced back at Alex's reflection and could see a small tear angling across his cheek. At the base of his neck and around his shoulders, more hair had fallen out, virtually covering the collar of his Spider-Man pajamas.

"I don't want Dad to see it."

"Baby, it's okay."

"Can you tell him that it's because of the chemo?"

She picked him up and hugged him, feeling his wiry arms wrap around her neck, his legs around her torso. She leaned in, inhaling the scent of him, and swallowed the lump in her throat. *You have to sound brave, Brooke. Strong. Positive.* "Remember what they told us, buddy?"

"What?" he said, nestling against her shoulder.

"They said it would grow back. Remember?"

"Are you sure?"

"Yes, I'm sure."

"You promise?"

"Yeah, baby," she said, rubbing his back and kissing the side of his face. "I promise."

THIRTY-ONE

I'm still trying to figure out which genius chef keeps putting green beans on the same plate as pizza," Kaitlyn said, sitting in front of Macey at the East Shore cafeteria. She studied her plate in partial disgust, making sure that none of the beans had the gall to touch either of her two slices.

"What are you, ten years old?" Macey asked, laughing and stabbing at the beans on her plate. "Ever try eating one? They are actually pretty good for you."

"I have no problem with green beans," Kaitlyn said. "I just can't get used to them being served with pizza. It's like ketchup and ice cream. Certain things don't belong together. It's food taboo."

"Look. I'm eating it," Macey said. "It doesn't bother me."

"I've also seen pictures of you diving out of a perfectly good airplane. So that explains that."

"Doesn't sound as weird as hanging out on a dark bridge in the wee hours of the morning," Macey said. "When do I get the full story?"

"Patience, Dr. Lewis," Kaitlyn said. "Trust me when I say it's all good."

Macey began patting at the side of her neck, and Kaitlyn felt goose bumps cover her arms. She turned to face the cafeteria entrance as a rowdy cluster of construction workers trampled through the hallway and then out the main door.

"So Zach asked you to go somewhere with him this weekend?" Macey asked, taking her hand off the back of her neck.

Kaitlyn nodded as she completed the separation between the

260

beans and the pizza. "Just when I was fully prepared to give Zach his newfound space, he asked me to go."

"Space? Like the space you gave him at church on Sunday? Not exactly beans and pizza, Kaitlyn. You were sitting right next to him."

"Shush, Lewis," Kaitlyn said. "Between you and me, I don't think I ever gave him my best. Or gave the hospital my best for that matter."

"Nurses don't get better than you, Kait."

"I'm going to do better."

"I don't see how that's possible, but it sounds good. So what are you and Zach going to do?"

"I'm not sure," Kaitlyn said. "But he told me it would explain some things. He also said to wear old clothes."

"Explain some things?" Macey asked. "Like what?"

"I'm not sure."

"I knew you were going to go out with him again," Macey said.

"Zip it, Lewis. Before I sic HR on you."

"I'm allowed to harass you whenever I want," Macey said, her eyebrows furrowing. She looked around the room as if confused, then up at the ceiling. "What's that buzzing sound?"

"I don't hear anything," Kaitlyn said. She put her fork down and laced her fingers together. "But on the Zach thing, I didn't think I'd ever want to spend time with him outside of the hospital again, Macey. I was sure of it. I know it hasn't been that long, but something's different about him, don't you think? It's like a switch was flipped."

"You won't get any argument from me," she said. "He's way more focused on the kids here, less self-centered. And who would've ever guessed that he'd be in church three weeks in a row? Heck—*once*, for that matter?"

Kaitlyn agreed. "Who would've ever guessed that *we* would be there three weeks in a row?"

"Kenneth," Macey said. "That's who."

"I wonder why Kenneth wasn't there on Sunday?"

"Are you two talking about me again?"

They looked up, and Kenneth was casually standing next to their table, dressed in his usual construction outfit of jeans and a flannel shirt.

"Hello, Kaitlyn," he said. "Hello, Macey."

"Kenneth!" Macey said, choking on her swallow of soda. "Hi."

Kaitlyn looked back up at the carpenter and oddly felt like a child, hanging out with a favorite parent.

He is the buzz Macey was talking about.

"We were just saying that we didn't see you at church on Sunday," Macey added.

"Interesting," Kenneth said as several hospital employees looked over at them. "I was there."

"We didn't see you," Macey said curiously.

"You're right." He nodded, quickly stepping back. "Listen, guys, I didn't mean to interrupt. I saw you two in here, and I wanted to swing in and say hi."

"You're welcome to join us," Macey said.

"Thanks, but I better be going," he said. "The superintendent doesn't really approve of us being in here."

"We have you covered," Macey said. "Please join us."

"I really have to leave," he said, cocking his thumb back over his right shoulder. "But I hope to see you guys again on Sunday. And I'll make sure you see me too." He gave them each a smile, then turned and made his way out the door.

Both women watched as he disappeared around the corner.

"I feel like an idiot," Macey said, tossing her crumpled napkin on the table. "I really didn't know what to say to him. Why didn't you say anything?"

"Don't know," Kaitlyn said. "He probably thinks we are a couple of gossips. Of *course* he walks in right as we're talking about him."

Macey shook her head, grabbed the napkin, and then picked up a piece of pizza. "I don't think he thinks that at all, Kait."

"Maybe," Kaitlyn said, trying to read the strange look on Macey's face. She leaned closer, so she could lower her voice. "I feel like a little kid when he's around."

"Me too," Macey said.

Kaitlyn sipped her Diet Coke. "Don't you think if he was at church, we would have seen him? There were more people, but we would've seen him. Right? Since we were both looking?"

Macey paused. "Not necessarily," she said, giving her a conspiratorial look. She lifted her elbows to the top of the table and leaned forward. "Maybe we weren't looking hard enough. In the right *way*."

"What do you mean?" Kaitlyn asked.

"He said he was there," Macey said in a soft voice, sitting back. "You know exactly what I mean."

"Don't even say it." Kaitlyn looked over her shoulder and around to see if anyone was overhearing their crazy talk.

"Fine." Macey looked miffed.

"Listen." Kaitlyn lowered her voice. "Just because I said I think he's linked to God doesn't mean he is God."

"It has nothing to do with what you said."

"Listen. We don't want anybody knowing that the best doctor here thinks that God is a dues-paying member of the local carpenters' union. They'll send you to the eighth-floor psych ward instead of letting you keep working on Three."

"Ha-ha," Macey said. "But back to the church thing. I want to keep going. In fact, I'm going to call Pastor Jim and see if our little group wants to go back to that Pilot Inn for lunch after church this Sunday, my treat. You in? Or would you rather go someplace else in case that idiot Tim guy shows up again?"

"He'll never go back in there again," Kaitlyn said, thinking about the promise she heard Lila make Tim. "And your treat? I'm sure they can probably afford it now. There were more people there this week than last. I figured the hype would've died down."

"Blindness just doesn't up and go away," Macey said. "People want to know what happened. They want to be around a miracle. And then they tell people who tell more people. And Pastor Jim isn't half-bad at preaching."

"You're right," Kaitlyn said. "The day we went for the cross, there were probably twenty people there, tops. How many do you think were there Sunday?"

"Two, maybe three hundred," Macey answered. "Those people in the back stood for the whole hour."

"Pastor Jim keeps them on their toes, though, doesn't he?"

"Yes, he does. He makes me want to try and make more of my life. Live it differently."

"Me too," Kaitlyn said.

Macey finished off her first slice of pizza. "Just like Zach, I'm going to try. I really do want to do better."

"Just like Zach," Kaitlyn repeated. "Go figure."

• • •

Zach lowered the volume on the radio as he and Kaitlyn turned off the Van Horn exit of I-75, a mile north of Carlson. "You ever wonder what it's all about, Kait?" he asked, waving his hand in a sweep across the breadth of the windshield.

"What?" Kaitlyn asked, leaning forward to see what he was talking about.

"Life," he answered. He rolled the driver's side window down a few inches and lifted his cheek closer to feel the crisp air. "It's a perfect day, isn't it?"

It is a beautiful day, Kaitlyn thought. She smiled over at him, as interested in the man beside her and the changes she saw in him as she was in the bright, blue sky outside. "To be honest, Zach, I've been thinking a lot lately."

"Anything specific?"

She paused, studying him. He'd never shown an interest in anything deep before, let alone sought her opinion. Now he seemed more alive to her. "Like you, Zach."

"Like me?" he asked. He looked surprised—maybe even a little pleased—by her sincerity.

"The way you have acted over the last couple of weeks is . . . well, it's inspiring."

"Thanks," he said. "I appreciate that. The truth is that I've been more than inspired. I think I'm changing." He shrugged. "In fact, I'm pretty sure of that."

Kaitlyn studied his smile as he paused. It wasn't forced, like the Dr. Norman smiles she'd become accustomed to.

"I think that is part of the reason I'm with you today," Kaitlyn said. "I can see the difference in you."

"And I want to keep it up," he said. "Do you remember when Pastor Jim was talking to all of us about the past, the present, and the future? And how he pointed out that too many of us are so wrapped up in worrying about things we can't control that we ignore our obligations and blessings in the present?"

"I'm that way sometimes," Kaitlyn said, thinking he'd really never looked more handsome than he did today. "I think about the future all the time."

"There's nothing wrong with that," Zach said. "But the way I see it, *worrying* about the future is where we get into trouble. We should plan, but *start* with planning to do the right things—right now and the future will take care of itself."

"Like what things?"

"The things we're *called* to do, deep down," he said. "And in my case, those things are not all about me. They are about serving others. Like spending more time with each of our patients rather than just seeing them as names on my to-do list. Just doing that alone has made each day so much more . . . meaningful."

"I see that," she said, wondering if he'd missed his calling. He had made his point every bit as well as the minister had.

"And then there is the past," he whispered, giving her a rueful look. "We all make mistakes. All of us. I made a hundred with you. Someday I hope you can forgive me for those. But I had to go further back to deal with something in order to break free of it." He slowed the car down and tapped on the steering wheel. "I wasn't smart enough to realize the obvious."

"What's that?"

"That there's nothing we can do about the past. Blown careers, divorces, opportunities that we missed or didn't handle quite right. The past is over. We can't go back and fix it. We can only accept what it was. And what it wasn't."

She nodded. "You're right—I guess we all make bad choices.

And it's so easy to live every day dwelling on those mistakes that we eat up the now."

"Exactly," he said, nodding. "And the *now* is our only opportunity to be aware—to change. We only have today, and hopefully tomorrow. And we need to do the right things—not just for ourselves but for those around us."

She studied him again. Was he even the same person anymore? "What was it, Zach? The thing in your past? Can you tell me?"

Zach pulled the car over onto the left shoulder of the road and rolled into some high weeds. They were in the middle of nowhere. She thought he was just wanting to focus before he told her what it was.

He put the car in park and turned off the engine. "You of all people deserve an explanation."

"An explanation for what?" Kaitlyn asked.

"For the way I was," he said.

"It's funny you say that, Zach. Because I have an explanation for the way I was as well. And I wanted you to be the first to know."

"I appreciate that," Zach said. "And I figured while we were here, I'd also appreciate if you'd help me fix something up a little bit, if you don't mind."

Here? Kaitlyn leaned across the front seat to look out the driver's side window. "A cemetery?"

"C'mon," he said, giving her a gentle smile. "There's something I need to show you."

● ● ●

Zach watched another tear slip down Kaitlyn's cheek.

She was kneeling at the foot of the grave and hadn't said a word in five minutes. She was wearing faded jeans and an old green and gold sweatshirt that had *Wayne State University* on the front. Her palms were flat on the tops of her legs and the light breeze that flitted through the cemetery tossed a small tuft of hair back and forth across her forehead as she stared at Amy's headstone. To her sides were the grass clippers and tiny rake she had dropped as he had told her about his little sister and the day he met Kenneth at the cemetery.

"Amy is okay," Zach said, placing the flower pot and chrysanthemums on the ground. He crouched and then sat next to Kaitlyn. "I never really knew that until recently."

"Things happen," Kaitlyn whispered, breaking her silence. "Don't they?"

"Yeah," he said. "I guess that's one way of putting it."

"Amy was only ten," Kaitlyn said. She laced her fingers together and paused before taking a deep breath. "Things started happening to me with my dad when I was about that age."

"What kind of things?" Zach said.

Kaitlyn finally turned away from the headstone and looked him in the eye.

"Things," she said.

Something in her eyes that told him exactly what she meant. He would have given away everything he owned to make the pain in her eyes go away. He put his arm around her shoulder and pulled her closer.

"I've got you," he said.

"I was going to ask you why you never told me about Amy," Kaitlyn said. "But obviously there are things I never told you. Things I'd like to tell you now."

"I'm listening," he said.

She leaned her head against his shoulder. "Because of what happened, I never liked myself, Zach. So I guess I needed other people to like me."

"What do you mean?"

"Mostly men."

"Men?"

"Lots of men," she said, lifting her head. "It's weird how we were just talking about living in the past. I've spent my whole life living in the past, trying to figure out why things happened and what I could have done differently. And when I couldn't come up with answers, the solution was for me to drink until I was drunk . . . until I didn't care." She paused and then buried her face in his shoulder before whispering, "And when I said there were lots of men, I mean *lots*."

"Lots of men?" he asked, more surprised about her drinking. "I don't understand. And I've never seen you drunk."

"You haven't," she said. "And never at work. If that ever happens I understand that you will have to do what you have to do. But it won't happen. Like you, Kenneth helped me to start working my way through my pain. My drinking problem was more of a reality problem and though I still don't have all the answers about my past, I have found a solution to help me deal with it. To deal with anything."

"What's that?"

Kaitlyn turned and pointed to their right. "See it?"

"I do," Zach said, remembering seeing it the last time he was at the cemetery. Kaitlyn was pointing at the top of the cross on the other side of the hill.

They were quiet for a couple minutes.

"I'm sorry about all of this," she said.

Zach never felt closer to anyone in his life. He pulled her in closer still and kissed her on her forehead.

"It's okay," he whispered, taking his turn pointing toward the hill. "You don't need my acceptance, but you've got it. All the forgiveness you'll ever need, that any of us will ever need, started right there on that cross. I'm glad I told you the things I did and am even more thankful about what you've shared with me today. Another thing we talked about in the car was how we are supposed to serve others and how we are supposed to be here for one another. I want you to know there is no one higher on my list than you."

She stared at him with wide eyes that were filled with hope. "Really?"

"Yeah," he answered. "Like you said, things happen. The past is over with and there is nothing we can do about it."

"And we have right now, don't we?"

He winked at her and said, "And a pretty bright future as well."

Her eyes lit up and she smiled. And right there he would have given away everything he owned to make it last forever.

THIRTY-TWO

For many people, The Pilot Inn was too loud.
Not for Jim.

The sound of it all, the *sight* of it all—he loved every second.

In the diner, there were older couples, younger couples, some of their children, and what seemed to be quite a few of their children's children. They laughed, smiled, and mouthed words over plastic wicker baskets of French fries, chicken strips, hamburgers, and clear plastic pitchers of different-colored sodas.

Returning from the restroom, he saw that the areas around the pool tables, dartboards, and jukebox were primarily clusters of college-aged kids and other twentysomethings who wielded single bottles of beer or mixed drinks. His smile weakened as he looked up at the bar at the patrons who *had* to be there—the regulars. These were the ones who gave up their lives to an alternative higher power. *Lord, help them*, he thought, glancing up at the faded lights along the mirror behind the bar, mercifully dimming the reflections of the ghosts who hopelessly stared back at it.

"Man, we suck!" someone yelled in a hoarse voice behind him.

Jim turned around and watched a replay of the pass that had put the Detroit Lions down fourteen to zero only five minutes into the game. He looked up at the TV. It wasn't the one-handed catch that amazed him. It was the size of that television. He walked under it and through the swinging doors, returning to the dining room. What a day it had been. After church, they had anonymously dropped off four carloads of food, clothing, and a generous envelope to Cash Baylee's food bank over in Rockwood, and now sat with hot burgers and chicken fingers awaiting them all.

"Isn't this fun, James?" Shirley said, taking his hand as he returned to his seat next to her. "What are you looking at?"

"Everything," he said, looking around at the table full of loved ones, as well as those beyond them. "Absolutely everything."

"Do you want to say grace?" she asked.

"Of course. Shall we give thanks?" He lifted his hands. Shirley took his left hand again, and Macey took his right. The rest of the table followed suit, and they all dropped their heads.

Only Macey, Shirley, Brooke, and Kenneth could hear him saying the prayer in the bustling diner, but it didn't matter. Every one of them felt it, Jim believed. Down at the far end, Ian, Kaitlyn, Zach, Alex, and Charlie looked up a moment after they'd said their amens.

We're so blessed, Lord, he thought. *So blessed. Thank you, Lord. Whatever comes, thank you for this day.*

• • •

"Quit patronizing me," Macey said playfully. Jim looked to his left over Macey's shoulder at Kenneth. The carpenter wasn't talking. He was nodding his head and listening to the young doctor. Macey had told Jim that she was going to ask Kenneth some interesting questions; apparently, she'd already started.

"What?" Kenneth said. "You asked me how I fixed the cross, and I told you."

Macey rocked in her seat. "I need a better answer than 'God-given ability.'"

"What else would I need?" he asked. "It seems like you've been given an ability in your line of work."

"I studied to learn what I do," Macey said. "I think what you did was a miracle."

Kenneth threw his hands up. "It was."

"Will you please stop?" Macey said. "It's driving me crazy how that cross went up so fast."

271

"Will I please stop?" Kenneth said, repeating her question and nudging her with his shoulder. "I don't think so."

Macey nudged back. "Seriously, Kenneth, you seem to be at the center of the miracle fest. Of everything that is good."

"That's because I am—"

"Well, well, well. What do you know," a smoke-rasped voice barked from only a few feet inside the front door. Tim Shempner with a couple of drunken buddies at his sides. "Lookie here. Look who's back! The Pilot bimbo and her band of Coke-drinking Jesus freaks!" He took a step forward. "Where's the big retard today?"

Jim froze. Lila and her baseball bat were off for the day, so Shempner had dared to return.

The diner quieted as Shempner walked up behind Kaitlyn and tugged sharply at the back of her hair. He looked like he'd been up all night and reeked of booze and sour body odor. He and his friends slid into an empty booth behind Kaitlyn.

Zach stood.

"Relax, Romeo!" Shempner shouted. "Where's the waitress? We need some menus!"

Jim pushed back his seat to stand and approach the drunken man, but Kenneth put a hand on his shoulder.

Kaitlyn turned around and faced Shempner with her shoulders back and a neutral expression on her face. Jim admired her strength.

"Why do you have to be this way?" Kaitlyn said. "Stay and eat, but remember this is the *family* side of The Pilot Inn . . . not the bar."

"Shut up," Shempner said, belching. "I don't need your permission for anything."

A waitress tentatively came over and handed three menus to the men. She took their orders for beers and shots and hurried off to the kitchen.

Kaitlyn sat down, sighing while fiddling with a French fry. Shempner and his buddies hunched together, talking.

Shempner rose and leaned over Kaitlyn's shoulder, took a fry, and popped it into his mouth, giving the rest of the table an insolent look.

Zach was visibly clenching his jaw, ready to pounce at any moment.

"I've got this, Zach. Don't move," Kaitlyn said. She turned around and looked Shempner in the eye. "Please leave us alone, Tim."

"And if I don't?" He leaned down and pushed her hair over her shoulder, looking at her neck like he wanted to kiss it. "Lila isn't here to save you today!"

"She doesn't have to be here to save me," Kaitlyn said, brushing aside his hand. "Now I'm going to ask you one more time. Please stop."

"*Pleeeaaase . . . pleeeeaaaase,*" Shempner whined, mocking Kaitlyn. "I'll make you say—"

"That's enough!" someone yelled.

Jim looked up. It was Ian.

He was about five feet from Shempner. Charlie and Alex had followed him back from the video games and were standing behind him.

"And you are?" Shempner asked.

"I'm Ian Tobias. And I think you're leaving."

"Only after I kick your butt!" Shempner ground out, getting in Ian's face.

"I love getting my butt kicked," Ian said, a confident smile creasing his lips. "Let's head out back."

Shempner paused. One of his buddies let a cackle slip, which was followed up with the muted sound of laughter. Tim hesitated.

"That's what I thought," Ian said quietly. "Such a big man with *women*. But not so fast to take on another man. Now, apologize to Kaitlyn and to everyone at our table. No. Make that the entire diner." He turned to pick up Alex.

Shempner grinned and lunged forward, kicking Ian's back. Ian's head snapped back and his arms fanned out, sending him sprawling forward. His arm hit Alex's chest, and the boy went flying backward.

"No!" Brooke screamed, jumping up from the other side of the table.

Panic flooded Charlie's face. He dropped to a knee and put his hand behind Alex's head, who was gasping for the air that had just been knocked out of him.

Ian brought himself to one knee as Macey, Kaitlyn, and Zach raced to Alex's side opposite Charlie. "We've got him now, Charlie," Macey said. "We'll help him. Don't worry." Charlie rose and backed away.

"Look at my finger, Alex," Macey said, calmly holding her hand up in front of his face. "Look at my finger. Look right here."

"Alex?" Zach said.

"He's all right," Macey said, sensing pressure from the circle of bystanders that had formed around them. She pulled the top of Alex's shirt back down. "The port's okay."

"Please," Jim said, trying to create some space. People were spilling over from the bar side to gather around. "Please, friends, please. She's a doctor. Pull back."

"He's going to kill him!" a young woman yelled. "Help!"

"Somebody do something!" another voice cried.

"James!" Shirley shouted from behind him. "*James!*"

Jim turned from Alex and looked at the center of yet another circle that had formed. It was something he'd never imagined. *No.*

"Charlie!" he yelled, working his way quickly through the crowd to the edge of the other circle. "Charlie, no!"

Charlie's lips were coiled back and his teeth were gritted. His exhales were not breaths, but intermittent growls that were clearly frightening people. His arms were perfectly straight in front of him and vibrated only with the thrashing of the weight they held.

Charlie had Tim Shempner by the throat.

Shempner's boots kicked and dangled in the air as Charlie served as both executioner and gallows. Shempner clawed at Charlie's hands until they bled, desperately seeking release.

"No, son!" Jim said. "Charlie, no!"

Shempner's face became a light shade of purple as Charlie lifted him higher in the air.

"Charlie!" Jim yelled again, reaching up and pulling down on Charlie's arm. He could see the veins pulsing in his son's hands and forearms, as well as his temples.

"Alex is okay!" Shirley yelled, coming to his other side. "Look, Charlie! Look!"

"Alex is okay!" Jim echoed, still pulling on Charlie's closest arm with all his weight, desperate now. *Please, Lord, don't let him kill him. Please, Lord. . .*

Charlie looked down at his father, then at his mother, and then back toward where Alex was. Alex was now on his feet, standing between Ian and Brooke. Kaitlyn handed Alex his ball cap, and Alex put it back on. Alex then rubbed the tears from his eyes and shook his head in disapproval at Charlie.

Charlie stared back at Shempner, giving him a message that words could never say. Shempner's hands dropped to his sides, and he was slobbering at the corners of his mouth when Kenneth reached up and took Charlie by the wrist.

"It's okay, Charlie," the carpenter said. Charlie immediately let go, and Shempner fell to the floor like a rag, bringing his own hands to his throat and gasping for air.

"Way to kick his butt, big man!" somebody yelled.

"Please, no," Jim said, holding up his hands. "Please."

Charlie turned toward Alex, and everybody got out of his way. He walked over and Alex held out his arms for a hug. Charlie picked him up, and Alex rested his head on his shoulder. Charlie lowered his cheek to the top of Alex's head, and they both closed their eyes as if they were equally glad it was over.

• • •

Macey and Kenneth sat back down at the table. She realized her hands were trembling when she reached for her glass of water. "Unreal, huh?" she said to him.

"Looked pretty real to me," Kenneth said calmly. "Nice work, with Alex."

"He's lucky. *Very* lucky."

"What if he wasn't?" Kenneth asked, taking a sip of his own water as everyone began returning to their own tables.

"What's that supposed to mean?" Macey asked.

"What if you couldn't help him?"

"I don't know," Macey said, frowning. "What kind of question is that?"

"What if your best wasn't good enough, Macey Lewis? What would you do?"

"Are you messing with me again?"

"I wasn't messing with you before," Kenneth said. "I thought maybe you should think about that."

Macey squinted and tilted her head. "Don't you think that's kind of an odd thing to say?"

"No, Macey," Kenneth said. He stood and walked around the other side of the table. "Kaitlyn saying I took a magic carpet to visit Mary Springsted is an odd thing to say."

Macey glanced up at him. "What did you just say?"

He put his palms flat on the table and smiled. "I think you heard me."

"But there is no way you could have possibly . . ." Macey stopped and then just stared, stone-faced, as the carpenter turned and walked out the door.

THIRTY-THREE

Macey stepped into the consultation room, and the first thing she saw was Ian, balancing Alex on his left knee. Like father, like son—the two of them wore matching smiles that reminded her of a ventriloquist act. Ian would make up for his absence in Alex's life. He already had, in an important way.

"Good morning, guys," Macey said. She shook Brooke's hand and then Ian's. "How is your back feeling?"

Ian reached his hand around his side and tapped it. "It only took three days, but it's like new."

Macey tilted her head and gave him a look that said she knew better. "That was quite a kick you took. Are you pressing charges?"

"Nah," Ian said. "Everything turned out all right. I think that Tim Shempner guy has enough problems already. And if I press charges, he might retaliate by pressing charges against Charlie. What's Kaitlyn going to do about him?"

"Got a restraining order," Macey said, lifting a copy of *Highlights* off a seat before sitting down. "He can't come within five hundred feet of her."

"Good," Brooke said. "Thank God."

"That may be in everyone's best interest for now—particularly until he gets the help he obviously needs."

Ian looked at Brooke in a way that said he was more than okay with the outcome. "Maybe what Shempner needs most is Charlie's kind of help."

"Yeah," Alex said attentively. "Charlie kicked his butt, huh?"

"Alex!" Brooke said.

Ian swallowed a grin and tapped on Alex's baseball cap. "Hey, you."

Alex looked up at his father. "That's what that man said at—"

"We don't talk that way, partner."

"Okay, Dad. I'm sorry."

Brooke smiled at Macey, who winked back at her. The doctor guessed it was probably the six hundredth time that Alex had used the word *dad* in just under a week. And those were only the ones she was around to hear.

Macey leaned forward in her chair and put her elbows on her knees. "And how about you, Mr. Alex? How're you feeling?"

"I'm pretty good," Alex said.

She could see that he appeared a little more drawn than usual. Despite his upbeat tone, he was a bit peaked. "It's okay if you're not feeling well. You can tell me."

"I'm a little sleepy sometimes," he said.

"That's okay," Macey assured him.

"He hasn't been himself the last couple of days," Brooke said. "He also threw up last night."

Macey nodded, not surprised. "I have some news for you guys."

"Lay it on us," Ian said, wrapping his arms around Alex.

"We already have Alex's results back from today. We also have the parental blood test results back."

"Okay," Ian and Brooke said together.

"First," Macey said, "Alex's white blood cell count came down, which is encouraging. So we will go ahead today with the same regimen." She smiled at Ian. "And second, even though it's extremely rare, and we need to run a few more tests, we believe we have a marrow match for Alex. It's also convenient that this person is local—really local."

"Kind of like you're-lookin'-at-him local?" Ian asked calmly, his eyebrows bunching together.

"Are you serious?" Brooke said, her mouth dropping open.

"Yes," Macey said. "Congratulations."

"That's good news for us, partner," Ian said, pulling down on the bill of Alex's cap, who quickly readjusted it.

"Yes, it is," Macey said. "We are extremely fortunate to have you as a potential match. Having a marrow transplant as an option is an incredible advantage. If needed, that is."

"Thank you, God!" Brooke said, squeezing her knees together and looking thankfully at the ceiling. "Thank you, God. Thank you, God."

"Thank you, God," Ian repeated. He lowered his chin to the top of Alex's head and met the doctor's eyes. She guessed that he was thinking about the last five—almost six—years and about all the gifts he'd never given Alex.

And now he had the one his son may need the most.

• • •

A week later, Ian joined Pastor Jim at the window in the Lindy living room. It was getting dark, and the year's first snow was fluttering straight down in thick, quarter-sized flakes.

"It's beautiful," Pastor Jim said. "I haven't seen snow in such a long time."

Brooke and Shirley entered the living room. They'd been with Alex.

"How is he doing?" Ian asked.

Shirley looked outside. "The chemotherapy seems to be hitting our little man a bit harder this week."

Charlie came into the living room, and Ian noticed that even the big guy seemed stressed.

Ian went down the hallway to Alex's bedroom. His son was lying on his side, asleep. He looked milky and thinner than he had a week earlier—for that matter, since just that morning. Ian sat in the chair next to the bed, stared at him a moment, and then closed his eyes. It was hard to believe that less than a month ago, he'd been sitting in that little pub back in Milwaukee, swapping divorce horror stories with some bartender he'd never see again. They'd gotten into a big discussion. About important things. Topics he couldn't remember now.

About things I thought were important.

He ran his hand across the top of Alex's head, wondering how his son had coped all this time without a dad. He'd had Pastor Jim, which made Ian thankful. *But it's not the same.* It wasn't fair, for the kid to have to go through all of this, but that was going to change. He was going to help Brooke give Alex the life he deserved.

"Fatherhood," Pastor Jim said quietly, standing in the bedroom doorway. "It's good stuff."

"Yes, it is," Ian said.

"He's a little sicker than normal, eh?"

"Looks that way," Ian said, pulling the blanket up to Alex's shoulders.

"He'll be made well," Pastor Jim said. Ian liked the way he said it. It sounded like it was already done.

"Pastor Jim," Ian said, "can I talk to you about something?"

"Sure. Anything." The tall man took a seat on a kid-sized stool and Ian smiled at the sight of it. But Pastor Jim looked like there was no place he'd rather be.

"I remember you from when I was eleven or twelve years old," Ian said, keeping his voice down so he wouldn't wake Alex. "And I certainly couldn't forget Charlie."

Pastor Jim smiled. "He's hard to forget, isn't he? In more ways than one."

"I know a lot of people aren't going to forget him at The Pilot Inn. It's not too often that a grown man is picked up off the ground by his throat."

Pastor Jim grimaced and nodded. "I really don't know why, but Mr. Shempner has never been too kind to Charlie. And obviously, Charlie never did anything about it . . . until then."

"He was just protecting Alex."

"Absolutely," Pastor Jim said. "Though I don't condone what happened, I suspect Mr. Shempner won't be coming up to our table for a while."

"I think you're right," Ian said. He would never admit it to Pastor Jim, but a part of him—a really big part of him—got a nice charge out of the look on Tim Shempner's face when Charlie was serving up some payback.

"So on to what you wanted to talk about," Pastor Jim said. "Is it about your situation?"

"My situation?"

Pastor Jim gave Ian a wise, fatherly look. "I'm guessing you feel a little morally awkward about your, ah, situation," he said, waving between Alex and Ian, "particularly when you're around me. Because of my profession. Is that right?" Ian could tell he was being cautious with his words in case Alex woke up and heard them.

"Yeah. That's exactly it. I feel awkward."

"And you're wondering what a man of God thinks about your responsibilities as a father, especially when your son is living under his roof?"

"Pastor Jim," Ian said. "You've gotta know that I plan to do my best to help Brooke and Alex. And I know how this all must look, but believe it or not, I generally try to do the right thing and—"

"The right thing?"

"Yes," Ian said. "I try to do the right thing. But this," he waved at Alex, "changes so many things. I just arrived and I feel like I'm supposed to be Dad of the Year or something." He rubbed his temples. "It's happening too fast."

Pastor Jim stopped. "I already know you're going to do the right thing."

Ian looked at him. The old-fashioned and morally *right thing* to do was marry the mother of his child. "So you think I ought to marry Brooke?" he whispered, soft enough that he was sure Alex couldn't hear.

"Are you serious?" Pastor Jim asked, arching a brow.

"I figured you wanted me to . . . you know . . . the whole 'having a child out of wedlock' thing . . ." He thought back to meeting up with Brooke again. And thinking about anything but a wedding . . . It seemed like a lifetime ago. Was he even the same man?

"Little late for the dance on that one, don't you think?" Pastor Jim said.

Ian stole a quick look at him, and then let out a breath.

"I guess so," Ian said. "In fact, we aren't even planning on dating." He dared to look at the minister again.

Pastor Jim leaned forward and rested his forearms on his knees. "Ian, always seek God's guidance for your life. And be the best father you can be to Alex. That's the right thing to do. I'm just thankful you're here now. Our little guy is happier than I've ever seen him, even sick as he is."

Ian looked over at his son. If he only did what the minister said, he'd be doing the right thing.

Seek God's guidance. Be a good dad. *That, I can do.*

THIRTY-FOUR

Macey leaned against the windowsill in her office as she waited for the results of Alex's weekly blood test. Despite the eleven inches of snow that blanketed the Detroit area, the construction of the hospital's new wing was nearing its much-anticipated completion.

She glanced down to the parking lot, once again seeking out the old F-150. Though she couldn't see it, she knew it was out there. She knew he was there—whoever he was.

She stepped back to her desk to open her e-mail and read the test results.

Flat. She was surprised. Alex's white blood cell count had not gone up or down much at all. She closed the screen, grabbed Alex's chart, and headed toward the consultation room, where she knocked quickly on the door before entering.

Ian and Brooke were on either side of Alex, who looked like he'd gone through a rough week. The balance of his hair was nothing but a sparse collection of short orange threads; he appeared exhausted and pale, with purplish-blue circles under his eyes. He'd obviously lost weight.

What if you couldn't help him? What if your best wasn't good enough?

As Kenneth's words flit in and out of her head, another voice—this time her own—told her that a race had begun, and they were starting to fall behind.

She shook it off. Alex wasn't going to lose. She wasn't going to lose. They weren't going to lose. She was Macey Lewis, and her best had always worked—always.

She just needed full control. 24/7 control. Admit him.

"Hello, everybody," Macey said confidently. "How are we doing?"

"Not so great. Alex's appetite has been way off," Brooke said without preamble. "And what he has eaten, he's had a hard time keeping down."

"Add to that a week of diarrhea," Ian said, "and the poor kid is miserable. I thought you said he'd be feeling better by now."

Macey was used to this stage with parents—they were feeling the weight of the treatment too. They often got mad at the doctors and nurses, wanting to cast blame. It was just part of the process. She lowered herself to one knee. "Not feeling too well, Alex?"

Alex lifted his head off Brooke's shoulder barely long enough to shake it.

"We're going to make you better, okay?" Macey said. She straightened. "He's pretty dehydrated."

"Well, yeah," Brooke said. "Sorry. It's been . . ."

"I know," Macey said. "It's a lot. Hang in there." She opened Alex's file. "We got the test results. Alex's numbers were relatively unchanged."

"Is that bad?" Brooke asked.

"I was looking for a bit of a decrease," Macey admitted. "But now I'm hesitant to ramp up his regimen because he's struggling. I think we should do another week of the same treatment, but this time in-house. That way we can monitor him more closely. As well as keep this dehydration business in line."

"You want to check him in?" Ian asked, casting an alarmed look at Brooke. Macey recognized the sound of parental fear.

"It's simply precautionary," she said. "We need to make sure he is getting proper rest and nutrition, and I can also monitor him a bit more closely."

"Was there something we should have done differently?" Brooke asked.

"Not at all," Macey said, holding her hand up. "You guys are doing an excellent job."

"How long?" Brooke asked, giving Macey a panicked look that the doctor had seen hundreds—maybe thousands—of times before.

"Let's plan on a week and see how he responds," Macey said. "It's where he needs to be, and you can be here 24/7 if you want."

"Okay," Brooke said quietly. She poked lightly at Alex's leg. "You want to stay at the hospital tonight, buddy?"

Alex hunched his shoulders indifferently.

"Mr. Brave will stop by almost every day," Macey promised, prompting a tiny smile from Alex.

"When do you want him?" Ian asked.

Macey stood, opened the manila folder she had been holding, and then jotted something quickly on its inside cover. She looked at Alex, then collectively at all three of them. She snapped the folder closed. "Right now."

● ● ●

"I see that Alex has joined us," Zach said, sticking his head into Macey's office. "It's a little early for that, isn't it?"

Macey turned around and looked blankly at the other doctor. She couldn't tell him how she felt. She had conditioned herself. *I don't get nervous, I don't get worried, and I certainly don't show fear. I have all the answers. I've been told I'm the best because I am.*

Then why am I freaking out?

Zach stepped into the office. "Macey? We see kids this sick in treatment every week of the year. What's up? You need to talk?"

He was being sincere. For starters, he'd never asked her if she needed to talk, but again, she'd never really needed to before. Now she did—not just about Alex, but about a lot of things. She didn't know where to begin. All she could do was stare at him.

He gave her a compassionate look and then quietly closed the door. "May I?" Zach asked, pointing at the couch.

"Please," she muttered, putting her elbows on her desk and her head in her hands.

He sat on the arm of the couch. He leaned forward with his left elbow on his left knee and his fist under his chin. "As Kaitlyn would say, 'You look like your dog is missing, Dr. Lewis.'"

"Something's missing," Macey said. She looked down, bit gently on her lip, and then sheepishly raised her head to him. "I'm concerned."

"About Alex?"

"Yes," she answered. "I believe it's aggressive—extremely aggressive."

"Okay," Zach said softly. "You know what to do. You've seen this before."

"Not like this, Zach. Regardless of what I do, he's not responding as expected."

"Macey, you know how this goes. You take your best stab at the regimen, adjust, and try again. It's what we do, week in and week out."

She took a deep breath and blew it out. "I don't know. I can't put my finger on it, Zach. There's just something . . . different."

"Different in the numbers?"

"In the numbers, in his appearance . . ."

"Every kid is different," he said.

"I know," she said. "I just have a bad feeling about it."

Zach stood up and walked around the desk, grabbed a chair, turned it around, and sat down on it backward. He perched his elbows up on the back of the seat and looked at her with the quiet understanding of a big brother. "Macey. Are you too close to this one?"

"No," she said, right away.

"With you getting close to Brooke, the Lindys—"

"No, Zach. I'm okay. Really." It would be the worst if he forced her to give up the case. "I mean, obviously, it makes it trickier, knowing them. Coming to love them. But I'm not doing anything for Alex that I wouldn't do for any other patient."

"Except admitting him a good two months before most other patients."

She sighed. "It's my gut, Zach. My gut tells me he should be here."

"Then you know you have my support," he said. "With all that's been going on around here lately, I'm beginning to understand following the lead of a power higher than mere medicine."

"Thanks, Zach."

They shared a smile, then Zach's smile fell. "Listen, Macey. Any way you dice it, if my son was sick, I'd trust him to no one but you."

Macey nodded, because she knew he meant it. And because it was the first time that they'd ever had this kind of conversation. "I appreciate it, Zach. That means a lot to me."

"You're welcome," he said. "Now just do your best. And say a few prayers."

She smiled. "That's exactly what I was doing when you came in here."

"That's good," Zach said, rising. He set the chair back in place and moved toward the door.

"Listen to us," she said. "Can you believe you and I are talking about praying? It's weird, huh?"

"Bizarre." He put his hand on the knob. "But what's weirder is that I think I like it." He gave her a wink.

"Zach," she said as he opened the door. "One more thing, if you don't mind."

"Of course. Shoot."

Macey stood and walked halfway across the office. She stopped and lifted her hands to the sides of her face as Zach stood in the doorway. "I know this may sound strange, but something has me concerned." She lowered her hands from her cheeks and crossed her arms. "He asked me what I would do if my best wasn't good enough."

"Who said that?"

"Him," Macey answered, lifting a brow.

Zach ran his hand across his chin. "Kenneth?"

"Yes. And if he meant what I think he meant, I feel like he knows something is going to go wrong with Alex."

"Kenneth asked you what you would do if your best wasn't good enough?" Zach repeated, obviously thinking it through, giving it weight.

"Yeah," Macey said. "And if it were anyone but him saying that—I mean, anyone—it wouldn't bother me." She could see he agreed. It made her heartbeat speed up.

Zach looked away, then back to her. "Are you sure he was talking about Alex?"

"Yes."

"Let's hope you're wrong," he said.

THIRTY-FIVE

The little girl's long, brown hair dipped down her back as she tilted her head up. Her eyes rounded in amazement, as if she were looking up at a giant. "How tall are you, mister?" she asked in a small but curious voice.

Charlie just smiled at the girl and ducked out of the elevator onto the third floor at East Shore. Ian followed behind, smiling. He turned around as the doors slid shut. "Almost seven feet," he whispered.

The little girl's eyes widened.

Charlie and Ian made their way past the waiting room and then past the nurses' station before taking the first left down a brightly lit hallway to Room 364.

"Knock, knock," Ian said, tapping on the door and pushing it open.

He and Charlie each stepped around a navy blue curtain with a three-foot SpongeBob SquarePants embroidered in the middle. Alex was curled up on the bed, sleeping with his mouth slightly open. He had an IV in his arm, and his head was propped up on a pillow that had been folded carefully in two. His right foot stuck out the end of his blanket.

Brooke was also asleep. She was lying on a reclining chair to Alex's right, and like her son, she had dark circles under her eyes.

Charlie walked up to Alex's left and removed a portable lunch tray that held a Styrofoam cup of water and a barely touched plastic container of Lucky Charms. He reached over and touched Alex's forehead lightly with the palm of his hand. Alex's eyes opened and were little more than a tired pair of slits. They widened when he saw Charlie. He looked at Charlie's hand and then at the TicTac it held. He barely shook his head and then struggled to clear his throat. "I'm not allowed, Charlie."

Charlie gave Alex a puzzled look and then popped it into his own mouth.

"Hey, partner," Ian said quietly from the foot of the bed.

"Hi, Dad," Alex said. Spoken at full throttle, the words only came out as a weak whisper. "We missed church today."

"I know. We missed you there."

Brooke's eyes opened and she stretched.

"Hello, sleeping beauty," Ian said. "Why don't you go home and let us take over? You need a break."

Brooke yawned. "Did you call Clippers for me?"

"Yep," Ian said. "They said to take as much time as you need and that you and pip-squeak here are in their prayers."

Ian turned his head and could see that Charlie had lowered his face within a foot of Alex's. They were studying each other with perfectly straight expressions.

"Do you know that this is the longest they have gone without seeing each other?" Brooke said. "They've never been apart for longer than a day."

"What are they doing?" Ian asked.

"First one to smile loses," Brooke said faintly. "It's one of their games."

An IV alarm beeped next to Charlie's head, causing him to jump. Alex lifted his head, started laughing, and then proceeded to cough up a tiny patch of vomit, which slowly dribbled down his chin.

"I've got it," Ian said, grabbing a washcloth folded on the sink to wipe Alex's chin. "There ya go, partner. It's like it never happened."

"That's the third time today," Brooke said. "And he still has diarrhea."

"Has Macey been in?" Ian asked.

"Oh yeah," Brooke said. "She and Kaitlyn have been in and out continuously since he was admitted. It's like he's getting preferential treatment."

"Did somebody say my name?" Kaitlyn asked, bouncing into the room. "Excuse me there, big guy," she added, stepping around Charlie and pressing her thumb firmly against a green button on the machine next to Alex. She removed the empty IV bag, turned around, and looked up at Charlie. "How are you, Charlie?"

Charlie smiled.

Kaitlyn put her hand on top of Alex's. "You sure seem glad to see Charlie."

"I just throwed up again," Alex announced.

"That's okay, honey," Kaitlyn said.

"Where is Mr. Brave?" Alex asked. "I think Charlie would like him."

"I'm not sure, but hang on a second," the nurse said, stepping back around Charlie and then disappearing around the navy pull curtain.

"Hey, Charlie, look!" Alex said, pointing at his IV. "I forgot to show you this." He tugged at the tape around the needle in his arm. "Look, Charlie, this doesn't even hurt!"

"Alexander, stop pulling on that!" Brooke said.

Alex's head flipped back at his mother. "But it doesn't hurt, Mom."

"That's 'cause he is so brave!" a high-pitched voice said from behind the curtain. They all turned around.

Alex laughed and pointed at Mr. Brave. The puppet's head arched around the corner of the curtain.

"Man, are you ever a big guy!" Mr. Brave said in a tone of awe. "Are you Charlie?"

Charlie's mouth opened, and he smiled at the puppet as Alex laughed. Charlie held up his index finger to Alex and then slowly tiptoed to the edge of the curtain to peek around it. He grinned at Kaitlyn with an I-know-it's-you look on his face.

"He's looking at you, Nurse Kaitlyn," Mr. Brave said. "Charlie sees you."

The nurse came back around the corner and smiled at Ian and

Brooke. "It looks like we've found some additional therapy for Mr. Alex, and it's called Charlie."

Brooke agreed. "Alex seems ten times better. That sparkle is back in his eyes, and his coloring even looks better with his BFF in the room."

"The best of all medicines," the nurse said, lifting Alex's head and adjusting his pillow. "Is Charlie your best friend forever?"

"Heck yeah," Alex said, grabbing his Styrofoam cup and sucking in a straw full of water.

Brooke stood up and stretched. "I'm going to go grab a shower. I'll be back in a couple of hours."

Ian hugged her, and then she hugged Charlie. "You're good medicine for him, Charlie. Thanks for coming to be with him."

Charlie nodded and then returned to Alex, while Ian and Brooke stepped outside with Kaitlyn.

"How are things looking?" Ian asked her.

Kaitlyn looked down at his chart. "Dr. Lewis wants to keep him here for a few more days. And then we're going to check his blood again."

"And then what?" Ian asked.

"Then we'll see where we are," Kaitlyn said carefully.

"Shouldn't his numbers come down?" Ian asked.

"They certainly should," Kaitlyn said. "But it's equally important to see how the rest of his system responds to his treatment. Macey wants him eating more, retaining it, and she also wants him better hydrated."

"When is she going to check his blood again?" Brooke asked the nurse.

Kaitlyn flipped through a couple pages in the chart and ran her finger down to the center. "Looks like Wednesday."

•   •   •

On Wednesday, Jim thought the sun glistened on the snow like a blanket of tiny diamonds. He put his arm around Shirley as they looked out over the snow-glazed pines that bent around the back of the church.

"It's pretty, isn't it?" Jim asked.

"As a picture," Shirley said.

Jim was thinking how quiet it was, inside and out. "Do you know that Sunday was the first service Brooke and Alex missed since they came into our lives?"

Shirley didn't say anything. She gave his arm a little squeeze and walked over to the sink.

"You know," Jim said, "if it warms up a little, it'd make great packing for a snowman. I'll see if Charlie wants to make one for Alex to greet him when he comes home Saturday. We could build a doozy."

"Let's hope he comes home Saturday, James."

Jim had never met another person with Shirley's faith, and that faith never made her hesitate to speak plainly. He looked back to the snow-laden branches. Alex had lost seven pounds and had been in the hospital for almost a week now. There probably wouldn't be a snowman in the yard this weekend.

"I'm kind of surprised Kaitlyn and Zach are joining us tomorrow," Shirley said.

"I'm glad. It will help it seem less lonely."

Jim looked back out the window and took his turn at not saying anything.

It was hard to believe tomorrow was Thanksgiving. *Help me concentrate on the blessings, Lord. The amazing blessings. And not what I'm missing.*

● ● ●

Alex tapped the roof of his mouth and then the inside of his cheek with his tongue. It all burned, and he wanted to cry. He was hungry, but it hurt when he ate. He was thirsty, his head hurt, and the thing in his arm was getting sore. He blinked at his dad, who was standing at the side of the bed.

Maybe Dad can make it all go away.

"I know this isn't much fun for you," Dad said, taking Alex's hand and rubbing the top of it gently with his thumb. "What can I do for you, partner?"

"I don't know," Alex said, hunching his left shoulder. It slid out of his Spider-Man pajama top. "I'm a little hungry, but it hurts when I chew."

"Let's try some of this," Dad said, peeling the top off of a small container of cherry Jell-O that was on Alex's tray. "Do you want some water too?"

"Yeah," Alex whispered, carefully licking his bottom lip. "Can I go home today? Please?"

"I'm not sure, partner," Dad said, moving around to the side of the bed, trying not to wake Mom, who had fallen asleep in the chair she'd been glued to for most of the week. They were waiting for Dr. Lewis, who was supposed to come back with the test results.

"But I want to go home for Thanksgiving tomorrow," Alex said. "I want to see Charlie. If I don't, who will eat the other turkey leg?"

"I want you home too," Dad said, holding a cup of water in his palm and bending the straw for him to take a drink. "I'll see if the Lindys can save you a turkey leg. And I'll see if I can get Charlie up here tonight or tomorrow to see you, okay?"

"Okay," Alex said. He drew in a little taste of water. It soothed his mouth, making it feel cooler. It also felt like he could breathe better. He went for more, this time taking in too much. He choked for a second, coughed, and water streamed down the sides of his mouth.

"Slow down, buddy," Dad said. "Slow down."

Dad held the back of his hand to Alex's forehead. "You are a little warm, partner."

Alex gazed at his dad, wondering if he could maybe fix it.

"Does the water make you feel better?"

"Yeah," Alex said, opening his mouth slightly while Dad gave him half of a plastic spoonful of Jell-O. After only two bites, Alex shook his head. He didn't want any more. It tasted funny. Everything tasted funny ever since he started chemo syrupy.

Dad finished the rest of his Jell-O and went back around to the foot of the bed. Behind him on a shelf was a box of those funny rubber gloves. Dad pulled one out and then dangled it under his chin like a rooster's beard, making Alex smile a little. Then he pulled it to his mouth for three quick puffs that blew it up, making it look like a fat, bodiless hand. He held it over his head and then let it go, making it rattle and then fly in a funny circle above the bed before bumping against Mom's forehead and landing on her shoulder.

Alex let out a laugh that made his throat hurt super bad. But he smiled, looking at the dead glove on Mom's shoulder.

"What's so funny?" Mom asked in a lazy voice, her eyes still closed. "What's up with you two?"

"Nothing," Dad said, looking over at Alex.

"Nothing," Alex echoed. He felt like crying again. He didn't want to be here anymore.

Dad came up beside him and felt his forehead again. "I'm calling Kaitlyn," he said to Mom.

"I want to go home," Alex said, half crying. His mouth still burned, his eyes hurt, and his throat now felt as if he'd swallowed broken glass. He had to go to the bathroom, he was on the verge of throwing up again, and the back of his neck was going *boom, boom, boom.*

"I know, buddy," Mom said, looking at him like she knew just how he felt. She kissed his cheek and then looked up at Dad. "He's warmer than usual." Her eyes looked all big and scared, which made Alex more scared.

"I know," Dad said. "Macey is supposed to be in any minute."

Mom offered Alex some water, but he turned away.

The drape pulled back, and Dr. Lewis entered the room. "Hi, everybody," she said. "How are we doing today?"

"Not so great," Mom said. She looked like she was gonna cry, which made Alex feel like crying too. Alex noticed that Dr. Lewis wasn't carrying the manila folder that she normally held under her arm as she stepped right up next to the bed and looked at him.

Nurse Kaitlyn came around the curtain, wearing her standard smile. She scooched in beside Dad and pressed the same button that he'd used to have her come to the room. "How are we doing? It looks like somebody turned Alex's temperature up, huh?"

"That's normal, though, right?" Mom asked, her voice all high and squeaky-like. "The fever?"

"He's okay," Dr. Lewis said, sounding like she knew. She looked down at Alex. "I know you don't feel well, Alex. We are going to fix you up, okay? You're doing great."

Alex nodded.

"Let's pull our chairs over here for a few minutes," Dr. Lewis said, gesturing past the blue curtain into the other side of the room. "Kaitlyn, can you entertain Mr. Alex while I speak to Mom and Dad for a few minutes?"

"Sure!" Kaitlyn said. "How 'bout a visit from Mr. Brave?"

Alex shrugged. He knew Dr. Lewis was going to talk to Mom and Dad about him, but he didn't feel good enough to care. And today he didn't really care if he saw Mr. Brave ever again.

I just wanna go home.

* * *

Ian wasn't a doctor, but one thing that helped him move up the ranks of the plant was his ability to read people. *Something's definitely wrong.* With one look at Brooke, he knew she knew it too. They all sat down, and Macey leaned toward the edge of her seat and laced her fingers together.

"There's a problem, isn't there?" Ian asked.

"Ian and Brooke," Macey said, "all kids are different. They all have different treatments, and they all respond differently."

"Tell us," Ian said. He didn't like the tone in the doctor's voice, confirming his suspicions. "Straight up."

"I wouldn't do it any other way," Macey said. "Here it is. Alex's white blood cell test came back, and his count went up."

"That's bad," Brooke said.

Macey nodded somberly. "The cancer's very aggressive."

Aggressive.

Ian didn't like that word. It had tiny fangs that carried poison—poison that could make the heart skip beats and then pound with sickening cold flashes.

Brooke beat him to the punch and repeated it. "Aggressive?"

"Yes," the doctor said.

"What's the plan, then?" Ian asked. "What do we do?"

"Like I said, all kids are different. They all respond differently. As tough as Alex is, I'm concerned about the toll his treatment is taking on him. With that being said, I believe we need to move on against the disease."

"You're worried about the toll it's taking?" Ian asked. Reality had an interesting way of constantly redefining itself. *I have a son. My son has leukemia. The leukemia is both aggressive and taking its toll.*

Macey nodded yet again. "He's now down eleven pounds in a little over a month. He is still not eating well, and at this pace, we're going to have a hard time keeping him comfortable. We need to move forward before he loses more ground. There are some significant hills to climb ahead of us."

Brooke looked like she was in agony. Their little boy was going to suffer some more. It was like sending a wounded soldier back to the front.

"How aggressive is it?" Ian asked, standing up and looking around the edge of the curtain. Alex was perfectly still, his small hand in Kaitlyn's. She lifted a finger to her lips. He was asleep. Ian sat back down and asked the same question. "How aggressive?"

"It's early in his treatment," Macey said. "But I know we are now looking at a high-risk leukemia—one where regular treatment is not effective enough to keep the cancer away."

"*High-risk?*" Ian said.

"He is going to be okay," Brooke said, taking a deep breath. She tilted her head toward the ceiling and closed her eyes. "He is going to be okay. He is going to be okay. Only believe. Only believe."

Ian put his hand on Brooke's shoulder. He knew she was scared. He was scared, too, but something about Macey's confidence had earned his trust. He looked back at the doctor. "What do you plan to do next?"

"Treating leukemia is sometimes like playing a game of cat and mouse. You treat and then test, treat and then test again, constantly adjusting until you get consistent results, with the ultimate goal being remission."

"And with Alex," Ian said, "it's like chasing a very fast mouse."

"You could say that," Macey said. Her eyes flicked from Ian to Brooke and back again. "You wanted it straight . . ."

"Let's have it," Ian said.

"I believe with just chemo, the cancer will keep coming back, making it more difficult to treat, because the cancer itself can develop a drug resistance."

"So what do you do then?"

"We up the chemo. Try to kill it before it can outrun it, in a sense."

"So then," Brooke said, "why aren't you doing that?"

"We could," Macey said. She rose and walked to the window, putting her hands in her white coat pockets. "It's definitely an option."

"But you're hesitating," Ian said. "Because?"

Macey turned around, took a long step back toward them, and crossed her arms. "Because it could kill him," she said quietly.

"No," Brooke said, bringing her hand to her mouth and shaking her head. "You have to help him. Before it gets to that point."

Ian reached over and took Brooke's hand. "What's your best plan, Macey? What would you do if this was your kid?"

"We need to go in and knock it all out," she said. "Fast."

"How are you going to do that?"

"The transplant. It's our best chance. And that chance is inside of *you* right now, Ian."

"Best chance?" Brooke asked.

Ian gently put his hand under Brooke's chin and had her face him. "It's gonna be okay, Brooke. Macey knows what she is doing."

"I know," Brooke sniffled. "He is going to be made well, remember? He is going to be all right. I believe—I believe."

"That's right," Macey repeated, the familiar words providing comfort in an uncomfortable moment. "Only believe."

But there was something in her eyes that made Ian think she didn't.

THIRTY-SIX

"What a day," Jim said, feeling extra comfortable in his La-Z-Boy. "We get to eat turkey *and* watch Thanksgiving football on television. It has been quite a while for me. Praise God."

"Good for you," Kaitlyn said, sitting on the couch next to Zach and Charlie. She nudged Zach with her elbow to look at Charlie.

Charlie was wearing headphones that could only reach his ears by being put on from the back of his head instead of from the top. He was listening to Brooke's old iPod. Kaitlyn smiled, watching as his lips rounded in amazement. His head slowly moved back and forth as he pressed the mystery button—the button that magically changed the songs he was hearing.

"So you said that it went pretty well at the shelter this morning?" Zach asked.

"It went really well," Jim said, reaching over and grabbing a handful of potato chips out of a plastic bowl on Charlie's lap. He held his hand out to Kaitlyn, and she took one. "A lot of people showed up to help."

"Many from St. Thomas?" Zach asked. "I know Kenneth was there."

"We had quite a few, and he was," Jim said. "Did you talk to him today?"

"Sort of," Zach said dismissively. He tapped Charlie on the leg. "You ready for some turkey, big man? It smells like it's getting close." Zach rubbed his hands together in anticipation and smiled at the rest of them. "I've had way too many Thanksgiving dinners in the hospital cafeteria. This will be a serious treat."

Charlie took the headphones off, nodded like he understood, and put the headphones back on.

"I'm thinking the big guy would pass on his turkey to have his little buddy back home," Kaitlyn said.

"Undoubtedly," Jim said. "When would you expect Alex to be out of the hospital?"

"It depends," Zach answered. "Each patient is different."

Jim grabbed a couple more chips. "So they are doing some more tests on Ian today?"

"On Alex too," he answered. "Dr. Lewis wants to make absolutely sure they are both ready for the transplant."

"They're both in the best possible hands," Kaitlyn said.

"I believe that," Jim said. "But when do you think they will do the bone marrow transplant? In a couple of days?"

"Oh no," Kaitlyn said. "It will be longer than that."

"And Alex will be in the hospital for quite a while," Zach said. "The bone marrow transplant will allow Macey to get more aggressive with the cancer through chemo, radiation, or both. We want to wipe it out and then make a replacement with healthy marrow. Make sense?"

Jim laced his fingers on top of his lap. "So out with the old and in with the new?"

Zach leaned forward on the couch. "More like out with the bad and in with the good."

"How long do you think it will take?" Jim asked.

"That's a good question." Zach smiled, and the sight of it did Jim good. The man was changed. He thought back to the day he'd met him, when he came to help with the cross. He was a totally different man. He'd been freed.

Zach stood and walked over to the window. "It takes as long as it takes the team to kill whatever residual cancer cells remain in Alex, while making sure his immune system doesn't reject the new marrow from Ian."

"How dangerous is it?" Jim asked. "Macey told Ian and Brooke that there are risks."

"Practically none for Ian."

"And for Alex?"

"Like Kaitlyn said, we have to trust that Alex is in the best hands."

"He is. He's in God's hands," Jim said.

"He really is in God's hands," Zach repeated. Jim was surprised by the way he said it. He actually sounded a little sad.

Shirley came in from the kitchen. "James, I'd like to ask you something I haven't asked you in a long time."

Jim swiveled around in the La-Z-Boy. "What's that, hon?"

Steam from the potatoes was still disappearing from Shirley's glasses. "Would you like to carve the turkey?"

"If I can remember how," he said, smiling and rising to his feet.

"Charlie," Shirley said, pulling off his headphones. "Would you come and mash the potatoes for me, please?"

He nodded.

"Put me to work too," Zach said. He gave Kaitlyn a kiss on her cheek and followed Charlie into the kitchen.

* * *

Shirley took Zach's place on the couch. "I hope Zach wasn't mad that James was asking all those questions. I could hear them talking."

"Not at all," Kaitlyn said. She sensed that something new was weighing on Zach's mind, but was sure it wasn't Pastor Jim's questions. "Don't worry about that, Shirley. It's perfectly normal to ask questions at a time like this."

"It's just that Brooke made it sound like the bone marrow transplant was their only option." Shirley paused. "Is Alex in that bad of shape?"

"He's really sick," Kaitlyn said.

Shirley shook her head. "But Kenneth told Pastor Jim . . ." She caught herself and shook her head. "Never mind. It's all so foreign to us, and when a child is involved . . ."

"Tell me about it," Kaitlyn said. "It's my life. But for obvious reasons, little Alex is the patient that holds our hearts."

"Come to the table, you two," Zach called.

The two women entered the kitchen, and Kaitlyn found herself stopping before she sat down. She looked around the kitchen, from the table, already loaded with food, to the people, still scattered. Pastor Jim was humming an upbeat tune she didn't recognize, working on carving the turkey. He directed Zach to bring the cranberries as he placed a steaming dish of mashed potatoes on the table, and Charlie had the iPod on again. Shirley walked behind him, took the headphones off, and set them aside, squeezing his shoulders. She sat down at one end of the table and smiled at Kaitlyn. "Well, I think it just might be all done. You begin the day wondering . . ."

"I can imagine," Kaitlyn said. "Someday I'll have to try my hand at it."

Shirley's eyes widened. "You've never made a Thanksgiving meal?"

"Not yet," Kaitlyn said. "Most years I seem to draw the Thanksgiving shift card at work. By some miracle I didn't this year." *By some miracle. Did she just utter those words?* But they didn't feel foreign; they felt right.

Kaitlyn sat down next to Zach, and Pastor Jim came to the table with a silver platter stacked with thin slices of turkey. He placed it in the center and then sat down at the opposite end of the table from Shirley. He pointed at the turkey and then lifted his hands. "The Ginsu master has performed his magic. This bird is carved."

"You haven't lost your touch," Shirley said.

"Looks perfect," Zach added.

These truly were people of God, continuing to embrace life in spite of adversities. There were plenty of families at the hospital even now, walking the halls, wringing their hands, weeping in fear. But Alex's people weren't worrying; it was like they all felt a peace about the situation. Momentary worries for sure, as with Shirley, but overall, a peace. It was so different from anything she'd ever experienced, and she found it stunning.

Shirley looked over at Kaitlyn and smiled.

"Shall we pray?" Pastor Jim asked, still holding his hands up.

"Let's do it," Zach said.

They all joined hands, and Pastor Jim led them through a prayer. Kaitlyn listened carefully as the minister thanked God for looking over Alex. Then he thanked God for bringing them together and for the food. Next he thanked God for the growth of the church before finally asking God to remember those less fortunate.

Kaitlyn noticed that there was something peculiar about the tone in Pastor Jim's voice when he prayed for Alex. He didn't pray as *if* God were going to take care of the boy. He prayed as if God had *already* taken care of him.

They all said, "Amen," and Kaitlyn glanced around the table one more time at the faces of these genuinely good people. She was glad they were now part of her life. She looked up at Zach, beside her, and it was then that she knew.

She nudged him on the side of his leg and whispered in his ear, "I think I've fallen in love with you again, Zach Norman."

Zach pulled his head back, eyes wide. He smiled, paused, and then leaned over to whisper back, "I don't think I ever stopped loving you."

Kaitlyn poked at Zach's arm, then nodded for him to look over at Charlie. He already had a mouthful of turkey and was putting three rolls' worth of butter onto a single roll.

She bit lightly on her lip and thought, *Don't you worry, Charlie. We'll have your friend home in no time. Because clearly, God has his hand on this house.*

THIRTY-SEVEN

B rooke walked quietly into the fellowship hall, hugged Shirley, and then plopped down on the couch without saying a word.

"Honey, you look so tired," Shirley said, wearing the motherly face that Brooke had seen quite a bit of lately. And she had to admit, it looked good to her.

"I am so tired," Brooke said, her eyes straying past Shirley and back to the doors that separated them from the sanctuary. She raised her hands to rub her eyes. "Today is Saturday, right? How long was I at the hospital?"

"Yes." Shirley unplugged an extension cord from the vacuum and wound it around her arm. "And the answer is four days. Remember what Dr. Lewis told you about not neglecting your own health during this?"

"I know, I know," Brooke said. "I'm going to head back down to the house and take a shower."

"Did you eat while you were up there?"

"Probably not enough, but I'll be okay. It's hard to eat when your stomach is in knots." Brooke slid up to the front of the cushion and stretched her arms over her head to yawn. "Somebody is in the sanctuary."

"It's probably James," Shirley said. "Or Charlie. He is all out of sorts without Alex around. You know how my son feels about yours."

"I know."

"So you said they put a catheter in Alex?"

"Yeah." Brooke was disappointed in herself for answering so

305

casually. She wondered if she was getting numbed by the ongoing struggle. "Zach did it this morning. It's something called a Hickman catheter, which is an intravenous line."

"What's it for?"

"It's to get Alex ready for the bone marrow transplant. It allows him to get the medicine and blood stuff he needs, and it allows the staff to withdraw a bunch of blood samples from him without having to poke needles in him all the time."

"Ian went back to the hospital this morning?" Shirley asked. "For the same thing they did yesterday?"

"Yeah," Brooke said. "It's the stuff that's supposed to help boost Ian's marrow stem cells before he makes his donation to Alex." Brooke yawned again, causing her eyes to water. "They were giving him more of that today when I was leaving the hospital."

"When are they actually going to do the transplant?"

"Pretty soon," Brooke said. "Kaitlyn said they may go in as early as tomorrow to harvest Ian's bone marrow. I guess they have to do a few more tests. But like I said, it all depends on when Macey thinks Alex is ready to go."

"The sooner the better," Shirley said. "Let's get through this and get Alex home."

"He's going to be in the hospital for eight more weeks," Brooke said. "*Two more months.*"

"Eight weeks?" Shirley said, sounding surprised. She slowly took her glasses off and then pulled a piece of tissue from her pocket to rub the lenses. "My goodness, honey. Why so long?"

"It takes time to see if the procedure was a success," Brooke said. "The radiation is going to knock his immune system down to practically nothing. That way, Alex's immune system doesn't reject Ian's bone marrow. And then it takes time for it to be able to reproduce on its own—I think Macey called it engraftment or something like that."

"He's going to be all right," Shirley said, standing up. She put her glasses back on and leaned toward Brooke. "I need to get up there and see Alex myself. It's been a couple of days and I miss him. I can tell Charlie wants to get back up there too."

"You should probably go tonight, then," Brooke said. "And bring Charlie if you want, because Macey says she may only want us in there one at a time after they do the transplant."

"Why is that?"

"She said that when they knock his immune system down that far, he will have very little defense against even the most common things. She also said that they want to keep him in the most sterile environment possible. He can't even have gifts like plants, fruit, flowers—nothing like that. They don't want him in contact with anything, and it sounds like that may even include some of us."

"That poor little thing," Shirley said. "God love him."

Brooke suddenly wanted more than ever to get back to the hospital, pick Alex up, and hold him. "I guess when we're in the room with him, we are going to be wearing masks, gloves, the whole nine yards."

"Well, if that's what has to be done to get him well, so be it," Shirley said, holding out her hand. "C'mon, let's go to the house. You need to get some rest."

Brooke took Shirley's hand and stood. "It's going to be tough on him, Shirley, and I feel so helpless."

"He is going to get through this." Shirley pulled Brooke into her arms.

"It's so much on his little body." Brooke sighed, pulling away. "Macey said on top of him being vulnerable to infections and viruses, he may also bleed a lot. And then he is going to be taking all kinds of medications, getting blood transfusions—it's just . . ." She paused, wondering for the umpteenth time why it was happening to Alex, why it was happening to her. She closed her eyes and slowly exhaled. She gave Shirley an exhausted look and then continued to convince herself, *He is going to be okay. He is going to be okay. He is going to be okay . . .*

Shirley held one of the fellowship hall doors open and pointed into the sanctuary. "I'm telling you he will pull through this. We will all get through this. All of these things that they are doing now—this is how Alex gets better."

"I know, I know," Brooke said. "It just seems so unfair, Shirley. And I'm sick of saying that, and I'm sick of thinking that."

"Come here," Shirley said, stopping and putting her arm around Brooke as they reached the last pew. "This will pass, honey. I just know our little Alex will be made well."

"Eight weeks," Brooke said, laying her head on Shirley's shoulder and wiping at her eyes with the pad of her thumb. "He missed Thanksgiving, and over the next eight weeks, he's going to spend his sixth birthday and then Christmas in the hospital. It's not fair."

"Let's sit down again for a second," Shirley said, motioning Brooke to the nearest pew.

"If I sit down again, Shirley, I'll fall asleep," Brooke said. She brought her hands up to her cheeks. "I don't want to lose him. I can't lose him. I am not going to lose him."

"No, you are not," Shirley said, putting a hand on each of Brooke's shoulders. "Honey, look at me."

Brooke did.

"Brooke, I know the feeling of being a mother and being totally helpless. I know what it is to hear that voice inside telling you to help, telling you to do something, but you can't."

She was talking about Charlie. When he was a baby. "I still can't imagine Charlie ever being small," Brooke said.

"And then you start to ask yourself why? Why is this happening to him? Why is this happening to me? And you want to believe . . . and more often than not, you do believe. I think it's important to know that if we didn't experience pain and hardship, we would never know the full measure of triumphs and joys."

"I don't know, Shirley." Brooke gave her a small smile. "I might settle for a half measure of joy and triumph if I could bring my boy home tomorrow."

Shirley returned her smile. "I know, honey. I know all about it. But trust me, down the line, you'll be glad you held out for the full measure."

"I'm trying to believe," Brooke said as they walked toward the church entrance. "I don't know how many times I've told myself,

'Only believe' since we found out Alex was sick—since Kenneth said that to Pastor Jim."

"Yes," Shirley said. "I know it's tough not to worry, but trust that God will see it through. Now let's go get you something to eat. A little food, a little nap, a little shower, and you'll feel like yourself again."

"Thank you, Shirley." Brooke took her arm as they walked down the hill. "I really don't know where I'd be without you guys."

"We don't know where we'd be without you and Alex either," Shirley said. "So let's get through this and bring Alexander home."

THIRTY-EIGHT

Macey hooked her index finger under the Hickman catheter, and Alex's eyes followed her every move as his father's bone marrow flowed through the thin tube into his fragile body. Alex kept very still and looked very small in his bed, temporarily located in the Bone Marrow Transplant unit.

"How you feeling, Alex?" she asked through her mask.

"Okay," he said faintly.

"Remember what I told you?"

"I think so."

"If you start to feel funny, I want you to tell me." She drew a circle in the air a few inches above his chest. "Especially in here, okay?"

"Okay."

"Good job," she said. "I'm going to bring your mom and dad in."

"Okay," he said again.

Macey went beyond the curtain to the far side of the room and through a small door to where Ian and Brooke sat anxiously waiting. She pulled down her mask and removed her gloves. "He is going to be hooked up for a while. Are you guys ready?"

"I think so. Is everything going okay?" Brooke asked.

"As well as can be expected," she answered, nodding at Ian. "How's your hip feeling?"

"Feels fine," Ian said.

Macey grinned. "That's interesting. People compare making a marrow donation to getting hit in the hip with a baseball bat, or having a really hard fall on the ice."

"I feel fine," Ian said. "I really do."

"I'm starting to see where Alex gets his bravado from," Macey said, winking at Brooke.

"Alex looked so tired earlier," Brooke said. "Does the radiation do that?"

"He is tired," she said. "All of this is very taxing on the body, particularly little bodies. It is important that you understand that it's every bit as psychologically tiring as it is physically. And, as we discussed, it's going to get worse."

"Eight weeks' worth?" Brooke asked.

Macey reached behind her and grabbed a pair of surgical masks. "He is going to have good days and bad days, but once we get over the hump, you will notice quite a difference for the better." She clapped her hands together and pointed toward the curtain. "Masks, gloves, and caps. Once you're suited up, you can see him."

• • •

Alex thought it was funny seeing Mom and Dad with all of the hospital stuff on. He was starting to feel a little bit funny in his tummy and his neck, but he didn't want to say anything to Dr. Lewis.

"You are doing it, buddy," Mom said. "You are doing so good."

"Yeah, you are, partner," Dad said. "Just be still and relax, okay?"

Alex tilted his head slightly, and despite the warm, almost burning feeling in his neck, he remained still, only moving his eyes back and forth to whoever was talking. His mouth still hurt, and he wanted to go home. He knew it had snowed outside, and he wanted to make a snowman with a carrot nose with Charlie. He thought about the last time he and Charlie had made a snowman and how one of the deer had eaten the nose off the next day. He remembered how Mrs. Lindy had given them another carrot for another nose and how the deer had eaten that one too.

He also wanted Charlie to pull him on that funny sled again. He tried to think of the name of it. *A botagan?* It was now feeling warm inside his tummy but suddenly so cold on the outside of his body. He tried not to think about it, but it was getting worse. He remembered when Charlie was pulling him on that—*toboggan, not bota-*

gan—and how Charlie slipped and fell down. He remembered how hard he laughed when Charlie got up, brushed himself off, took one step, and fell down again. His eyes shifted back to his dad, and he wondered if he would get more Christmas presents now that he had a dad. His arms were starting to hurt a little, but not enough to cry. He was tired, but he didn't want to sleep.

"We have a little surprise for you, Alex," Dad said. "We can't have too many people in here, so I'll be back in about half an hour."

Alex watched as his dad went around the other side of the curtain. This one was a plain white curtain. He liked the SpongeBob one in the other room lots better. He wondered why his dad left and also wanted to know what the surprise was. He felt a prickly feeling in his legs, and he was getting colder—not on the inside, where it was warm, but the outside.

"I think somebody is getting the chills," Dr. Lewis said, gently raising the blanket to cover as much of Alex as possible without interfering with any of his several connections. "That feel better, Alex?"

"Yeah," he whispered.

"Good," Dr. Lewis said. "I'm going to leave for a little bit, too, while you get your surprise. But I'll be back in about ten minutes."

"Okay," he said.

Dr. Lewis looked at Mom and said, "Kaitlyn will be here in a minute."

"Sounds good," Mom said.

Alex watched as Dr. Lewis touched that machine next to him and then started writing something down in the folder. And then she disappeared behind the curtain.

"You feeling okay, baby?" Mom asked, her eyes looking funny between the mask and the cap.

Alex didn't answer. He didn't feel as cold as he had earlier, but his skin felt prickly, and his neck and stomach were hurting him even more. He wondered if he could go home right after this was done.

Nurse Kaitlyn appeared at the corner of the curtain.

"We have a surprise for you, Alex," she said.

Mom smiled as Nurse Kaitlyn counted. "One—two—and three." Nurse Kaitlyn pulled the curtain back, and Charlie was standing there with a mask on. He had what Mom called "surgical caps" taped over his big hands instead of gloves, his mask looked like a small white nose, and the cap on his head fit like something a real swimmer would wear.

Alex laughed as Nurse Kaitlyn pulled the big chair from the other side of the room to the foot of the bed. She guided Charlie to the chair, who waved at Mom before sitting down. Nurse Kaitlyn patted Charlie on the shoulder and pulled out Mr. Brave, who was also wearing a tiny cap and surgical mask. Mom laughed real hard.

"We need you to stay right there," Nurse Kaitlyn said. "Okay, Charlie?"

"He won't move," Mom said.

"I know he won't," Nurse Kaitlyn said. She held the puppet up and Mr. Brave said, "Everything is going great, guys!"

"Okay," Alex said.

"Who is your bestest best friend ever?" Mr. Brave asked.

"Charlie!" Alex said.

As Nurse Kaitlyn and Mr. Brave left the room, Charlie leaned forward and waved his hello. Then he looked over at Mom, who looked sleepy.

Alex noticed the lines that ran across Charlie's forehead and knew that there were things Charlie didn't understand. There were things that he probably was curious about.

"You want to know why I'm here, don't you, Charlie?" Alex asked, yawning. He guessed that Charlie also wanted him back home to watch TV, play hide-and-seek, and eat bologna sandwiches.

Charlie held up his hands with the masks on them and lightly patted them together.

"I gotta get this bone marrow stuff in me," he said. "So I can get better. Then I can come home."

Alex looked over at his mother, who was sleeping. Sleeping seemed like a really good idea. He smiled again at Charlie and closed his eyes.

• • •

Brooke's head jerked, and her heart felt like it kicked in her chest, popping her out of sleep. As she caught her breath and the room swung in and out of focus, she could see that Macey had returned and was standing behind Charlie. *Yes, Brooke . . . you're at the hospital. Alex is sick. This is really happening.*

"I didn't mean to wake you," the doctor said, stepping to the other side of the bed to toggle a switch on one of the machines that was attached to Alex.

"Oh, it's fine," Brooke said, a little embarrassed she'd dozed off. She looked at Charlie, who looked like he hadn't moved since he arrived. It was like he was Alex's personal body guard. She sat up in the chair and wondered how long she was out. It could have been five minutes or five hours. All she knew was that she was still exhausted.

"Excuse me one second," Macey said, coming around to Brooke's side of the bed. The doctor leaned behind Alex and adjusted a pair of knobs on a different machine, adding a soothing hum to the room, making Brooke even sleepier.

Brooke rubbed her eyes and took a deep breath. Alex had shifted his head on the pillow away from Charlie and was facing her. The dark circles under his eyes had become more apparent, and it seemed like he was smiling in his sleep. Brooke smiled back at him. He was a little angel. He practically looked like a doll. *He is going to get better, she thought. In fact, he is getting better right now. Please, Lord, make him better!*

"One more second here," Macey said, putting her foot on the side rail a little closer to Brooke. "Sorry about the intrusion."

"No problem," Brooke said, unable to take her eyes off of Macey's tennis shoe—the way her foot was positioned on the rail and the light blue Nike logo.

"That should do it," Macey said.

"Your shoe," Brooke said. It reminded her of something . . .

"Yeah," Macey said. "I threw them into the washer, and that one came out faded. I don't mind, though. I'm not trying to make a fashion statement."

The shore. It was on the shore at the park.

"Shirley and I were walking along the lake a while back, and we found a single Nike tennis shoe laying in the sand. It looked just like yours."

"Only one shoe?" Macey asked, letting out a little laugh.

"Yeah," Brooke said.

"I've seen one on the side of the road before," Macey said, "but never at the lake." She walked back around Brooke and stopped next to Charlie. "It's good to see Alex, isn't it, Charlie?"

Charlie smiled at her and nodded.

"I'll be back in fifteen minutes or so," Macey said. "Everything is going smoothly, okay?"

Brooke was looking back at Alex. She didn't answer.

"Did you hear me, Brooke?" Macey asked.

Right near the Nike tennis shoe—the one with the faded Nike logo.

"I'll be back in about fifteen minutes," Macey repeated.

Brooke just kept staring at Alex. One of his eyes opened and looked at her, then closed.

"You all right, Brooke?"

"The doll," Brooke said dreamily.

"The doll?" Macey asked. "What do you mean?"

Brooke could feel the tears dampening her surgical mask.

"What doll?" Macey asked, coming back around Charlie and kneeling next to Brooke's chair. "What's wrong?"

Brooke couldn't take her eyes off of Alex, nor her mind's eye off the doll. The baby-doll she and Shirley had seen, near the tennis shoe. She remembered that most of its hair had fallen out. She remembered how the lake water had stained dark circles under its eyes. She remembered how one of those eyes seemed pasted shut and how the other eye had just stared at her. It looked dead.

"Brooke?" Macey said. "What is it?" She took her hand.

"I'm okay," Brooke muttered, still crying. But she wasn't.

She remembered thinking about the little girl who lost the doll.

Wondering how the little girl must have felt, knowing she'd never see her baby again. Wondering how long the little girl must have cried, hopelessly wanting to hold her baby just one more time.

But she didn't get to. Her baby was gone, carried away in the water . . .

THIRTY-NINE

I'll call you in about an hour," Zach said, kissing Kaitlyn on her cheek before she made her way out of the fellowship hall. He turned and waited for Pastor Jim to finish talking to an older couple.

"You look like a man deep in thought," Pastor Jim said.

"Thoughts," Zach said, feeling like a man with a secret. "And it won't cost you a penny to hear some of them."

"Let's head back to the office," Pastor Jim said. He gestured toward the narrow hallway that led to the back of the church.

Zach followed him.

"Are you going to be at the hospital this afternoon?" Pastor Jim asked. He stopped in the hallway and turned the thermostat down. "Shirley and I were going to run up there around three-ish."

"Not today," Zach said. "Kaitlyn and I both have the day off, and we were going to head up to Birch Run for a couple of hours and shop."

"Ah, Frankenmuth," Pastor Jim said. "Haven't been there in years. It's beautiful."

"It is."

Pastor Jim opened the door to his office and flicked on the light switch. "With us heading over to see Alex every night, I hope you guys don't run out of those masks and gloves."

Zach smiled. "Well, prepping Charlie is like outfitting five people, but I think we'll be okay." He paused, thinking about how faithful the Lindys had been. A visit every night since Alex's blood marrow transfusion, almost a week ago, and many days before then.

They truly embodied the meaning of extended family. "You have all been incredibly supportive of Alex, Pastor Jim."

Pastor Jim smiled. "Ahh, it's the least we could do. By the grace of God, they say he is doing well and everything seems to be going as planned."

By the grace of God? Zach thought. *As planned?* He could still see the look on Macey's face when she shared what Kenneth had asked her about her best not being good enough. That single look had let him know that her normal mountain of confidence hadn't just been reduced, it had been eliminated.

And Macey was right, wasn't she? Had it been anyone but Kenneth who had said it . . .

"Have a seat," Pastor Jim said, clearing off the top of his desk.

"Nice office."

"I used to spend a lot of time in here," he said, stacking books he had just taken off his desk onto a small table behind him. "Excuse the mess. I was going through these, trying to get organized, and in the process, became more unorganized."

"I certainly know that feeling," Zach said, pointing at a photograph on the wall. "Who is that good-looking couple?"

"Forty-three years ago," Pastor Jim said, smiling and running his finger across the wood that framed his wedding picture. "I am lucky. To me, she's every bit as beautiful today as she was then."

"You are both lucky. You seem very happy."

"We are." Pastor Jim sat down and closed the Bible in front of him. "You and Kaitlyn certainly seem to be hitting it off lately, but I'm guessing you're not here to discuss my marriage services."

"Not yet," he said, pausing. "It's that obvious that something's bothering me?"

"I'm not sure if *bother* is the word I would use," the minister said. "Preoccupied, maybe?"

"More than maybe."

"Let's give it a whirl," Pastor Jim said. "What's on your mind?"

Zach put his hands flat on top of the desk. He wasn't quite sure where to start. "I'm new to a lot of this, Pastor Jim. So please bear with me."

"You can say whatever you want in here, Zach. Take your time."

"You see, I've experienced something that's allowed me to be very confident in my knowledge of God's presence. But despite my confidence, I guess I still have questions about the Lord and the way . . . well, the way some things end up happening."

"You're not the only one," Pastor Jim said, his kind and patient smile bending his lips. "Maybe we can help each other."

"I want to know more about why God allows things to happen. Bad things. Like this, with little Alex. I meet up with kids like him every day."

"God has a plan," Pastor Jim said. "And everything does happen for a reason. In fact, Paul tells us to 'know that all things work together for good to those who love God, to those who are called according to his purpose.'"

"But then, why do bad things happen to good people?"

"His promise isn't that bad things don't happen, Zach. His promise is that God can turn every circumstance into something good. *Every* circumstance. Sometimes we just need to look." He sighed heavily and lifted one eyebrow. "Sometimes it takes a lot of time to see it. Sometimes we don't get to see it at all—but somehow our suffering aids others. The key is trusting the Master, through it all."

Zach thought about Amy. About how he'd been striving so hard, and for so long, to somehow make up for her death. To pay penance for a crime he did not commit. And then he thought again about Macey's best not being good enough for Alex, and how she might have to soon come to a similar realization. *Some things are out of our control.*

"Make sense?" Pastor Jim asked.

"Yes." He took a deep breath. "But then why pray at all? For healing? For change?"

Pastor Jim gave him a gentle smile. "Because he loves to hear from his children. You and me. And you never know if he simply wants us to ask before he grants it to us." He tapped his lips. "In really simplistic terms, it's kind of like a kid asking for a cookie. If it's the right time, not too close to a meal, then sure, we say yes. But if it's going to spoil a meal, or if the kid has had nothing but junk to eat all day, we say no. Right?"

"Right."

"But the kid can't really see that. All he can see is the cookie, and how yummy it looks, and how he wants it right now. Only someone with a greater perspective can make the wise decision. And the wise kid accepts and trusts that person."

"I understand," Zach said. "But what if we're not talking cookies? What if we're talking someone's *life*?"

Pastor Jim seemed to hesitate, and their met eyes again. "Are you talking about Alex?"

"Yes. And others . . ."

Pastor Jim sighed. "Obviously, the stakes are totally different, but the same principle applies. Regardless of what the outcome is, Zach, and as much sense as it does or doesn't make, we really are not capable of understanding it all. We're left with one decision: to trust or not to trust. Because we are not in control as much as we'd like to be. I mean, we're to use our God-given brains, to follow where God leads. But we're sinful, fallible people in a fallen world. There are a ton of dynamics at play."

Zach stared at him for a long moment. "It's strange. But I do have this weird feeling that everything is going to be okay, Pastor Jim. Regardless of what happens. *I know it.*"

"That's all that really counts here," Pastor Jim said. "Let go, and let God take care of it, no matter how it feels at the time."

Kenneth's words to Macey ran through Zach's mind again, speaking to him as much to her, it seemed.

What if your best wasn't good enough?

Zach stood. "But what I really want is for everyone . . ." He stopped, and the images of people flitted across his mind, like a slideshow in his head—first there was Kaitlyn, then Macey, Brooke, Ian, Shirley . . . and finally Charlie. "What I really want is for *everyone else* to know that whatever happens, it really is all for a reason. I want everyone to believe that. I just want them to have—"

"Faith?" Pastor Jim interrupted calmly.

Zach looked at the cross on the wall behind Pastor Jim. He

wanted everyone to feel the way he did . . . at peace and secure with whatever was to come. He brought the tips of his fingers to his forehead and thought about Alex and how the boy fit into that equation.

"Faith?" Pastor Jim asked again.

"I don't know," he said.

"Think about it. Something tells me you do."

Zach looked away from the pastor, to the cross. A lot of things had happened in his life for reasons he couldn't understand. Maybe he never would. But somehow, it was still okay. He'd been freed from making it all make sense, freed from making Amy's death—and the patients he'd lost—count. Because their God had already counted them. It was up to Christ to save them, not Zach. *Not me. Not me! And not Macey either . . .*

Even though it had taken him close to forty-one years, it was at that exact moment that Zach Norman knew he had something he never had before. He looked at Pastor Jim.

"Yes, Pastor Jim," he said. "Faith."

FORTY

I'm just a little tired," Alex said, rolling carefully onto his side. It hurt to move much. He scratched right above his belly button and ran his tongue around his top gums. He was tired of feeling tired, and even though the inside of his mouth was sore and the inside of his nose was feeling scratchy, he did feel pretty good today. He had been in this room for a long time, close to a month, Mom had said, and he was hoping maybe he could go home today. Mom promised that it was gonna be pretty soon.

Maybe if I pretend I'm okay, they'll let me go, he thought. But even the thought of pretending made him sleepier still.

"Do you want me to turn the DVD off, then?" Dad asked, pointing up at the small television mounted on the wall. "You look like you need to take a nap."

"No," Alex said, making his eyes open wider. Willy Wonka had just walked out of his factory.

Pastor Jim was sitting in the chair next to Dad, playing cards. He set down a card. "If you ever try to pause, stop, or change a movie with Alex or Charlie in the room, you do so at your own risk."

"Yeah, Pastor Jim," Alex said playfully. He licked his lips again. "Hey, Pastor Jim?"

"What, Wonka boy?"

"My nose hasn't bleeded today."

"That's great," Pastor Jim said, his mask making his new eyes look really new.

"It's okay even if it does, partner," Dad said. "You're doing really good."

"Yeah, I know," Alex said. "Does that mean I can maybe go home?"

"We still have a little bit to go, partner."

"Okay," Alex said. That didn't seem like too long.

"Hello, Mr. Alex," Nurse Kaitlyn said, entering the room. She pressed the buttons and wrote some numbers in the same folder that Dr. Lewis carried. "I just saw your mother outside."

"Unbelievable," Dad said, smiling and shaking his head. "Brooke can't stay at home for longer than a couple of hours, can she?"

"And I think she wants to see *the boss* as soon as possible," Nurse Kaitlyn said, tilting the edge of the folder at Alex.

"I'm the boss?" Alex asked. He liked that idea.

"Yes, you are, Alex," the nurse said. "You sure seem chipper today."

"Yeah," Alex said, not having any idea what Nurse Kaitlyn meant. Based on her smile and the way she said it, he decided that *chipper* was something good.

"Is Brooke here by herself?" Pastor Jim asked.

"No," Nurse Kaitlyn said. "Shirley is out there with her." The nurse closed the folder and looked at Alex. "Hey, Bossman, you sure have a lot of people who care about you."

"That's good," Alex said, wondering, *If I had a candy bar with a golden ticket, could I go to meet Willy Wonka?* He didn't ever remember seeing a golden ticket before, just the silver wrapper part that he and Charlie tore in two pieces when they shared.

"Why don't we run down to the cafeteria and get something to eat?" Dad asked Pastor Jim. Then Dad checked his phone. "I gotta head over to work for a few minutes after that."

"Okay," Pastor Jim said. "Then I can come back up and take Shirley home in an hour or so."

"That'll work," Dad said as he and Pastor Jim stood.

"I'll see you in a little bit, Alex," Pastor Jim said.

"Okay, Pastor Jim." He always felt a little sad when any of them left. He wanted to be home, with all of them. All the time.

Dad rubbed his head. "I'll be back tonight. You get some rest. Deal?"

"Deal," Alex said. "And then maybe you can take me home."

"Not yet, partner. But you'll be home before you know it."

• • •

"This food is pretty darn good," Pastor Jim said, stabbing his fork into the East Shore cafeteria's version of chicken Caesar salad. "Hospital food or not."

Ian nodded and then took another bite of pepperoni pizza. "Brooke and I've been down here probably four or five times with Kaitlyn. She continuously steers us toward the pizza as some type of precautionary measure so we avoid the other food. It's not all bad."

"You spending the night here tonight?"

"Probably," Ian said. "They have only been letting one of us stay, and Brooke needs a break that's longer than two hours."

"But will she agree to it? That's the question," Pastor Jim said.

"I think so. I think she finally believes that Alex is stable. And that she can trust me to watch him sleep." Ian tossed the minister a wry grin.

Pastor Jim smiled, closed his eyes, and flattened his palm on the table. "I just want this to be over so they can both move on. I feel so bad for Alex, lying up there, hooked up to all those things. And for Brooke, fretting over him every day."

"They're both troupers. They'll get through this. We all will."

"It will all be okay," Pastor Jim said.

"It has to be," Ian said. He took the napkin off his lap, folded it neatly, and placed it on top of the table.

"You're a lucky man," Pastor Jim said. "And I know that you know what I mean."

"I know," Ian said. "In more ways than one." He thought about all that'd happened to him—he'd gained a son, some true friends, and for the first time, something that resembled a relationship with God.

"God is good," Pastor Jim said, smiling not so shyly. "Everything good comes from him. It's awesome."

Ian's cell phone chirped and he answered it by the end of the second ring.

"What?" he said, darting up. He felt like ice water was pouring down the inside of his chest. "We're on our way."

"What?" Pastor Jim asked, his smile vanishing.

"Alex is having a seizure," he said, and then he turned and ran.

FORTY-ONE

Ian raced past the third-floor nurses' station and down the isolated hall that led toward the BMT corridor. They slowed at the solid double doors that led into the unit, and Ian slammed his fist against the shiny metal square button on the wall that automatically opened them. Ian could see Shirley and Brooke standing down the hallway. Brooke was crying and had her face buried in Shirley's shoulder; the two women stood outside of the door that led to yet another hallway and then to Alex's room.

"What happened?" Ian asked. "Where is he?"

"It was terrible," Brooke said, lifting her face and then letting go of Shirley to hug Ian. "His eyes rolled back, and he was shaking so hard. And then . . ."

"And then what?" Ian asked, pulling back and looking at Brooke as he held her out in front of him by her shoulders. "Brooke, *is he all right*?"

"And then they put all of these ice packs on him . . ."

"They said he is going to be all right," Shirley said. "Try to—"

"I want to know what happened!" Ian said, putting his hands on his head. "He was fine just a second ago! Where's Dr. Lewis?" he bellowed down the hall, toward a nurse.

"Please, Ian," Shirley said, taking a step toward him. "They said for us to stay out here. Macey's in there with him."

"I'm going in there!"

"Please, Ian," Shirley said again, blocking his way. "We're not—"

"He needs me!"

"Yes, he does," Shirley said. "But he needs *them* more right now."

Ian glanced at Brooke, who seemed to agree with Shirley. He glanced over at Pastor Jim who gave him a fatherly nod, and then Ian tilted his head up to the ceiling and closed his eyes. He had never felt so helpless.

"C'mon," Shirley said, holding out her arms as if she were talking him off of a ledge.

"I don't understand it," Ian said, running his hand through his hair again. "We just left here, and he seemed fine."

"He was fine," Brooke said, her eyebrows wilting as she glared back at the door. "And then all of a sudden, his hands went into little fists and his eyes rolled back." She paused, noticing that the door was moving. Macey came out and pulled down her surgical mask.

"Is he all right?" Ian asked. "What happened?"

"It's called a febrile seizure," she said. "He's okay. It's caused by an abrupt increase in body temperature."

"But how in the world did that happen?" Ian asked. "All of the things he is hooked up to. You can read his temperature right there on the machine. We just left the room about—"

"Ian," Macey said, holding up her hand. "Febrile seizures can happen in a matter of seconds. We are prepared for when things like this happen. What's important is that he is stable right now."

"But why—what caused the increase in his temperature? I don't understand."

"There are several things that could have caused it."

"Like what?"

"Ian," Macey said again, this time putting her hand on his arm. "It may only be a side effect of the transplant, but we are taking blood cultures right now to make sure."

"Make sure of what?"

"That it's not something else."

"When can we go in there?"

"When they're done," Macey said firmly. "I don't want you in there right now."

"Why not? Why can't we go in there?" The more she said he couldn't, the more he wanted it.

"Because," Macey said in a way that entertained no argument.

"He's going to be very uncomfortable while they take those cultures. You guys are his protectors—"

"Exactly. As his protectors, we—"

"*No*," Macey said, lifting her hand. She took a deep breath and dropped her hand. "These cultures are going to be painful for him. It's this simple: I don't want him to watch you watch us hurt him. There's nothing you can do to help him, and trust me, he won't understand."

"Oh," Ian said, glancing at Brooke and regretting that he'd asked. Now all he could imagine was Alex screaming, reaching out for him, begging him to make it stop. *Dad.*

"They're probably done already, okay? Just hang tight for a minute. I'll be right back."

She opened the door and then pulled it closed behind her.

Brooke began to weep again, and she walked to Pastor Jim who took her in his arms.

"It's probably over already," Ian said, desperately repeating Macey's words.

"He's going to be okay," Shirley said. "She said he's stable. That's the important thing."

"Stable?" Brooke said, through choking tears. "If you could've seen him, Ian . . . His back arched off the bed and the sound of him choking on his tongue . . . They all came running in and put their hands over the bed rails, so he wouldn't thrash against them."

The door opened back up, and Kaitlyn stepped out.

"He's all right," she said, motioning with her hand to Brooke and Ian. "But he wants to see you two."

Ian and Brooke followed Kaitlyn through the door and into the small area where they put on their masks, gloves, and caps.

Macey stepped out from behind the curtain, and even though she had on a mask, Ian recognized that her game face was still on. "We've asked Alex to be still for a bit," she said. "We'll come back in a little while to remove the ice packs, then we'll see if we can get him to take a little nap. He has to be exhausted. So let's all stay real low-key, okay?" She looked at both of them.

They quickly agreed and pulled back the curtain. Alex was lying there with ice packs around his groin and under his armpits. Ian felt his chest constrict at the sight of Alex's face, pasty and pale. The few strands of hair he had left were now sweaty and glued to his head like fresh scratches. It looked like his freckles had disappeared. His eyes were sunken, darker, and more hollow. His cheeks were puffy, and both sides of his nose were tear-soaked.

"Oh, Alex," Brooke said. "I'm so sorry you had to go through that, baby."

Alex's eyebrows huddled together, and his bottom lip covered the top one. He looked disappointed, like he didn't want them to know he had been crying.

"Hey, partner," Ian said.

Alex tried to talk and cleared his throat, wincing in pain. He swallowed delicately and paused. "Does this mean I don't get to go home pretty soon?" A new tear was forming at the corner of his left eye.

"I don't think so, buddy," Brooke said.

Alex's eyes shifted to his father, and Ian knew that he hoped for a different answer from him. The sharp teeth of helplessness bit once again into the edge of Ian's heart as the tear slowly cascaded down Alex's cheek. It made *him* want to cry.

"Just try to rest, partner," Ian said, trying to force cheer and confidence in his voice. Alex seemed easily ten times—no, a hundred times—more sickly than when he'd seen him an hour ago. He looked like a little old man, and what tugged even more at Ian's heartstrings was the fact that Alex appeared to be ashamed of himself. Like he'd failed. And there was something else, something he couldn't quite identify.

And then, looking at Brooke, he knew what it was.

It probably was plain as day on his own face too.

His brave little man, less than a week away from his sixth birthday, could neither fight it nor hide it any longer.

Alex was scared.

FORTY-TWO

I know you're out there," Macey said, gazing out of her small office window over the parking lot and into the construction site. "And I know you hear me."

She turned the small crank to crack open the window and was slapped by a gust of crisp December air. She looked down at the muddy, slush-banked puddles that littered the parking lot like hundreds of tiny lakes and guessed it was no more than ten degrees outside.

Where are you?

She lifted her elbows to the windowsill and cradled her head in her palms as she surveyed the fenced-in area that was reserved for the construction crew. She noticed the mounds of plowed snow, dirtied from exhaust, along with the three different plywood walkways that had been assembled over the icy muck that led from the parking area to the different entrances of the new wing.

A half dozen men stood outside a foreman's trailer, sipping coffee and listening to a heavyset man who wore coveralls that were way too clean. He pointed in all different directions, and their heads followed his finger as frozen puffs of air came out of his mouth with every word.

"So you think you're the boss out there?" she said to the heavy man, having a sneaking suspicion that at least one of his employees had a more impressive resume.

"Who are you talking to?" Kaitlyn asked, standing in Macey's doorway.

"Myself," she said, her eyes quickly running down a row of cars and trucks that had all been glazed by a powdery film from winter roads. She turned around and clapped her hands together, trying to snap herself out of her preoccupied mind-set. "Whatcha got?"

"Good news," Kaitlyn said. "Dr. Mueller said no growth after twenty-four hours for Alexander."

"That doesn't surprise me," Macey said, taking a copy of the e-mail from the nurse. "I never thought that this was a bacterial infection."

"What are you thinking, then?"

Macey took her hair out of its ponytail and let it fall across her shoulders. She sat at her desk and tapped her fingers nervously on the arm of her chair and then suddenly stopped. "I'm thinking he doesn't look good, Kaitlyn."

Never, ever, had they shared such words. A peculiar silence separated them, and then the nurse said, "No, he doesn't."

Macey's heart sank. Kaitlyn had a lot more experience on the pediatric oncology wing than Macey. If she agreed, then . . . It really was bad.

"What's your plan?" Kaitlyn asked, coming to sit down.

"No growth after twenty-four hours with the first culture is good news," Macey said, backing up, thinking it all through for the hundredth time.

The nurse nodded.

"And I have to respect the test results. But I have to treat the patient, not the test results."

"What are you are saying?" Kaitlyn asked. "Even though the culture looks good . . ."

"I'm saying something isn't right here, Kaitlyn."

"You'll get it," the nurse said. "That is what we do. We fix things that aren't right. And I've never seen a doc better at it than you. If it can be fixed, you will do it. Just stay focused."

"But," Macey said, feeling like she couldn't breathe, "what if it can't be fixed? What if it's out of our hands, Kait? What if there is nothing we can do about it?"

"That happens in our business too, Macey," she said somberly. "All we can do is our best. You know that as well as—"

"Our best?" Macey interrupted. Kaitlyn's words seemed to slap her in the face. She sat back in the chair. Then the carpenter's words shot through her. *What if your best wasn't good enough?*

"I'm going to run down and get something to eat," Kaitlyn said, frowning. "Do you want to go?"

"No. You go ahead. I need some time."

"Want me to bring anything back up?"

"I'll take whatever you're having, with a diet Coke," Macey said. "Why don't you bring yours up and we'll both eat here?"

"Okay, I'll be right back." Kaitlyn pointed at the office door. "Open or closed?"

"Close it, if you don't mind, Kait. Thanks."

Macey wandered back to the window. She felt like she had dipped her toe in the same pool that Ian had taken a few laps in earlier—*helplessness*. Her head cleared momentarily, and she found herself mechanically scanning a couple more rows of cars and pickups.

"I know you're out there," she said. "I know it."

Newer truck—newer truck—car—car—car—vacant spot—newer truck with a huge dent in driver's side door.

Down another couple rows. And then a few more.

Car—car—older truck—car—older truck—empty parking spot with a stack of wet cardboard surrounded by orange cones—newer truck—car—car—Dumpster—back end of a truck.

There. An older pickup truck.

Macey squinted and pressed her forehead against the glass as she looked straight down and to her left at the rear of the older truck.

The truck.

A flash of relief and fear rounded through her stomach. Part of her felt like she had just found a lost set of keys. The rest of her felt as if she had spotted the school bully from a distance and was desperately kidding herself that she had time to hide.

A knock sounded at her door, three times. Kaitlyn? Back so fast?

Macey opened the door and gasped.

Kenneth was standing in the hallway.

Her shoulders flinched upward, and she felt like an ice-cold mallet had struck the side of her heart. Her mouth closed, muffling her shriek, and she instinctively stepped backward.

"Hello, Macey," he said softly, his eyes filled with compassion.

She stood there, speechless, her heart hammering.

"Sorry to frighten you," he said, hooking his thumbs casually into the tops of his front jean pockets. "I was just down the hall, talking with Zach, and thought I would pop in and see how you're doing."

"You know how I'm doing," she said, finding her voice. "Why bother?"

Kenneth tilted his head. "Think so, eh?"

Macey nodded. "And so far, it looks like my best really isn't good enough with Alex. What do I do now? Just quit on him?"

"Why would you do that?" He gestured to the center of her office, and she waved him in. He quietly shut the door behind him.

"I knew you were talking about Alex when you said what you did to me at the diner—about my best not being good enough."

"Tell me why you would quit on him."

"Why don't *you* tell me?" she asked, not really sure how comfortable she was with her own audacity. "You are the big man with the plan."

Kenneth smiled casually, and she didn't like it.

Macey crossed her arms and stepped even closer. "You run the show and the rest of us are nothing more than puppets on a stage, going through the motions."

He smiled again, but it seemed a little different to her. Their eyes met, and he said, "You make it sound like you have no free will. Like you have no control over your actions."

"No," she said, maintaining their eye contact as she took another step toward him. She lifted her hand and pointed at his chest. "What I'm saying is that I have no control over what *you* do."

"That's true," he said matter-of-factly.

"What do I tell Alex's people?" she asked, taking a step back. "What do I tell those good, *Christian* people? Maybe I will just tell them that I'm doing everything I can, but someone *bigger* and *badder* than us wants Alex dead."

He stood deadly still, as if her words had wounded him. *Good,* she thought. *Good!*

"I'm not the enemy, Macey."

"Aren't you?" she asked. "Aren't you the one who basically told me my best wasn't good enough?"

"Does that make me your enemy?"

She shook her head, pushing her hair from her face. "I'm telling you I'm going to fight you on this."

"Fight me?"

"I know I can't win, but I'll still fight."

"I'm sure you will."

She had a feeling she'd already crossed a line with him, so she figured she might as well stay there. "I can beat the cancer, and I can beat whatever caused that seizure yesterday. But I can't beat destiny. I can't beat you and your will, but I'm going to try."

"I believe you."

Macey turned and shook her head as she walked toward her desk. She spun back around. She wanted just one answer and knew there would never be a better time to ask. "Why a little boy? Why Alex?" She thought about Zach and the age-old question. "That's the least you can do for me. Tell me why God lets children suffer and die? Why the little ones, Kenneth?"

"You are all little ones. Every one of you."

She clenched her fists and banged them at her sides. "But he is *five years old!* He will be six in only a few days."

Kenneth went to the window and looked out, saying nothing for the span of a minute. "Macey, you said you can't win. *Win* is an interesting word, don't you think?"

"I know I can't win," she muttered. "Deep down, I know that." She rose and walked away, wanting some distance from him. He was just too . . . close.

Kenneth turned around and didn't say anything.

"The odds have been stacked against this kid from the get-go," she said. "Right?"

He didn't answer, just stared at her.

"I've studied case after case," Macey said. "I've prepared for every possible situation. I've done things with kids that other doctors called miracles. I want to help. I want to make a difference, but with Alex, it's all about you, Kenneth. All about that mystery plan of yours. Cancer doesn't move this fast, and that seizure you gave him—and I want to reiterate the fact that *you gave it to him*—knocked three-quarters of the wind out of that kid's sail yesterday. Why don't you squeeze his kidneys a little today and make sure he suffers some more? And don't kid yourself. He *is* suffering."

Kenneth crossed his arms and let her words hang in the air between them. "Let's say I am who you think I am."

"You *are* who I think you are!" she screamed.

"Let's say that is the case." He stepped around the desk, leaned against it. "If that's true, tomorrow morning a beautiful little boy will be without suffering, without pain, in that proverbial perfect world—a paradise—and he will be there forever. How do you lose in that, Macey? How is that not winning?"

"He is a little boy!" she shouted. "And you can save him!" This wasn't going how she'd envisioned. She wanted his help, and she wanted it right away. "The cross. Mary Springsted. Pastor Jim's sight. Zach's faith. My faith—and whatever happened with you and Kaitlyn out on that bridge. These are all miracles. I'm asking you for one more—just one more."

He remained where he was, still, listening, and she took a few steps toward him.

"I see what you wanted me to learn. That it's not all up to me. That people's lives are ultimately in God's hands alone. If you'd only stop now," she pleaded. "The way Alex is right now, I can fix him. I can make him better. I know I can. Please, Kenneth."

The carpenter uncrossed his arms and lowered them to his sides. "I'm sorry, Macey."

She stepped back from him, fighting tears. "Why this little boy?" she asked. "You know it all. You've already seen it all. You have all the answers. Tell me why. Why Alex?"

"You wouldn't understand."

Someone knocked on the door behind the carpenter and then opened it. Kaitlyn, holding a white paper bag in her left hand and a cup holder in her right. Her eyes widened.

"Hello, Kaitlyn," Kenneth said, before turning back to Macey. "I've gotta get back to work now."

"Why'd you even come?" Macey asked, sinking to a chair as defeat washed through her. "Seriously . . . why'd you even bother coming?"

Kenneth approached and looked down at her. "Because you wanted me to."

She paused and then reluctantly looked up into his face, hating the fact that he was right. "I'm still going to fight you on this."

"I know you'll do your best," he said, turning and heading back to the door. He looked over his shoulder. "But don't prolong it."

Kenneth nodded at Kaitlyn, who quickly stepped aside as he went out the door.

The nurse peeked curiously back down the hallway and then turned to Macey. "What was that about?"

Macey stared blankly at the open door.

"Out with it. Tell me," Kaitlyn said, setting the bag and drinks on the table.

"Tomorrow," Macey muttered, looking out the window.

"What's tomorrow?" Kaitlyn asked.

"Alex," she said sadly. "Kenneth just told me he will be dead in the morning."

FORTY-THREE

I f you need anything at all, just let one of us know."

"Thanks," Brooke said, unable to remember the nurse's name. She pointed at Alex as he slept. "As long as he is okay, I'm okay."

The nurse's cheeks lifted above the top corners of her mask as she smiled. Brooke recognized the smile as a fellow mom's.

The nurse glanced over at Pastor Jim, who was seated at the foot of the bed, and then back at Brooke. "Kaitlyn will be back in a few minutes."

"Very good," Pastor Jim said as the nurse adjusted a bead necklace that caught Brooke's eye.

"I like your necklace," Brooke said. "One of the little patients make that for you?"

"My daughter made it for me," the nurse said, and immediately Brooke's face fell.

The nurse clicked her pen closed and hooked it over the upper edge of what Brooke and Ian had labeled *the* manila folder. Alex's file. His chart. It had been passed back and forth between them like a medical baton in a relay race that Brooke desperately wanted to end—in a good way.

"Thank you for your help," Pastor Jim said as the nurse went around the curtain and out the door.

"Pastor Jim," Brooke said, thinking about the necklace. "I can't remember what that nurse said her name was."

"Diane," he said.

"That's right," Brooke said.

"They're all doing a fine job," Pastor Jim said.

"But there are so many of them today. Even before you got here, since around two this afternoon, there have been all kinds of extra nurses coming in and out of here. Even Macey and Kaitlyn have been in here ten times more than usual."

"Our boy's in good hands," Pastor Jim said, scratching at his left ear and adjusting his surgical cap. He leaned forward on his chair and dropped his elbows on top of his knees as he stared at Alex. "I'm thankful for all of the help he's getting."

"Me too, but I don't like the idea of an infectious disease specialist, or whatever he was called, being here."

"They just want to be sure nothing else caused his seizure," Pastor Jim said. "And from what you said, the results of that first culture they took looked pretty good."

"Yeah, but I still don't understand how it's possible for whatever they are looking for—the bacteria, or whatever it is—to *not* be there after twenty-four hours, but to still be able to show up after forty-eight or seventy-two hours. It doesn't make sense to me."

"Me either," Pastor Jim said. "But whatever they're doing is all part of how he will be made well. That I know."

"Why can't he be well now? How much more does he have to endure?" Brooke asked.

"I'm not sure," he said, speaking softly. He waved his hand in a small circle above the bed. "But I would like to tell you how I feel about some of this, if that's okay."

"Of course," Brooke said. "I always want to know what you think, Pastor Jim."

Pastor Jim's eyes stayed fixed on Alex. "You know, Brooke, I sit here and look at Alex, and I remember the day he was born. He's made such a difference in all of our lives—your life, Charlie's, and of course, mine and Shirley's." His head never moved, but his eyes shifted to Brooke, and they stared at each other for a few seconds.

"You're gonna make me cry, Pastor Jim."

"Go ahead and cry, then, sweetie. I may join you."

"I've never seen you cry," she said, swallowing hard around a ball in her throat.

Pastor Jim looked back at Alex and rested his hands on the edge of the bed. "It's hard for me to describe the way I feel, Brooke. All that I'm thinking."

"Go ahead and try. I'll listen."

Pastor Jim turned to Brooke and lowered his voice. "We have an enemy with us, honey. We live in a fallen world and still experience so many consequences like sickness and even death, but I look at Alex—"

"Don't say death, Pastor Jim," she whispered, fresh tears streaming down her cheeks. Was he saying what she thought he was saying? *Please, God, no . . .*

"Don't get ahead of me. Just hear me out," Pastor Jim said, his hands lifting back off the bed. "I look at Alex right now—I look at him the way he is right this second—all of those things hooked up to him, how pale he is, how thin he is, and how his hair has fallen out. As hard as I look, I just can't see his spark right now—you know, that spark of his that lights up every room he goes in?"

"Yeah," Brooke whispered, her heart pounding. She knew exactly what he meant.

Pastor Jim pointed back at Alex. "And there he is, exactly where I would never want him to be, looking the way he is, and still . . . there is absolutely no doubt in my mind . . . I really can't explain it, but I am *certain*, Brooke."

The growing strength of his tone encouraged her. "Certain of what?" she whispered, wiping her eyes.

"That God is going to make him better."

"I like when you say that, Pastor Jim."

"I wouldn't say it if I didn't believe it. The Lord has never given me so much confidence about anything in my life, Brooke. I'm not talking about wishful thinking here. To me, it's a certainty. I have no doubt at all. Not a shred."

"Not a shred?" Brooke repeated.

"None," he said. "And I want God to give it to you. I want you to be the one without any doubt that Alexander will be made well."

"How about both of us having it?" Brooke said.

"Only believe," Pastor Jim said.

"Yeah."

"Never forget that," he said, nodding at Alex, who stirred lightly in the bed. "You just keep being a wonderful mother. Let the professionals do their work here, and the Lord will do his."

"Okay," Brooke said. Something Pastor Jim said made her want to tell him about another necklace. Not the one Nurse Diane was wearing, but the necklace that belonged to her. *And her mother.* "My mom was a wonderful mother too. And that necklace Nurse Diane was wearing reminded me of something I want to share with you."

"Lay it on me," Pastor Jim said.

Brooke took a deep breath, holding off more tears.

"I don't think a day has gone by where I don't think about it," she said. "In fact, I'm sure of it."

"Think about what?"

"A necklace my mother and I made," she said. "Alex is the only one I've told about it since my parents died."

"Why is that?"

"I guess because making the necklace was *our* moment," Brooke said. "Not mine and Alex's, but me and my mother's. It's what I remember most about her."

"Making a necklace?"

"Yeah," Brooke said. "It was craft day at my preschool. I was four. We made the necklace out of dental floss, macaroni, Mod Podge, and a little piece of cardboard. They took a Polaroid photo of us. I was sitting on her lap. We were wearing matching outfits and both of us had ponytails pulled over our left shoulders. We glued the photo to the little piece of cardboard. Then we cut it into the shape of a heart, poked a hole in the top, and slid it on to the necklace."

"That's special, Brooke."

"Yeah," Brooke said. "We took turns wearing it. She'd wear it one day and I'd wear it the next. That went on for probably three months."

"Awesome," Pastor Jim said.

"One day I was on the playground when it was my turn to wear it. It was unusually warm out and when I went to take my coat off, the cardboard heart popped off. I couldn't find it. The whole class looked for it in the grass for probably twenty minutes until finally, we found it. Even after I had it back in my hands, I was still crying so hard that they let me call and talk to my mom so I'd calm down."

Don't cry, Brookie. The reason it fell off is because we love each other so much the necklace just couldn't hold it all.

"Sounds like somebody really loved her mother," Pastor Jim said.

"She was everything to me," Brooke said. "But she was wearing the necklace the day she and my father died and I never saw it again. Dumb thing only cost twenty cents to make but I'd give all my money to get it back."

Pastor Jim nodded and pointed at the bed. Alex was awake.

"Hey, sleepyhead," Brooke said. "That was a short nap."

Alex's left eye was only half as open as his right.

"Mom," he whispered. "Me and Charlie have way more than twenty cents saved. I'll buy you a new necklace."

"Thank you, buddy," Brooke said. "But that necklace wasn't special because of what it cost. It was special because me and your grandma made it together."

"Oh," Alex said. She could barely hear him. His eyes would close and then slowly reopen. "Well, you said she had it when she went to heaven. If I don't get better and I go to heaven, too, I promise to find Grandma and ask her where it's at so you can get it back."

"Don't say that, baby. You are getting better right now."

"I know," he said.

"They are bringing you some more ice chips for your mouth."

Alex squinted at the food tray on the side of the bed and then fell back asleep. Brooke wondered if the lining of his mouth and the area behind his eyes still hurt him or if his stomach still felt funny. She wanted to know what he was thinking about. Maybe it was about his new baseball mitt and how his dad had promised to show him how to play when the snow melted. Ian had even given him a hint about a new bike for his birthday—one that Alex insisted not have baby wheels on it.

Kaitlyn slid the curtain open, and Alex's eyes opened a bit again.

"Here you go, Mr. Alex," she said, stepping to the side of the bed and handing Brooke a Styrofoam cup of ice chips. "Feeling a little warm still?"

Alex's eyelids bobbed up and down, and then he nodded.

"He keeps falling asleep and waking up," Brooke said. "He hasn't stayed awake longer than a few minutes all day long."

"He's wiped," Kaitlyn said. "Not unusual after what he's gone through."

"He falls asleep even with *Charlie and the Chocolate Factory* on," Brooke said, scooping a few ice chips to the tip of a small plastic spoon and holding it out in front of Alex. "Even with Willy Wonka on, huh, buddy?"

"He's still running a low-grade fever," Kaitlyn said, glancing at Alex's food tray that was untouched.

Alex's bottom lip dropped, and Brooke tipped a pair of ice chips off the spoon into his mouth. He dabbed at the ice with his tongue, and his bloodshot eyes watered. He tried to say something, but Brooke could only make out a couple of the words.

"What, buddy?" she asked, lowering her head within a few inches of his mouth. "See Charlie what?"

"See Charlie," he whispered.

Brooke forced a smile. "Maybe when you wake up next time, Charlie will be here with those caps on his hands."

Alex had trapped a few ice chips between his tongue and the inside of his cheek. As they dissolved against the roof of his mouth, he fell back asleep.

"There he goes again," Brooke said.

"Let him rest," Kaitlyn said, glancing at a monitor behind Alex. "He needs it."

"There's blood on the spoon, Kaitlyn," she said, trying not to panic as she looked at the bright red against the bright white plastic.

"Low platelets," the nurse said. "I want all three of you to try to relax, and I'll be back in a few minutes."

Brooke lifted her feet up to the edge of her seat as Kaitlyn left. She crouched forward and rested her arms across her knees.

"Why don't you go ahead and take a little nap?" Pastor Jim said.

"You look exhausted, Brooke. I'll do nothing but stare at our boy and pray over him."

"Thanks, Pastor Jim. I'm glad you're here."

"Me too," he said.

"Can you believe what he said about finding my mother in heaven?"

"Somebody really loves his mother," Pastor Jim said.

Brooke watched as Pastor Jim pulled out a pocket-sized New Testament. St. Thomas had been fortunate enough to recently receive two hundred of them from the Gideons, and he hadn't been able resist the temptation of keeping one for himself.

Brooke slid her hip against the lower part of the chair's right armrest and tried to get comfortable. Her sleep had become nothing more than a series of interrupted dozes, each loaded with its own dream sequence where none of this had ever happened. Each of the dreams took her to places like Lakeside Metropark, where Alex and his full head of bright red hair swung daringly on the swings, or to Church Road, where a healthy and vibrant Alex—a boy with a spark—threw rocks at invisible monsters. Other times the dreams would allow her to watch as Alex played with Charlie behind the church or irritated everyone by accidentally resetting the TV remote control in the basement. Regardless, the dreams were nothing more than teases, dashed when she woke up to reality.

Invisible monster? she thought, lifting her head and glancing at Alex over the bed's side rail. *Keep fighting it, buddy.*

She lowered her head again and peeked back at Pastor Jim as he flipped through the tiny Bible. He put it back in his pocket, stood up, and lowered his head while stretching his arm out over the end of the bed toward Alex. He began to say the Lord's Prayer, and the tranquility of his voice made Brooke sleepier.

Her eyes fell closed again. She was back at the Metropark and could see a flock of geese flying over her head. They now seemed dark and were flying in slow motion.

"Hallowed be thy name . . ."

The lake was like black glass. It was perfectly still except for the reflections of the three geese as they headed toward Canada. *Three?*

There were just twenty or thirty of them. And where did Shirley go? Wasn't Shirley just here?

She kept walking, and Pastor Jim kept praying. She could hear his voice like a narrator in a movie.

"Thy kingdom come . . ."

She continued to walk down the shore. The sand felt like cool flour between her toes, and the only thing she could hear were the sounds of her own breath and heart. She looked up the bank and then up the hill to where Charlie had just picked Alex up out of the leaf pile. They weren't there. There were no leaves, no more swing sets, no more playground. It was all gone.

"Thy will be done . . ."

She could hear something. It was coming from above her. It was faint, and it had a pulse. Little flashes of light behind the solid gray sky beckoned her. She looked farther down the shoreline. Someone was standing there, waiting for her. It was a man.

She walked toward him. With each step, the pulse grew stronger. Its buzz became louder and more pronounced. It was an old man—a very old man with a beard and shiny white hair. He was holding something.

She kept walking, and the buzz got louder with each step she took. But she kept going, knowing that whatever the old man was holding, she wanted it. It was the reason she was there. It was why *they* were there.

She was no more than twenty feet from the old man when she stopped. Something about him looked familiar. She felt comfortable, as if she knew him, as if she'd always known him. He looked like he wanted to show her something.

He turned his head toward the sky and pointed with his left hand. That light in the sky grew brighter and flashed in perfect unison with each pulse of the vibrating noise, the noise that now came in hollow booms, outwardly warning her of something. She closed her eyes and covered her ears. The noise was unbearable.

And then it stopped.

She opened her eyes, and the old man was smiling at her. Yes, it was a familiar smile—a smile that told her everything was all right. It told her that everything was going to be okay.

The old man lifted his arms straight out in front of him. In his hands was the doll. The doll from the lake.

It was brand-new.

Both of its eyes were glassy and bright, and its thick red hair shined. The man held it out a little farther, and Brooke stepped forward.

You've got it right, the old man said in a familiar voice.

The buzzing sound was back and grew louder and louder . . .

Brooke's head slid off the armrest, and she sprung up in her chair. Kaitlyn was hitting a switch that killed an alarm at the other side of the bed. The nurse then removed something that was attached to Alex's finger and thumbed at another button on a machine next to Alex's IV bag. Kaitlyn immediately wrapped a Velcro cuff around Alex's arm and began to take his blood pressure manually.

"What's wrong?" Brooke asked, gripping the sides of the seat and questioning herself as to whether this was real or another bizarre dream.

"Alexander was sleeping, and that alarm went off," Pastor Jim said, looking stricken. He was on his feet.

Nurse Diane appeared from behind the curtain and gestured to Brooke. "Brooke, I need you back here for a minute."

"What's wrong?" Brooke said. "Why are you doing that, Kaitlyn?"

"Diane, call the code," Kaitlyn said sternly, beginning chest compressions on Alex.

"What's happening?" Brooke asked again, her mouth dry. She tried to move closer to Alex before being held back by Pastor Jim. "Why are you doing that? Is he breathing?"

Macey and two other people rushed into the room and took their sides on the bed.

"I'll take the lead," the tallest one said.

Brooke cringed.

"Brooke, Pastor, please come with me," Diane beckoned again.

"No!" Brooke said. "Tell me what's happening!"

"Brooke, you gotta let us do our job," Kaitlyn said.

Pastor Jim grabbed Brooke and pulled her out of the room as the code team continued working on Alex.

And as the door finally closed, the last thing Brooke saw was the expression on Macey's face.

It wasn't good.

FORTY-FOUR

Just under an hour had passed before they could hear the monotone hum of muffled voices behind the door.

Ian stopped pacing.

Brooke lifted her head off Shirley's shoulder.

Pastor Jim opened his eyes and stood up, away from the wall where he'd been leaning.

When the latch finally clicked open, they watched as the youngest of the nurses pushed the door all the way open and then held it against the wall. Diane was next, slowly backing out and pulling at the foot of a gurney while the tall one at the far end stared straight ahead and pushed forward.

"Alex," Brooke said, rising. Ian stood next to her as the team wheeled him by. He'd been stripped of his Spider-Man pajama top and was flat on his back, with his arms motionless at his sides. Two other members from the code team flanked the gurney, one of them managing a pair of IVs, and the other holding and squeezing one of those breathing bags Brooke had seen on television over Alex's face.

Macey was right behind them, and waved to Ian and Brooke. "You two only. Let's go."

"We'll be in the waiting room," Shirley called as Brooke hurried to catch up with Ian, who was already right behind Macey.

"Where are you taking him?" Ian asked.

"We're going up to the ICU," Macey said, her voice now that of someone on a mission. They paused at the thick, gray doors that led out of the BMT unit and waited for them to open.

Brooke turned around and looked at Pastor Jim.

No doubts, Pastor Jim?

He nodded, as if he could hear her, and Brooke turned and followed Alex and the team out.

They stopped in front of an elevator marked Authorized Personnel Only. Brooke stared at it, anxious to look at anything but Alex, looking like he was still battling for his life as the nurse squeezed, and squeezed, and squeezed the bag . . .

Macey took Brooke by the arm and then grabbed Ian's, leading them into the elevator first, and over to the corner, out of the way. "When we get up there, you guys are going to have to wait a little longer until they get him situated. I'll come right out and sit with you in the waiting room to go over all that's happened."

The tall nurse pressed 4 on the first row of numbers, and the doors closed. The elevator was uncomfortably quiet, with the exception of the puffing sound that came from the bag over Alex's face. Brooke's boat of confidence was taking in water, and she could tell by the way Ian was looking at the gurney that his was too.

She forced herself to glance down at the side of Alex's face, which had been practically consumed by the mask. His small jawline was more pronounced than ever, and she reached her hand out, because his little eyelids looked so pink and were—

"Please don't touch him, Miss Thomas," the tall nurse said, causing Brooke to pull her hand back as if she had grazed the side of a hot stove. The nurse gave her an apologetic smile. "It's good for him to hear you, though." She gestured forward. "Please say something to him."

Brooke swallowed hard. "Alex, baby, I'm here," she said. "So's your dad." She felt like she was talking to a picture of Alex. What was before her wasn't her son, not her vibrant, bouncy boy . . .

Ian brushed away a tear like he hoped no one saw it. "Hey, partner. You gotta get better so we can go shop for that bike you want."

The elevator door opened, and they swung a right and made it past a nurses' station that Brooke guessed was three times bigger than the one down on the third floor, with nurses that disappeared behind banks of computers. The code team led them to another corridor.

Macey slowed down and then pointed to a crowded waiting room. "Please wait in there. I'll be back in a few minutes."

Brooke watched the gurney make its way down the hall. Ian was already sitting in the waiting room and had his head tilted back with his hands over his eyes. She went in and sat next to him, and he glanced over at her.

"You okay?" he asked.

"It's like this isn't really happening," she said, absorbing the tension reserved specifically for ICU waiting rooms. It was as if the twenty to thirty people in there simultaneously realized that their priorities had always been out of order. "How about you?"

"It's the worst nightmare I've ever had. It won't end, and it keeps getting worse."

"He's going to get better," Brooke said, trying to stop hyperventilating. "He has to."

"He will," Ian said. But Brooke thought he sounded only half sure.

Macey entered the room and pulled up a folding chair to sit in front of them. "Only a few more minutes until you can see him, you guys."

"What happened, Macey?" Brooke asked.

She licked her lips and then looked them both in the eye. "Alex quit breathing."

A shiver ran down Brooke's back. *He quit breathing? As in, never to begin breathing again?*

"Is he going to be all right?" Ian asked, his voice faint.

"We're doing everything we can," Macey said. "Now we just have to wait."

Brooke felt light-headed. The words sounded powerless. *Doing everything we can. As in, there's nothing else we can do. It's up to somebody else. Somebody Else.*

A nurse showed up at the waiting room door. She pointed at Brooke and Ian, and Macey nodded back.

"Ah, here's Alex's new nurse," Macey said. "The intensive care unit has its own nurses, and she's one of our best."

"Hello," the nurse said, holding out her hand. "I'm Talia." Her shiny-brown hair was pulled neatly into a shoulder-length ponytail. The resilient look in her dark brown eyes and the firmness in her handshake let Brooke know that it was all about business on this floor and that Talia had the confidence it took to be up here.

Which was fine with Brooke.

"Listen, Mom and Dad," the nurse said. She lowered her voice so only the three of them could hear her. "Before we go back, I want you to prepare yourselves, okay?"

"For what?" Ian asked.

"First of all, Alex is unconscious, and he's on a ventilator, so you're going to see a tube in his mouth. Beyond that, there are a few different machines that help us monitor him, so you're going to see wires running in all different directions. It can be tough seeing your son this way. Don't let it alarm you, and try to keep in mind that all of these things are necessary, all right?"

Brooke looked at Ian and then at Talia. "Okay."

"Do we know when he will wake up?" Ian asked, glancing at Brooke as he fidgeted with the cuff of his shirt.

He doesn't know, Brooke thought, a shred of panic sliding down her throat. *Ian doesn't know whether or not Alex will be okay.*

"We don't know that," the nurse said. "But I will be here with you all night." She smiled confidently.

"Why don't we head back?" Macey said.

Talia led them down the hallway, and Brooke tried to figure out exactly what it was about open hospital room doors that made her want to look in them. They were like eye magnets, and when she did look, it almost always seemed like someone was looking back at her.

They went through another set of thick double doors beneath a sign that read Corridor C, signaling to Brooke that Alex was once again in some type of isolation. The nurse took them into another room, where they all put on masks, gloves, and surgical caps, confirming Brooke's suspicion. They walked down to yet another room that had the block letters CUBE with the number 9 attached to the door. The nurse opened that door, and they all walked in.

There was a bathroom to their immediate left, followed by eight to ten feet of solid beige wall, and then a thin white curtain—not unlike the room he had just left. Talia pulled the curtain back, and they saw Alex lying there.

Ian gasped.

"Oh, buddy," Brooke whispered as thousands of tiny pinpoints danced nervously across the lining of her stomach.

The back portion of the bed had been slightly elevated, giving the impression that Alex was sitting up. His head was perfectly still and cocked back at what looked like an uncomfortable angle. Just looking at the tube that his mouth was taped around made Brooke want to gag. Alex's thin, bare chest was crisscrossed with more tape, which held down countless wires that tailed off toward machines to his left. His right arm was tucked under the sheet, and his left arm was draped off to his side. His little legs stuck out at forty-five-degree angles from under the blanket as tiny drops of urine skittered slowly through a catheter into a drainage bag on the side of the bed.

Despite Talia's words of warning, it was too much.

Ian stepped in front of Brooke, blocking her view. He slowly turned around and looked at her. She recognized the hollow helplessness in his eyes. *You are helpless*, she thought. *And so am I.*

"Come on," Macey said softly, inviting them to sit down.

"There are chairs over there," Talia said, pointing toward the side of the bed.

"Talia, I'm going to stay here with them for a bit," Macey said.

"Okay, I'll be back shortly."

Brooke firmly gripped the armrests and looked at the white piece of tape stretched across the top of Alex's tiny right hand. *My buddy's little hand.* Brooke wondered how many times she'd gone into the basement with a wet paper towel and found Alex sleeping. It was that same little hand she'd lift and wipe clean of Cheetos, popcorn butter, melted chocolate, or anything else he'd eaten while watching TV. It was the same little hand he held up to her last summer as Charlie carried him, running across the front yard toward the house, the swell of a bee sting forming a tiny red mound between his two little knuckles. He'd howled at her, tears racing down his face, wanting her to *please fix it, to please make it all better, to please make the stinging stop . . .*

How many other times had she bandaged and soothed that little hand?

Now she couldn't help. There was nothing she could do.

Brooke looked back to Alex's small face and knew that he was somewhere in there, quietly crying for her to come, wanting her to somehow help him—to make him better. To *please make it all go away.*

The sickening feeling of helplessness throbbed between her chest and stomach. She closed her eyes and thought of the look Pastor Jim had just given her downstairs. And then she remembered his words.

It's what he wanted her to do.

It's all she could do.

Only believe.

FORTY-FIVE

The Lindys reluctantly went home when it was apparent that nothing immediate was going to happen, but they'd been sitting at the house for nearly six hours, staring at a plate of untouched cookies and drinking Jim's especially strong coffee, as if they'd set up their own waiting room. Intermittently, they prayed. They were hoping for something that even resembled favorable news in the periodic updates they were getting from both Ian and Brooke.

"What did she say?" Jim asked, tilting forward on the La-Z-Boy when Shirley came back from answering the phone.

Shirley sat on the couch, and as Jim awaited Shirley's answer, he could sense a tiny bubble of hope that fluttered invisibly around the room, bouncing back and forth between his unwavering faith that Alex would be made well and Shirley's increasing conviction that things were getting progressively worse.

"The same thing," Shirley said. "She said the same thing that she told you an hour ago."

"Alex still hasn't woken up?"

"He hasn't moved an inch on that bed."

"Did the new nurse say anything? What are the doctors saying?"

"Macey just left," Shirley said, removing her glasses and gently rubbing her eyes. "She's been there this whole time and will be back up there around five thirty in the morning."

"What time is it?"

Shirley looked at her watch. "It's 11:50 p.m."

"And Macey just left?"

"Yes."

"God love her," Jim said, his eyebrows rising. He stood and started toward the front window. "How did Brooke sound?"

"She sounds exhausted," Shirley said. "And I'm sure Ian is too."

Jim stood at the window. In the reflection, he could see Shirley and Charlie behind him, both staring and waiting for him to say the right words. He looked out the window and down the snowy driveway into the darkness that led out to Church Road. There was another face—another expression—that came to mind. It was Brooke's. He could still see the glance she gave him as they took Alex away to the Intensive Care Unit. Brooke had always trusted what he told her—and more importantly, she trusted in God. Still, that look she had given him let him know that she wanted just one more nod of reassurance. And he'd given it to her. *Because Alex is going to be okay.*

Jim tensed and then relaxed as his eyes settled on St. Thomas. Even in the dark, there it was. He could see it perfectly—the outline of the cross in front of the church.

Tell her, James . . . only believe, and he will be made well.

He turned around. "I feel like I need to be back up at the hospital with them."

Shirley crossed her arms. "They won't let us in the ICU at this hour, James."

"I feel like I need to talk to them," he said. "To tell her again. To tell them both."

"Tell them what?" Shirley asked. "Let me guess—to only believe?"

"Yes," he said. "To only believe."

Shirley stood up from the couch and took her turn at the window. She put her hands on top of her head and then slowly looked up at him. "James, you've been telling Brooke that all along."

"I know, honey," he said. "And Brooke does believe. I know she does."

"I know she does too," Shirley said, pausing as if trying to choose her words carefully. "But . . . aren't we *all* ultimately made well? If we only believe?"

Jim frowned, a cool sliver of fear poking at his heart.

Shirley continued. "Ian sounded scared on the phone," she said. "And he doesn't seem like the type of person who gets scared. You should have heard his voice."

Jim stepped closer to her and held out his hand. "Shirley, we have no control over what is happening, and it's important that—"

"And I'm scared too," Shirley interrupted, her voice skipping and her lip beginning to quiver. "I have a really, really bad feeling about this."

He put his hand on her shoulder. "Shirley, what is important is that—"

"Can you please answer the question?" she pleaded, like she felt ashamed to ask. "My faith is stronger than ever, but, James, aren't we all—all of us—ultimately made well *if we only believe?*"

"Yes," Jim said wearily. She was entirely right. "The answer is yes."

Shirley was silent for a long moment. "Brooke's hung her hat on what Kenneth told you since the day she found out Alex had leukemia."

Jim looked deep into her eyes, and he could tell by the expression on her face that she was fighting an unwelcome notion that had begun to dance back and forth across her mind—the idea of life without Alex.

"Tell me," Shirley whispered as a single tear weaved its way down her cheek. "Tell me *where* we are all made well if we only believe."

Jim settled his hands on Shirley's shoulders, but struggled to say what he had to. He looked back at Charlie, and fought off his own tears.

"Answer me, James Lindy," Shirley said. "You know the answer to that question."

Jim closed his eyes. Kenneth was right. And now, Shirley was right.

Why hadn't I seen it?

Jim knew where believers were made well. He pulled Shirley closer and hugged her, sickened as he whispered the two words he never thought he would regret saying.

"In heaven."

FORTY-SIX

I sn't it pretty?" Brooke asked.

"Yeah," Ian said.

Neither of them had said a word in close to three hours as they sat side-by-side next to Alex's bed. Out the window and beyond the hospital parking lot was the southern edge of North Jefferson Avenue and the small business district of downtown Carlson. Even though Brooke's cell phone read 5:07 a.m., the Christmas lights that the Rotary Club had draped across the town's storefronts and street-lights were still on. They pumped an artificial sense of life into the empty streets.

"Did you sleep at all?" Brooke asked.

"A little," Ian said. "I was out for an hour or so. You?"

"I don't know," Brooke said, glancing over at Alex. "I think I did, but I'm really not sure."

Ian considered what she said and he began to second-guess himself, not sure if he slept after all. He sure didn't feel like he had, and if he did, it hadn't been beneficial. He knew he'd gotten up to use the restroom and that Talia had come in and out of the room maybe fifteen times in the last few hours to check on Alex. *Fifteen times?* he thought. *Or did I dream that?* It was hard to tell. He was a notch past exhausted, and part of his subconscious was trying to convince him that none of this was real. It was all one big dream— or maybe he was an actor in a depressing movie or playing a part in a video for some sad song.

Cat's in the Cradle.

Ian looked at Alex's profile—nothing more than a still shadow—and thought about the ball mitt he'd just bought for him. You would have thought he'd handed Alex a bag of gold or had given him a brand-new car. His son had watched in amazement as he performed the age-old ritual of properly breaking in the baseball glove. First, he'd rubbed a half jar of Vaseline into the glove's pocket, then he put a baseball in it, and finally, he wrapped a shoestring around it before tossing it under a mattress—Alex's mattress—the same day they'd admitted him to the hospital.

The respirator inhaled and clicked, then exhaled and clicked. As Ian watched his son, the respirator seemed to get louder as the part of his mind that had muted it for the last eleven hours took a much-needed break.

"Can I ask you something?" Brooke asked. "And I want you to be honest with me."

"Sure, Brooke," he said, closing his burning eyes.

She pulled her leg up on the chair and rested her chin on her knee. "What is going through your head right now?"

It wasn't the exact question Ian expected, but a distant relative. He hesitated and then answered honestly. "What's *not* going through my head? That might be a better question."

"I know," Brooke whispered. "It's too much."

Ian's mind drifted back to where it had spent most of the night—not in and out of what he thought was sleep—but in the middle of a cruel tug-of-war between pure sadness and wishful thinking about Alex. He agreed with Brooke. It really was too much. "It's almost like I can't breathe."

"Like you're being suffocated?" she asked, then nodded, as if answering her own question.

"Exactly," Ian said. "It's like a giant glass bubble has been placed over my life, and I'm trapped here in a new world. I feel like I can't take a full breath until Alex gets better. And like we're running out of air—like time is running short—and I want to pick him up, break that glass, and take him with me. But I can't. All I can do is sit here and watch, drowning in the knowledge that there's nothing I can do."

He leaned forward and put his hand up on the side rail and

pointed at Alex. "Since I met him, I envisioned so many things that we were going to do. Reading to him, teaching him how to ride a bike, coaching him at football, basketball, golf—anything he wanted to do. I was dying to—"

Ian stopped and glanced over at Brooke, wanting to erase the word he'd just used. "I was *wanting* to spend time with him. Make some memories together. Make up for our lost time."

Ian could faintly hear the words to that sad song coming from some distorted channel playing in the back of his mind.

"You can still do those things with him, Ian. You still can."

He put his hand on the side of her arm. "Nothing else matters to me more than him getting better, Brooke. Nothing. And I don't want to say this, but—"

"Don't say it," she said wearily.

Ian dipped his head back toward the floor and waited. "Maybe we need to realize that—"

"Ian, *no*."

"Brooke, there's a good chance he won't get better." She had to get ready, be prepared.

"Please don't say that, Ian. I don't want to hear that. You shouldn't even be saying that! Here! In his room, where he can hear you!"

He looked at Alex, his tiny chest inflating and deflating, all due to the ventilator. Was he even in there anymore? Was he coming back to them? "Brooke, I know we aren't supposed to think like—"

"Can I tell you something?" Brooke interrupted. "And I really have no idea what made me think of this, but I want to tell you."

"Okay," Ian said reluctantly.

Brooke pulled her other foot up on the chair and rested her arms across the tops of her knees. "I remember when I worked at the plant. Alex was a little over a year old. It was a Friday, and Pastor Jim and Shirley had taken Charlie to the doctor's office with an ear infection, so I took Alex to work with me. It was the only time he ever went there. Remember the nurseries there?"

"Yeah," Ian said.

"They were pretty fancy too," Brooke said. "Among the six rooms, there was close to a hundred kids."

"That's a heckuva lot," Ian said.

"Yeah," Brooke agreed. "They did a good job trying to accommodate single parents. And it was free. I just never took him there before." She paused and then said, "I was only an hour or two into my shift, and I kept imagining I could hear Alex crying. After around ten minutes, I knew I wasn't imagining it. The strange thing about it was that he was on the other side of the plant—not to mention that the production noise was so loud I couldn't hear the worker next to me talking. But still, I knew it was Alex who was crying. I could hear him."

"Kind of a motherly instinct thing?"

"I guess." Brooke nodded. "You were my supervisor that day, Ian. And you let me go check on him. When I got there, I realized that part of that wing had a power failure, and three of the nurseries were filled with kids who were freaking out about the dark, including Alex. Among all those crying kids, in the midst of all that noise, I could still hear his cry, and I knew which room it was coming from. I remember opening the door to the nursery. It was still pretty dark, and they had a little emergency generator light on that barely lit anything, and guess what?"

"What?"

"Alex was right there. Right near the door, leaning against a little fence, holding his arms over the edge. He quit crying and he said, 'Mommy.'"

"So he was already at the gate like he knew you were coming?"

"Yeah," Brooke said. "It's one of those connections I guess that mothers can have with their kids."

"I've heard about stuff like that before."

Brooke glimpsed at Alex and bit her lip. "But I know what you're probably feeling. Why you're saying . . ." She shook her head and wrapped her arms around herself. "Because I can't—I just can't feel that connection right now. I look at that bed, and I don't know where he is. That's my son there. That's *our* son right there. That's really Alex. This is all real."

"Too real," Ian said.

"But there's another connection," Brooke said, her composure changing. "There's something else that I feel." She hesitated.

"Go on."

"God's going to make Alex better. I know it." Brooke dropped her feet back on the floor and pointed at the bed. "Pastor Jim told me to believe, and he'd be made well. What I feel is something I simply can't explain. But just like I knew Alex was crying at the plant, I know God is going to make him better. *I know it.*"

The door opened on the other side of the curtain, and Brooke and Ian turned to see who it was.

"Good morning," Macey said, stepping around the curtain and standing at the foot of the bed.

"Good morning," Ian said. The doctor looked like she hadn't gotten much more sleep than they had.

"Why don't we go out in the hallway for a minute?" Macey asked.

Ian looked at Brooke and then at Macey. A bit of that instinct that Brooke was just talking about was telling him that things had gone from bad to worse. "What's wrong?"

"Something *else* is wrong?" Brooke asked. "Is something happening?"

"Let's step out in the hall for a minute," Macey repeated. She walked out and they followed her.

Macey crossed her arms and paused. "I just met with Talia and Dr. Kelly. We are concerned."

Ian felt Brooke gripping his arm, and he put his hand on top of hers.

"We've had him on two relatively heavy IVs for his heart and blood pressure."

"Yes," Ian said. "And?"

"And he's not responding like we hoped he would."

"What does that mean?" Ian asked.

"We're concerned that his blood pressure has been down so long that maybe there hasn't been adequate blood flow and oxygen getting to his brain."

"Charlie's brain didn't have enough oxygen," Brooke said. "Is Alex going to be—"

"Brain damaged?" Ian asked.

"I'm not prepared to say that," Macey said, holding up her hands. "But we have a tech on his way up here that is going to run an EEG in a little bit."

"How long does it take to get the results?" Ian asked.

"It will take him probably twenty minutes to set it up and then thirty to forty minutes to record. We have a neurologist making a special stop by here at seven to read it."

That glass over Ian's life had suddenly gotten smaller. "What are we supposed to do? What can we do?"

"Pray," Brooke said.

Macey nodded. "Why don't you two run down and get something to eat? The cafeteria just opened."

"I'm not leaving him," Brooke said.

"Me neither," Ian added.

"Please," Macey said. "I'll be here with him."

Ian and Brooke looked at each other, and then Ian took Brooke's arm. "C'mon. Let's go down for a little bit. We're probably going to be here for a while."

"Okay," Brooke conceded. "But I want to go back in the room real quick, before we go."

They went back in and Ian looked at Alex. He was doing everything he could to make that connection with his son that Brooke had talked about. As hard as he tried, he just couldn't feel it. *Where are you, partner? I know you're in there.*

Brooke stroked Alex's arm and bent down to kiss his head. "We'll be right back, buddy." She turned to walk out the door and Ian went to grab her coat. He paused at the window, overlooking downtown Carlson. Something seemed different out there, and whatever it was somehow managed to sadden him even further.

He made his way to the door and stopped. He turned around and went back to look out the window.

"What's wrong?" Brooke asked.

"The Christmas lights," he said.

"What about them?"

"Nothing," he said, quietly staring at Alex's reflection in the window.

The lights had gone off.

FORTY-SEVEN

Dr. Monica Kelly rubbed the edges of the photograph and then tucked it neatly back into the small leather planner in her desk drawer. The picture served as her daily reminder. Every morning before heading out to the floor, she not only checked her normally unpredictable schedule but also counted her blessings.

This morning she was counting a little more.

As head intensivist at East Shore's ICU, Dr. Kelly was the first to see the results of Alexander Thomas's EEG that had just arrived from Neurology. She stepped away from her computer and grabbed a copy of the report off the printer in the far corner of her office. She put the report in a blue folder and slid it under her arm before returning to the desk. She picked up the phone.

"Talia, can you grab Dr. Lewis? I'll be out in about two minutes."

"She's right here," the nurse answered.

"I'll be right there."

Dr. Kelly hung up the phone and stared at the desk drawer.

She opened it back up and took the photo back out of the planner. It was a little over five years old. She held it and looked at her two children—her two *healthy* children—as they played on the swings in the backyard. Jennifer was seven in the picture and was pushing little Jack, who would have been two at the time. He was smiling from ear to ear, hanging on for dear life, not caring in the least about the purple Kool-Aid that had stained both the sides of his mouth and the front of his T-shirt.

Dr. Kelly was going to give them each an extra hug tonight when she got home. She kissed the photo, put it back, and left her office.

As she turned the corner of the hallway, she saw Talia and Dr. Lewis standing side-by-side against the far end of the nurses' station. As Dr. Kelly marched down the corridor toward them, she purposely looked at the floor, not wanting to knock the legs out from underneath what little hope Dr. Lewis had left. Not yet.

• • •

"Good morning," Macey said.

"Good morning." Dr. Kelly handed the blue folder to Macey, who quickly opened it. It didn't take long for one of the words at the bottom of the report to jump off the page and punch her in the gut.

Flat.

Macey's head pulled back in disappointment, and she could feel a heavy cloak of sympathy from the other two. She shook her head and closed the folder.

"I'm sorry," Dr. Kelly whispered.

Macey glanced at the ceiling. "I've got to go tell the parents."

"I'm sorry, Dr. Lewis," Talia added.

"So am I," Macey said. Even though this was an inevitable part of the business, no other doctor or nurse had *ever* told her they were sorry, and it made her feel uneasy.

There was nothing I could do.

"Are you all right?" Dr. Kelly asked.

"He's a good kid," Macey said. *Was a good kid.*

"Of course," Dr. Kelly said softly.

Macey closed the folder again. "They are a good family."

"I'm sure they are," Dr. Kelly said. "We'll still run another EEG in twenty-four hours, and then we'll see what the family wants to do."

"All right," Macey said.

Talia tapped Macey's elbow. "Do you want me to go with you?"

"I've got it," she said. "Thank you, though, Talia." Macey turned and slowly walked away. Uneasiness began shifting back and forth between her stomach and her throat, growing with each step closer toward Alex's room.

"Dr. Lewis?" Talia said.

She stopped. It felt good to stop. She turned around. "Yes?"

"Dr. Lewis, I want to show you something real quick," the nurse said, tilting her head toward Dr. Kelly as if she were asking permission. The doctor nodded toward her.

Macey walked back to the station, and Talia flipped open yet another folder and made a circle with her finger around a series of blood pressure readings. "Look right here."

She studied the numbers. They didn't make any sense.

"Look at what we were giving him—what we're *still* giving him. Alexander has been on maximum dosage, and his blood pressure hasn't even entertained the idea of staying up. I've never seen anything like it."

Macey glanced suspiciously at Dr. Kelly and then back to the chart.

"Me neither," Dr. Kelly said, lifting her eyebrows and giving her head a little shake. "Not quite like that."

Macey stared at the numbers, reading them three times, then four. "Nor have I. I guess sometimes the cards are stacked against you."

"I know I can't erase your disappointment," Dr. Kelly said. "And I would never say that he had *no* chance. But it certainly looks that way here."

You have no idea, Macey thought.

Dr. Kelly put her elbows on top of the station counter and made a proposal. "We could put him on bypass if you want. He's not the best candidate, but I'd back you on it. See if something changes."

Macey closed her eyes and pinched lightly at her forehead. She shook her head, thinking about Alex—what was left of Alex—hooked to a machine for the next five, ten, or twenty years.

She heard the carpenter's voice again.

Don't prolong it.

"No way," she said, dropping her hand on the countertop. She had no interest in playing God with Alexander Thomas. There was too much competition hanging out at East Shore.

"No way?" Dr. Kelly repeated.

"No way am I putting this family through that. Particularly with these EEG results."

"Of course," Dr. Kelly said. "I respect that decision."

"Are you sure you don't want me to go with you?" Talia asked, looking at her with concern.

"Thank you," Macey said. "I think I've got it."

She turned again and made her way down the hallway to corridor C. She finally stopped and wasn't sure how much time was passing as she stared at the 9 on the door. Would this ever get easier? Giving parents the worst news possible?

But Brooke and Ian were not simply the parents of her patient; they'd also become good friends. She was in no way ready to run through that door with this bomb strapped to her back.

C'mon, Lewis. Let's go. There's no such thing as ready. There's only willing. She opened up the door, walked in, and gently pulled back the curtain.

Ian immediately propped up in his seat, looking eager for good news.

The bottom of Macey's heart felt like it had been dunked in cold water. She looked in Ian's eyes, knowing what a good father he was. And how little time he'd had to try his hand at it.

Brooke was still looking at Alex, and Macey joined her. His head had been turned since the EEG was taken. He was now facing them, and the thick tube that led out of his mouth into the respirator had been replaced and freshly taped.

Macey pulled a chair to the foot of the bed. She ran her hand uncomfortably along the side of her face and then crossed her arms. The respirator seemed like it was the only sound in the room. Inhale—*click*. Exhale—*click*. Inhale—*click*. Alex's little chest went up and down.

"What did the EEG say?" Brooke asked.

"It's not good, you guys."

"What do you mean?" Brooke asked, crouching forward. "It's not good?"

"It was flat," Macey responded, her voice light and apologetic. "The EEG came back flat."

"What does that mean?" Brooke asked in a way that suggested she wasn't quite ready to panic.

"It means . . ."

"He's brain-dead," Ian said numbly, looking back at Alex. "That's what it means, right?"

Macey frowned, watching the shades of sorrow spread across his face. "We are going to do another EEG tomorrow morning. Until we have that report—"

"Brain-dead?" Brooke said, the pitch in her voice heightening. "No, that's impossible. It's not supposed to happen like this. I want to talk to Pastor Jim. I need to talk to Pastor Jim!"

"We'll call him, Brooke," Ian said. He put his arm around her and then turned back to the doctor. "What do we do now?"

"Wait," Macey answered. "All we can do is wait."

"Wait for what?" Brooke asked.

Macey couldn't answer the question. Not yet, anyhow. All she knew was that she had to get to the window.

"Wait for what, Macey?" Brooke repeated.

Macey glanced at both Ian and Brooke. She had done nothing for them, in the end. Everything she had ever worked for—everything she had ever done—was crashing into this one moment of failure. She was at God's mercy and couldn't do anything about it.

"Macey?" Ian asked.

God's mercy.

"Excuse me," she muttered, walking over to the window to look outside.

This time there was no overweight boss, no searching the vast construction site.

He was right there.

The first vehicle she looked at was the truck, and Kenneth was standing in the center of the bed with his arms crossed, looking right up at her.

"Macey?" Brooke asked, wanting an answer to her question. "What is it?"

Macey stared down at the carpenter.

Let me ask you something, big man. Mary Springsted, the cross, Zach Norman, Pastor Jim's eyesight—you hold the power. You know all the answers to every question ever asked. I'm going to ask again. Why these people? They are some of your biggest fans. Why this boy?

Kenneth didn't move.

"Macey!" Brooke shouted, crying now. "Why aren't you answering me?"

But Macey could only put her head closer to the glass. *What are we waiting for, Kenneth?*

Kenneth just stared.

I'm not a quitter. I did my best. But I can't win. I can't beat you.

Kenneth lowered his arms to his sides and then tilted his head to his right. Macey could feel his stare running right through her.

I'm not prolonging this. I did what you said. You're prolonging it. Why?

Kenneth stepped off the back of the tailgate onto the ground.

"Tell us," Ian said. "Go ahead and tell us. We know why you're hesitating. Why you don't want to say it."

I didn't prolong it, Kenneth. Why are you? Tell me.

Brooke was sobbing.

Kenneth turned and walked toward the new wing.

"Don't you walk away from me," Macey grit out, belatedly realizing it was aloud.

Ian rose and joined her at the window, just as Kenneth slipped behind a construction trailer.

Brooke was choking, she was crying so hard. Ian turned to kneel beside her and missed Kenneth appearing on the far side of the trailer, heading down the wooden walkway.

Macey's face was an inch from the glass and her inner voice screamed at a fevered pitch. *Tell me, Kenneth! What are you waiting for?*

Kenneth stopped in his tracks, and Macey held her breath. She waited, and he still didn't move. Behind her, the respirator continued to raise little Alex's chest, then let it fall. As it would for hours, days, months . . .

"You win," she whispered.

Kenneth slowly turned around. There was something different about his stare this time. It didn't run through her. It *filled* her.

"You win," she repeated.

"Who are you talking to?" Ian asked.

Macey pulled back a little farther from the window and waited. And then she did something she never thought she would be capable of doing. She let go. She surrendered.

She waited a moment longer, and she and the carpenter continued to stare at each other. She took a deep breath, paused again, and then she finally said it.

"Take him."

The oxygen saturation alarm sounded, wailing and turning Ian's head.

"What is that?" Brooke screamed, trying to get around Ian to Alex.

The blood pressure alarm was next.

"No!" Brooke screamed. "No! Please, no!"

The heart monitor went off last.

Macey spun around and yanked a white spiral cord on the wall, calling the Code Blue. The last one.

"I want to talk to Pastor Jim!" Brooke cried, drowned out by the chorus of alarms as she clung to Ian. "Please! Please!"

Within thirty seconds, five ICU members were working on Alex. Two more showed up and failed to usher Brooke out of the room. Ian had to pick her up and carry her out into the hallway, with Macey right behind them.

"What are we supposed to do now?" Ian asked.

Macey answered him with a question and felt like she was handing him the nails to a tiny coffin. "How long do you want to do this?"

"What are you talking about?" Brooke asked, clinging to Ian's arm. "It's not supposed to be like this! I want to talk to Pastor Jim!"

"How long?" Macey repeated. "Until you let him go?"

"What are you saying?" Brooke asked, trying to catch her breath. "We can't let him go! God is going to make him better!"

Macey shook her head. "No, Brooke. We can keep his body going, but . . ."

"Well you just keep him going!" Brooke screamed.

Macey felt like she had switched into autopilot. Feelings were gone, and words just came. "The part of Alex's brain that lets him breathe can go on for years, Brooke. *Years.*"

"What are you suggesting we do?" Ian asked.

"Listen to me," Macey said. "Please listen to me. Even if Alex were to somehow come out of this, he won't be the same little boy you knew."

"No, no, no!" Brooke cried. "He is gonna get better. He's *supposed* to. I believed. I believed!" She put her fist to her mouth, staring at Macey like she was a monster. Behind her, another nurse and orderly ran into Alex's room. "I want to call Pastor Jim."

"I want you to call him too," Macey said, taking Brooke's arm. "I want you to call him and have him come up here right now with Shirley, Charlie, and whoever else you want."

"What do we do until then?" Ian asked.

"Please do something, Macey," Brooke said. "I love him so much."

"I know you do," Macey said, emotion suddenly returning to the stage and forcing her to fight off her own tears. "Brooke and Ian—I love Alex too. I love that little boy. But he isn't here anymore. And he won't be." She dropped her voice. "Please, you guys, please."

"Please . . . what?" Brooke asked, dread in her eyes.

"Please do the right thing."

"What's the right thing?"

Don't cry, Macey Lewis. Don't you dare cry.

Macey closed her eyes and then struggled to slowly open them back up. "Let him go," she whispered.

Brooke stepped back as if she'd been slapped. She looked up at Ian.

"He's already gone," Ian said, his own eyes beginning to well.

Brooke covered her ears and looked at Macey.

Brooke was completely lost and searching for another answer that wouldn't come—ever.

"I am sorry," Macey said. "I'm so sorry."

"Don't side with her, Ian. Help me," Brooke pleaded, cringing and making fists that pounded at her sides. "We have to stand up for Alex!"

"Stand up for him by doing what's best for him." Macey reached out to put her hand on Brooke's shoulder.

"No," Brooke said in a child's voice, edging away. Then she went completely silent.

"Brooke," Macey said. She held her arms open, waiting, and Brooke broke then, looking as if she was going to collapse.

Brooke stepped slowly forward, her arms at her sides, and leaned against the doctor. Macey wrapped her arms around her.

"Let him go," Macey whispered.

Ian put his arms around both of them and repeated Macey's words. "He won't be the same little boy we knew . . ."

"But he was so excited," Brooke said, sniffling and shifting her head on Macey's shoulder. "He was so excited about getting a bike that didn't have training wheels. And he wanted a lunchbox with a thermos in it, because he was going to go to school on the big kids' bus for the whole day, and he—"

"It's time," Macey said softly. "It's time to free him."

There was a pause. Macey could feel Brooke's heart thumping against her ribs.

"My baby is gone," Brooke muttered. "He's gone already, isn't he?"

"Yes," Macey whispered.

Brooke shifted her face from Macey's shoulder to Ian's chest. He held her, and then they both turned and looked at Alex's door, clinging to each other.

"Go ahead, buddy," Brooke said, closing her eyes. "Go ahead."

Ian nodded at Macey as his lip quivered. "Let him go."

Macey put her arms around them and watched as the tears began to race down the sides of Ian's face.

"I'll go inform the team of your wishes," she said.

FORTY-EIGHT

Brooke hadn't said a word in fifteen minutes; she wasn't all there at the moment. Neither was Ian.

The capital *E* in the East Shore sign on the wall kept coming in and out of focus as she stared dreamily down the hallway. There wasn't any sound. Everything was fuzzy and moving slowly.

Whatever was in her brain that was now cushioning her from the blow of Alex's death had transformed Corridor C into a colorless, emotionless wasteland. She didn't cry. She couldn't seem to form words. She couldn't seem to care.

Her head stayed glued to Ian's shoulder as the last two members of the code team finally came out of the room. To her, they were like faceless apparitions, characters from an ongoing nightmare, gliding past. She clung to Ian's arm and turned her head back toward C-9. The door was still open, and inside was her dead child.

Dead child. Alex is dead.

She could already imagine Alex in that bed, and the thought of it added another drip of the natural painkiller that made things blurrier still.

Macey came out from around the door. It was time.

She lifted her head off of Ian's arm. Every movement took effort, as if her body had been cracked open and filled with sand.

"Did you get ahold of Pastor Jim?" Macey asked, looking with compassion from one to the other. Brooke focused in on her face long enough to see that she was hurting too.

"They should be up here any minute," Ian said.

"Do you want to wait for them?"

"No," he said, looking down at Brooke. "I think . . . I think it'd be good for us to see him alone, first."

Brooke nodded. Not because she agreed. But because dimly, she thought it would be what was expected of a mother. *Why can't I feel anything?*

"All right," Macey said, holding the door open. "I'll come with you."

They walked in the room and stood behind the curtain. Brooke momentarily panicked, thinking they'd all forgotten to don masks and gloves, but then remembered they weren't needed.

Not needed . . .

Macey began to slowly pull the curtain back, but Brooke looked away, out the window at snow floating down in thick, wet flakes into the parking lot below. Alex loved to play in the snow. Brooke had bought him a new sled for his birthday . . . It was in the garage.

Who will I give that to now? Can I return it? Maybe Charlie wants it . . .

The sound of the top curtain rings moving drew her attention, the only sound in the room. There was no longer any soft beeping or chirping coming from the monitors. There was no more puffing and clicking from the respirator.

The curtain slid open enough to expose the machines to the right of Alex's bed, all off now, their flickering numbers replaced by blank screens. *Time to watch over another patient.*

Not Alex. Never again, Alex.

Macey finished opening the curtain and stood on the opposite side, waiting. Brooke knew she should look down, force herself to look at Alex, but she couldn't.

She looked up and to her right at Ian. She tried to take in the empty look on his face as he stared at their dead son. Slowly, she turned her head back toward the bed, and there Alex was.

The breathing tube had been taken out of his mouth, and his IVs had been removed. The back of the bed was propped up, and the side rails were lowered. Alex's head was positioned straight forward, centered in his pillow, with his chin tilted up slightly. The sheet had been pulled up to just below his shoulders, barely exposing the port in the top of his chest. His arms were draped straight down to his sides, and his tiny hands were flat on the sheet. His mouth was slightly open, and a small voice inside of Brooke said, *Wake up, buddy, wake up. The Pop-Tarts are done. Charlie's waiting for you. He wants to watch a show.*

Ian stepped to the side of the bed. He stared, as if he were on guard, frozen by the brutal, blunt unfairness of what was before them.

On legs that didn't feel like her own, Brooke walked past Macey and went to the other side of the bed. She wasn't sure how long it took her to get there. Alex's cheeks were a little puffy and stretched into a dark pink color from the tube that had been in his mouth. A new bruise was starting to appear on the side of his neck, and she could see a sliver of an opening in his right eye. Still, he looked like he was sleeping, and she sadly wondered if he was running around in heaven, talking about everything that had happened to him over the last five years.

Six. He was going to be six on Saturday.

"Go ahead and sit on the bed, if you want," Macey said.

Brooke put her hand on the sheet and then quickly pulled it back.

Ian stepped closer. "I want to touch him. Can I, Macey?"

"Yes," Macey said, prompting Ian to put his hand on the side of Alex's face. "Go ahead and hold him, if you want." Brooke thought she heard the doctor's voice crack.

Brooke sat her hip on the edge of the bed, and Alex moved slightly up and down with her weight. For a moment she thought he had moved on his own and her heart leaped. She imagined for a second that they were all wrong—that he was still there—that he'd been made well because she really had believed.

But her skyrocketing hope came crashing down as Ian cradled the side of Alex's neck in his hand. Ian's face didn't light up with joy. Instead he silently bent down and tenderly kissed Alex's head.

Brooke looked back at Macey. It now seemed as if they were each playing their little parts in this big nightmare. She wanted to cry it out, but the tears just wouldn't come.

"They're here," Macey said quietly, looking toward the door, and then at Brooke and Ian. "Do you want them to wait?"

Brooke just stared at her, not able to decide. Ian answered, "Have them come in."

Macey stepped back and gave way to Pastor Jim, who gave the doctor a hug before stepping around the curtain to the foot of the bed. He looked at Alex, and then glanced at Brooke as she blinked heavily without saying a word.

Ian went over and hugged Pastor Jim. As they separated, Pastor Jim touched the side of Ian's face, and when their eyes met, Ian merely nodded.

Pastor Jim came to Brooke's side then, and she stood and stared up at him thinking, *You said. You said if I only believed . . .*

"I'm sorry, honey," Pastor Jim whispered. "I didn't mean to mislead you."

Brooke's lip quivered and the two words melted away at the back of her mind. *Only believe.*

Pastor Jim hugged her, but she wasn't hugging back. Her arms dangled loosely at her sides. She looked to the door and saw Shirley step through it.

Charlie was with her.

Shirley guided Charlie by the arm to the opposite side of the bed. Charlie's expression went from one of cautious obedience—one that knew not to touch anything and to stay out of the way—to one of uncontrollable joy when he saw Alex. He'd noticed that Alex no longer had the wires plugged into him, so he must have thought that good things were happening. Charlie slowly lifted his finger up to his lips, making a *shh* motion for everyone to be quiet, as if he didn't want anyone to wake his friend up.

"Does he know?" Ian asked, his voice strangled.

"We told him," Shirley said, "but it will take him a bit to accept it. To understand." Shirley tried to stifle her sobs and came around to hug Brooke. "I'm so sorry, Brooke."

Brooke didn't say anything. She wanted to talk. She wanted to cry. But she couldn't. She just watched as Pastor Jim placed his hand on the side of Alex's head and then bowed his own.

Pastor Jim turned around and took Brooke's arm. "I know you believed. And I need you to believe me, honey. Alexander *has* been made well." He tilted his head toward Alex. "I want you to take Alex's hand." He guided her back to the edge of the bed. "Everybody, please join me."

Brooke lifted Alex's right hand, waiting in vain for him to move.

They joined hands all the way around the bed, and Charlie followed suit, providing the last link by reaching down and picking up Alex's left hand. They all bowed their heads.

"Lord," Pastor Jim said, pausing, "we want to thank you for welcoming Alex—"

"Hang on, James," Shirley whispered.

"Charlie?" Ian said. "It's okay, Charlie."

Charlie had let go of Alex's hand and stepped back from the bed. He looked at his mother and then his father. He reached down with two fingers and lightly tapped at the top of Alex's hand. He glanced up at Brooke, ran his hand across his chin, and then picked Alex's hand back up. Brooke knew that Charlie didn't like the way Alex's hand felt.

Charlie turned his head toward Pastor Jim. He tapped again at Alex's hand, pressed his thumb against it, and rubbed it in a tiny circle. He looked over at Ian, who was shaking his head and weeping, and then looked at Shirley, who'd begun to cry again.

Charlie crouched over the edge of the bed and put his arm above Alex's head. He touched the side of Alex's cheek and then dipped his shoulder and head next to Alex's face. He gently tapped at Alex's forehead with his finger and then patiently waited.

Brooke just stared. *He wants to see who smiles first.*

No more smiles.

Charlie glanced desperately at Pastor Jim when Alex didn't respond. It was at that moment that Brooke knew Charlie understood that Alex was gone. Not sleeping, but gone forever. Charlie's eyes rounded as he stood, pulled a TicTac container out of his pocket, and then picked Alex's arm back off the bed. He took Alex's hand, opened it, and put the TicTac in his palm. He then coiled Alex's hand around the candy and carefully placed Alex's arm back at his side.

"Take his hand, son," Pastor Jim said.

Slowly, reluctantly, Charlie did as he was told, completing their circle.

"This is not the last time you'll hold his hand, Charles Lindy," Pastor Jim said. "Someday, when you're reunited in heaven, you'll hold it again. I promise." He looked around the group. "Let's pray. Father, we thank you that even in our sadness, Alex is experiencing total joy right now. We ask that you comfort us, as we mourn his loss, and yet celebrate in the knowledge that he is with you . . ."

As Pastor Jim prayed, Brooke looked up and around at all the people who loved Alex best. Behind her and Shirley, at the foot of the bed, Macey, Kaitlyn, and Zach stood, heads bowed. Macey's lip was trembling, and tears were running down Kaitlyn's face.

Pastor Jim finished his prayer and nodded at the doctors and the nurse. "Thanks for being here, friends. Would you join us in the chapel?"

Brooke noticed none of them answered. They just stared at the bed, as was everyone else.

Charlie had lowered himself to one knee and was leaning against the side of the bed. His left arm was draped across Alex's chest, and his enormous head was resting on her dead son's bare shoulder. Charlie's eyes were closed, and Brooke could see the pair of tears that were slowly heading down his cheek. She couldn't help noticing that with each breath Charlie took, Alex's head shifted ever so slightly on the pillow.

"Please excuse me," Macey said, stepping back to the other side of the curtain.

Brooke went quietly to the foot of the bed and edged around the curtain too.

Macey was standing at the window. Brooke remembered how Macey had stared out that window . . . right before Alex died. And right now, looking anywhere but at Alex was what Brooke needed most. She stepped up beside Macey, and the doctor wrapped her arm around her waist. Together, they looked out, into the snow.

"It's gone," Macey said softly.

What's gone? Brooke wanted to ask. But she couldn't make her lips form the words.

"His truck," Macey said dully. "Kenneth is gone."

Then the doctor turned and left the room.

FORTY-NINE

The Authorized Personnel Only elevator beeped three times, and then its door hummed and closed behind her. Macey was back on the third floor and felt fortunate that nobody was in the hallway. She glanced to her left through the small window of the gray double doors that led back to the Bone Marrow Transplant Unit. Down on the right-hand side, she could see the door of the room Alex had been in before they took him up to the ICU.

She closed her eyes and then sighed as a dose of sorrow filtered through her like water through sand. She turned and made her way down the hallway. She didn't want anybody to see her. What she really wanted was to go home and stick her head under her pillow. She wanted to let it all out. But she couldn't do it here.

Anywhere but here. Don't you dare cry here, Macey Lewis. All you have to do is get to your office. Just make it there.

She passed the nurses' station unseen and then started down the hall toward her office. She'd almost made it when she heard Zach's voice behind her. "Macey!"

She stopped and froze like a teenager whose late-night plans of disappearing out the back door had just been thwarted. She stood in front of her office and didn't respond. *I have to get inside, because I'm about to lose it.* She opened the door and went inside, almost making it to her desk when she heard Kaitlyn's voice.

"Macey?"

She couldn't answer. She only gasped for breath, widening her eyes, trying to hold on just a little longer . . .

She knew both Kaitlyn and Zach were in the doorway, but she couldn't face them. They already knew the truth.

"He was right," Macey said, keeping her back to them. She frowned and bit her lip. "My best wasn't good enough."

"You gave it everything you had," Kaitlyn said. "That's all anyone could ever ask."

"Macey," Zach said. She could hear him come in the office. "You have to believe me when I say that Alex is in a good place—the best place. I know for a *fact* that he is all right."

"I know *you* know," she said. She leaned forward and put her palms flat on her desk, holding herself up. She shook her head and paused. "What I don't know is about all of *this* anymore."

"All of what?" Kaitlyn asked.

"The hospital. My work. How do I know I'm making any difference with these kids here? Any difference at all?"

"What do you mean?" Zach said.

Macey lifted her arms and put her hands behind her head. She took a deep breath and turned to face them. "I'm not in control of anything here. I always thought I was saving kids' lives. That's why I became a doctor—to do just that. But now I know—and I think you two also know—that we really aren't the ones in control of much at all."

Zach studied her. "I understand. I became a doctor to save kids' lives too—mostly to make up for the one I couldn't save." His sister. Kaitlyn had told her about their visit to her gravesite and Zach's experience there with Kenneth.

"It doesn't seem fair," Macey said. "It *isn't* fair. At the end of the day, regardless of what we do here, if a certain *Somebody* thinks a child's life on earth is over, there's absolutely nothing we can do about it."

"Looks that way," Zach said. "We do our best. But ultimate power is not our own."

Macey crossed her arms. "And you accept it just like that?"

"Yeah," he said, with the hint of a smile.

It irritated her, his peace. "Pastor Jim was blind for twenty years," Macey said. "Charlie has never said a word, and did you know that Brooke's parents were killed in a motorcycle accident?"

"Yes," he said.

"And now this," she added, preparing to ask the question once again. It was the same question that was without an acceptable answer. "Why? Why these people? These people who do good things for God? And more importantly, what does God have in store for them *next*?"

"I don't know," Zach said.

Her shoulders slumped, and she shook her head. "Alex was five years old. He was a good kid, a good son, and a good friend to somebody who doesn't have a whole lot of friends. Now he's gone. Does a loving God let things like that happen to people?"

"Yes, he does."

"Why? Tell me why."

"I said I don't know, Macey. But I know that someday we will."

"I could have saved him, Zach. If God had let me. And if he won't let me . . . why even bother?"

"Look at me," he said, stepping closer to her. "There's something you need to know."

"What?" she asked, crossing her arms.

He took her by the shoulders and spoke quickly. "Alex won't be the last patient you'll ever lose. I promise you that. But God will still use you, Macey. He smiles whenever any of us use the gift he's given us. And he's given you a doozy. There are kids here who need you, Macey, and you better believe there will be more. Do you hear me?"

She turned away.

"Don't you dare give up, Macey Lewis," Kaitlyn said, stepping closer. "We *all* need you here."

Macey swallowed hard, then covered her face.

"Don't hold it in," Zach said. "I know how you feel. It's okay, Macey. Let it go. Let it go now."

"What?" Macey asked. "Let what go?"

"Play tough all you want," he said. "But there's something else I want to tell you. Turn around and look at me."

Hesitantly, she did.

"Here is why you'll keep doing it, regardless of the heartache," Zach said. "Guess what God does with the kids he isn't quite ready for?"

"What?" she said.

Zach grinned, and then his smile slowly faded. "He puts them in your hands, Macey Lewis. Your hands."

"You don't know that."

"Yes, I do."

She looked back at him. "How?"

"Because Kenneth told me. He told me to tell you that. And he also told me that I would know when to say it. And that time is now."

"God puts them in my hands?" she asked in a tiny voice, her head lowering.

"Yes," Zach said. He put his finger under her chin and gently lifted her head. "And don't you ever forget that."

Macey just stared at him. She could still hear Alex calling her "Doc Lewis" and constantly asking her when he could go home.

It was at that moment she realized that he already was home. She then became perfectly still and lowered her head again. She took a deep breath and could feel her shoulders start to shake—and then her bottom lip. She closed her eyes tightly, desperately fighting the first tear from coming.

"It's okay," Zach said, holding out his arms.

Macey slowly looked at Kaitlyn, then Zach. When their eyes met, she could somehow feel Zach's faith, and knew he was right. It really was okay. She leaned forward to hug him, sighed, and began to sob.

Kaitlyn joined them and the three of them clung together, shaking as they all wept.

FIFTY

The small chapel at East Shore was located on the first floor, directly through the main entrance and past the greeting center. It was tucked neatly between the gift shop and the main elevators, and its exterior was bricked in a deep brown, both separating and identifying it distinctly from the light tan drywall and paneling that ran the balance of the same hallway.

Brown double doors with thick black handles led to an interior that was carpeted in light beige. Twelve darkly stained pews were angled inward, split by an aisle that ran from the entrance to a two-step, rounded platform, which held a small altar and standard pulpit.

A dark wooden cross that matched the pews was mounted on the front wall, dramatically lit in the otherwise shadowy pulpit area. It instantly evoked a spirit of contemplation, perfect for those who came here with desperate requests, or those reeling from bad news, seeking a place to anchor.

Jim was standing at the pulpit, looking at Brooke in the first row next to Ian. Her cheeks were pale, and he hadn't heard her say a word since seeing Alex dead. She was staring vacantly at the floor with her hands in her lap and her head on Ian's shoulder. Directly behind them were Shirley and Charlie, who were only a few feet from Kaitlyn, Zach, and Macey.

Jim rested his arms on the pulpit and closed his eyes. *Lord, thank you for blessing our lives with Alex, and thank you for welcoming him into your kingdom. I ask that you give us strength and ask that you give me the right words to—*

He heard the creak of the floor and opened his eyes. Zach was up on the landing and walked right past him. Jim turned around and, in amazement, watched Zach kneel before the cross and bow his head. *Thank you, Lord,* Jim prayed silently. *How far you've brought this man—*

Charlie stood and stepped out into the main aisle. He ran his hand across the top of his head and down along the side of his face as he went up on the curved platform and took three huge steps to join Zach. They all watched as he went to one knee and dipped his head, imitating Zach. Zach and Charlie shared a long look, and Jim could see the tears that had begun to stream once again down his son's face. Zach put his hand on Charlie's shoulder and then squeezed the base of his neck. Then they both bowed their heads again.

Shirley joined them, next to Charlie.

Kaitlyn nodded at Macey, then they stood up and walked up the aisle and onto the dais. They kneeled to Zach's left.

Jim could see Ian saying something to Brooke. Brooke didn't respond, and Ian pulled Brooke closer, wrapping his arm around her before putting his chin on top of her head. Then he whispered in her ear. It still didn't look like Brooke said anything; she just leaned forward, and Ian helped her to her feet. They seemed stiff and sore from the weeks of bedside vigil, but Jim knew that pain would soon go away, leaving only their sore hearts. They walked like an old couple up the two steps, and Ian held Brooke, guiding her as they slowly angled to the right side of the huddle to kneel next to Shirley.

Jim left the pulpit. He went up behind the others, and took a knee, purposefully wedging himself between Shirley and Brooke. Brooke's arms were at her sides, and she was staring at the carpet. She slowly turned her head and glanced up at him, and it pained Jim to see that her eyes no longer held the certainty, the unwavering confidence in him, that she'd long had.

"I'm sorry," he whispered. He knew it wasn't enough, but it was all he could say. He wanted more than ever for her to say something back.

Brooke just stared at him for a few seconds. Her mouth barely opened, and he thought she was about to say something. She turned her head all the way toward him and then suddenly stopped and leaned back to look past him.

Jim looked over his shoulder, and Kaitlyn was patting the sides of her face.

Zach lowered his hand and put it on her back. "You okay?"

Kaitlyn slid her hands across the back of her neck. She shook her head and loudly said, "I can feel that buzz. I can feel him."

"Who?" Zach asked.

"He's here," Kaitlyn said.

"Who is here?"

"Him," she answered. The nurse stood and turned around, looking toward the back of the chapel.

Kenneth was standing near the back door.

They all stood and turned to face him.

Jim noticed that the snow that had fallen on the shoulders and arms of the carpenter's coat still hadn't melted. His hair was matted and wet, and he ran his fingers through it, moving it straight back off his forehead. He just stood there, and it was clear he was looking at Brooke.

Kenneth finally slid his hands into his coat pockets, and as he slowly walked up the aisle, droplets of melting slush slid off the top edges of his tattered work boots, leaving a trail of water spots on the carpet behind him.

He stopped between the first and second pews, never taking his eyes off of Brooke. It was utterly silent as the two stared at each other. Brooke finally broke her silence.

"I believed."

Kenneth didn't flinch.

"Did you hear me?" she said, loud enough for a tiny echo. "I *believed.*"

Kenneth didn't move.

"You told Pastor Jim that if I only believed, Alex would be made well."

Kenneth took his hands out of his pockets and walked to within a few feet of the two steps.

Jim suddenly thought about Alex. He wondered if his body was still up in the hospital room. "Alex is with God, Brooke. Kenneth was right. He *has* been made well."

She ignored him, focusing only on Kenneth.

"What am I going to do without Alex?" Brooke asked, tears filling her eyes. She leaned out from under Ian's arm and walked to the edge of the steps before stopping and crossing her arms. "What am I supposed to do now?"

"Continue on," Jim said.

Kenneth looked up at Shirley, the doctors, and then Kaitlyn. Zach nodded at Kenneth, but Kenneth just turned his head back to Brooke once again.

Brooke went down the steps, and stood right in front of Kenneth. She threw her arms up and let them drop. Then she lifted one back up and pointed at the carpenter. "I thought you *knew* God, you know that? There are people in this room who actually thought you were something bigger than just a carpenter. They, *we*, thought you had a direct line to God. But I guess not. In the end, it turns out you're just a carpenter."

They all waited for Kenneth to say something. He didn't.

"What do you want?" Ian asked, leaving the others to join Brooke, directly in front of Kenneth.

"It's my fault," Jim said. "I misunderstood what Kenneth said. He was right. I was wrong."

"Thank you, James," the carpenter said calmly. "Thank you."

Jim held his hands up. He had no idea what Kenneth was talking about. "Thank you for what?"

"You tell them what to do," Kenneth said. "They rarely do it, but you certainly tell them, and you always have. I thank you for that."

"And you," he added softly, nodding at Brooke. "I thank you too. You were told to only believe."

"But I was also told he'd be made well. What about that?"

"Why are you doing this?" Ian growled, clearly fed up. "What's your point, man? Our son just died."

Brooke put her hands over her face and started crying, and it seemed to make Ian even angrier.

Kenneth reached over and gently started to pull Brooke's hands from her face, and Ian laid hold of the carpenter's wrist, looking like he was about to punch him.

"It's all right, Ian," Kenneth said. He took his free hand and placed it on top of Ian's shoulder.

Ian squinted and looked bewildered. He let go of Kenneth's wrist and his hand fell limply to his side, his mouth dropping open.

"It's okay to cry, Brooke," Kenneth said. "There are no quick fixes for feelings of loss. It hurts and you will miss Alex. But as you mourn, know that when you are at your weakest . . . God is at his strongest."

"He was only five," Brooke said.

"Let him talk," Ian whispered.

"But he was only five!"

"He's with God," Kenneth said, glancing behind Brooke at Kaitlyn, Macey, and Zach. "And this has brought others closer to God. You will see Alex again and again means forever."

"My parents were in their twenties."

"Five, twenty-five, sixty, or one hundred. Does it matter?" Kenneth said. "What greater thing could you possibly want for someone you love . . . than for them to be with the Father in heaven? And as a mother, can you think of a better place for Alex to be?"

"He was supposed to get better."

Kenneth nodded. "You were told to believe, Brooke."

"I already told you," Brooke cried. "I really did believe, and now Alex is gone."

"Yes, you did," Kenneth said. The smallest hint of a smile creased his lips. "Your belief was real. It was beautiful. It was without reservation."

"But it didn't do him any good. Tell me why this would happen to us. We did everything we were supposed to do and—"

"James," Kenneth said, interrupting Brooke. "People say it all the time. But does everything really happen for a reason?"

"Yes," Jim whispered.

"No," Kenneth said, shaking his head. He paused and then asked, "Where is that written?"

Jim thought about it and then walked over to the pulpit and grabbed the Bible. He squeezed it gently with both hands before setting it back down. The carpenter was right. "It doesn't say that. But it does tell us that all things work together for the good to those who love God, to those who are called according to his purpose."

"So, why are you here?" Brooke whispered. "Just tell me. Why are you here?"

"I am here for only one reason," Kenneth said. "And that is *the* reason."

Jim waited, absorbing the carpenter's words. He looked at the others, then back to Kenneth. "*What* is the reason?"

Kenneth looked away and stared at Charlie for a good ten seconds before bowing his head.

The room had gone quiet again. Even Brooke quieted. It was as if they all held their breath, none of them clear on how this could possibly turn out.

Except for Jim. Jim could see it.

One tear trickled down the center of the carpenter's left cheek. It worked its way over to his jaw and then fell to the front of his coat.

Kenneth turned his face up to the ceiling, hands outstretched. And then he began to cry. After a long minute, he looked straight back at Brooke, who cried with him.

Zach stepped around Kaitlyn, as if to console Kenneth, but the carpenter lifted his arm for the doctor to be still.

"Brooke," Kenneth said, wiping a tear from his cheek. "God doesn't expect you to be perfect. And he doesn't expect you to understand his perfection."

"Why are you crying?" Brooke asked.

"Because of the way you loved Alex," he said, staring straight into her eyes. "There are mysteries in this life, but make no mistake about it. Alex has been made well." Kenneth glanced over toward the doctors. "Tell her, Zach."

"Alex is more alive than ever," Zach said.

Kenneth remained right in front of Brooke. She covered her face with her hands again and began to cry harder.

"You believed Alex would be made well as if he already was—as if it was a given," Kenneth said. "You did your part, Brooke. And perfect faith is sometimes rewarded with perfect certainty."

The carpenter reached up and lowered Brooke's right hand from her face and they stared at each other, tears streaming down both of their faces. Kenneth took her hand and turned it over, her palm up. He reached into his pocket, pulled something out, and then put it in Brooke's hand.

Brooke let out a gasp and began to shake.

"How?" she said. "I don't understand."

"Someone made you a promise," Kenneth said. "Remember?"

Brooke turned and looked at Pastor Jim. She held out her hand and Jim immediately saw it.

It was the macaroni necklace.

Brooke squinted and touched it with her other hand. She held it up in front of her face and Jim could see the cardboard heart with the photo of Brooke and her mother on it. Matching outfits and ponytails.

"He did it," Brooke said. "Alex found my mother. Found her in heaven."

Jim swallowed heavily and caught his breath.

"I know a little boy that loves his mother," he said.

Brooke smiled at him and turned back to Kenneth. "Thank you," she said.

Kenneth smiled back.

Brooke held the necklace against the side of her face and fell to her knees. Then she slowly looked up at Kenneth. "Who are you?"

Kenneth glanced at Pastor Jim and smiled yet again.

"You never figured out the verse did you . . . 7:16?"

"No," Jim said. "The verse was 8:50 that told her to only believe. The time was 7:16 when I regained my sight. You somehow knew that."

Kenneth's eyes shifted from Brooke to Jim, and the carpenter held up his hand. "Verse 7:16 is also from the book of Luke."

Jim cast a confused glance at the others on the landing. "But Luke 7:16 doesn't have anything to do with someone getting their sight back. I know the verse, Kenneth."

"I know you do, James."

Jim thought about the verse, and the back of his neck suddenly warmed. "But, Kenneth, Luke 7:16—"

"Can you read it for us?" Kenneth asked.

Jim stepped to the pulpit, opened the Bible, and thumbed quickly to the verse.

"From the book of Luke," he said, looking obediently at Kenneth, "chapter 7, verse 16." Jim looked over at Shirley and then down at the Bible and began to read.

> "They were all filled with awe and praised God. 'A great prophet has appeared among us,' they said."

Jim's eyes scanned what followed. The words seemed to jump off the page. His stomach tightened, and then he cautiously glanced up from the Bible toward the carpenter. He couldn't look. He tried again, but he just couldn't look at Kenneth.

Good Lord.

Jim turned toward Shirley and then looked at the two doctors. Macey was rubbing at her neck, as was Kaitlyn, and Jim couldn't stop himself from doing the same thing. Jim picked the Bible up and walked directly behind Brooke with his head down. He tried again and failed to look at Kenneth. The verse was perfect. Now it all made sense.

Brooke wiped her eyes and looked up at Kenneth again before whispering, "Please tell me who you are."

"Answer her question, James," Kenneth said. "Answer it. Finish the verse."

Jim didn't have to read it. He already knew it, but he opened the Bible back up and read it anyhow.

> "God has come to help his people."

They all looked at one another and the room became quiet, except for Brooke's crying.

Nobody said a word as Kenneth stepped off the platform. The room had gone quiet yet again, and they all just watched in silence as he walked purposefully down the aisle toward the chapel entrance.

"Thank you," Jim said.

The carpenter stopped a few feet short of the door. He didn't move, and was still facing the exit.

"What is the reason?" Jim asked, bowing his head.

Kenneth waited for a few long seconds. And then he slowly turned around.

Jim could feel the sweat in his palms separating his hand from the Bible. He took a step forward. "You said you were here for only one reason . . . what is it?"

"Look at me, James," Kenneth said, and Jim did.

Kenneth held up his fists and then slowly fanned his arms out to his sides. "You know the reason, James Lindy."

"I know," Jim said. "But I was hoping everyone could hear it from you."

The carpenter nodded and then uncoiled his fists, exposing his palms.

"The reason is God loves you."

And then Kenneth turned and made his way out the door.

EPILOGUE

Ten Months Later

"You're gonna need a bigger boat," Zach said, talking to Pastor Jim and passing a clear Tupperware bowl filled with pretzels to Ian on the other side of the couch in the Lindy living room. Ian grabbed a handful and then dropped them into his other palm.

"What's that?" Pastor Jim asked, looking puzzled. "A bigger boat?"

"It's from *Jaws*," Ian said. "The boat they were using wasn't big enough to get the job done. You don't remember that?"

Pastor Jim threw his hands up in the air and then dropped them to his lap. "You know what? I've never seen *Jaws*."

Zach shifted to the edge of the couch and grinned. "What I'm trying to say is that we're going to need a bigger church. We've been at full capacity for too long and more want to come."

"I'm hoping you're right," Pastor Jim said. "But we are the church, Zach. Our message is not confined to any four walls. God wants his message to spread. He wants everyone to hear."

"I like that," Zach said.

"Me too," Ian added.

Shirley popped her head in the living room. "We're going to sing to the birthday boy now."

"Okay, honey," Pastor Jim said. The three of them stood and went into the kitchen.

Macey was sitting next to Kaitlyn and Shirley on one side of the table. Opposite them was Charlie and Brooke, and they were all wearing cone birthday hats. Zach sat down and had to smile when he looked again across the table. It was obvious that the rubber band attached to Charlie's hat didn't even come close to reaching under his chin, so he had tried to put it on a different way. The hat was on his forehead, pointing straight out, the band around his ears, making Charlie both the tallest and only unicorn in the room.

"Look at Charlie," Kaitlyn whispered, leaning her head on Zach's shoulder.

He kissed her and whispered back, "Look at Brooke."

Brooke had walked over to the counter and her face was one of pure joy as she carried the birthday cake back to the table and set it in front of Charlie. She took out a lighter, lit all thirty-nine candles, and then sat down.

Charlie wiggled in his seat in growing anticipation. Zach knew he was waiting for them to sing so he could tear into the cake.

When they were done singing, Charlie closed his eyes for no longer than three seconds to make a wish, cocked his head back, and then tilted forward, blowing as hard as he could on the candles that were scattered across the chocolate cake. All of the tiny flames leaned away and then slowly recoiled back toward him before they went out. He straightened his back, lifted his chin, and threw his arms up in victory as little trails of smoke headed toward the ceiling.

"Good job, Charlie!" Brooke said as everyone surrounding the kitchen table applauded—with the exception of Charlie, who'd gotten distracted by the smoke from the candles.

"I'll bet I know what he wished for," Shirley said.

"I think I know too," Ian said, grabbing a party favor and blowing into it, uncoiling its snakelike paper tongue rapidly into the side of Charlie's head.

Ian leaned next to him and kissed Brooke on the cheek. "What do you say?"

"It's up to you," she said, pointing back at Charlie.

Ian turned around just in time to see Charlie's cheeks puff on his own party favor and launch his retaliatory strike off of Ian's chin.

"Get him, Charlie!" Pastor Jim yelled.

"I think Mr. and Mrs. Tobias have an announcement," Shirley said.

Ian smiled at Brooke. "You want to tell them, or you want me to?"

"Go ahead," she said.

"Stand up with me," Ian said.

Brooke did. Ian put his arm back around her and then put his other hand on Brooke's baby bump. She put her hands over his and her face lit up again.

"We weren't going to say anything," Ian said. "But the timing couldn't be better. Charlie got his wish. We found out yesterday that it's a boy."

As everyone applauded again, Pastor Jim came up beside Zach.

"There's something here I want you to see," the minister whispered. He handed Zach a folded newspaper, the morning's *Carlson Herald*. "Tell me that truck doesn't look familiar."

Zach lifted a brow and took the paper from the pastor before excusing himself for a moment and stepping back into the living room. He unfolded the paper and his eyes widened, immediately recognizing the battered Ford F-150. He quickly read the article under the photograph.

Driver Missing from Train Crash

CARLSON—Investigators are looking for the driver of a vehicle that was struck by a westbound train early Friday morning.

Carlson police said the crash was the first in over forty years at the Old Gibraltar Road central crossing, despite the site's not having crossing gates to protect drivers.

Police said, "Early indications lead us to believe that a collision occurred shortly after 3:00 a.m. with an unregistered 1996 Ford F-150 that was heading east toward Gibraltar. It is believed, at this stage, the truck was forced some 220 feet north into the old McLouth Steel property. The locomotive engineer has confirmed the truck was moving across the tracks prior to impact, leaving us to believe it was occupied. We are extremely concerned for the welfare of the individual operating that vehicle."

Anyone who may have information regarding this crash is being asked to notify the Carlson Police Department.

Detroit-Access Rail was not available for comment.

There were no other witnesses.

"No other witnesses," Zach whispered. "We'll see about that."

Though he hadn't seen the carpenter since that day in the hospital chapel, Zach knew it was his truck.

He never leaves us.

His eyes climbed up the page to the photo of the mangled F-150 lying next to a telephone pole in a dark ditch off of Old Gibraltar Road. Behind it, two train cars were visible, covered with graffiti. And then he saw it. The two words, in blocky tagger printing. He laughed aloud and glanced out the window and up the hill at St. Thomas just in time to see three deer prance playfully around the front corner of the church. They slowed near the cross. He remembered the first time he'd seen the cross and how hopeless he thought it was. But it had risen. It had been made new.

Zach looked back at the photo one last time and the words on the boxcar.

He closed his eyes and thought about those words and what they meant to him. About how he'd come to know love, true Love, and all that had helped him overcome. When he finally opened his eyes, he wiped away a tear and looked up again to the cross. It was there that his life had truly begun.

"And where I'll stay," he promised in a whisper, nodding. And then he said the two words that had been so neatly painted on the side of the train.

"Only believe."

• • •

"Someone is here to see you, Timmy."

He didn't feel like answering. Even if he did, she wouldn't be able to hear him. The old bat couldn't hear half the things he said from five feet away, so why bother answering now?

"Timmy?" she yelled from the base of the stairs.

Her voice was warbly, and he figured with the disease that made her shake all the time, that white-haired head of hers was probably bobbling all over the place. What a pain she was becoming.

"Timmy? Are you asleep?"

Not anymore, you idiot.

He could hear the creak in the stairs. Must be important, because she was on her way up. He glanced at the clock. It was 11:39 a.m., and with that miserable back of hers, it would take her just about forever to get up to his room. *I'll just grab a little more shut-eye before she gets here . . .*

There was a knock on his door and Tim Shempner woke back up, startled. *I actually did go back to sleep*, he thought with a laugh under his breath. He rolled over in bed and looked at the clock. It was 11:43 a.m. It took her four minutes to get up the stairs. He hoped it hurt, so she wouldn't bother to do it again.

"Timmy?"

"Not now, Grandma!"

The door handle turned, and Shempner could see those crooked blue fingers that were holding the side of the door as his grandmother struggled to push it open over the carpet, against a mountain of dirty clothes. Even though it was her house, she had a *lot* to learn about respecting his privacy.

"Someone is here for you," she said, giving him that disappointed look that was really starting to get on his nerves. She shook her head, and it was the shake she actually had control of. "Timmy, honey, I asked you not to smoke in the house. Are you smoking up here again?"

"No, Grandma."

"What do you want me to tell those men downstairs?"

"Who are they?"

"I'm worried that they may be the police. Are you in trouble again?"

"No, Grandma. Tell them I'm sick."

"I'm not going to lie," she said. "I'll tell them you are tired."

"You do that, Grandma."

She grimaced as she pulled back on the door and suddenly stopped. "Do you think that you could get around to cutting the grass today?"

No, but I might get around to hiding your heart medicine.

Shempner covered his head with the sheet and ignored her. She finally gave up and closed the door.

He sat up and reached for his pack of cigarettes on the night-stand. It was empty, but there was a good half of one, a little bent up but still smokable, resting in the ashtray. He lit it and looked out the window.

Things had to get better.

It had been pretty close to a year since Kaitlyn had the big re-tard attack him at The Pilot Inn. Between the restraining order that drunk whore put on him and the constant humiliation from every-one in town, he figured his best play was to get out of Dodge for a while and come out to Arizona and mooch off Grandma for a bit.

Though it was normally a couple hundred degrees in this hot-box she called home, it hadn't been that hard for him to make ends meet. She didn't charge him any rent, he ate for free, and between his unemployment checks and the occasional ten or twenty dollar bill he'd lift out of her purse while she dozed in her chair, he wasn't in any real hurry to get a job.

Grandma had also told him that she'd decided to include him in the latest version of her will. It wasn't but a couple weeks ago that he'd actually thought she'd punched out in the middle of one of her naps. He had already been counting the money as he held a mirror under her mouth to see if she was breathing. She practically gave *him* a heart attack when her eyes popped open and she asked him what he was doing.

It was all good, though. She was eighty-seven and hopefully it wouldn't be much longer. *If this heat keeps up, it'll help, he thought.* Old people died in the heat all the time. And Tim had been encouraging her to save money and keep the air conditioning off . . .

He thought he heard a man's voice. Apparently, Grandma wasn't going to be able to fend them off. He snubbed out his cigarette and put his jeans on to go see what they wanted. He figured it probably had something to do with not paying his court costs and fines back in Michigan, but wasn't quite sure if they could even issue a warrant out here for that.

He went downstairs but found only Grandma, sitting in her chair. He shoved back a wave of irritation. He'd gotten up for nothing? "Were they cops, Grandma?"

"I asked them if they were the police, and they said no."

Shempner sat on the couch. "Then who were they?"

"I don't know," she said. "There were three of them, and the one who did all the talking left something for you. I put it in the kitchen."

Good thing it wasn't the cops. He needed more legal problems like he needed cancer.

"What did they leave me?" Shempner asked. A pile of tickets? Court paperwork? "They made you sign for it, right?"

"What? No? Oh, Timmy, it's beautiful," she said. "You just have to see it."

Shempner shook his head. Getting a straight answer out of the crazy old coot was like pulling teeth. He stood and made his way into the kitchen.

He immediately saw it and stopped.

Shempner squinted, and his mouth opened slightly. The side of his neck was becoming uncomfortably warm, and the strength was pouring out of his legs. He swore under his breath. *What's happening to me?* He leaned heavily against the refrigerator, but his hand slid slowly down the cool stainless steel of the refrigerator door as he sank to his knees, that warm feeling attacking every inch of his body.

He tried to lift his arms. He couldn't.

He tried to look away, but the whole time he was in the kitchen, he just couldn't take his eyes off it.

Over on the table.

It was the single most beautiful thing he'd ever seen.

It was perfect.

It was an apple.

DID YOU ENJOY *THE REASON*?

Please spread the word
and tell your friends and church about it!

Also, please follow William Sirls

on Facebook,

Twitter @WilliamSirls,

or at WilliamSirls.com

AUTHOR'S NOTE

Two little red wagons . . .

I can vividly remember walking down a hallway at a Detroit hospital back in early 2004. To say that things needed to be put in perspective for me at that time may be the greatest understatement of my lifetime. I had just gone through a divorce, I was in the middle of some activities that were hurting a lot of good people—activities that would ultimately lead me to federal prison—and my oldest daughter had just been diagnosed with type 1 diabetes. I guess I was more than a little self-absorbed and found I was drowning in the middle of my own pity party.

That's when I saw the first one.

A young boy—I'm guessing maybe two or three years old—was being pulled in a little red wagon. He was wearing superhero pajamas, and his hair had fallen out. He looked awful. Both his mother and father were clearly exhausted and experiencing a level of stress that to this day is something I can only imagine. At that time, I had no idea that I was looking at Ian, Brooke, and Alex. I can still see that little boy looking up and smiling at his parents, and when they smiled back, nothing else in the world seemed to be happening. Their exchange was one of the most beautiful things I had ever seen. I wanted those smiles to be a result of something—of anything— and I wanted them to last, because in too many cases, they don't. That's when the idea for this book danced through my head.

Like so many inspirational moments, the promises I made to myself that day didn't last. I still couldn't be the better person I wanted to be. I had arrived at another one of those proverbial forks in the road and had somehow convinced myself that I could dig my way out of an enormous hole that I had created. I made the same terrible choices over and over again, and as I tried to fix a problem, I inevitably created more.

I continued to head in the wrong direction over the next four years and brought a lot of unknowing participants with me. In the middle of that destruction, I had somehow managed to scribble here and there writings to the tune of over one thousand pages about a stranger who shows up at a hospital in the small town of Carlson, Michigan. I guess I wanted him to do more than fix sick little kids—I wanted him to fix me. The problem was that I really didn't have the faintest idea who this stranger was, so I ended up tossing the story in a drawer.

In May of 2007, while on pretrial for wire fraud and money laundering charges, I was allowed to visit an uncle of mine in North Carolina. I had gone down there with a friend, and we were sitting in a restaurant just south of Asheville, waiting for my uncle to meet us for breakfast. He was going to lead us through the winding roads into the mountains where he lived.

That's when I saw the second one.

There were a few rows of booths in that restaurant, and in the row to my left, there was another young boy who was sitting in another little red wagon. He had a full head of hair and had one of those piercing laughs that came from nothing other than pure joy and an appreciation of being alive. I initially found it a little odd that his mother was spoon-feeding him. The kid continued to laugh and didn't seem to have a care in the world. He also didn't have any arms or legs. I didn't say anything about the little boy to my uncle or my friend, and I suddenly realized I had spent my whole life worrying about the wrong things. I was a little over six months from heading off to prison, and I felt like the luckiest man in the world. Needless to say, I thought about the kid in Detroit again and about my unfinished story. The book and its author were about to get a three-year overhaul.

On December 4, 2007, I reported to the United States Penitentiary–Hazelton, in Bruceton Mills, West Virginia. Prison is something I would never wish on anyone, but at the same time, there are few things I would trade for the experience. It was a much needed "time-out" that not only gave me the opportunity to figure out who I really was but also to figure out what was important—and what was missing in my life. The same thing that was missing in my life was also absent from the earliest version of the book, and I started to make some changes. When I refer to something missing, I'm talking about that "buzz" that Kaitlyn Harby felt. There is no doubt in my mind that the cause of that buzz is, in fact, very real and isn't just there when you need it—it's always there. You just have to be open to it and trust that it doesn't have to be found in a prison, a cemetery, a little bar, or the parking lot of a hospital. It can be found anywhere. I hope that makes some sense.

When I was released, I was lucky enough to be given the opportunity and the time (a word I now respect more than ever) to take all the changed pieces and try to put them together. The one thousand pages (despite adding a few characters) quickly became eight hundred. I was fortunate to be able to work with Chris Cancilliari, who helped me knock it down to the five hundred pages that ultimately went to the publisher to become what you are holding. Chris—how many phone calls and e-mails did we exchange? I never knew the difference between three dots and an em dash, but I hope to harass you more in the future. Thanks for tolerating my OCD and for turning my drivel into something that made sense. It was truly a lot of fun, and I hope to do it again.

I have a lot of other people to thank. This book has been on a journey, so please be patient with me.

Thank you Ginny Simpson, Norm Fenton, and Jack Kelly . . . I couldn't have done this without you.

Brooke, thanks for your support with everything.

I also want to thank everyone that read the earliest and latest versions of the prepublished book, particularly: Bob Deragisch, Kim Falkowski-Lewis, Debbie Vendlinski, Rich and Leann Hedke, Judi McNair, Liz Zeller, Jacqueline Lynch, Rose Williams, Helen McCord, Lorene Miller, Dawn Overstreet, Aunt Paulette Pedigo,

Cousin Susan Shelton, Ray Johnson, Uncle Bill Sirls, Janet Krust, Yvonne Cancilliari, Lila Marcum, Kimberly Brown, Jim Steere, Patti Hogue, Mike Stedman, Tom Ayers, Russell Bradley Fenton, Tim Cooke, Brian Noble, Mark Drew, JoEllen Hurst, Susan Tant, Fred Bisaro, Lynn (LJ) Bisaro, Katie Thompson, Jes Stout-Fortenberry, Kaley Azambuja, Rhonda Raft, Pat Pittsnogle, David Mikels, Victoria Stahl, Jacqui Clark, Lori Howard, Mindy Hartwell, Michele Hangen, Macy West Griffin, Deidre Black, Robin Beitler, David Hill, Annette Bishop, Ryan Armey, Sandy Overton, Karla Dorman, Kathy Curtis, Kristina Wright, Misti Begeman, Jeff and Michelle Katz, Anne Craymer, Helen Beerline, Amanda Salazar, Mary Morgan Shirley, Allison Samoluk, Cindy Viehmann, Jane Jennings, Susan Vermeire, Savannah Patin, Anna Schumann , Bonnie Plummer, Everett Plummer, and Betty Attinger. Sometimes you can't see the forest for the trees, and you guys were incredible.

A very special thanks to Chris Sonksen, lead pastor at South Hills Church in Corona, California. I appreciate the guidance you gave me on the book and for sharing your thoughts on the 23rd Psalm. It was the single most amazing sermon I have ever heard.

Pastor Chris Harrell. PCH . . . you are my spiritual ninja. Thank you, brother.

Hunter Wright and his team at Ignition Church in Knoxville. Thanks for making me feel so welcome on my visit there. I've been blessed to see a lot of churches over the last couple of years and Ignition is one of those where you can literally feel God working though His people. For those of you that are from Knoxville or plan on being in the area, I encourage you to visit Ignition Church as they have something very special happening there.

Thanks also go to the team at Westbow, including Joel Pierson, D. Spindler, Jamie Brazel, Megan Schindele, Andy Mays, Stefanie Holzbacher, Jeremy Weddle, Amanda Parsons, Richard Robertson, Shelley Rogers Landes and Chris Bass. Professionalism and good people are a great combination.

I can't forget my buddy with the English accent, Alan Bower. Alan is in the publishing business for the right reasons. He loves publishing and loves authors. Thank you for your advice, voice of reason, and your friendship. Thanks also go to his better half, Erica Dooley-Dorocke. What a difference you two truly do make.

Thank you to all my friends at Thomas Nelson. I have learned a great deal from you.

Thanks to Paige Collins and Jennifer Willingham from Icon Media Group, and to Carlton Garborg and David Sluka with Broad-Street Publishing. I've learned that this business is all about vision and the four of you have it. You are truly awesome.

My friend and editor, Natalie Hanemann. You are the best and have taught me more about writing than I have learned from everyone and everywhere else combined. There is nobody that I would rather have helping me with my storytelling than you. You've pushed me to get better, and I'm very lucky to have your help. Thank you.

Lisa Bergren. Thank you LTB!

Elizabeth Sluka. Thank you for your help. What an amazing eye you have. I look forward to reading your books in the future.

I have two beautiful daughters and a family I love very much. I thank you for being you and for your patience. I'd mention your names here, but I've already done that, haven't I?

I want to apologize once again to the "31." You deserved much better than what you got from me. I don't know if I can ever make it right, but I promise you it won't be for lack of effort.

Finally, I want to thank the reader. I hope you enjoyed reading this as much as I did writing it—and that it somehow makes a difference in your life.

William Sirls
Gibraltar, Michigan

DISCUSSION QUESTIONS

1. Kenneth hands Kaitlyn an apple and asks her what would happen to it if it had a worm inside of it. What do you think the apple and worm represent?
2. Early in the book, Zach Norman calls God a "bully." If God allows something bad to happen, does that mean it is part of God's will? Why or why not?
3. Pastor Jim encourages his congregation to spend less time worrying about what they don't have and more time being thankful for what they do have. Do you find yourself doing this? What has God given you that you are most thankful for?
4. Do you know anyone that harbors ill will and resentment toward someone who has harmed them? What would you say to help them try to forgive that person?
5. Would you agree or disagree that when we forgive others, we are really letting ourselves off the hook? Why or why not?
6. Pastor Jim explains to Brooke that God doesn't keep us from tests and trials, but he helps us get through them. What are your thoughts on this?
7. At what point do you think Zach Norman knew he had faith? Why? Can you describe the moment you knew you had it?
8. If we pray for something and it doesn't happen, does that mean the prayer wasn't answered?
9. What lesson did Macey Lewis need to learn?

10. Do you believe that God smiles when we use the unique gifts that he has given us? Take a few minutes and think about what your gift or gifts may be. Are you putting your gift to use? How do you feel when you do?
11. How could God make something good come from the death of a child?
12. Who is Kenneth to you?
13. In the epilogue, who are the three visitors that Tim Shempner's grandmother encounters? Are they anywhere else in the book?
14. Who do you believe is the main character in the book and why?